PRAISE FOR
The Black Widow

#1 *NEW YORK TIMES* BESTSELLER • #1 *USA TODAY* BESTSELLER
#1 *WALL STREET JOURNAL* BESTSELLER

AN AMAZON EDITORS' BOOK OF THE YEAR   AN IBOOKS
BOOK OF THE MONTH • A *KIRKUS REVIEWS* BEST FICTION
BOOK OF THE YEAR

"An exceptional spy thriller, well written and timely, weaving history seamlessly into a sumptuous page-turner of a novel. . . . Longtime fans will revel in familiar faces . . . and Silva's understated but deft writing. . . . For newcomers, well, what are you waiting for?"   —*Minneapolis Star Tribune*

"Slow-burn suspense. . . . We stayed up way too late . . . but we justified the sleeplessness as a learning opportunity: amidst the action, Silva gives a surprisingly thorough crash course in the history of ISIS and the Middle East."   —iBooks Reviews

"Heart-stopping."   —*Washington Post*

"Silva builds suspense like a symphony conductor . . . but the novel also affords a sobering, insightful, and multifaceted look at the overwhelming complexities of the seemingly interminable war in the Middle East. And, for series fans, Silva introduces a new and richly conceived character who is likely to become a regular cast member. A winner on all fronts."
    —*Booklist* (starred review)

"To say that Daniel Silva is a bestselling author is a bit like saying Henry Aaron was a decent home-run hitter."
    —*Dallas News*

"A literary powder keg."   —*Huffington Post*

"Fascinating, suspenseful, and bated-breath exciting."
    —*Publishers Weekly* (starred review)

"From the devastating beginning in Paris to the terrifying end in Washington, D.C., *The Black Widow* holds us in its grip—a thriller that any fan will devour from cover to cover. . . . It establishes Silva, who already has eighteen spy novels to his credit, as the foremost author of the genre."   —Bookreporter.com

THE BLACK WIDOW

ALSO BY DANIEL SILVA

House of Spies

The English Spy

The Heist

The English Girl

The Fallen Angel

Portrait of a Spy

The Rembrandt Affair

The Defector

Moscow Rules

The Secret Servant

The Messenger

Prince of Fire

A Death in Vienna

The Confessor

The English Assassin

The Kill Artist

The Marching Season

The Mark of the Assassin

The Unlikely Spy

THE BLACK WIDOW

DANIEL SILVA

HARPER
PERENNIAL

The Black Widow
Copyright © 2016 by Daniel Silva.
All rights reserved.

Published by Harper Perennial, an imprint of HarperCollins Publishers Ltd

First published in Canada by HarperCollins Publishers Ltd
in an original trade paperback edition: 2016
First HarperCollins Publishers Ltd mass market edition: 2017
This Harper Perennial trade paperback edition: 2018

HarperCollins books may be purchased for educational, business,
or sales promotional use through our Special Markets Department.

HarperCollins Publishers Ltd
Bay Adelaide Centre, East Tower
22 Adelaide Street West, 41st Floor
Toronto, Ontario, Canada
M5H 4E3

www.harpercollins.ca

Map designed by Nick Springer

Library and Archives Canada Cataloguing in Publication
information is available upon request.

ISBN 978-1-44345-648-7

Printed and bound in the United States
LSC/H 9 8 7 6 5 4 3 2 1

For Stephen L. Carter, for friendship and faith.
And, as always, for my wife, Jamie,
and my children, Lily and Nicholas.

The black flags will come from the East, led by mighty men, with long hair and beards, their surnames taken from their home towns.

—THE HADITH

Give me a girl at an impressionable age, and she is mine for life.

—MURIEL SPARK, *The Prime of Miss Jean Brodie*

I COMMENCED WORK ON THIS NOVEL before the Islamic terrorist group known as ISIS carried out a wave of shootings and bombings in Paris and Brussels that left more than 160 people dead. After briefly considering setting aside the typescript, I chose to complete it as originally conceived, as though the tragic events had not yet occurred in the imaginary world where my characters live and work. The similarities between the real and fictitious attacks, including the links to the Brussels district of Molenbeek, are entirely coincidental. I take no pride in my prescience. I only wish that the murderous, millenarian terrorism of the Islamic State lived solely on the pages of this story.

BLACK SEA
RUSSIA
GEORGIA
AZERBAIJAN
ARMENIA
Ankara
TURKEY
Mosul
IRAN
Raqqa
SYRIA
CYPRUS
MEDITERRANEAN SEA
Palmyra
LEBANON
Beirut
Damascus
Ramadi
Fallujah
Baghdad
Tiberias
IRAQ
Netanya
Nahalal
Tel Aviv
Amman
Jerusalem
ISRAEL
JORDAN
KUWAIT
SAUDI ARABIA
RED SEA
Riyadh
EGYPT
0
250 km.
200 mi.
Copyright © MMXVI Springer Cartographics LLC

PART ONE

RUE DES ROSIERS

1

THE MARAIS, PARIS

IT WAS TOULOUSE THAT WOULD prove to be Hannah Weinberg's undoing. That night she telephoned Alain Lambert, a contact at the Interior Ministry, and told him that this time something would have to be done. Alain promised a swift response. It would be bold, he assured Hannah, boldness being the default response of a fonctionnaire when in reality he planned to do nothing at all. The following morning the minister himself paid a visit to the site of the attack and issued a vague call for "dialogue and healing." To the parents of the three victims he offered only regrets. "We will do better," he said before returning hastily to Paris. "We must."

They were twelve years of age, the victims, two boys and a girl, all Jewish, though the French media neglected to mention their religion in the first reports. Nor did they bother to point out that the six attackers were Muslim, only that they were youths who resided in a suburb, a banlieue, east of the city center. The description of the attack was vague to the point of inaccuracy. According to French radio, an altercation of some sort had occurred outside a patisserie. Three were injured, one seriously. The police were investigating. No arrests had been made.

In truth, it had not been an altercation but a well-planned ambush. And the attackers were not youths, they were men in their early twenties who had ventured into the center of Toulouse in search of Jews to harm. That their victims were children seemed to trouble them not. The two young boys were kicked, spat upon, and then beaten bloody. The girl was pinned to the pavement and her face slashed with a knife. Before fleeing, the six attackers turned to a group of stunned bystanders and shouted, "Khaybar, Khaybar, ya-Yahud!" Though the witnesses did not know it, the Arabic chant was a reference to the seventh-century Muslim conquest of a Jewish oasis near the holy city of Medina. Its message was unmistakable. The armies of Muhammad, the six men were saying, were coming for the Jews of France.

Regrettably, the attack in Toulouse was not without precedent or ample warning. France was presently in the grip of the worst spasm of violence against Jews since the Holocaust. Synagogues had been firebombed, gravestones toppled, shops looted, homes vandalized and marked with threatening graffiti. In all, there had been more than four thousand documented attacks during the past year alone, each carefully recorded and investigated by Hannah and her team at the Isaac Weinberg Center for the Study of Anti-Semitism in France.

Named for Hannah's paternal grandfather, the center had opened its doors under heavy security ten years earlier. It was now the most respected such institution in France, and Hannah Weinberg was regarded as the foremost chronicler of the country's new wave of anti-Semitism. Her supporters referred to her as a "memory militant," a woman who would stop at nothing to pressure France into protecting its besieged

Jewish minority. Her detractors were far less charitable. Consequently, Hannah had long ago stopped reading the things that were written about her in the press or in the sewers of the Internet.

The Weinberg Center stood on the rue des Rosiers, the most prominent street in the city's most visible Jewish neighborhood. Hannah's apartment was around the corner on the rue Pavée. The nameplate on the intercom read MME BERTRAND, one of the few steps she took to safeguard her security. She resided in the flat alone, surrounded by the possessions of three generations of her family, including a modest collection of paintings and several hundred antique lunettes, her secret passion. At fifty-five, she was unmarried and childless. Occasionally, when work permitted, she allowed herself a lover. Alain Lambert, her contact at the Interior Ministry, had once been a pleasant distraction during a particularly tense period of anti-Jewish incidents. He rang Hannah at home late after his master's visit to Toulouse.

"So much for boldness," she said acidly. "He should be ashamed of himself."

"We did the best we could."

"Your best wasn't good enough."

"It's better not to throw oil on the fire at a time like this."

"That's the same thing they said in the summer of nineteen forty-two."

"Let's not get overly emotional."

"You leave me no choice but to issue a statement, Alain."

"Choose your words carefully. We're the only ones standing between you and them."

Hannah hung up the phone. Then she opened the top drawer of the writing desk and removed a single key. It unlocked a door at the end of the hall. Behind it was the room of a child, Hannah's room, frozen in time. A four-poster bed with a lace canopy. Shelves stacked with stuffed animals and toys. A faded pinup of a heartthrob American actor. And hanging above the French provincial dresser, invisible in the darkness, was a painting by Vincent van Gogh. *Marguerite Gachet at Her Dressing Table* . . . Hannah trailed a fingertip over the brushstrokes and thought of the man who had carried out the painting's one and only restoration. How would he respond at a time like this? No, she thought, smiling. That wouldn't do.

She climbed into her childhood bed and, much to her surprise, fell into a dreamless sleep. And when she woke she had settled on a plan.

FOR THE BETTER PART OF THE NEXT WEEK, HANNAH AND HER team toiled under conditions of strict operational security. Potential participants were quietly approached, arms were twisted, donors were tapped. Two of Hannah's most reliable sources of funding demurred, for like the minister of the interior they thought it better to not *jeter de l'huile sur le feu*— throw oil on the fire. To make up for the shortfall, Hannah had no choice but to dip into her personal finances, which were considerable. This, too, was fodder for her enemies.

Lastly, there was the small matter of what to call Hannah's endeavor. Rachel Lévy, head of the center's publicity department, thought blandness and a trace of obfuscation would be the best approach, but Hannah overruled her. When synagogues were burning, she said, caution was a luxury they could not afford. It was Hannah's wish to sound an alarm, to issue a clarion call for action. She scribbled a few words on a slip of notepaper and placed it on Rachel's cluttered desk.

"That should get their attention."

At that point, no one of any consequence had agreed to

attend—no one but a gadfly American blogger and cable television commentator who would have accepted an invitation to his own funeral. But then Arthur Goldman, the eminent historian of anti-Semitism from Cambridge, said he might be willing to make the trip down to Paris—provided, of course, that Hannah agreed to put him up for two nights in his favorite suite at the Crillon. With Goldman's commitment, Hannah snared Maxwell Strauss from Yale, who never passed up an opportunity to appear on the same stage as his rival. The rest of the participants quickly fell into place. The director of the United States Holocaust Memorial Museum signed on, as did two important memoirists of survival and an expert on the French Holocaust from Yad Vashem. A novelist was added, more for her immense popularity than her historical insight, along with a politician from the French far right who rarely had a kind word to say about anyone. Several Muslim spiritual and community leaders were invited to attend. All declined. So, too, did the interior minister. Alain Lambert broke the news to Hannah personally.

"Did you really think he would attend a conference with so provocative a title?"

"Heaven forbid your master ever do anything provocative, Alain."

"What about security?"

"We've always looked after ourselves."

"No Israelis, Hannah. It will give the entire affair a bad odor."

Rachel Lévy issued the press release the next day. The media were invited to cover the conference; a limited number of seats were made available to the public. A few hours later, on a busy street in the Twentieth Arrondissement, a religious Jew was set upon by a man with a hatchet and gravely wounded. Before making his escape, the assailant waved the bloody weapon and shouted, "Khaybar, Khaybar, ya-Yahud!" The police were said to be investigating.

FOR REASONS OF BOTH HASTE AND SECURITY, A PERIOD OF JUST five busy days separated the press release from the start of the conference itself. Consequently, Hannah waited until the last minute to prepare her opening remarks. On the eve of the gathering, she sat alone in her library, a pen scratching furiously across a yellow legal pad.

It was, she thought, an appropriate place to compose such a document, for the library had once been her grandfather's. Born in the Lublin district of Poland, he had fled to Paris in 1936, four years before the arrival of Hitler's Wehrmacht. On the morning of July 16, 1942—the day known as Jeudi Noir, or Black Thursday—French police officers carrying stacks of blue deportation cards arrested Isaac Weinberg and his wife, along with nearly thirteen thousand other foreign-born Jews. Isaac Weinberg had managed to conceal two things before the dreaded knock at the door: his only child, a young son named Marc, and the van Gogh. Marc Weinberg survived the war in hiding, and in 1952 he managed to reclaim the apartment on the rue Pavée from the French family who had settled into it after Jeudi Noir. Miraculously, the painting was precisely where Isaac Weinberg had left it, hidden under the floorboards of the library, beneath the desk where Hannah now sat.

Three weeks after their arrest, Isaac Weinberg and his wife were deported to Auschwitz and gassed upon arrival. They were just two of the more than 75,000 Jews from France who perished in the death camps of Nazi Germany, a permanent stain on French history. But could it ever happen again? And was it time for the 475,000 Jews of France, the third-largest

Jewish community in the world, to pack their bags and leave? This was the question Hannah had posed in the title of her conference. Many Jews had already abandoned France. Fifteen thousand had immigrated to Israel during the past year, and more were leaving every day. Hannah, however, had no plans to join them. Regardless of what her enemies might say, she considered herself French first and Jewish second. The idea of living somewhere other than the Fourth Arrondissement of Paris was abhorrent to her. Still, she felt duty-bound to warn her fellow French Jews of the gathering storm. The threat was not yet existential. But when a building is burning, Hannah wrote now, the best course of action is to find the nearest exit.

She finished a first draft shortly before midnight. It was too strident, she thought, and perhaps a bit too angry. She softened its roughest edges and added several depressing statistics to bolster her case. Then she typed it into her laptop, printed a copy, and managed to find her bed by two. The alarm woke her at seven; she drank a bowl of café au lait on the way to the shower. Afterward, she sat before her vanity in a toweling robe, staring at her face in the mirror. Her father, in a moment of brutal honesty, had once said of his only daughter that God had been generous when giving her brains but parsimonious with her looks. Her hair was wavy and dark and streaked with gray that she had allowed to encroach without resistance. Her nose was prominent and aquiline, her eyes were wide and brown. It had never been a particularly pretty face, but no one had ever mistaken her for a fool, either. At a moment like this, she thought, her looks were an asset.

She applied a bit of makeup to hide the circles beneath her eyes and arranged her hair with more care than usual. Then she dressed quickly—a dark woolen skirt and sweater, dark stockings, a pair of low-heeled pumps—and headed downstairs. After crossing the interior courtyard, she opened the main doorway of the building a few inches and peered into the street. It was a few minutes after eight; Parisians and tourists were making their way swiftly along the pavement beneath a gray early-spring sky. No one, it seemed, was waiting for an intelligent-looking woman in her mid-fifties to emerge from the apartment building at Number 24.

She did so now and headed past a row of chic clothing boutiques to the rue des Rosiers. For a few paces it seemed like an ordinary Paris street in a rather upscale arrondissement. Then Hannah came upon a kosher pizzeria and several falafel stands with signs written in Hebrew, and the true character of the street was revealed. She imagined how it must have looked early on the morning of Jeudi Noir. The helpless detainees clambering into open-top trucks, each clutching their allotted one suitcase. The neighbors staring down from open windows, some silent and ashamed, others barely able to contain their glee at the misfortune of a reviled minority. Hannah clung to this image—the image of Parisians waving goodbye to doomed Jews—as she moved through the flat light, her heels tapping rhythmically over the paving stones.

The Weinberg Center stood at the quiet end of the street, in a four-story building that before the war had housed a Yiddish-language newspaper and a coat factory. A line of several dozen people stretched from the doorway where two dark-suited security guards, young men in their twenties, were carefully searching all those who wished to enter. Hannah slipped past them and made her way upstairs to the VIP reception. Arthur Goldman and Max Strauss were eyeing each other warily across the room over cups of weak *américain*. The famous novelist was speaking seriously to one of the memoirists; the head of the Holocaust Museum was exchanging notes with the specialist from Yad Vashem, who was a longtime friend. Only the gadfly American commentator seemed to have no one to talk to. He was piling croissants and brioche onto his plate as though he hadn't seen food in days. "Don't worry," said Hannah, smiling. "We're planning to take a break for lunch."

She spent a moment or two with each of the panelists before heading down the hall to her office. Alone, she reread her opening remarks until Rachel Lévy poked her head through the doorway and pointed to her wristwatch.

"What's the crowd like?" asked Hannah.

"More than we can handle."

"And the media?"

"Everyone came, including the *New York Times* and the BBC."

Just then, Hannah's mobile phone chimed. It was a text from Alain Lambert at the Interior Ministry. Reading it, she frowned.

"What does it say?" asked Rachel.

"Just Alain being Alain."

Hannah placed the mobile on her desk and, gathering her papers, went out. Rachel Lévy waited until she was gone before picking up the mobile and entering Hannah's not-so-secret security code. The text from Alain Lambert appeared, four words in length.

BE CAREFUL MY DEAR . . .

THE WEINBERG CENTER HAD INSUFFICIENT SPACE FOR A FORmal auditorium, but the room on its uppermost floor was one of the finest in the Marais. A row of greenhouse-like windows gave it a magnificent view across the rooftops toward the Seine, and upon its walls hung several large black-and-white photographs of life in the district before the morning of

Jeudi Noir. All those depicted had perished in the Holocaust, including Isaac Weinberg, who had been photographed in his library three months before disaster struck. As Hannah passed the picture, she trailed a forefinger over its surface, as she had touched the brushstrokes of the van Gogh. Only Hannah knew of the secret connection between the painting, her grandfather, and the center that bore his name. No, she thought suddenly. That wasn't quite true. The restorer knew of the connection, too.

A long rectangular table had been placed atop a raised platform in front of the windows, and two hundred chairs had been arranged on the open floor like soldiers on a parade ground. Each of the chairs was occupied, and another hundred or so spectators lined the rear wall. Hannah took her assigned seat—she had volunteered to serve as a separation barrier between Goldman and Strauss—and listened as Rachel Lévy instructed the audience to silence their mobile phones. Finally, her turn came to speak. She switched on her microphone and looked down at the first line of her opening statement. *It is a national tragedy that a conference such as this is even taking place* . . . And then she heard the sound in the street below, a popping, like the snap of firecrackers, followed by a man shouting in Arabic.

"Khaybar, Khaybar, ya-Yahud!"

Hannah stepped from the platform and moved quickly to the floor-to-ceiling windows.

"Dear God," she whispered.

Turning, she shouted at the panelists to move away from the windows, but the roar of the detonation swallowed her warning. Instantly, the room was a tornado of flying glass, chairs, masonry, articles of clothing, and human limbs. Hannah knew she was toppling forward, though she had no sense of whether she was rising or falling. Once, she thought she glimpsed Rachel Lévy spinning like a ballerina. Then Rachel, like all else, was lost to her.

At last, she came to rest, perhaps on her back, perhaps on her side, perhaps in the street, perhaps in a tomb of brick and concrete. The silence was oppressive. So, too, was the smoke and the dust. She tried to wipe the grit from her eyes, but her right arm would not respond. Then Hannah realized she had no right arm. Nor did she seem to have a right leg. She turned her head slightly and saw a man lying beside her. "Professor Strauss, is that you?" But the man said nothing. He was dead. Soon, thought Hannah, I'll be dead, too.

All at once she was frightfully cold. She supposed it was the loss of blood. Or perhaps it was the breath of wind that briefly cleared the black smoke from in front of her face. She realized then that she and the man who might have been Professor Strauss were lying together amid the rubble in the rue des Rosiers. And standing over them, peering downward over the barrel of a military-style automatic rifle, was a figure dressed entirely in black. A balaclava masked the face, but the eyes were visible. They were shockingly beautiful, two kaleidoscopes of hazel and copper. "Please," said Hannah softly, but the eyes behind the mask only brightened with zeal. Then there was a flash of white light, and Hannah found herself walking along a hallway, her missing limbs restored. She passed through the door of her childhood bedroom and groped in the darkness for the van Gogh. But the painting, it seemed, was already gone. And in a moment Hannah was gone, too.

2

RUE DE GRENELLE, PARIS

LATER, THE FRENCH AUTHORITIES WOULD determine that the bomb weighed in excess of five hundred kilograms. It had been contained in a white Renault Trafic transit van and was detonated, according to numerous security cameras along the street, at ten o'clock precisely, the scheduled start time of the Weinberg Center conference. The attackers, it seemed, were nothing if not punctual.

In retrospect, the weapon was unnecessarily large for so modest a target. The French experts concluded that a charge of perhaps two hundred kilograms would have been more than sufficient to level the offices and kill or wound all those inside. At five hundred kilograms, however, the bomb toppled buildings and shattered windows the entire length of the rue des Rosiers. The shock wave was so violent—Paris actually recorded an earthquake for the first time in longer than anyone could remember—that the damage extended belowground as well. Water and gas mains cracked throughout the arrondissement, and a Métro train jumped the tracks while approaching the station at the Hôtel de Ville. More than two hundred passengers were injured, many severely. The Paris police initially thought the train had been bombed, too, and in response they ordered an evacuation of the entire Métro system. Life in the city quickly ground to a halt. For the attackers, it was an unexpected windfall.

The enormous force of the blast dug a crater in the rue des Rosiers twenty feet in depth. Nothing remained of the Renault Trafic, though the left rear cargo door, curiously intact, was found floating in the Seine near Notre-Dame, having traveled a distance of nearly a kilometer. In time, investigators would determine that the vehicle had been stolen in Vaulx-en-Velin, a bleak Muslim-majority suburb of Lyon. It had been driven to Paris on the eve of the attack—by whom, it was never established—and left outside a kitchen-and-bath store on the boulevard Saint-Germain. There it would remain until ten minutes past eight the following morning, when a man collected it. He was clean-shaven, approximately five foot ten inches in height, and was wearing a billed cap and sunglasses. He drove the streets of central Paris—aimlessly, or so it appeared—until nine twenty, when he picked up an accomplice outside the Gare du Nord. Initially, the French police and intelligence services operated under the assumption that the second attacker was male, too. Later, after analyzing all available video images, they concluded that the accomplice was in fact a woman.

By the time the Renault reached the Marais, both occupants had concealed their faces with balaclava masks. And when they emerged from the vehicle outside the Weinberg Center, both were heavily armed with Kalashnikov assault rifles, handguns, and grenades. The center's two security guards were killed instantly, as were four other people who had yet to be cleared into the building. A passerby bravely attempted to intervene and was mercilessly slaughtered. The remaining pedestrians in the narrow street wisely fled.

The gunfire outside the Weinberg Center ceased at 9:59:30, and the two masked attackers moved calmly west along the rue des Rosiers to the rue Vieille-du-Temple, where they entered a popular boulangerie. Eight customers were waiting in an orderly queue. All were killed, including the woman behind the counter, who pleaded for her life before being shot several times.

It was at that instant, as the woman was collapsing to the floor, that the bomb inside the van exploded. The force of the blast shattered the windows of the boulangerie, but otherwise the building remained undamaged. The two attackers did not immediately flee the carnage they had inflicted. Instead, they returned to the rue des Rosiers, where a single surviving security camera recorded them moving methodically through the debris, executing the wounded and the dying. Among their victims was Hannah Weinberg, who was shot twice despite the fact that she had almost no chance of survival. The attackers' cruelty was matched only by their competence. The woman was seen calmly clearing a jammed round from her Kalashnikov before killing a badly wounded man who, a moment earlier, had been seated on the fourth floor of the building.

For several hours after the attack, the Marais remained cordoned off, inaccessible to all but emergency workers and investigators. Finally, in late afternoon, when the last of the fires had been extinguished and the site was determined to be free of secondary explosives, the French president arrived. After touring the devastation, he declared it "a Holocaust in the heart of Paris." The remark did not meet with a favorable reception in some of the more restive banlieues. In one, there erupted a spontaneous celebration that was quickly snuffed out by riot police. Most of the newspapers ignored the incident. A senior French police official called it "an unpleasant distraction" from the immediate task at hand, which was finding the perpetrators.

Their escape from the Marais, like everything else about the operation, had been meticulously planned and executed. A Peugeot Satelis motorbike had been left for them on a nearby street, along with a pair of black helmets. They traveled north, the male driving, the woman clinging to his waist, passing unnoticed through the stream of approaching police cars and ambulances. A traffic camera photographed them for the last time near the hamlet of Villeron, in the Val-d'Oise department. By midday they were the targets of the largest manhunt in French history.

The National Police and the gendarmerie saw to the roadblocks, the identity checks, the smashed windows of abandoned warehouses, and the severed padlocks of suspected hideouts. But inside a graceful old building located on the rue de Grenelle, eighty-four men and women were engaged in a search of a far different kind. Known only as the Alpha Group, they were members of a secret unit of the DGSI, France's internal security service. The Group, as it was known informally, had been formed six years earlier, in the aftermath of a jihadist suicide bombing outside a landmark restaurant on the Avenue des Champs-Élysées. It specialized in human penetration of France's sprawling jihadist underground and had been granted the authority to take "active measures" to remove potential Islamic terrorists from circulation before the Islamic terrorists could take active measures against the Republic or its citizenry. It was said of Paul Rousseau, Alpha Group's chief, that he had plotted more bombings than Osama bin Laden, a charge he did not dispute, though he was quick to point out that none of his bombs actually exploded. The officers of Alpha Group were skilled practitioners in the art of deception. And Paul Rousseau was their undisputed leader and lodestar.

With his tweed jackets, tousled gray hair, and ever-present pipe, Rousseau seemed more suited to the role of absentminded professor than ruthless secret policeman, and not without good reason. Academia was where he began his career and where, in darker moments, he sometimes longed to return. A respected scholar of nineteenth-century French literature, Rousseau had been serving on the faculty of Paris-Sorbonne University when a friend in French intelligence asked him to take a job with the DST, France's internal security service. The year was 1983, and the country was beset by a wave of bombings and assassinations carried out by the left-wing terrorist group known as Direct Action. Rousseau joined a unit dedicated to Direct Action's destruction and, with a series of brilliant operations, brought the group to its knees.

He remained with the DST, battling successive waves of leftist and Middle East–based terrorism, until 2004, when his beloved wife Collette died after a long struggle with leukemia. Inconsolable, he retired to his modest villa in the Luberon and commenced work on a planned multivolume biography of Proust. Then came the bombing on the Champs-Élysées. Rousseau agreed to lay down his pen and return to the fight, but only on one condition. He had no interest in tailing suspected terrorists, listening to their telephone conversations, or reading their maniacal musings on the Internet. He wanted to go on offense. The chief agreed, as did the interior minister, and Alpha Group was born. In the six years of its existence, it had foiled more than a dozen major attacks on French soil. Rousseau viewed the bombing of the Weinberg Center not merely as a failure of intelligence but as a personal affront. Late that afternoon, with the French capital in turmoil, he rang the chief of the DGSI to offer his resignation. The chief, of course, refused it. "But for your penance," he said, "you shall find the monster responsible for this outrage and bring me his head on a plate."

Rousseau did not care for the allusion, for he had no intention of emulating the conduct of the very creatures he was fighting. Even so, he and his unit threw themselves into the task with a devotion that matched the religious zealotry of their adversaries. Alpha Group's specialty was the human factor, and it was to humans they turned for information. In cafés, train stations, and back alleys across the country, Rousseau's case officers met quietly with their agents of penetration— the preachers, the recruiters, the streetwise hustlers, the well-meaning moderates, the blank-eyed lost souls who had found a home in radical Islam's global Ummah of death. Some spied out of conscience. Others spied for money. And there were some who spied because Rousseau and his operatives had given them no other choice. Not one claimed to know that an attack had been in the planning—not even the hustlers, who claimed to know everything, especially when money was involved. Nor could any of Alpha Group's assets identify the two perpetrators. It was possible they were self-starters, lone wolves, followers of a leaderless jihad who had constructed a five-hundred-kilogram bomb under the noses of French intelligence and then delivered it expertly to their target. Possible, thought Rousseau, but highly unlikely. Somewhere, there was an operational mastermind, a man who had conceived the attack, recruited the operatives, and guided them skillfully to their target. And it was the head of this man that Paul Rousseau would deliver to his chief.

And so, as the whole of the French security establishment searched for the two perpetrators of the Weinberg Center attack, Rousseau's gaze was already fixed resolutely upon a distant shore. Like all good captains in times of trouble, he remained on the bridge of his vessel, which in Rousseau's case was his office on the fifth floor. An air of academic clutter hung over the room, along with the fruited scent of Rousseau's pipe tobacco, a habit he indulged in violation of numerous official edicts regarding smoking in government offices. Beneath his bulletproof windows—they had been forced upon him by his chief—lay the intersection of the rue de Grenelle and the tranquil little rue Amélie. The building itself had no street entrance, only a black gate that gave onto a small courtyard and car park. A discreet brass plaque proclaimed that the building housed something called the International Society for French Literature, a particularly Rousseauian touch. For the sake of the unit's cover, it published a thin quarterly, which Rousseau insisted on editing himself. At last count it had a readership of twelve. All had been thoroughly vetted.

Inside the building, however, all subterfuge ended. The technical support staff occupied the basement; the watchers, the ground floor. On the second floor was Alpha Group's overflowing Registry—Rousseau preferred old-fashioned paper dossiers to digital files—and the third and fourth floors were the preserve of the agent runners. Most came and went through the gate on the rue de Grenelle, either on foot or by government car. Others entered through a secret passageway linking the building and the dowdy little antique shop next door, which was owned by an elderly Frenchman who had served in a secret capacity during the war in Algeria. Paul Rousseau was the only member of Alpha Group who had been allowed to read the shopkeeper's appalling file.

A visitor to the fifth floor might have mistaken it for the office of a private Swiss bank. It was somber and shadowed and quiet, save for the Chopin that occasionally drifted through Paul Rousseau's open door. His long-suffering secretary, the implacable Madame Treville, occupied an orderly desk in the anteroom, and at the opposite end of a narrow hall was the office of Rousseau's deputy, Christian Bouchard. Bouchard was all things Rousseau was not—young, fit, sharply dressed, and far too good-looking. Most of all, Bouchard was ambitious. The chief of the DGSI had foisted him upon Rousseau, and it was widely assumed he would one day be Alpha Group's chief. Rousseau resented him only a little, for Bouchard, despite his obvious shortcomings, was extremely good at his job. Ruthless, too. When there was bureaucratic dirty work to be done, invariably it was Bouchard who saw to it.

Three days after the Weinberg Center bombing, with the terrorists still at large, there was a meeting of department heads at the Interior Ministry. Rousseau loathed such gatherings—they invariably devolved into political point-scoring contests—so he sent Bouchard in his stead. It was approaching eight that evening when the deputy finally returned to the rue de Grenelle. Entering Rousseau's office, he wordlessly placed two photographs on the desk. They showed an olive-skinned woman in her mid-twenties with an oval face and eyes that were like kaleidoscopes of hazel and copper. In the first photo her hair was shoulder length and brushed straight back from her unblemished forehead. In the second it was covered by a hijab of unadorned black silk.

"They're calling her the black widow," said Bouchard.

"Catchy," said Rousseau with a frown. He picked up the second photo, the one where the woman was piously attired, and stared into the bottomless eyes. "What's her real name?"

"Safia Bourihane."

"Algerian?"

"By way of Aulnay-sous-Bois."

Aulnay-sous-Bois was a banlieue north of Paris. Its crime-ridden public housing estates—in France they were known as HLMs, or *habitation à loyer modéré*—were some of the most violent in the country. The police rarely ventured there. Even Rousseau advised his streetwise case officers to meet their Aulnay-based sources on less dangerous ground.

"She's twenty-nine years old and was born in France," Bouchard was saying. "Even so, she's always described herself as a Muslim first and a Frenchwoman second."

"Who found her?"

"Lucien."

Lucien Jacquard was the chief of the DGSI's counterterrorism division. Nominally, Alpha Group was under his control. In practice, however, Rousseau reported over Jacquard's head to the chief. To avoid potential conflicts, he briefed Jacquard on active Alpha Group cases but jealously guarded the names of his sources and the unit's operational methods. Alpha Group was essentially a service within a service, one that Lucien Jacquard wished to bring firmly under his control.

"How much does he have on her?" asked Rousseau, still staring into the eyes of the woman.

"She popped up on Lucien's radar about three years ago."

"Why?"

"Her boyfriend."

Bouchard placed another photograph on the desk. It showed a man in his early thirties with cropped dark hair and the wispy beard of a devout Muslim.

"Algerian?"

"Tunisian, actually. He was the real thing. Good with electronics. Computers, too. He spent time in Iraq and Yemen before making his way to Syria."

"Al-Qaeda?"

"No," said Bouchard. "ISIS."

Rousseau looked up sharply. "Where is he now?"

"Paradise, apparently."

"What happened?"

"Killed in a coalition air strike."

"And the woman?"

"She traveled to Syria last year."

"How long was she there?"

"At least six months."

"Doing what?"

"Obviously, she did a bit of weapons training."

"And when she returned to Paris?"

"Lucien put her under surveillance. And then . . ." Bouchard shrugged.

"He dropped it?"

Bouchard nodded.

"Why?"

"The usual reasons. Too many targets, too few resources."

"She was a ticking time bomb."

"Lucien didn't think so. Apparently, she cleaned up her act when she came back to France. She wasn't associating with known radicals, and her Internet activity was benign. She even stopped wearing the hijab."

"Which is exactly what she was told to do by the man who masterminded the attack. She was obviously part of a sophisticated network."

"Lucien concurs. In fact, he advised the minister that it's only a matter of time before they hit us again."

"How did the minister take the news?"

"By ordering Lucien to turn over all his files to us."

Rousseau permitted himself a brief smile at the expense of his rival. "I want everything, Christian. Especially the watch reports after her return from Syria."

"Lucien promised to send the files over first thing in the morning."

"How good of him." Rousseau looked down at the photograph of the woman they were calling "la veuve noire"—the black widow. "Where do you suppose she is?"

"If I had to guess, I'd say she's back in Syria by now, along with her accomplice."

"One wonders why they didn't wish to die for the cause." Rousseau gathered up the three photographs and returned them to his deputy. "Any other news?"

"An interesting development regarding the Weinberg woman. It seems her art collection included a lost painting by Vincent van Gogh."

"Really?"

"And guess who she decided to leave it to."

By his expression, Rousseau made it clear he was in no mood for games, so Bouchard quickly supplied the name.

"I thought he was dead."

"Apparently not."

"Why didn't he attend the funeral?"

"Who's to say he didn't?"

"Have we told him about the painting?"

"The ministry would prefer that it remain in France."

"So the answer is no?"

Bouchard was silent.

"Someone should remind the ministry that four of the victims of the Weinberg Center bombing were citizens of the State of Israel."

"Your point?"

"I suspect we'll be hearing from him soon."

Bouchard withdrew, leaving Rousseau alone. He dimmed his desk lamp and pressed the play button on his bookshelf stereo system, and in a moment the opening notes of Chopin's Piano Concerto No. 1 in E Minor crept into the silence. Traffic moved along the rue de Grenelle, and to the east, rising above the Seine embankments, glowed the lights of the

Eiffel Tower. Rousseau saw none of it; in his thoughts he was watching a young man moving swiftly across a courtyard with a gun in his outstretched hand. He was a legend, this man, a gifted deceiver and assassin who had been fighting terrorists longer than even Rousseau. It would be an honor to work with him rather than against him. Soon, Rousseau thought with certainty. *Soon . . .*

3

BEIRUT

Though Paul Rousseau did not know it then, the seeds for just such an operational union had already been sown. For on that very same evening, as Rousseau was walking toward his sad little bachelor's apartment on the rue Saint-Jacques, a car was speeding along Beirut's seafront Corniche. The car was black in color, German in manufacture, and imposing in size. The man in back was long and lanky, with pale, bloodless skin and eyes the color of glacial ice. His expression projected a sense of profound boredom, but the fingers of his right hand, which were tapping lightly on the armrest, betrayed the true state of his emotions. He wore a pair of slim-fitting jeans, a dark woolen pullover, and a leather jacket. Beneath the jacket, wedged inside the waistband of the trousers, was a 9mm Belgian-made pistol he had collected from a contact at the airport—there being no shortage of weapons, large or small, in Lebanon. In his breast pocket was a billfold filled with cash, along with a well-traveled Canadian passport that identified him as David Rostov. Like most things about the man, the passport was a lie. His real name was Mikhail

Abramov, and he was employed by the secret intelligence service of the State of Israel. The service had a long and deliberately misleading name that had very little to do with the true nature of its work. Men such as Mikhail referred to it as the Office and nothing else.

He looked into the rearview mirror and waited for the eyes of the driver to meet his. The driver's name was Sami Haddad. He was a Maronite, a former member of the Lebanese Forces Christian militia, and a longtime contract employee of the Office. He had the gentle forgiving eyes of a priest and the swollen hands of a prizefighter. He was old enough to remember when Beirut was the Paris of the Middle East—and old enough to have fought in the long civil war that had torn the country to pieces. There was nothing Sami Haddad didn't know about Lebanon and its dangerous politics, and nothing he couldn't lay his hands on in a hurry—weapons, boats, cars, drugs, girls. He had once procured a mountain lion on short notice because the target of an Office recruitment, an alcoholic prince from a Gulf Arab dynasty, admired predatory cats. His loyalty to the Office was beyond question. So were his instincts for trouble.

"Relax," said Sami Haddad, finding Mikhail's eyes in the mirror. "We're not being followed."

Mikhail peered over his shoulder at the lights of the traffic following them along the Corniche. Any one of the cars might have contained a team of killers or kidnappers from Hezbollah or one of the extreme jihadist organizations that had taken root in the Palestinian refugee camps of the south—organizations that made al-Qaeda seem like dowdy old Islamic moderates. It was his third visit to Beirut in the past year. Each time, he had entered the country with the same passport, protected by the same cover story. He was David Rostov, an itinerant businessman of Russian-Canadian descent who acquired illicit antiquities in the Middle East for a largely European clientele. Beirut was one of his favorite hunting grounds, for in Beirut anything was possible. He had once been offered a seven-foot Roman statue, remarkably intact, of a wounded Amazon. The cost of the piece was $2 million, shipping included. Over endless cups of sweet Turkish coffee, he convinced the seller, a prominent dealer from a well-known family, to drop his price by half a million. And then he walked away, earning for himself the reputation of both a shrewd negotiator and a tough customer, which was a good reputation to have in a place like Beirut.

He checked the time on his Samsung mobile. Sami Haddad noticed. Sami noticed everything.

"What time is he expecting you?"

"Ten o'clock."

"Late."

"Money never sleeps, Sami."

"Tell me about it."

"Shall we go straight to the hotel, or do you want to take a drive first?"

"Your call."

"Let's go to the hotel."

"Let's take a drive."

"No problem."

Sami Haddad turned off the Corniche into a street lined with colonial French buildings. Mikhail knew it well. Twelve years earlier, while serving in the Sayeret Matkal special forces, he had killed a terrorist from Hezbollah as he lay sleeping in the bed of a safe house. To be a member of such an elite unit was the dream of every Israeli boy, and it was a particularly noteworthy achievement for a boy from Moscow. A boy who had to fight every day of his life because his ancestors happened to be Jewish. A boy whose father, an important

Soviet academic, had been locked away in a psychiatric hospital because he dared to question the wisdom of the Party. The boy had arrived in Israel at the age of sixteen. He had learned to speak Hebrew in a month and within a year had lost all traces of a Russian accent. He was like the millions who had come before him, the early Zionist pioneers who had fled to Palestine to escape the persecution and pogroms of Eastern Europe, the human wrecks who came spilling out of the death camps after the war. He had shed the baggage and the weakness of his past. He was a new person, a new Jew. He was an Israeli.

"We're still clean," said Sami Haddad.

"Then what are you waiting for?" replied Mikhail.

Sami wound his way back to the Corniche and headed to the marina. Rising above it were the twin glass-and-steel towers of the Four Seasons Hotel. Sami guided the car into the drive and looked into the mirror for instructions.

"Call me when he arrives," said Mikhail. "Let me know whether he has a friend."

"He never goes anywhere without a friend."

Mikhail collected his briefcase and overnight bag from the opposite seat and opened the door.

"Be careful in there," said Sami Haddad. "Don't talk to strangers."

Mikhail climbed out and, whistling tunelessly, breezed past the valets into the lobby. A dark-suited security man eyed him warily but allowed him to enter without a search. He crossed a thick carpet that swallowed his footfalls and presented himself at the imposing reception desk. Standing behind it, illuminated by a cone of overhead light, was a pretty black-haired woman of twenty-five. Mikhail knew that the woman was a Palestinian and that her father, a fighter from the old days, had fled Lebanon with Arafat in 1982, long before she was born. Several other employees of the hotel also had troubling connections. Two members of Hezbollah worked in the kitchen, and there were several known jihadis in housekeeping. Mikhail reckoned that approximately ten percent of the staff would have killed him if informed of his true identity and occupation.

He smiled at the woman, and the woman smiled coolly in return.

"Good evening, Mr. Rostov. So good to see you again." Her painted nails clattered on a keyboard while Mikhail grew lightheaded from the stench of overripe azaleas. "We have you for just one night."

"A pity," said Mikhail with another smile.

"Do you require assistance with your luggage?"

"I can manage."

"We've upgraded you to a deluxe sea-view room. It's on the fourteenth floor." She handed him his packet of room keys and gestured toward the elevators like a flight attendant pointing out the location of the emergency exits. "Welcome back."

Mikhail carried his bag and briefcase into the elevator foyer. An empty carriage waited, its doors open. He stepped inside and, grateful for the solitude, pressed the call button for the fourteenth floor. But as the doors were closing, a hand poked through the breach and a man entered. He was thickset, with a heavy ridge over his brow and a jawbone built to take a punch. His eyes met Mikhail's briefly in the reflection of the doors. A nod was exchanged, but no words passed between them. The man pressed the button for the twentieth floor, almost as an afterthought, and picked at his thumbnail as the carriage rose. Mikhail pretended to check his e-mail on his mobile and while doing so surreptitiously snapped the blunt-headed man's photograph. He forwarded the photo to King Saul Boulevard, the location of the Office's anonymous

Tel Aviv headquarters, while walking along the corridor to his room. A glance around the door frame revealed no evidence of tampering. He swiped his card key and, bracing himself for attack, entered.

The sound of Vivaldi greeted him—a favorite of arms smugglers, heroin dealers, and terrorists the world over, he thought as he switched off the radio. The bed had already been turned down, a chocolate lay on the pillow. He went to the window and saw the roof of Sami Haddad's car parked along the Corniche. Beyond was the marina, and beyond the marina the blackness of the Mediterranean. Somewhere out there was his back door. He was no longer allowed to come to Beirut without an offshore escape hatch. The next chief had plans for him—or so he had heard through the Office grapevine. For a secure institution, it was a notoriously gossipy place.

Just then, Mikhail's mobile blossomed with light. It was a message from King Saul Boulevard stating that the computers could not identify the man who had joined him in the elevator. It advised him to proceed with caution, whatever that meant. He drew the blackout shade and the curtains and switched off the room lights one by one until the darkness was absolute. Then he sat at the foot of the bed, his gaze focused on the thin strip of light at the bottom of the door, and waited for the phone to ring.

IT WAS NOT UNUSUAL FOR THE SOURCE TO BE LATE. HE WAS, AS he reminded Mikhail at every opportunity, a very busy man. Therefore, it was no surprise that ten o'clock came and went with no call from Sami Haddad. Finally, at quarter past, the mobile flared.

"He's entering the lobby. He has two friends, both armed."

Mikhail killed the call and remained seated for an additional ten minutes. Then, gun in hand, he moved to the entrance hall and placed his ear against the door. Hearing nothing outside, he returned the gun to the small of his back and stepped into the corridor, which was deserted except for a single male member of the housekeeping staff. Upstairs, the roof bar was the usual scene—rich Lebanese, Emiratis in their flowing white kanduras, Chinese businessmen flushed with drink, drug dealers, whores, gamblers, adventure seekers, fools. The sea wind toyed with the hair of the women and made wavelets in the pool. The throbbing music, spun by a professional DJ, was a sonic crime against humanity.

Mikhail made his way to the farthest corner of the rooftop, where Clovis Mansour, scion of the Mansour antiquities-dealing dynasty, sat alone on a white couch facing the Mediterranean. He was posed as if for a magazine shoot, with a glass of champagne in one hand and a cigarette smoldering in the other. He wore a dark Italian suit and a white open-neck shirt that was handmade for him by his man in London. His gold wristwatch was the size of a sundial. His cologne hung around him like a cloak.

"You're late, *habibi*," he said as Mikhail lowered himself onto the couch opposite. "I was about to leave."

"No, you weren't."

Mikhail surveyed the interior of the bar. Mansour's two bodyguards were picking at a bowl of pistachios at an adjacent table. The man from the elevator was leaning against the balustrade. He was pretending to admire the view of the sea while holding a mobile phone to his ear.

"Know him?" asked Mikhail.

"Never seen him before. Drink?"

"No, thanks."

"It's better if you drink."

Mansour flagged down a passing waiter and ordered a second glass of champagne. Mikhail drew a buff-colored envelope from his coat pocket and placed it on the low table.

"What's that?" asked Mansour.

"A token of our esteem."

"Money?"

Mikhail nodded.

"I don't work for you because I need the money, *habibi*. After all, I have plenty of money. I work for you because I want to stay in business."

"My superiors prefer it if money changes hands."

"Your superiors are cheap blackmailers."

"I'd look inside the envelope before calling them cheap."

Mansour did. He raised an eyebrow and slipped the envelope into the breast pocket of his suit jacket.

"What have you got for me, Clovis?"

"Paris," said the antiquities dealer.

"What about Paris?"

"I know who did it."

"How?"

"I can't say for certain," said Mansour, "but it's possible I helped him pay for it."

4

BEIRUT—TEL AVIV

IT WAS HALF PAST TWO in the morning by the time Mikhail finally returned to his room. He saw no evidence to suggest it had been disturbed in his absence; even the little foiled chocolate lay at precisely the same angle atop his pillow. After sniffing it for traces of arsenic, he nibbled at a corner thoughtfully. Then, in an uncharacteristic fit of nerves, he hauled every piece of furniture that wasn't bolted down into the entrance hall and piled it against the door. His barricade complete, he opened the curtains and the blackout shade and searched for his bolt-hole among the shipping lights in the Mediterranean. Instantly, he reproached himself for entertaining such a thought. The escape hatch was to be utilized only in cases of extreme emergency. Possession of a piece of intelligence did not fall into that category, even if the piece of intelligence had the potential to prevent another catastrophe like Paris.

They call him Saladin . . .

Mikhail stretched out on the bed, his back propped against the headboard, the gun at his side, and stared at the shadowy mass of his fortifications. It was, he thought, a truly undignified sight. He switched on the television and surfed the airwaves of a Middle East gone mad until boredom drove him toward the doorstep of sleep. To keep himself alert he guzzled a cola from the fridge bar and thought about a woman he had foolishly let slip through his fingers. She was a beautiful American of flawless Protestant pedigree who had worked for the CIA and, occasionally, for the Office. She was living in New York now, where she oversaw a special collection of paintings at the Museum of Modern Art. He'd heard she was seeing a man quite seriously, a bond trader, of all things. He contemplated calling her, just to hear the sound of her voice, but decided it would be unwise. Like Russia, she was lost to him.

What's his real name, Clovis?

I'm not sure he ever had one.

Where's he from?

He might have been from Iraq once, but now he's a son of the caliphate . . .

Finally, the sky beyond Mikhail's window turned blueblack with the coming dawn. He put his room in order and thirty minutes later slumped bleary-eyed into the back of Sami Haddad's car.

"How did it go?" asked the Lebanese.

"Total waste of time," replied Mikhail through an elaborate yawn.

"Where now?"

"Tel Aviv."

"It's not such an easy drive, my friend."

"Then perhaps you should take me to the airport instead."

His flight was at half past eight. He sailed through passport control as a smiling, somewhat drowsy Canadian and settled into his first-class seat aboard a Middle East Airlines jet bound for Rome. To shield himself from his neighbor, a

Turkish salesman of disreputable appearance, he pretended to read the morning papers. In reality, he was considering all the possible reasons why an aircraft operated by the government of Lebanon might fail to reach its destination safely. For once, he thought glumly, his death would have consequences, for the intelligence would die with him.

How much money are we talking about, Clovis?

Four million, maybe five.

Which is it?

Closer to five . . .

The plane landed in Rome without incident, though it took Mikhail the better part of two hours to clear the organized stampede that was Fiumicino's passport control. His stay in Italy was brief, long enough for him to switch identities and board another airplane, an El Al flight bound for Tel Aviv. An Office car waited at Ben Gurion; it whisked him north to King Saul Boulevard. The building at the western end of the street was, like Paul Rousseau's outpost on the rue de Grenelle, a lie in plain sight. No emblem hung over its entrance, no brass lettering proclaimed the identity of its occupant. In fact, there was nothing at all to suggest it was the headquarters of one of the world's most feared and respected intelligence services. A closer inspection of the structure, however, would have revealed the existence of a building within a building, one with its own power supply, its own water and sewer lines, and its own secure communications system. Employees carried two keys. One opened an unmarked door in the lobby; the other operated the lift. Those who committed the unpardonable sin of losing one or both of their keys were banished to the Judean Wilderness, never to be seen or heard from again.

Like most field agents, Mikhail entered the building through the underground parking garage and then made his way upward to the executive floor. Because the hour was late—

the security cameras recorded the time as half past nine—the corridor was as quiet as a school that had been emptied of children. From the half-open door at the end of the hall stretched a slender rhombus of light. Mikhail knocked softly and, hearing no reply, entered. Stuffed into an executive leather chair behind a desk of smoked glass was Uzi Navot, the soon-to-be former chief of the Office. He was frowning at an open file as though it were a bill he could not afford to pay. At his elbow was an open box of Viennese butter cookies. Only two remained, not a good sign.

At length, Navot looked up and with a dismissive movement of his hand instructed Mikhail to sit. He wore a striped dress shirt that had been cut for a thinner man and a pair of the rimless spectacles beloved by German intellectuals and Swiss bankers. His hair, once strawberry blond, was gray stubble; his blue eyes were bloodshot. He rolled up his shirtsleeves, exposing his massive forearms, and contemplated Mikhail for a long moment with thinly veiled hostility. It wasn't the reception Mikhail had expected, but then one never knew quite what to expect when one encountered Uzi Navot these days. There were rumors his successor intended to keep him on in some capacity—blasphemy in a service that regarded regular turnover at the top almost as a matter of religious doctrine—but officially his future was unclear.

"Any problems on the way out of Beirut?" Navot asked at last, as though the question had occurred to him suddenly.

"None," answered Mikhail.

Navot snared a stray cookie crumb with the tip of a thick forefinger. "Surveillance?"

"Nothing we could see."

"And the man who rode the hotel elevator with you? Did you ever see him again?"

"At the roof bar."

"Anything suspicious?"

"Everyone in Beirut looks suspicious. That's why it's Beirut."

Navot flicked the cookie crumb onto the plate. Then he removed a photograph from the file and dealt it across the desktop toward Mikhail. It showed a man sitting in the front seat of a luxury automobile, at the edge of a seaside boulevard. The windows of the car were shattered. The man was a bloody tattered mess, and quite obviously dead.

"Recognize him?" asked Navot.

Mikhail squinted in concentration.

"Look carefully at the car."

Mikhail did. And then he understood. The dead man was Sami Haddad.

"When did they get him?"

"Not long after he dropped you at the airport. And they were just getting started."

Navot spun another photo across the desk, a ruined building on an elegant street in downtown Beirut. It was Gallerie Mansour on the rue Madame Curie. Limbs and heads littered the pavement. For once the carnage wasn't human. It was Clovis Mansour's magnificent professional inventory.

"I was hoping," Navot resumed after a moment, "that my last days as chief would pass without incident. Instead, I have to deal with the loss of our best contract employee in Beirut and an asset we spent a great deal of time and effort recruiting."

"Better than a dead field agent."

"I'll be the judge of that." Navot accepted the two photographs and returned them to the file. "What did Mansour have for you?"

"The man who was behind Paris."

"Who is he?"

"They call him Saladin."

"Saladin? Well," Navot said, closing the file, "at least that's a start."

NAVOT REMAINED IN HIS OFFICE LONG AFTER MIKHAIL HAD taken his leave. The desk was empty except for his leather-bound executive notepad, on which he had scrawled a single word. *Saladin* . . . Only a man of great self-esteem would grant himself a code name like that, only a man of great ambition. The real Saladin had united the Muslim world under the Ayyubid dynasty and recaptured Jerusalem from the Crusaders. Perhaps this new Saladin was similarly inclined. For his coming-out party he had flattened a Jewish target in the middle of Paris, thus attacking two countries, two civilizations, at the same time. Surely, thought Navot, the success of the attack had only whetted his lust for infidel blood. It was only a matter of time before he struck again.

For the moment, Saladin was a French problem. But the fact that four Israeli citizens had perished in the attack gave Navot standing in Paris. So, too, did the name that Clovis Mansour had whispered into Mikhail's ear in Beirut. In fact, with a bit of skilled salesmanship, the name alone might be enough to secure the Office a seat at the operational table. Navot was confident in his powers of persuasion. A former field agent and recruiter of spies, he had the ability to spin straw into gold. All he needed was someone to look after the Office's interest in any joint Franco-Israeli undertaking. He had but one candidate in mind, a legendary field agent who had been running operations on French soil since he was a boy of twenty-two. What's more, the operative in question had known Hannah Weinberg personally. Unfortunately, the prime minister had other plans for him.

Navot checked the time; it was ten fifteen. He reached for his phone and dialed Travel.

"I need to fly to Paris tomorrow morning."

"The six o'clock or the nine?"

"The six," said Navot despondently.

"When are you coming back?"

"Tomorrow night."

"Done."

Navot rang off and then placed a final call. The question he posed was one he had asked many times before.

"How long before he's finished?"

"He's close."

"How close?"

"Maybe tonight, tomorrow at the latest."

Navot replaced the receiver and allowed his gaze to wander the spacious office that soon would no longer be his.

Tomorrow at the latest . . .

Maybe, he thought, or maybe not.

5

ISRAEL MUSEUM, JERUSALEM

IN THE FAR CORNER OF the conservation lab, a black curtain stretched from the white ceiling to the white floor. Behind it was a matching pair of oaken Italian easels, two halogen lamps, a Nikon camera mounted atop a tripod, a palette, a tiny bale of cotton wool, an ancient CD player smudged with several different colors of paint, and a trolley laden with pigments, medium, solvents, wooden dowels, and several Winsor & Newton Series 7 sable-hair paintbrushes. For the better part of the past four months, the restorer had labored there alone, sometimes late at night, sometimes long before dawn. He wore no museum credentials, for his true place of employment was elsewhere. The staff conservators had been advised not to mention his presence or even to speak his name. Nor were they to discuss the large painting, an Italian Old Master altarpiece, propped upon his easels. The painting, like the restorer, had a dangerous and tragic past.

He was below average in height—five foot eight, perhaps, no more—and slender of build. His face was high at the forehead and narrow at the chin, with wide prominent cheekbones and a long, bony nose that looked as though it had been carved from wood. The dark hair was cropped short and stained with gray at the temples, the eyes were an unnatural shade of green. His age was one of the most closely guarded secrets in Israel. Not long ago, when his obituary appeared in newspapers around the world, no verifiable date of birth ever found its way into print. The reports of his death had been part of an elaborate operation to deceive his enemies in Moscow and Tehran. They had believed the stories to be true, a miscalculation that allowed the restorer to take vengeance against them. Not long after his return to Jerusalem, his wife gave birth to a set of twins, a girl named Irene after his mother, and a son called Raphael. They were now—mother, daughter, son—three of the most closely guarded people in the State of Israel. So, too, was the restorer. He came and went in an armored American-made SUV, accompanied by a bodyguard, a fawn-eyed killer of twenty-five, who sat outside the door of the conservation lab whenever he was present.

His appearance at the museum, on a black and wet Wednesday in December a few days after the birth of his children, had come as a shock, and a profound relief, to the rest of the conservation staff. They had been warned he did not like to be observed while working. Still, they routinely poked their heads into his little curtained grotto merely to glimpse the altarpiece with their own eyes. Truth be told, he couldn't blame them. The painting, Caravaggio's *Nativity with St. Francis and St. Lawrence*, was arguably the world's most famous missing work of art. Stolen from the Oratorio di San Lorenzo in Palermo in October 1969, it was now formally in the possession of the Vatican. The Holy See had wisely decided to withhold news of the painting's recovery until the restoration was complete. Like many Vatican pronouncements, the official version of events would bear little resemblance to the truth. It would not mention the fact that a legendary Israeli intelligence officer named Gabriel Allon had found the missing painting hanging in a church in the northern Italian town of Brienno. Nor would it mention that the same legendary intelligence officer had been entrusted with the task of restoring it.

During his long career he had carried out several unusual restorations—he had once repaired a Rembrandt portrait that had been pierced by a bullet—but the Caravaggio altarpiece propped upon Gabriel's easels was without question the most damaged canvas he had ever seen. Little was known of its long journey from the Oratorio di San Lorenzo to the church where he had found it. The stories, however, were legion. It had been kept by a Mafia don as a prize and brought out for important meetings of his henchmen. It had been chewed by rats, damaged in a flood, and burned in a fire. Gabriel was certain of only one thing: the painting's wounds, while grievous, were not fatal. But Ephraim Cohen, the museum's chief of conservation, was dubious. Upon seeing the painting for the first time, he advised Gabriel to administer last rites and return the altarpiece to the Vatican in the same wooden coffin in which it had arrived.

"Ye of little faith," Gabriel had said.

"No," replied Cohen. "Me of limited talent."

Cohen, like the other members of the staff, had heard the stories—the stories of deadlines missed, of commissions abandoned, of church reopenings delayed. The snail-like pace of Gabriel's work habits was legendary, almost as legendary as his exploits on the secret battlefields of Europe and the Middle East. But they soon discovered that his slowness was voluntary rather than instinctive. The craft of restoration, he explained to Cohen one evening while swiftly repairing the tattered face of Saint Francis, was a bit like making love. It was best done slowly and with painstaking attention to detail, with occasional breaks for rest and refreshment. But in a pinch, if the craftsman and his subject matter were adequately acquainted, a restoration could be done at extraordinary speed, with more or less the same result.

"You and Caravaggio are old friends?" asked Cohen.

"We've collaborated in the past."

"So the rumors are true then?"

Gabriel had been painting with his right hand. Now he moved the brush to his left and worked with equal dexterity.

"What rumors are those?" he asked after a moment.

"That you were the one who restored the *Deposition* for the Vatican Museums a few years ago."

"You should never listen to rumors, Ephraim, especially when they concern me."

"Or the news," said Cohen darkly.

His hours were erratic and unpredictable. An entire day might pass with no sign of him. Then Cohen would arrive at the museum to find a large portion of the canvas miraculously restored. Surely, he thought, he had a secret helper. Or perhaps Caravaggio himself was stealing into the museum at night, a sword in one hand, a brush in the other, to assist with the work. After one nocturnal session—a particularly productive visit during which the Virgin was returned to her former glory—Cohen actually checked the security footage. He found that Gabriel had entered the lab at half past ten in the evening and had departed at seven twenty the next morning. Not even the fawn-eyed bodyguard had been with him. Perhaps it was true, thought Cohen, as he watched the ghostly figure moving at one frame per second along a half-lit hall. Perhaps he was an archangel after all.

When he was present during normal business hours, there was always music. *La Bohème* was a particular favorite. Indeed, he played it so often that Cohen, who spoke not a word of

Italian, could soon sing "Che gelida manina" from memory. Once Gabriel entered his curtained grotto, he never reappeared until the session was complete. There were no strolls in the museum's sculpture garden to clear his head, no trips to the staff lunchroom for a jolt of caffeine. Only the music, and the soft *tap-tap-tap* of his brush, and the occasional click of his Nikon camera as he recorded his relentless progress. Before leaving the laboratory he would clean his brushes and his palette and put his trolley in order—precisely, noted Cohen, so he would be able to detect whether anyone touched his things in his absence. Then the music would go silent, the halogen lamps would dim, and with little more than a cordial nod to the others he would be gone.

By early April, with the winter rains a memory and the days warm and bright, he was hurling himself headlong toward a finish line only he could see. All that remained was the winged angel of the Lord, an ivory-skinned boy who floated in the upper reaches of the composition. It was a curious choice to leave for last, thought Cohen, for the boy angel had suffered serious injury. His limbs were scarred by heavy paint losses, his white garment was in tatters. Only his right hand, which was pointed heavenward, was undamaged. Gabriel restored the angel in a series of marathon sessions. They were noteworthy for their silence—there was no music during this period—and for the fact that, as he was repairing the angel's auburn hair, a large bomb exploded in Paris. He stood for a long time before the lab's small television, his palette slowly drying, watching as the bodies were pulled from the rubble. And when a photograph of a woman named Hannah Weinberg appeared on the screen, he flinched as though struck by an invisible blow. Afterward, his expression darkened and his green eyes seemed to burn with anger. Cohen was tempted to ask the legend whether he had known the woman, but decided against it. One could talk to him about paintings and the weather, but when bombs exploded it was probably better to keep one's distance.

On the last day, the day of Uzi Navot's journey to Paris, Gabriel arrived at the lab before dawn and remained in his little grotto long after the museum had closed for the night. Ephraim Cohen found an excuse to stay late because he sensed the end was near and wanted to be present to witness it. Shortly after eight o'clock he heard the familiar sound of the legend laying his brush—a Winsor & Newton Series 7— on the aluminum tray of his trolley. Cohen peered furtively through the slender gap in the curtain and saw him standing before the canvas, a hand resting against his chin, his head tilted slightly to the side. He remained in the same position, motionless as the figures in the painting, until the fawn-eyed bodyguard entered the lab and pressed a mobile phone urgently into his palm. Reluctantly, he lifted it to his ear, listened in silence, and murmured something Cohen couldn't quite make out. A moment later both he and the bodyguard were gone.

Alone, Ephraim Cohen slipped through the curtain and stood before the canvas, scarcely able to draw a breath. Finally, he plucked the Winsor & Newton paintbrush from the trolley and slipped it into the pocket of his smock. It wasn't fair, he thought, as he doused the halogen lamps. Perhaps he really was an archangel after all.

6

MA'ALE HAHAMISHA, ISRAEL

THE OLD KIBBUTZ OF MA'ALE HAHAMISHA occupied a strategic hilltop in the craggy western approaches to Jerusalem, not far from the Arab town of Abu Ghosh. Founded during the Arab Revolt of 1936–39, it was one of fifty-seven so-called tower and stockade settlements hastily erected across British-ruled Palestine in a desperate bid to secure the Zionist endeavor and, ultimately, reclaim the ancient kingdom of Israel. It derived its name and very identity from an act of revenge. Translated into English, Ma'ale Hahamisha meant "the Ascent of the Five." It was a not-so-subtle reminder that an Arab terrorist from a nearby village had died at the hands of five of the kibbutz's Jews.

Despite the violent circumstances of its birth, the kibbutz grew prosperous from its cauliflower and peaches and its charming mountain hotel. Ari Shamron, the twice-former chief of the Office and éminence grise of Israeli intelligence, often used the hotel as a meeting place when King Saul Boulevard or a safe flat wouldn't do. One such meeting occurred on a brilliant afternoon in September 1972. On that occasion

Shamron's reluctant guest was a promising young painter named Gabriel Allon, whom Shamron had plucked from the Bezalel Academy of Art and Design. The Palestinian terrorist group Black September had just murdered eleven Israeli athletes and coaches at the Olympic games in Munich, and Shamron wanted Gabriel, a native German speaker who had spent time in Europe, to serve as his instrument of vengeance. Gabriel, with the defiance of youth, had told Shamron to find someone else. And Shamron, not for the last time, had bent him to his will.

The operation was code-named Wrath of God, a phrase chosen by Shamron to give his undertaking the patina of divine sanction. For three years Gabriel and a small team of operatives stalked their prey across Western Europe and the Middle East, killing at night and in broad daylight, living in fear that at any moment they might be arrested by local authorities and charged as murderers. In all, twelve members of Black September died at their hands. Gabriel personally killed six of the terrorists with a .22-caliber Beretta pistol. Whenever possible, he shot his victims eleven times, one bullet for each murdered Jew. When finally he returned to Israel, his temples were gray from stress and exhaustion. Shamron called them smudges of ash on the prince of fire.

It had been Gabriel's intention to resume his career as an artist, but each time he stood before a canvas he saw only the faces of the men he had killed. And so with Shamron's blessing he traveled to Venice as an expatriate Italian named Mario Delvecchio to study restoration. When his apprenticeship was complete, he returned to the Office and to the waiting arms of Ari Shamron. Posing as a gifted if taciturn European-based art restorer, he eliminated some of Israel's most dangerous foes—including Abu Jihad, Yasir Arafat's talented second-in-command, whom he killed in front of his wife and children in Tunis. Arafat returned the favor by ordering a terrorist to place a bomb beneath Gabriel's car in Vienna. The explosion killed his young son Daniel and seriously wounded Leah, his first wife. She resided now in a psychiatric hospital on the other side of the ridge from Ma'ale Hahamisha, trapped in a prison of memory and a body ravaged by fire. The hospital was located in the old Arab village of Deir Yassin, where Jewish fighters from the Irgun and Lehi paramilitary organizations massacred more than a hundred Palestinians on the night of April 9, 1948. It was a cruel irony—that the shattered wife of Israel's avenging angel should reside among the ghosts of Deir Yassin—but such was life in the twice–Promised Land. The past was inescapable. Arab and Jew were bound together by hatred, blood, and victimhood. And for their punishment they would be forced to live together as feuding neighbors for all eternity.

The years after the bombing in Vienna were for Gabriel the lost years. He lived as a hermit in Cornwall, he wandered Europe quietly restoring paintings, he tried to forget. Eventually, Shamron came calling yet again, and the bond between Gabriel and the Office was renewed. Acting at his mentor's behest, he carried off some of the most celebrated operations in the history of Israeli intelligence. His was the career against which all others would be measured, especially Uzi Navot's. Like the Arabs and Jews of Palestine, Gabriel and Navot were inextricably bound. They were the sons of Ari Shamron, the trusted heirs of the service he had built and nurtured. Gabriel, the elder son, had been confident of the father's love, but Navot had always struggled to win his approval. He had been given the job as chief only because Gabriel had turned it down. Now, remarried, a father once more, Gabriel was finally ready to assume his rightful place in the executive suite of King Saul Boulevard. For Uzi Navot it was a *nakba*, the word the Arabs used to describe the catastrophe of their flight from the land of Palestine.

The old hotel in Ma'ale Hahamisha was less than a mile from the 1967 border, and from its terrace restaurant it was possible to see the orderly yellow lights of Jewish settlements spilling down the hillside into the West Bank. The terrace was in darkness, except for a few windblown candles flickering dimly on the empty tables. Navot sat alone in a distant corner, the same corner where Shamron had been waiting on that ·September afternoon in 1972. Gabriel sat down next to him and turned up the collar of his leather jacket against the cold. Navot was silent. He was staring down at the lights of Har Adar, the first Israeli settlement over the old Green Line.

"Mazel tov," he said at last.

"For what?"

"The painting," said Navot. "I hear it's almost finished."

"Where did you hear a thing like that?"

"I've been monitoring your progress. So has the prime minister." Navot regarded Gabriel through his small rimless spectacles. "Is it really done?"

"I think so."

"What does that mean?"

"It means that I want to take one more look at it in the morning. If I like what I see, I'll apply a coat of varnish and send it back to the Vatican."

"And only ten days past your deadline."

"Eleven, actually. But who's counting?"

"I was." Navot gave a rueful smile. "I enjoyed the reprieve, however brief."

A silence descended between them. It was far from companionable.

"In case it's slipped your mind," Navot said at last, "it's time for you to sign your new contract and move into my office. In fact, I was planning to pack up my things today, but I had to make one more trip as chief."

"Where?"

"I had a piece of intelligence that I needed to share with our French brethren about the bombing of the Weinberg Center. I also wanted to make certain they were pursuing the perpetrators with appropriate vigor. After all, four Israeli citizens were killed, not to mention a woman who once did a very large favor for the Office."

"Do they know about our links to her?"

"The French?"

"Yes, Uzi, the French."

"I sent a team into her apartment to have a look around after the attack."

"And?"

"The team found no mention of a certain Israeli intelligence officer who once borrowed her van Gogh in order to find a terrorist. Nor was there any reference to one Zizi al-Bakari, investment manager for the House of Saud and CEO of Jihad, Incorporated." Navot paused, then added, "May he rest in peace."

"What about the painting?"

"It was in its usual place. In hindsight, the team should have taken it."

"Why?"

"As you no doubt remember, our Hannah was never married. No siblings, either. Her will was quite explicit when it came to the painting. Unfortunately, French intelligence got to her lawyer before he could make contact with us."

"What are you talking about, Uzi?"

"It seems Hannah trusted only one person in the world to look after her van Gogh."

"Who?"

"You, of course. But there's just one problem," Navot added. "The French have taken the painting hostage. And they're asking a rather high ransom."

"How much?"

"The French don't want money, Gabriel. The French want *you*."

7

MA'ALE HAHAMISHA, ISRAEL

NAVOT LAID A PHOTOGRAPH ON the table, a street in Beirut littered with the ancient debris of an antiquities gallery.

"I assume you saw this."

Gabriel nodded slowly. He had read about Clovis Mansour's death in the newspapers. Given the events in Paris, the bombing in Beirut had received only minor press coverage. Not a single news outlet attempted to link the two events, nor was there any suggestion in the media that Clovis Mansour was on the payroll of any foreign intelligence service. In point of fact, he received money from at least four: the CIA, MI6, the Jordanian GID, and the Office. Gabriel knew this because, in preparation for taking over as chief, he had been devouring briefing books on all current operations and assets.

"Clovis was one of our best sources in Beirut," Navot was saying, "especially when it came to matters involving money. Lately, he'd been keeping an eye on ISIS's involvement in the illicit antiquities trade, which is why he requested a crash meeting the day after the bomb exploded in Paris."

"Who did you send?"

Navot answered.

"Since when is Mikhail an agent runner?"

Navot laid another photograph on the table. It had been taken by an overhead security camera and was of moderate quality. It showed two men sitting at a small round table. One was Clovis Mansour. As usual he was impeccably attired, but the man opposite looked as though he had borrowed clothing for the occasion. In the center of the table, resting on what appeared to be a swath of baize cloth, was a head, life-size, its eyes staring blankly into space. Gabriel recognized it as Roman in origin. He reckoned the poorly dressed man had more of the statue, perhaps the entire piece. The perfectly intact head was merely his calling card.

"There's no date or time code."

"It was the twenty-second of November, at four fifteen in the afternoon."

"Who's the chap with the Roman head?"

"His business card identified him as Iyad al-Hamzah."

"Lebanese?"

"Syrian," answered Navot. "Apparently, he rolled into town with a truckload of antiquities to sell—Greek, Roman, Persian, all high-quality, many bearing the telltale signs of recent excavation. Among the places he attempted to unload his wares was Gallerie Mansour. Clovis expressed interest in several items, but after making a few quiet inquiries he decided to take a pass."

"Why?"

"Because the word on the street was that the gentleman from Syria was using the sale of looted antiquities to raise money for the Islamic State. Evidently, the money wasn't intended for ISIS's general fund. The Syrian gentleman was working on behalf of a high-ranking ISIS leader who was building a terror network capable of attacking targets in the West."

"Does the ISIS leader have a name?"

"They call him Saladin."

Gabriel looked up from the photograph. "How grandiose."

"I couldn't agree more."

"I don't suppose Clovis managed to learn his real name?"

"No such luck."

"Where's he from?"

"The senior ISIS commanders are all Iraqis. They regard the Syrians as pack mules."

Gabriel looked down at the photograph again. "Why didn't Clovis tell us about this sooner?"

"It seems to have slipped his mind."

"Or maybe he's lying."

"Clovis Mansour? Lying? How could you suggest such a thing?"

"He's a Lebanese antiquities dealer."

"What's your theory?" asked Navot.

"I have a feeling Clovis made a great deal of money selling those antiquities. And when a bomb exploded in the heart of Paris, he thought it might be wise to hedge his bets. So he came to us with a pretty story about how he was too virtuous to deal with the likes of ISIS."

"That pretty story," said Navot, "cost Clovis his life."

"How do you know?"

"Because they killed Sami Haddad, too. I'll spare you the photo."

"Why just Clovis and Sami? Why not Mikhail, too?"

"I've been asking myself the same question."

"And?"

"I don't know why. I'm just glad they didn't kill him. It would have ruined my going-away party."

Gabriel returned the photograph. "How much did you tell the French?"

"Enough to let them know that the plot against the Weinberg Center originated in the caliphate. They weren't surprised. In fact, they were already well aware of the Syrian connection. Both of the attackers traveled there during the past year. One is a Frenchwoman of Algerian descent. Her male accomplice is a Belgian national from the Molenbeek district of Brussels."

"Belgium? How shocking," said Gabriel derisively.

Thousands of Muslims from France, Britain, and Germany had traveled to Syria to fight alongside ISIS, but tiny Belgium had earned the dubious distinction of being Western Europe's largest per capita supplier of manpower to the Islamic caliphate.

"Where are they now?" asked Gabriel.

"In a few minutes the French interior minister is going to announce they're back in Syria."

"How did they get there?"

"Air France to Istanbul on borrowed passports."

"But of course." There was a silence. Finally, Gabriel asked, "What does this have to do with me, Uzi?"

"The French are concerned that ISIS has managed to construct a sophisticated network on French soil."

"Is that so?"

"The French are also concerned," said Navot, ignoring the remark, "that this network intends to strike again in short order. Obviously, they would like to roll it up before the next attack. And they'd like you to help them do it."

"Why me?"

"It seems you have an admirer inside the French security service. His name is Paul Rousseau. He runs a small operational unit called Alpha Group. He wants you to fly to Paris tomorrow morning for a meeting."

"And if I don't?"

"That painting will never leave French soil."

"I'm supposed to meet with the prime minister tomorrow. He's going to tell the world that I wasn't killed in that bombing on the Brompton Road. He's going to announce that I'm the new chief of the Office."

"Yes," said Navot dryly, "I know."

"Maybe *you* should be the one to work with the French."

"I suggested that."

"And?"

"They only want you." Navot paused, then added, "The story of my life."

Gabriel tried and failed to suppress a smile.

"There is a silver lining to this," Navot continued. "The prime minister thinks a joint operation with the French will help to repair our relations with a country that was once a valuable and trusted ally."

"Diplomacy by special ops?"

"In so many words."

"Well," said Gabriel, "you and the prime minister seem to have it all worked out."

"It was Paul Rousseau's idea, not ours."

"Was it really, Uzi?"

"What are you suggesting? That I engineered this to hold on to my job a little longer?"

"Did you?"

Navot waved his hand as though he were dispersing a foul odor. "Take the operation, Gabriel—for Hannah Weinberg, if for no other reason. Get inside the network. Find out who Saladin really is and where he's operating. And then put him down before another bomb explodes."

Gabriel gazed northward, toward the distant black mass

of mountains separating Israel from what remained of Syria. "You don't even know whether he really exists, Uzi. He's only a rumor."

"Someone planned that attack and moved the pieces into place under the noses of the French security services. It wasn't a twenty-nine-year-old woman from the banlieues and her friend from Brussels. And it wasn't a rumor."

Navot's phone flared like a match in the darkness. He raised it briefly to his ear before offering it to Gabriel.

"Who is it?"

"The prime minister."

"What does he want?"

"An answer."

Gabriel stared at the phone for a moment. "Tell him I have to have a word with the most powerful person in the State of Israel. Tell him I'll call first thing in the morning."

Navot relayed the message and rang off.

"What did he say?"

Navot smiled. "Good luck."

8

NARKISS STREET, JERUSALEM

THE GRUMBLE OF GABRIEL'S SUV disturbed the resolute quiet of Narkiss Street. He alighted from the backseat, passed through a metal gate, and headed up the garden walk to the entrance of a Jerusalem limestone apartment building. On the third-floor landing, he found the door to his flat slightly ajar. He opened it slowly, silently, and in the half-light saw Chiara seated at one end of the white couch, a child to her breast. The child was wrapped in a blanket. Only when Gabriel crept closer could he see it was Raphael. The boy had inherited his father's face and the face of a half-brother he would never know. Gabriel toyed with the downy dark hair and then leaned down to kiss Chiara's warm lips.

"If you wake him," she whispered, "I'll kill you."

Smiling, Gabriel slipped off his suede loafers and in stocking feet padded down the corridor to the nursery. Two cribs stood end to end against a wall covered by clouds. They had been painted by Chiara and then hastily repainted by Gabriel upon his return to Israel, after what was supposed to be his last operation. He stood at the railing of one of the cribs and gazed down at the child sleeping below. He didn't dare touch her. Raphael was already sleeping through the night, but Irene was a nocturnal creature who had learned how to blackmail her way into her parents' bed. She was smaller and trimmer than her corpulent sibling, but far more stubborn and determined. Gabriel thought she had the makings of a perfect spy, though he would never permit it. A doctor, a poet, a painter—anything but a spy. He would have no successor, there would be no dynasty. The House of Allon would fade with his passing.

Gabriel peered upward toward the spot where he had painted Daniel's face among the clouds, but the darkness rendered the image invisible. He left the nursery, closing the door soundlessly behind him, and went into the kitchen. The savor of meat braising in red wine and aromatics hung decadently in the air. He peered through the oven window and saw a covered orange casserole centered on the rack. Next to the stove, arranged as if for a recipe book, were the makings of Chiara's famous risotto: Arborio rice, grated cheese, butter, white wine, and a large measuring cup filled with homemade chicken stock. There was also a bottle of Galilean Syrah, unopened. Gabriel eased the cork from the neck, poured a glass, and returned to the sitting room.

Quietly, he settled into the armchair opposite Chiara. And he thought, not for the first time, that the little apartment in the old neighborhood of Nachlaot was too small for a family of four, and too far from King Saul Boulevard. It would be better to have a house in the secular belt of suburbs along the Coastal Plain, or a large apartment in one of the smart new towers that seemed to sprout overnight along the sea in Tel Aviv. But long ago, Jerusalem, God's fractured city upon a hill, had cast a spell over him. He loved the limestone buildings and the smell of the pine and the cold wind and rains in the winter. He loved the churches and the pilgrims and the Haredim who shouted at him because he drove a motorcar on the Sabbath. He even loved the Arabs in the Old City who eyed him warily as he passed their stalls in the souk, as if somehow they knew that he was the one who had eliminated so many of their patron saints of terror. And while not religious by practice, he loved to slip into the Jewish Quarter and stand before the weighty ashlars of the Western Wall. Gabriel was willing to accept territorial compromises in order to secure a lasting and viable peace with the Palestinians and the broader Arab world, but privately he regarded the Western Wall as nonnegotiable. There would never again be a border through the heart of Jerusalem, and Jews would never again have to request permission to visit their holiest site. The Wall was part of Israel now, and it would remain so until the day the country ceased to exist. In this volatile corner of the Mediterranean, kingdoms and empires came and went like the winter rains. One day the modern reincarnation of Israel would disappear, too. But not while Gabriel was alive, and certainly not while he was chief of the Office.

He drank some of the earthy, peppery Syrah and contemplated Chiara and Raphael as though they were figures in his own private nativity. The child had released his hold on his mother's breast and was lying drunken and sated in her arms. Chiara was staring down at him, her long curly hair, with its auburn and chestnut highlights, tumbling over one shoulder, her angular nose and jaw in semi-profile. Chiara's was a face of timeless beauty. In it Gabriel saw traces of Arabia and North Africa and Spain and all the other places her ancestors had wandered before finding themselves in the ancient Jewish ghetto of Venice. It was there, ten years earlier, in a small office off the ghetto's broad piazza, that Gabriel had seen her for the first time—the beautiful, opinionated, over-educated daughter of the city's chief rabbi. Unbeknownst to Gabriel, she was also an Office field agent, a *bat leveyha* female escort officer. She revealed herself to him a short time later in Rome, after an incident involving gunplay and the Italian police. Trapped alone with Chiara in a safe flat, Gabriel had wanted desperately to touch her. He had waited until the case was resolved and they had returned to Venice. There, in a canal house in Cannaregio, they made love for the first time, in a bed prepared with fresh linen. It was like making love to a figure painted by the hand of Veronese.

She was far too young for him, and he was much too old to be a father again—or so he had thought until the moment his two children, first Raphael, then Irene, emerged in a blur from the incision in Chiara's womb. Instantly, all that had come before seemed like stops along a journey to this place: the bombing in Vienna, the years of self-imposed exile, the long Hamlet-like struggle over whether it was proper for him to remarry and start another family. The shadow of Leah would always hang over this little home in the heart of Jerusalem, and the face of Daniel would always peer down on his half-siblings from his heavenly perch on the wall of the nursery. But after years of wandering in the wilderness, Gabriel Allon, the eternal stranger, the lost son of Ari Shamron, was finally home. He drank more of the blood-red Syrah and tried to compose the words he would use to tell Chiara that he was leaving for Paris because a woman she had never met had left him a van Gogh painting worth more than a hundred million dollars. The woman, like too many others he had met along his journey, was dead. And Gabriel was going to find the man responsible.

They call him Saladin . . .

Chiara placed a finger to her lips. Then, rising, she carried Raphael into the nursery. She returned a moment later and took the glass of wine from Gabriel's hand. She lifted it to her nose and breathed deeply of its rich scent but did not drink.

"It won't hurt them if you take a small sip."

"Soon." She returned the glass to Gabriel. "Is it finished?"

"Yes," he answered. "I think it is."

"That's good." She smiled. "What now?"

"HAVE YOU CONSIDERED THE POSSIBILITY," asked CHIARA, "that this is all an elaborate plot by Uzi to hang on to his job a little longer?"

"I have."

"And?"

"He swears it was all Paul Rousseau's idea."

Chiara skeptically folded the butter and the cheese into the risotto mixture. Then she spooned the rice onto two plates and to each added a thick slice of the osso buco Milanese.

"More juice," said Gabriel. "I like the juice."

"It's not stew, darling."

Gabriel tore away a crust of bread and swirled it along the bottom of the casserole pot.

"Peasant," sneered Chiara.

"I come from a long line of peasants."

"You? You're as bourgeois as they come."

Chiara dimmed the overhead lights, and they sat down at a small candlelit table in the kitchen.

"Why candles?" asked Gabriel.

"It's a special occasion."

"My last restoration."

"For a while, I suppose. But you can always restore paintings after you retire as chief."

"I'll be too old to hold a brush."

Gabriel poked the tines of his fork into the veal, and it fell from the thick bone. He prepared his first bite carefully, an equal amount of meat and risotto drenched in the rich marrowy juice, and slipped it reverently into his mouth.

"How is it?"

"I'll tell you after I regain consciousness."

The candlelight was dancing in Chiara's eyes. They were the color of caramel and flecked with honey, a combination that Gabriel had never been able to reproduce on canvas. He prepared another bite of the risotto and veal but was distracted by an image on the television. Rioting had erupted in several Parisian banlieues after the arrest of several men on terrorism-related charges, none in direct connection with the attack on the Weinberg Center.

"ISIS must be enjoying this," said Gabriel.

"The rioting?"

"It doesn't look like rioting to me. It looks like . . ."

"What, darling?"

"An intifada."

Chiara switched off the television and turned up the volume on the baby monitor. Designed by the Office's Technology department, it had a heavily encrypted signal so that Israel's enemies could not eavesdrop on the domestic life of its spy chief. For the moment it emitted only a low electrical hum.

"So what are you going to do?" she asked.

"I'm going to eat every bite of this delicious food. And then I'm going to soak up every last drop of juice in that pot."

"I was talking about Paris."

"Obviously, we have two choices."

"You have two choices, darling. I have two children."

Gabriel laid down his fork and stared levelly at his beautiful young wife. "Either way," he said after a conciliatory silence, "my paternity leave is over. I can assume my duties as chief, or I can work with the French."

"And thus take possession of a van Gogh painting worth at least a hundred million dollars."

"There is that," said Gabriel, picking up his fork again.

"Why do you suppose she decided to leave it to you?"

"Because she knew I would never do anything foolish with it."

"Like what?"

"Put it up for sale."

Chiara made a face.

"Don't even think about it."

"One can dream, can't one?"

"Only about osso buco and risotto."

Rising, Gabriel went to the counter and helped himself to another portion. Then he doused both rice and meat in juice, until his plate was in jeopardy of brimming over. Behind his back, Chiara hissed in disapproval.

"There's one more," he said, gesturing toward the casserole.

"I still have five kilos to lose."

"I like you the way you are."

"Spoken like a true Italian husband."

"I'm not Italian."

"What language are you speaking to me right now?"

"It's the food talking."

Gabriel sat down again and laid siege to the veal. From the monitor came the short cry of a child. Chiara cocked a vigilant ear toward the device and listened intently, as if to the footsteps of an intruder. Then, after a satisfactory interlude of silence, she relaxed again.

"So you intend to take the case—is that what you're saying?"

"I'm inclined to," answered Gabriel judiciously.

Chiara shook her head slowly.

"What have I done now?"

"You'll do anything to avoid taking over the Office, won't you?"

"Not anything."

"Running an operation isn't exactly a nine-to-five job."

"Neither is running the Office."

"But the Office is in Tel Aviv. The operation is in Paris."

"Paris is a four-hour flight."

"Four and a half," she corrected him.

"Besides," Gabriel plowed on, "just because the operation starts in Paris, that doesn't mean it will end there."

"Where will it end?"

Gabriel tilted his head to the left.

"In Mrs. Lieberman's apartment?"

"Syria."

"Ever been?"

"Only to Majdal Shams."

"That doesn't count."

Majdal Shams was a Druze town in the Golan Heights. Along its northern edge was a fence topped by swirls of razor wire, and beyond the fence was Syria. Jabhat al-Nusra, an al-Qaeda affiliate, controlled the territory along the border, but a two-hour car ride to the northeast was ISIS and the caliphate. Gabriel wondered how the American president would feel if ISIS were two hours from Indiana.

"I thought," said Chiara, "that we were going to stay out of the Syrian civil war. I thought we were going to sit by and do nothing while all our enemies killed each other."

"The next chief of the Office feels that policy would be unwise in the long term."

"Does he?"

"Have you ever heard of a man named Arnold Toynbee?"

"I have a master's degree in history. Toynbee was a British historian and economist, one of the giants of his day."

"And Toynbee," said Gabriel, "believed there were two great pivot points in the world that influenced events far beyond their borders. One was the Oxus-Jaxartes Basin in modern-day Pakistan and Afghanistan, or Af-Pak as our friends in America are fond of calling it."

"And the other?"

Again, Gabriel tilted his head to the left. "We hoped the problems of Syria would remain in Syria, but I'm afraid *hope* is not an acceptable strategy when it comes to national security. While we've been twiddling our thumbs, ISIS has been developing a sophisticated terror network with the ability to strike in the heart of the West. Maybe it's led by a man who calls himself Saladin. Maybe it's someone else. Either way, I'm going to tear the network to pieces, hopefully before they can strike again."

Chiara started to respond but was interrupted by the cry of an infant. It was Irene; her two-note wail was as familiar to Gabriel as the sound of a French siren on a wet Paris night. He started to rise but Chiara was on her feet first.

"Finish your dinner," she said. "I hear the food in Paris is terrible."

Gabriel heard her voice next over the monitor, speaking soothingly in Italian to an infant who was no longer crying. Alone, he switched on the television and finished his supper while, four and a half hours to the northwest by airplane, Paris burned.

For thirty minutes she did not return. Gabriel saw to the dishes and wiped down the kitchen counters, thoroughly, so that Chiara would not feel it necessary to reprise his efforts, which was usually the case. He added coffee and water to the automatic maker and then stole softly down the hall to the master bedroom. There he found his wife and daughter, Chiara supine atop the bed, Irene prone across her breasts, both sleeping soundly.

Gabriel stood in the doorway, his shoulder leaning against the woodwork, and allowed his eyes to travel slowly across the walls of the room. They were hung with paintings—three paintings by Gabriel's grandfather, the only three he had been able to track down, and several more by his mother. There was also a large portrait of a young man with prematurely gray temples and a gaunt, weary face haunted by the shadow of death. One day, thought Gabriel, his children would ask him about the troubled young man depicted in the portrait, and about the woman who had painted it. It was not a conversation he was looking forward to. Already, he feared their reaction. Would they pity him? Would they fear him? Would they think him a monster, a murderer? It was no matter; he had to tell them. It was better to hear the unhappy details of such a life from the lips of the man who had led it rather than from someone else. Mothers often portrayed fathers in too flattering a light. Obituaries rarely told the whole story, especially when their subjects led classified lives.

Gabriel lifted his daughter from Chiara's breast and carried her into the nursery. He placed her gently in her crib, covered her with a blanket, and stood over her for a moment until he was sure she was settled. Finally, he returned to the master bedroom. Chiara was still sleeping soundly, watched over by the brooding young man in the portrait. It's not me, he would tell his children. It's just someone I had to become. I am not a monster or a murderer. You exist in this place, you sleep peacefully in this land tonight, because of people like me.

9

THE MARAIS, PARIS

At TWENTY MINUTES PAST TEN the following morning, Christian Bouchard was standing in the arrivals hall of Charles de Gaulle, a tan raincoat over his crisp suit, a paper sign in his hand. The sign read SMITH. Even Bouchard found it less than convincing. He was watching the conveyor belt of humanity flowing into the hall from passport control—the international peddlers of goods and services, the seekers of asylum and employment, the tourists who had come to see a country that no longer existed. It was the job of the DGSI to sift through this daily deluge, identify the potential terrorists and agents of foreign intelligence, and monitor their movements until they left French soil. It was a near-impossible task. But for men such as Christian Bouchard, it meant there was no shortage of work or opportunities for career advancement. For better or worse, security was one of the few growth industries in France.

Just then, Bouchard's mobile vibrated in his coat pocket. It was a text message stating that the reason for his visit to Charles de Gaulle had just been admitted into France on an

Israeli passport bearing the name Gideon Argov. Two minutes later Bouchard spotted the selfsame Monsieur Argov, black leather jacket, black nylon overnight bag, adrift on the current of arriving passengers. Bouchard had seen him in surveillance photographs—there was that famous shot taken in the Gare de Lyon a few seconds before the explosion—but never had he seen the legend in the flesh. Bouchard had to admit he was sorely disappointed. The Israeli was five foot nothing and maybe, *maybe*, a hundred and fifty pounds. Still, there was a predatory swiftness in his gait and a slight outward bend to his legs that suggested speed and agility in his youth, which, thought Bouchard with misplaced arrogance, was quite some time ago.

Two paces behind him was a much younger man of nearly identical height and weight: dark hair, dark skin, the alert dark eyes of a Jew whose ancestors had lived in Arab lands. An employee of the Israeli Embassy was there to greet them, and together the three men—legend, bodyguard, and embassy functionary—filed outside to a waiting car. It headed directly into the center of Paris, followed by a second car in which Bouchard was the only passenger. He had anticipated his quarry would proceed directly to Madame Weinberg's apartment on the rue Pavée, where Paul Rousseau was at that moment waiting. Instead, the legend made a stop on the rue des Rosiers. At the far western end of the street was a barricade. Behind it were the ruins of the Weinberg Center.

By Bouchard's wristwatch, the Israeli remained at the barricade for three minutes. Then he headed eastward along the street, trailed by his bodyguard. After a few paces he paused in a shop window, a crude but effective touch of tradecraft that compelled Bouchard, who was discreetly following, to seek shelter in the boutique opposite. Instantly, a cloying saleswoman accosted him, and by the time he'd managed to extricate himself, the Israeli and his bodyguard had vanished. Bouchard stood frozen for a moment, staring up the length of the street. Then he wheeled round and saw the Israeli standing behind him, one hand pressed to his chin, head tilted to one side.

"Where's your sign?" he asked finally in French.

"My what?"

"Your sign. The one you were holding at the airport." The green eyes probed. "You must be Christian Bouchard."

"And you must be—"

"I must be," he interrupted with the terseness of a nail gun. "And I was assured there would be no surveillance."

"I wasn't watching you."

"Then what were you doing?"

"Rousseau asked me to make sure you arrived safely."

"You're here to protect me—is that what you're saying?" Bouchard was silent.

"Allow me to make one thing clear from the outset," said the legend. "I don't need protection."

THEY WALKED SIDE BY SIDE ALONG THE PAVEMENT, BOUCHARD in his smart suit and raincoat, Gabriel in his leather jacket and his grief, until they arrived at the entrance of the apartment house at Number 24. When Bouchard opened the outer door, he inadvertently opened a door in Gabriel's memory, too. It was ten years ago, early evening, a light rain falling like tears from the sky. Gabriel had come to Paris because he needed a van Gogh as bait in order to insert an agent into the entourage of Zizi al-Bakari, and he had heard from an old friend in London, a wildly eccentric art dealer named Julian Isherwood, that Hannah Weinberg was in possession of one. He had approached her without introduction on the very spot where he and Christian Bouchard stood now. She was holding an umbrella in one hand and with the other was stretching a key toward the lock. "I'm sorry to disappoint you," she had lied with admirable composure, "but I don't have a van Gogh. If you'd like to see some paintings by Vincent, I suggest you visit the Musée d'Orsay."

The memory dissipated. Gabriel followed Bouchard across an internal courtyard, into a foyer, and up a flight of carpeted stairs. On the fourth floor, nickeled light leaked weakly through a soiled window, illuminating two stately mahogany doors facing each other like duelists across the chessboard floor of the landing. The door on the right was absent a nameplate. Bouchard unlocked it and, stepping to one side, motioned for Gabriel to enter.

He paused in the formal entrance hall and surveyed his surroundings, as if for the first time. The room was decorated precisely as it had been on the morning of Jeudi Noir: stately brocaded furniture, heavy velvet curtains, an ormolu clock, still ticking away five minutes slow on the mantel. Again, the door to Gabriel's memory opened, and he glimpsed Hannah seated on the couch in a rather dowdy woolen skirt and thick sweater. She had just handed him a bottle of Sancerre and was watching intently as he removed the cork—watching his hands, he remembered, the hands of the avenger. "I'm very good at keeping secrets," she was saying. "Tell me why you want my van Gogh, Monsieur Allon. Perhaps we can reach some accommodation."

From the adjoining library there came the faint rustle of paper, like the turning of a page. Gabriel peered inside and saw a rumpled figure standing before a bookcase, a large leather-bound volume in his hand. "Dumas," the figure said without looking up. "And quite valuable."

He closed the book, returned it to the shelf, and studied

Gabriel as if contemplating a rare coin or a cage bird. Gabriel returned the gaze without expression. He had expected another version of Bouchard, a slick, cocky bastard who took wine with his midday meal and left the office promptly at five so he could spend an hour with his mistress before rushing home to his wife. Therefore, Paul Rousseau was a pleasant surprise.

"It's a pleasure to finally meet you," he said. "I only wish the circumstances were different. Madame Weinberg was a friend, was she not?"

Gabriel was silent.

"Is something wrong?" asked Rousseau.

"I'll let you know when I see the van Gogh."

"Ah, yes, the van Gogh. It's in the room at the end of the hall," said Rousseau. "But I suppose you already knew that."

SHE HAD KEPT A KEY, GABRIEL RECALLED, IN THE TOP DRAWER of the desk. Obviously, Rousseau and his men had not discovered it, because the lock had been dismantled. Otherwise, the room was as Gabriel remembered it: the same bed with a lace canopy, the same toys and stuffed animals, the same provincial dresser, above which hung the same painting, *Marguerite Gachet at Her Dressing Table*, oil on canvas, by Vincent van Gogh. Gabriel had carried out the painting's only restoration, in a rambling Victorian safe house outside London, shortly before its sale—private, of course—to Zizi al-Bakari. His work, he thought now, had held up well. The painting was perfect except for a thin horizontal line near the top of the image that Gabriel had made no attempt to repair. The line was Vincent's fault; he had leaned another canvas against poor Marguerite before she was sufficiently dry. Zizi al-Bakari, a connoisseur of art as well as jihadist terror, had regarded the line as proof of the painting's authenticity—and of the authenticity of the beautiful young American woman, a Harvard-educated art historian, who had sold it to him.

Of this, Paul Rousseau knew nothing. He was staring not at the painting but at Gabriel, his cage bird, his curio. "One wonders why she chose to hang it here rather than in her parlor," he said after a moment. "And why, in death, she chose to leave it to you, of all people."

Gabriel lifted his eyes from the painting and fixed them squarely on the face of Paul Rousseau. "Perhaps we should make one thing clear at the outset," he said. "We're not going to be closing out old accounts. Nor are we going to take any strolls down memory lane."

"Oh, no," Rousseau agreed hastily, "we haven't time for that. Still, it would be an interesting exercise, if only for its entertainment value."

"Be careful, Monsieur Rousseau. Memory lane is just around the next corner."

"So it is." Rousseau gave a capitulatory smile.

"We had a deal," said Gabriel. "I come to Paris, you give me the picture."

"No, Monsieur Allon. First you help me find the man who bombed the Weinberg Center, and *then* I give you the painting. I was very clear with your friend Uzi Navot." Rousseau looked quizzically at Gabriel. "He is a friend of yours, is he not?"

"He used to be," said Gabriel coolly.

They fell into a comfortable silence, each staring at the van Gogh, like strangers in a gallery.

"Vincent must have loved her very much to paint something so beautiful," Rousseau said at last. "And soon it will belong to you. I'm tempted to say you're a very lucky man, but I won't. You see, Monsieur Allon," he said, smiling sadly, "I've read your file."

10

RUE PAVÉE, PARIS

INTELLIGENCE SERVICES FROM DIFFERENT NATIONS do not cooperate because they enjoy it. They do so because, like divorced parents of small children, they sometimes find it necessary to work together for the greater good. Old rivalries do not vanish overnight. They slumber just beneath the surface, like the wounds of infidelities, forgotten anniversaries, and unmet emotional needs. The challenge for the two intelligence services is to create a zone of trust, a room where there are no secrets. Outside that room they are free to pursue their own interests. But once inside, each is compelled to lay bare its most cherished sources and methods for the other to see. Gabriel had much experience in this realm. A natural restorer, he had repaired the Office's relations with both the CIA and Britain's Secret Intelligence Service. France, however, was a more difficult proposition. It had long been an important operational theater for the Office, especially for Gabriel, whose litany of secret sins on French soil was long. What's more, France was an unabashed supporter of many of Israel's most implacable foes. In short, the intelligence services of Israel and France did not like each other much.

It was not always so. France armed Israel in its infancy, and without French help Israel would have never developed the nuclear deterrent that allowed it to survive in the hostile Middle East. But in the 1960s, after the disastrous war in Algeria, Charles de Gaulle set out to repair France's strained relations with the Arab world—and when Israel, largely with French aircraft, launched the Six-Day War with a surprise attack on Egypt's airfields, de Gaulle condemned it. He referred to Jews as "an elite people, sure of itself, domineering," and the rupture was complete.

Now, over coffee in the salon of the Weinberg family apartment on the rue Pavée, Gabriel and Rousseau set out to repair, at least temporarily, the legacy of mistrust. Their first order of business was to hammer out a basic operational accord, a blueprint for how the two services would work together, a division of labor and authority, the rules of the road. It was to be a true partnership, though for obvious reasons Rousseau would retain preeminence over any aspects of the operation that touched French soil. In return, Gabriel would be granted complete and total access to France's voluminous files on the thousands of Islamic extremists living within its borders: the watch reports, the e-mail and phone intercepts, the immigration records. That alone, he would say much later, had been worth the price of admission.

There were bumps in the road, but for the most part the negotiations went more smoothly than either Gabriel or Rousseau could have imagined. Perhaps it was because the two men were not so different. They were men of the arts, men of culture and learning who had devoted their lives to protecting their fellow citizens from those who would shed the blood of innocents over ideology or religion. Each had lost a spouse—one to illness, the other to terror—and each was well respected by their counterparts in Washington and London. Rousseau was no Gabriel Allon, but he had been fighting terrorists almost as long, and had the notches in his belt to prove it.

"There are some in the French political establishment," said Gabriel, "who would like to see me behind bars because of my previous activities."

"So I've heard."

"If I am to function here without cover, I require a document giving me blanket immunity, now and forever, amen."

"I'll see what I can do."

"And I'll see if I can find Saladin before he attacks again."

Rousseau frowned. "Too bad you weren't the one to negotiate the Iran nuclear deal."

"Too bad," agreed Gabriel.

By then, it was approaching four o'clock. Rousseau stood, yawned elaborately, stretched his arms wide, and suggested a walk. "Doctor's orders," he said. "It seems I'm too fat for my own good." They slipped from the entrance of Hannah Weinberg's apartment house and, with Bouchard and Gabriel's bodyguard in tow, walked along the Seine embankments toward Notre-Dame. They were a mismatched pair, the lumpy, tweedy former professor from the Sorbonne, the smallish figure in leather who seemed to float slightly above the surface of the paving stones. The sun was low in the western sky, blazing through a slit in the clouds. Rousseau shaded his eyes.

"Where do you intend to start?"

"The files, of course."

"You'll need help."

"Obviously."

"How many officers do you intend to bring into the country?"

"The exact number I need."

"I can give you a room in our headquarters on the rue de Grenelle."

"I prefer something a bit more private."

"I can arrange a safe house."

"So can I."

Gabriel paused at a news kiosk. On the front page of *Le Monde* were two photographs of Safia Bourihane, the Frenchwoman of Muslim heritage, the veiled killer from the caliphate. The headline was one word in length: CATASTROPHE!

"Whose catastrophe was it?" asked Gabriel.

"The inevitable inquiry will undoubtedly find that elements of my service made terrible mistakes. But are we truly to blame? We, the humble secret servants who stand with our fingers in the dike? Or does the blame lie elsewhere?"

"Where?"

"In Washington, for example." Rousseau set off along the embankment. "The invasion of Iraq turned the region into a cauldron. And when the new American president decided the time had come to withdraw, the cauldron boiled over. And then there was this folly we called the Arab Spring. Mubarak must go! Gaddafi must go! Assad must go!" He shook his head slowly. "It was madness, absolute madness. And now we are left with this. ISIS controls a swath of territory the size of the United Kingdom, right on the doorstep of Europe. Even Bin Laden would have never dared to dream of such a thing. And what does the American president tell us? ISIS is not Islamic. ISIS is the jayvee team." He frowned. "What does this mean? Jayvee?"

"I think it has something to do with basketball."

"And what does basketball have to do with a subject as serious as the rise of the caliphate?"

Gabriel only smiled.

"Does he truly believe this drivel, or is it an *ignorantia affectata*?"

"A willful ignorance?"

"Yes."

"You'd have to ask him."

"Do you know him?"

"We've met."

Rousseau was obviously tempted to ask Gabriel about the circumstances of his one and only meeting with the American president, but he carried on with his lecture on ISIS instead. "The truth is," he said, "ISIS is indeed Islamic. And it has more in common with Muhammad and his earliest followers—*al salaf al salih*—than some of the so-called experts care to admit. We are horrified when we read accounts of ISIS using crucifixion. We tell ourselves that these are the actions of barbarians, not men of faith. But ISIS doesn't crucify only because it is cruel. It crucifies because, according to the Koran, crucifixion is one of the proscribed punishments for the enemies of Islam. It crucifies because it *must*. We civilized Westerners find this almost impossible to comprehend."

"*We* don't," said Gabriel.

"That's because you live in the region. You are a people of the region," Rousseau added. "And you know full well what will happen if the likes of ISIS are ever let loose within the walls of your fortress. It will be . . ."

"A holocaust," said Gabriel.

Rousseau nodded thoughtfully. Then he led Gabriel across the Pont Notre-Dame, to the Île de la Cité. "So in the words of Lenin," he asked, "what is to be done?"

"I am merely a spy, Monsieur Rousseau, not a general or a prime minister."

"And if you were?"

"I would tear them out root and branch. I would turn them

into losers instead of winners. Take away the land," Gabriel added, "and there can be no Islamic State. And if there is no state, the caliphate will recede once more into history."

"Invasion didn't work in Iraq or Afghanistan," replied Rousseau, "and it won't work in Syria. Better to chip away at them from the air and with the help of regional allies. In the meantime, contain the infection so it doesn't spread to the rest of the Middle East and Europe."

"It's too late for that. The contagion is already here."

They crossed another bridge, the Petit Pont, and entered the Latin Quarter. Rousseau knew it well. He walked now with a purpose other than his health, down the boulevard Saint-Germain, into a narrow side street, until finally he stopped outside the doorway of an apartment building. It was as familiar to Gabriel as the entrance of Hannah Weinberg's building on the rue Pavée, though it had been many years since his last visit. He glanced at the intercom. Some of the names were still the same.

Presently, the door swung open and two people, a man and a woman in their mid-twenties, emerged. Rousseau caught the door before it could close and led Gabriel into the half-light of the foyer. A passageway gave onto the shadowed internal courtyard, where Rousseau paused for a second time and pointed toward a window on the uppermost floor.

"My wife and I lived right there. When she died I gave up the apartment and headed south. There were too many memories, too many ghosts." He pointed toward a window overlooking the opposite side of the courtyard. "A former student of mine lived over there. She was quite brilliant. Quite radical, too, as were most of my students in those days. Her name," he added, with a sidelong glance at Gabriel, "was Denise Jaubert."

Gabriel stared without expression at Rousseau, as though

the name meant nothing to him. In truth, he suspected he knew more about Denise Jaubert than did her former professor. She was indeed a radical. More important, she was the occasional lover of one Sabri al-Khalifa, leader of the Palestinian terror group Black September, mastermind of the Munich Olympics massacre.

"Late one afternoon," Rousseau resumed, "I was working at my desk when I heard laughter in the courtyard. It was Denise. She was with a man. Black hair, pale skin, strikingly handsome. Walking a few steps behind them was a smaller fellow with short hair. I couldn't see much of his face. You see, in spite of the overcast weather he was wearing dark glasses."

Rousseau looked at Gabriel, but Gabriel, in his thoughts, was walking across a Parisian courtyard, a few paces behind the man for whom the Office had spent seven long years searching.

"I wasn't the only one who noticed the man in the sunglasses," Rousseau said after a moment. "Denise's handsome companion noticed him, too. He tried to draw a pistol, but the smaller man drew first. I'll never forget how he moved forward while he was firing. It was . . . beautiful. There were ten shots. Then he inserted a second magazine into his weapon, placed the barrel of the gun against the man's ear, and fired one last shot. It's odd, but I don't recall him leaving. He just seemed to vanish." Rousseau looked at Gabriel. "And now he stands beside me."

Gabriel said nothing. He was staring down at the cobbles of the courtyard, the cobbles that had once run red with the blood of Sabri al-Khalifa.

"I must admit," said Rousseau, "that for a long time I thought you a murderer. The civilized world condemned your actions. But now the civilized world finds itself in the very same fight, and we are using the very same tactics. Drones, missiles, men in black in the middle of the night." He paused, then added, "It seems history has absolved you of your sins."

"I committed no sins," said Gabriel. "And I seek no absolution."

Just then, Rousseau's mobile chimed in his coat pocket, followed a few seconds later by Gabriel's. Once again, it was Gabriel who drew first. It was a priority message from King Saul Boulevard. The DGSI had sent a similar message to Rousseau.

"It appears the attack on the Weinberg Center was only the beginning." Rousseau returned the phone to his coat pocket and stared at the cobbles where Sabri al-Khalifa had fallen. "Will it end the same way for the one they call Saladin?"

"If we're lucky."

"How soon can you start?"

"Tonight."

II

AMSTERDAM—PARIS

LATER, IT WOULD BE DETERMINED with near certainty that the Paris and Amsterdam bombs were the lethal handiwork of the same man. Once again the mode of delivery was an ordinary white panel van, though in Amsterdam it was a Ford Transit rather than a Renault. It detonated at half past four precisely, in the center of Amsterdam's bustling Albert Cuyp Market. The vehicle had entered the market early that morning and had remained there undetected throughout the day as thousands of shoppers strolled obliviously past through the pale spring sunshine. The driver of the van was a woman, approximately thirty years of age, blond hair, long legs, narrow hips, blue jeans, a hooded sweatshirt, a fleece vest. This was established not with the help of witnesses but with closed-circuit video surveillance cameras. Police found no one among the living who could recall seeing her.

The market, regarded as Europe's largest, is located in the Old Side of the city. Opposing rows of stalls line the street, and behind the stalls are terraces of saddle-brown brick houses with shops and restaurants on the ground floor. Many of the vendors are from the Middle East and North Africa, a fact that several reporters and terrorism analysts were quick to point out during the first hours of the coverage. They saw it as evidence that the perpetrators were inspired by a creed other than radical Islam, though when pressed to name one, they could not. Finally, a scholar of Islam from Cambridge explained the seeming paradox. The Muslims of Amsterdam, she said, were living in a city of legalized drugs and prostitution where the laws of men held sway rather than the laws of Allah. In the eyes of the Muslim extremists, they were apostates. And the only punishment for apostasy was death.

Witnesses would recall not the thunderous bellow of the explosion but the deep, wintry silence that followed. In time, there was a moan, and a childlike sob, and the electronic pulse of a mobile phone pleading to be answered. For several minutes thick black smoke obscured the horror. Then, gradually, the smoke lifted and the devastation was revealed: the limbless and the lifeless, the sooty-faced survivors wandering dazed and partially disrobed through the debris, the shoes of a vendor scattered among the shoes of the dead. Everywhere there was split fruit and spilled blood and the aroma, suddenly nauseating, of roasted lamb seasoned with cumin and turmeric.

The claims of responsibility were not long in coming. The first was from an obscure cell in lawless Libya, followed soon after by al-Shabaab, the Somalia-based group that had terrorized East Africa. Finally, there appeared a video on a popular social media site. In it, a black-hooded man who spoke English with an East London accent declared that the attack was the work of ISIS, and that more attacks were to come. He then embarked, in a mixture of English and Arabic, on a rambling homily about the armies of Rome and a Syrian village called Dabiq. The television commentators were perplexed. The learned expert from Cambridge was not.

The reaction ranged from outrage to disbelief to smug recriminations. In Washington the American president condemned the bombing as "a wanton act of murder and barbarism," though, curiously, he made no mention of the perpetrators' motives or of Islam, radical or otherwise. His congressional opponents quickly laid blame for the attack squarely at his feet. Had he not precipitously withdrawn American troops from Iraq, they said, ISIS would never have taken root in neighboring Syria. The president's spokesman later dismissed suggestions that the time had come for American ground troops to take the fight directly to ISIS. "We have a strategy," he said. Then, with a straight face, he added, "It is working."

In the Netherlands, however, Dutch authorities had no interest in apportioning blame, for they were far too busy searching for survivors amid the rubble, and for the woman, approximately thirty years of age, blond hair, long legs, narrow hips, blue jeans, hooded sweatshirt, fleece vest, who had driven the bomb van into the market. For two days her name remained a mystery. Then a second video appeared on the same social media Web site, narrated by the same man who spoke with an East London accent. This time, he was not alone. Two veiled women stood next to him. One remained silent, the other spoke. She identified herself as Margreet Janssen, a convert to Islam from the Dutch coastal city of Noordwijk. She had planted the bomb, she said, to punish the blasphemers and the infidels in the name of Allah and Muhammad, peace be upon him.

Later that day the AIVD, the Dutch security and intelligence service, confirmed that Margreet Janssen had traveled to Syria eighteen months previously, had remained there for approximately six months, and had been allowed to return to the Netherlands after convincing the Dutch authorities that she had renounced her ties to ISIS and the global jihadist movement. The security service placed the woman under electronic and physical surveillance, but the surveillance was subsequently dropped when she exhibited no signs of continued involvement in radical Islamic activities. Obviously, said an AIVD spokesman, it was an error in judgment.

Within minutes the cyberrooms of the digital caliphate were ablaze with excited chatter. Margreet Janssen was suddenly the new symbol of the global jihad, a former Christian from a European country who was now a lethal member of the community of believers. But who was the other woman in the video? The one who did not speak? The answer came not from Amsterdam but from a fortress-like building in the Paris suburb of Levallois-Perret. The second woman, said the chief of the DGSI, was Safia Bourihane, one of the perpetrators of the attack on the Weinberg Center.

Before terminating its surveillance of Margreet Janssen, the AIVD had assembled a dense dossier of watch reports, photographs, e-mails, text messages, and Internet browsing histories, along with secondary files on friends, family members, associates, and fellow travelers in the global jihadist movement. Paul Rousseau received a copy of the dossier during a meeting at AIVD headquarters in The Hague, and upon his return to Paris he presented it to Gabriel in a quiet brasserie on the rue de Miromesnil, in the Eighth Arrondissement. The dossier had been digitized and stored on a secure flash drive. Rousseau slid it across the table beneath a napkin, with all the discretion of a gunshot in an empty chapel. It was no matter; the brasserie was deserted except for a small bald man wearing a well-cut suit and a lavish lavender necktie. He was drinking a glass of Côtes du Rhone and reading a copy of *Le Figaro*. It was filled with the news from Amsterdam. Gabriel slipped the flash drive into his coat pocket, making no effort to conceal his action, and asked Rousseau about the mood at AIVD headquarters.

"Somewhere between panic and resignation," answered Rousseau. "They're ramping up their surveillance of known Islamic extremists and searching for the man who built the bomb and the other elements of the network." He lowered his voice and added, "They were wondering whether I had any ideas."

"Did you mention Saladin?"

"It might have slipped my mind," said Rousseau with a sly smile. "But at some point we're going to have to go on the record with our friends here in Europe."

"They're your friends, not mine."

"You have a history with the Dutch services?"

"I've never had the pleasure of visiting the Netherlands."

"Somehow, I find that difficult to believe." Rousseau glanced at the small bald man sitting on the other side of the brasserie. "A friend of yours?"

"He runs a shop across the street."

"How do you know?"

"I saw him leave and lock the door."

"How observant of you." Rousseau peered into the darkening street. "Antiquités Scientifiques?"

"Old microscopes and the like," explained Gabriel.

"Interesting." Rousseau contemplated his coffee cup. "It seems I wasn't the only foreign visitor to AIVD headquarters yesterday. An American came, too."

"Agency?"

Rousseau nodded.

"Local or Langley?"

"The latter."

"Did he have a name?"

"Not one that my Dutch hosts wished to share with me. They did suggest, however, that American interest was high."

"How refreshing."

"Apparently, the White House is concerned that an attack on the American homeland this late in the president's second term might prove injurious to his legacy. The Agency is under enormous pressure to make sure it doesn't happen."

"I guess ISIS isn't the jayvee team after all."

"To that end," Rousseau continued, "the Agency is expecting full and complete cooperation from America's friends and partners here in Europe. The man from Langley is due in Paris tomorrow morning."

"It might be wise for you to spend some time with him."

"My name is already on the guest list."

Gabriel handed Rousseau a slip of paper, folded in quarters. "What's this?"

"A list of additional files we need."

"How much longer?"

"Soon," said Gabriel.

"That's what you said yesterday, and the day before." Rousseau slipped the list into the breast pocket of his tweed jacket. "Are you ever going to tell me where you and your helpers are working?"

"You mean you haven't figured it out yet?"

"We haven't tried."

"Somehow," said Gabriel, "I find that difficult to believe."

He rose without another word and went into the street. Rousseau watched him walk away along the darkened pavement, followed discreetly by two of Alpha Group's best surveillance men. The little bald man with the lavender necktie laid a few bills on his table and departed, leaving Rousseau alone in the brasserie with no company other than his mobile phone. Five minutes elapsed before it finally illuminated. It was a text message from Christian Bouchard. "Merde," said Rousseau softly. Allon had lost them again.

12

PARIS

IT WAS WITH A PAIR of routine countersurveillance moves—a reversal of course along a one-way street, a brief stop in a bistro that had a rear service exit off the kitchen—that Gabriel slipped away from the finest watchers of Paul Rousseau's Alpha Group. Afterward, he made his way, on foot, by Métro, and in a taxi, to a small apartment building along the edge of the Bois de Boulogne. According to the intercom panel, the occupant of 4B was someone named Guzman. Gabriel thumbed the button, waited for the snap of the automatic locks, and entered.

Upstairs, Mikhail Abramov unchained the door to him. The air was bitter with smoke. Gabriel peered into the kitchen and saw Eli Lavon attempting to extinguish a fire he had started in the microwave. Lavon was a diminutive figure, with a head of wispy unkempt hair and a face that was entirely forgettable. His looks, like most things about him, were deceiving. A natural predator and chameleon, Lavon was regarded as the finest street surveillance artist the Office ever produced. Ari Shamron had famously said of Lavon that he could disappear while shaking your hand. It wasn't far from the truth.

"How long did it take you to lose them this time?" Lavon asked as he tossed a misshapen lump of charred plastic into the sink.

"Less time than it took you to burn down the safe flat."

"A small mix-up with the time setting. You know me, I've never really been good with numbers."

Which wasn't true. Lavon also happened to be a skilled financial investigator who singlehandedly had managed to track down millions of dollars' worth of looted Holocaust assets. An archaeologist by training, he was a natural digger.

Gabriel entered the sitting room. Yaakov Rossman, a veteran agent runner and a fluent speaker of Arabic, appeared to be contemplating an act of violence against his notebook computer. Yossi Gavish and Rimona Stern were sprawled on the couch like a couple of undergraduates. Yossi was a top officer in Research, which is how the Office referred to its analytical division. Tall, tweedy, and balding, he had read classics at All Souls and spoke Hebrew with a pronounced English accent. He had also done a bit of acting—Shakespearean, mainly— and was a gifted cellist. Rimona served in the Office unit that spied on Iran's nuclear program. She had sandstone-colored hair, childbearing hips, and a temper she had inherited from Ari Shamron, who was her uncle. Gabriel had known her since she was a small child. Indeed, his fondest memories of Rimona were of a fearless young girl on a kick scooter careening down the steep drive of her famous uncle's house.

The five field agents and analysts were members of an elite team of operatives known as Barak, the Hebrew word for lightning, for their ability to gather and strike quickly. They had fought and sometimes bled together on a string of secret battlefields stretching from Moscow to the Caribbean, and in the process had carried out some of the most fabled operations in the history of Israeli intelligence. Gabriel was the team's founder and leader, but a sixth member, Dina Sarid, was its conscience and institutional memory. Dina was the Office's top terrorism specialist, a human database who could recite the time, place, perpetrators, and casualty toll of every act of Palestinian or Islamic terrorism committed against Israel and the West. Her talent was to see connections where others saw only a blizzard of names, numbers, and words.

She was small in stature, with coal-black hair that fell about a soft, childlike face. At present, she was standing before a seemingly haphazard collage of surveillance photos, e-mails, text messages, and phone conversations. It was the same place she had been standing, three hours earlier, when Gabriel had left the safe flat for his meeting with Paul Rousseau. Dina was in the grip of the fever, the frightful creative rage that came over her each time a bomb exploded. Gabriel had induced the fever many times before. Judging by her expression, it was about to break. He crossed the room and stood beside her.

"What are you looking at?" he asked after a moment.

Dina took two steps forward, limping slightly, and pointed toward a surveillance photo of Safia Bourihane. It had been taken before her first trip to Syria, in an Arab-style café in the heavily immigrant Paris banlieue of Saint-Denis. Safia had recently taken the veil. Her companion, a young woman, was veiled, too. There were several other women in the café, along with four men, Algerians, Moroccans, sharing a table near the counter. Another man, angular face, clean-shaven, slightly out of focus, sat alone. He wore a dark business suit, no tie, and was working on a notebook computer. He might have been an Arab—or he might have been a Frenchman or an Italian. For the moment he was of no concern to Dina Sarid. She was gazing, spellbound, at the face of Safia Bourihane.

"She looks normal, doesn't she? Happy, even. You'd never suspect she'd spent the entire morning talking to an ISIS recruiter on the Internet. The recruiter asked her to leave her family and travel to Syria to help build the caliphate. And what do you suppose Safia told him?"

"She said she wanted to stay in France. She said she wanted to marry a nice boy from a good family and have children who would grow up to be fully assimilated French citizens. She said she wanted no part of a caliphate run by men who behead and crucify and burn their enemies alive."

"Isn't it pretty to think so." Dina shook her head slowly. "What went wrong, Gabriel? Why have more than five hundred young Western women joined the ranks of ISIS? Why are the bearded ones the new rock stars of Islam? Why are killers cool?" Dina had devoted her life to the study of terrorism and Islamic extremism, and yet she had no answers. "We thought they would be repulsed by the violence of ISIS. We were wrong. We assumed assimilation was the answer. But the more they assimilated, the less they liked what they saw. And so when a recruiter from ISIS comes knocking on their digital door, they're vulnerable."

"You're too charitable, Dina."

"They're children." She paused, then added, "Impressionable girls."

"Not all of them."

"That's true. Many are educated, much more educated than the men who've joined ISIS. They're forbidden to fight, the women, so they take on important support roles. In many respects, it's the women who are actually building the caliphate. Most of them will also take a husband—a husband who's likely to soon be a martyr. One in four women will become widows. *Black* widows," she added. "Indoctrinated, embittered, vengeful. And all it takes is a good recruiter or talent spotter to turn them into ticking time bombs." She pointed toward the slightly-out-of-focus figure seated alone in the Arab-style café. "Like him. Unfortunately, the French never noticed him. They were too busy looking at Safia's friend."

"Who is she?"

"She's a girl who watched a few beheading videos on the Internet. She's a waste of time, money, and manpower. But not Safia. Safia was trouble waiting to happen." Dina took a step to the right and indicated a second photograph. "Three days after Safia had coffee with her friend in Saint-Denis, she came to the center of Paris to do a bit of shopping. This picture was taken as she was walking along the arcades of the rue de Rivoli. And look who's walking a few steps behind her."

It was the same man from the café, the clean-shaven man with an angular face who might have been an Arab or a Frenchman or an Italian.

"How did they miss him?"

"Good question. And they missed him here, too."

Dina pointed toward a third photograph, the same day, an hour later. Safia Bourihane was leaving a women's clothing store on the Champs-Élysées. The same man was waiting outside on the pavement, pretending to consult a tourist guidebook.

"Send the photos to King Saul Boulevard," said Gabriel. "See if anything turns up."

"I already have."

"And?"

"King Saul Boulevard has never made his acquaintance."

"Maybe this will help." Gabriel held up the flash drive.

"What is it?"

"The life and times of Margreet Janssen."

"I wonder how long it will take to find Safia's secret admirer."

"I'd hurry if I were you. The Americans have her file, too."

"I'll beat them," she said. "I always do."

It took Dina fewer than thirty minutes to find the first surveillance photograph of Margreet Janssen and the man who had shadowed Safia Bourihane in Paris. An AIVD team had snapped the picture at a quaint Italian restaurant in central Amsterdam where Margreet, having left her dreary home in Noordwijk, was waiting tables for starvation wages. It wasn't difficult to spot him; he was dining alone with a volume of Sartre for protection. This time, the camera managed to capture him in focus, though he was somewhat different in appearance. A pair of round eyeglasses had softened the sharp edges of his face; a cardigan sweater lent him a librarian's unthreatening air. Margreet was his server, and judging from her wide smile she found him attractive—so attractive, in fact, that she agreed to meet him for drinks later at a bar on the edge of the red-light district. The evening ended with a well-executed slap, delivered with Margreet's right hand to the man's left cheek and witnessed by the same surveillance team. It was, thought Gabriel, a nice touch of tradecraft. The Dutch wrote the man off as a cad and never tried to establish his identity.

But what was the connection between the two women, other than the man who might have been an Arab or a Frenchman or an Italian? Dina found that, too. It was a Web site based in the Persian Gulf emirate of Qatar that sold clothing for Muslim women of piety and taste. Safia Bourihane had surfed it three weeks before the man's visit to Paris. Margreet Janssen had stopped there just ten days before the slap in Amsterdam. Dina suspected that the site contained a password-protected room where ISIS recruiters could invite promising young women for a private chat. These encrypted rooms had so far proved almost impenetrable to the intelligence services of Israel and the West. Even the mighty National Security Agency, America's omniscient signals intelligence service, was struggling to keep pace with ISIS's digital hydra.

There is no worse feeling for a professional spy than to be told something by an officer from another service that he should have already known himself. Paul Rousseau endured this indignity in a small café on the rue Cler, a fashionable pedestrian shopping street not far from the Eiffel Tower. The French police had erected barricades at the intersections of the cross streets and were checking the handbags and backpacks of everyone who dared to enter. Even Gabriel, who had nothing in his possession other than a manila envelope filled with photographs, was thoroughly searched before being allowed to pass.

"If this were ever to become public," said Rousseau, "it would be deeply embarrassing for my service. Heads would roll. Remember, this is France."

"Don't worry, Paul, your secret is safe with me."

Rousseau leafed again through the photos of Safia Bourihane and the man who for two days had followed her around Paris undetected by the DGSI.

"What do you suppose he was doing?"

"Watching her, of course."

"Why?"

"To make sure she was the right kind of girl. The question is," said Gabriel, "can you find him?"

"These photographs were taken more than a year ago."

"Yes?" asked Gabriel leadingly.

"It will be difficult. After all," said Rousseau, "we still haven't been able to find out where your team is working."

"That's because we're better than he is."

"Actually, his track record is rather good, too."

"He didn't travel to the café in Saint-Denis on a magic carpet," said Gabriel. "He took a train, or a bus, or he walked along a street with security cameras."

"Our network of CCTV cameras is nowhere near as extensive as yours or the British."

"But it exists, especially in a place like Saint-Denis."

"Yes," said Rousseau. "It exists."

"So find out how he got there. And then find out who he is. But whatever you do," Gabriel added, "do it quietly. And don't mention any of this to our friend from Langley."

Rousseau consulted his wristwatch.

"What time are you seeing him?"

"Eleven. His name is Taylor, by the way. Kyle Taylor. He's the chief of the CIA's Counterterrorism Center. Apparently, Monsieur Taylor is very ambitious. He's droned many terrorists. One more scalp, and he might be the next director of operations. At least, that's the rumor."

"That would come as news to the current director."

"Adrian Carter?"

Gabriel nodded.

"I've always liked Adrian," said Rousseau. "He's a decent soul, and rather too honest for a spy. One wonders how a man like that could survive so long in a place like Langley."

As it turned out, it took Rousseau's Alpha Group just forty-eight hours to determine that the man from the café in Saint-Denis had traveled to Paris from London aboard a Eurostar high-speed train. Surveillance photographs showed him disembarking at the Gare du Nord in late morning and boarding a Métro a few minutes later, bound for the northern suburbs of Paris. He departed Paris the morning after he was photographed on the rue de Rivoli and the Champs-Élysées, also aboard a Eurostar train, this one bound for London.

Unlike most international trains in Western Europe, the Eurostar requires passengers to clear passport control before boarding. Alpha Group quickly found their man in the manifests. He was Jalal Nasser, born in Amman, Jordan, in 1984, currently residing in the United Kingdom, address unknown. Rousseau dispatched a cable to MI5 in London and, in the dullest language possible, asked whether the British security service had a place of residence for one Jalal Nasser and whether it had reason to suspect his involvement in any form of Islamic extremism. His address arrived two hours later: 33 Chilton Street, Bethnal Green, East London. And, no, said MI5, it had no evidence to suggest that Nasser was anything more than what he claimed to be, which was a graduate student in economics at King's College. He had been enrolled there, on and off, for seven years.

Gabriel dispatched Mikhail to London, along with a pair of all-purpose field hands named Mordecai and Oded, and within a few hours of their arrival they managed to acquire a small flat in Chilton Street. They also managed to snap a photograph of Jalal Nasser, the eternal student, walking along Bethnal Green Road with a book bag over one shoulder. It appeared on Gabriel's mobile phone that evening as he was standing in the nursery of his apartment in Jerusalem, staring down at the two children sleeping peacefully in their cribs.

"They missed you terribly," said Chiara. "But if you wake them . . ."

"What?"

She smiled, took him by the hand, and led him into their bedroom.

"Quietly," she whispered as she loosened the buttons on her blouse. "Very quietly."

13

AMMAN, JORDAN

EARLY THE FOLLOWING MORNING Gabriel slipped from the apartment while Chiara and the children were still sleeping and climbed into the back of his armored SUV. His motorcade contained two additional vehicles filled with well-armed Office security agents. And instead of heading west toward Tel Aviv and King Saul Boulevard, it skirted the gray Ottoman walls of the Old City and spilled down the slopes of the Judean Hills, into the unforgiving flatlands of the West Bank. Stars clung to the cloudless sky above Jerusalem, oblivious to the sun that lay low and fiery above the cleft of the Jordan Valley. A few miles before Jericho was the turnoff for the Allenby Bridge, the historic crossing between the West Bank and the British-created Hashemite Kingdom of Jordan. The ramp on the Israeli half had been cleared of traffic for Gabriel's arrival; on the other side idled an impressive motorcade of Suburbans filled with mustachioed Bedouin soldiers. The head of Gabriel's security detail exchanged a few words with his Jordanian counterpart. Then the two motorcades merged into one and set off across the desert toward Amman.

Their destination was the headquarters of Jordan's General Intelligence Department, also known as the Mukhabarat, the Arabic word used to describe the all-pervasive secret services that safeguarded the fragile kingdoms, emirates, and republics of the Middle East. Surrounded by concentric rings of security men, a locked stainless steel attaché case in one hand, Gabriel strode swiftly across the marble lobby, up a flight of curved stairs, and into the office of Fareed Barakat, the GID's chief. It was a vast room, four or five times the size of the director's suite at King Saul Boulevard, and decorated with somber curtains, overstuffed chairs and couches, lustrous Persian carpets, and expensive trinkets that had been bestowed on Fareed by admiring spies and politicians around the world. It was the sort of place, thought Gabriel, where favors were dispensed, judgments were passed, and lives were destroyed. He had upgraded his usual attire for the occasion, exchanging his denim and leather for a trim gray suit and white shirt. Even so, his clothing paled in comparison to the worsted sartorial splendor that hung from the tall slender frame of Fareed Barakat. Fareed's suits were handmade for him by Anthony Sinclair in London. Like the current king of Jordan, the man he was sworn to protect, he had been expensively educated in Britain. He spoke English like a news presenter from the BBC.

"Gabriel Allon, at long last." Fareed's small black eyes shone like polished onyx. His nose was like the beak of a bird of prey. "It's good to finally meet you. After reading those stories about you in the newspaper, I was convinced I'd missed my chance."

"Reporters," said Gabriel disdainfully.

"Quite," agreed Fareed. "Your first time in Jordan?"

"I'm afraid so."

"No quiet visits to Amman on a borrowed passport? No operations against one of your many enemies?"

"I wouldn't dream of it."

"Wise man," said Fareed, smiling. "Better to play by the rules. You'll discover soon enough that I can be very helpful to you."

Israel and Jordan had more in common than a border and a shared British colonial past. They were both westward-looking countries trying to survive in a Middle East that was spinning dangerously out of control. They had fought two wars, in 1948 and 1967, but had formally made peace in the afterglow of the Oslo peace process. Even before that, however, the Office and the GID had maintained close, if cautious, ties. Jordan was universally considered the most fragile of the Arab states, and it was the job of the GID to keep the king's head on his shoulders and the chaos of the region at bay. Israel wanted the same thing, and in the GID had found a competent and reliable partner with whom they could do business. The GID was a bit more civilized than its brutal Iraqi and Egyptian counterparts, though no less ubiquitous. A vast network of informers watched over the Jordanian people and monitored their every word and deed. Even a stray unkind remark about the king or his family could result in a sojourn of indeterminate length in the GID's labyrinth of secret detention centers.

Uzi Navot had warned Gabriel about the rituals that accompanied any visit to Fareed's gilded lair: the endless cups of sticky-sweet Arab coffee, the cigarettes, the long stories of Fareed's many conquests, both professional and romantic. Fareed always spoke as though he couldn't quite believe his own luck, which added to his considerable charm. Where some men wearied under the burden of responsibility, Fareed thrived. He was the lord of a vast empire of secrets. He was a deeply contented man.

Throughout Fareed's monologue, Gabriel managed to keep a placid, attentive smile fixed firmly on his face. He laughed when appropriate and posed a leading question or two, and yet all the while his thoughts wandered to the photographs contained in the locked stainless steel briefcase at his ankle. He had never carried a briefcase before—not willingly at least, only for the sake of his cover. It felt like a ball and chain, an anvil. He supposed he should find someone to carry it for him. But inwardly he feared that such a move might nurture in him a taste for privilege that would spiral, inevitably, to a valet, a food taster, and a standing appointment at an exclusive Tel Aviv hair salon. Already, he missed the small thrill of piloting his own automobile down the ski-slope grade of Highway 1. Fareed Barakat would surely have found such sentiments curious. It was said of Fareed that he once jailed his own butler for allowing the Earl Grey tea to steep a minute too long.

At length, Fareed brought the topic of conversation around to the situation at King Saul Boulevard. He had heard about Gabriel's pending promotion, and Uzi Navot's impending demise. He had also heard—from where he refused to say—that Gabriel intended to keep Navot around in some capacity. He thought this a very bad idea, horrendous actually, and told Gabriel so. "Better to sweep the decks and make a fresh start of it." Gabriel smiled, praised Fareed for his shrewdness and wisdom, and said nothing more on the subject.

The Jordanian had also heard that Gabriel had recently become a father again. With the press of a button he summoned an aide, who entered the office bearing two gift-wrapped boxes, one enormous, the other quite small. Fareed insisted that Gabriel open both in his presence. The large box contained a motorized Mercedes toy car; the second box, the smaller, a strand of pearls.

"I hope you're not offended because the car is German."

"Not at all."

"The pearls are from Mikimoto."

"That's good to know." Gabriel closed the box. "I can't possibly accept these."

"You must. Otherwise, I'll be deeply offended."

Gabriel was suddenly sorry he had come to Amman without gifts of his own. But what was one supposed to give a man who jailed his butler for misbrewing a pot of tea? He had only the photographs, which he retrieved from the attaché case. The first showed a man walking along an East London street, a book bag over one shoulder, a man who might have been an Arab or a Frenchman or an Italian. Gabriel handed the photograph to Fareed Barakat, who gave it a brief glance. "Jalal Nasser," he said, returning the photograph to Gabriel with a smile. "What took you so long, my friend?"

14

GID HEADQUARTERS, AMMAN

FAREED BARAKAT KNEW MORE ABOUT ISIS than any other intelligence officer in the world, and with good reason. The movement had its roots in the grim Amman suburb of Zarqa, where, in a two-story house overlooking a derelict cemetery, there had once lived a man named Ahmad Fadil Nazzal al-Khalayleh, a heavy drinker, a vandal, a vicious street brawler who had so many tattoos the neighborhood children referred to him as "the green man." His mother was a devout Muslim who believed that only Islam could save her troubled son. She enrolled him for religious instruction at the al-Hussein Ben Ali Mosque, and it was there al-Khalayleh found his true calling. He quickly became a radical and a committed enemy of the Jordanian monarchy, which he was determined to topple with force. He spent several years inside the GID's secret prisons, including a stint in the notorious desert fortress at al-Jafr. The leader of his cellblock was Abu Muhammad al-Maqdisi, a firebrand preacher who was one of the foremost theoreticians of jihadism. In 1999, when a young, untested king ascended to the throne after the death of his father, he decided to release more than a thousand criminals and political prisoners in a traditional gesture of goodwill. Two of the men he freed were al-Maqdisi and his violent pupil from Zarqa.

By then, the former street brawler with many tattoos was known as Abu Musab al-Zarqawi. Not long after his release, he made his way to Afghanistan and pledged allegiance to Osama bin Laden. And in March 2003, with the American invasion of Iraq looming, he slipped into Baghdad and formed the resistance cells that would eventually come to be known as al-Qaeda in Iraq. The wave of beheadings and spectacular sectarian bombings carried out by Zarqawi and his associates pushed the country to the brink of all-out civil war. He was the prototype of a new kind of Islamic extremist, willing to use horrifying violence to shock and terrify. Even Ayman al-Zawahiri, al-Qaeda's second-in-command, rebuked him.

An American air strike ended Zarqawi's life in June 2006, and by the end of the decade al-Qaeda in Iraq had been decimated. But in 2011 two events conspired to revive its fortunes: the outbreak of civil war in Syria and the withdrawal of all U.S. forces from Iraq. Now known as ISIS, the group rose from the ashes and rushed into the power vacuum along the Syria–Iraq border. The land under its control stretched from the cradle of civilization to the doorstep of Europe. The Hashemite Kingdom of Jordan was squarely in its sights. So, too, was Israel.

Among the thousands of young Muslims from the Middle East and Europe who were drawn to the siren song of ISIS was a young Jordanian named Jalal Nasser. Like Zarqawi, Nasser was from a prominent East Bank tribe, the Bani Hassan, though his family was better off than the Khalaylehs of Zarqa. He attended a private secondary school in Amman and King's College in London. Soon after the outbreak of civil war in Syria, however, he met with an ISIS recruiter in Amman and inquired about making his way to the caliphate. The recruiter advised Jalal that he could be more useful elsewhere.

"In Europe?" asked Gabriel.

Fareed nodded.

"How do you know this?"

"Sources and methods," said Fareed, which meant he had no interest in answering Gabriel's question.

"Why not take him off the streets?"

"Jalal is from a good family, a family that has been loyal to the monarchy for a long time. If we had arrested him, it would have caused problems." A careful smile. "Collateral damage."

"So you put him on an airplane to London and waved good-bye."

"Not entirely. Every time he comes back to Amman, we bring him in for a little chat. And we watch him from time to time in England to make certain he isn't plotting against us."

"Did you tell the British about him?"

Silence.

"What about your friends at Langley?"

More silence.

"Why not?"

"Because we didn't want to turn a small problem into a big problem. These days, that seems to be the American way."

"Careful, Fareed. You never know who's listening."

"Not here," he said, glancing around his vast office. "It's perfectly secure."

"Says who?"

"Langley."

Gabriel smiled.

"So why are you so interested in Jalal?" asked Fareed.

Gabriel handed him another photograph.

"The woman from the Paris attack?"

Gabriel nodded. Then he instructed Fareed to look carefully at the man seated alone in the corner of the café, with an open laptop computer.

"Jalal?"

"In the flesh."

"Any chance it's a coincidence?"

Gabriel handed the Jordanian two more photos: Safia Bourihane and Jalal Nasser on the rue de Rivoli, Safia Bourihane and Jalal Nasser on the Champs-Élysées.

"I guess not."

"There's more."

Gabriel gave Fareed two more photos: Jalal Nasser with Margreet Janssen at a restaurant in Amsterdam, Jalal Nasser holding his recently slapped cheek on a street in the red-light district.

"Shit," said Fareed softly.

"The Office concurs."

Fareed returned the photos. "Who else knows about this?"

"Paul Rousseau."

"Alpha Group?"

Gabriel nodded.

"They're quite good."

"You've worked with them?"

"On occasion." Fareed shrugged. "As a rule, France's problems come from other parts of the Arab world."

"Not anymore." Gabriel returned the photos to his briefcase.

"I assume you have Jalal under watch."

"As of last night."

"Have you had a chance to peek at that laptop?"

"Not yet. You?"

"We drained it the last time we brought him in for a chat. It was clean as a whistle. But that doesn't mean anything. Jalal is very good with computers. They're all very good. And getting better by the day."

Fareed started to light one of his English cigarettes but stopped. It seemed that Gabriel's aversion to tobacco was well known to the GID.

"I don't suppose you've mentioned any of this to the Americans."

"Who?"

"What about the British?"

"In passing."

"There's no such thing when it comes to the British. Furthermore," said Fareed with his newsreader formality, "I know for a fact they're terrified that they're going to be hit next."

"They should be terrified."

Fareed ignited his gold lighter and touched his cigarette to the slender flame. "So what was Jalal's connection to Paris and Amsterdam?"

"I'm not sure yet. He might be just a recruiter or talent spotter. Or he might be the project manager." Gabriel was silent for a moment. "Or maybe," he said finally, "he's the one they call Saladin."

Fareed Barakat looked up sharply.

"Obviously," said Gabriel, "you've heard the name."

"Yes," conceded Fareed, "I've heard it."

"Is he?"

"Not a chance."

"Does he exist?"

"Saladin?" Fareed nodded slowly. "Yes, he exists."

"Who is he?"

"He's our worst nightmare. Other than that," said Fareed, "I haven't a clue."

15

GID HEADQUARTERS, AMMAN

OF THE TERRORIST'S NAMESAKE, HOWEVER, the GID chief knew a great deal. Salah ad-Din Yusuf ibn Ayyub, or Saladin, was born into a prominent family of Kurds, in the town of Tikrit, in approximately 1138. His father was a soldier of fortune. Young Saladin lived for a time in Baalbek, in present-day Lebanon, and in Damascus, where he drank wine, pursued women, and played polo by candlelight. Damascus was the city he preferred over all others. Later, he would describe Egypt, the financial hub of his empire, as a whore who tried to separate him from his faithful wife Damascus.

His realm stretched from Yemen to Tunisia and north to Syria. It was ruled over by a hodgepodge of princes, emirs, and greedy relatives, all held together by Saladin's diplomatic skills and considerable charisma. He used violence to great effect, but found it distasteful. To his favorite son, Zahir, he once remarked: "I warn you against shedding blood, indulging in it and making a habit of it, for blood never sleeps."

He was lame and sickly, watched over constantly by a team of twenty-one doctors, including the philosopher and Talmudic scholar Maimonides, who was appointed his court physician in Cairo. Lacking in personal vanity—in Jerusalem he once laughed uproariously when a courtier splashed his silk robes with mud—he had little interest in personal riches or earthly delights. He was happiest when surrounded by poets and men of learning, but mainly it was the concept of jihad, or holy war, that consumed him. He built mosques and Islamic centers of learning across his lands and lavished money and favors on preachers and religious scholars. His goal was to re-create the zeal that had allowed Islam's earliest followers to conquer half of the known world. And once the sacred rage had been rekindled, he focused it on the one prize that had eluded him: Jerusalem.

A smallish outpost fed by springs, the city occupied a strategic high ground at the crossroads of three continents, a geographical sin for which it would be punished throughout the ages. Besieged, plundered, captured and recaptured, Jerusalem had been ruled by Jebusites, Egyptians, Assyrians, Babylonians, Persians, Greeks, Romans, Byzantines, and, of course, the Jews. When Omar al-Khattab, a close confidant of Muhammad, conquered Jerusalem in 639 with a small band of Arab cameleers from the Hejaz and Yemen, it was a predominantly Christian city. Four and a half centuries later, Pope Urban II would dispatch an expeditionary force numbering several thousand European Christians to reclaim Jerusalem from the Muslims, whom he regarded as a people "alien to God." The Christian soldiers, who would one day be known as Crusaders, breached the city's defenses on the night of July 13, 1099, and slaughtered its inhabitants, including three thousand men, women, and children who had taken shelter inside the great al-Aqsa Mosque on the Temple Mount.

It was Saladin, the son of a Kurdish soldier of fortune from Tikrit, who would return the favor. After humiliating the thirst-crazed Crusader force at the Battle of Hattin near Tiberias—Saladin personally sliced off the arm of Raynald of Châtillon—the Muslims reclaimed Jerusalem after a negotiated surrender. Saladin tore down the large cross that had been erected atop the Dome of the Rock, scrubbed its courts with Damascene rosewater to remove the last foul traces of the infidel, and sold thousands of Christians into slavery or the harem. Jerusalem would remain under Islamic control until 1917, when the British seized it from the Ottoman Turks. And when the Ottoman Empire collapsed in 1924, so, too, did the last Muslim caliphate.

But now ISIS had declared a new caliphate. At present, it included only portions of western Iraq and eastern Syria, with Raqqa as its capital. Saladin, the new Saladin, was ISIS's chief of external operations—or so believed Fareed Barakat and the Jordanian General Intelligence Department. Unfortunately, the GID knew almost nothing else about Saladin, including his real name.

"Is he Iraqi?"

"He might be. Or he might be a Tunisian or a Saudi or an Egyptian or an Englishman or one of the other lunatics who've rushed to Syria to live in this new Islamic paradise of theirs."

"Surely, the GID doesn't believe that."

"We don't," Fareed conceded. "We think he's probably a former Iraqi military officer. Who knows? Maybe he's from Tikrit, just like Saladin."

"And Saddam."

"Ah, yes, let's not forget Saddam." Fareed exhaled a lungful of smoke toward the high ceiling of his office. "We had our problems with Saddam, but we warned the Americans they would rue the day they toppled him. They didn't listen, of course. Nor did they listen when we asked them to do something about Syria. Not our problem, they said. We're putting the Middle East in our rearview mirror. No more American wars in Muslim lands. And now look at the situation. A quarter of a million dead, hundreds of thousands more streaming into Europe, Russia and Iran working together to dominate the Middle East." He shook his head slowly. "Have I left anything out?"

"You forgot Saladin," said Gabriel.

"What do you want to do about him?"

"I suppose we could do nothing and hope he goes away."

"Hope is how we ended up with him in the first place," said Fareed. "Hope and hubris."

"So let's put him out of business, sooner rather than later."

"What about the Americans?"

"What about them?" asked Gabriel.

"They'll want a role."

"They can't have one, at least not yet."

"We could use their technology."

"We have technology, too."

"Not like the Americans," said Fareed. "They *own* cyber, cellular, and satellite."

"None of that means a thing if you don't know the target's real name."

"Point taken. So we work together? The Office and the GID?"

"And the French," added Gabriel.

"Who runs the show?"

When Gabriel offered no reply, Fareed frowned. The Jordanian didn't like diktats. But he also wasn't in the mood for a quarrel with the man who in all likelihood would be running the Office for a very long time.

"I won't be treated like a domestic servant. Do you understand me? I get enough of that from the Americans. Too often, they think of us as a branch office of Langley."

"I would never dream of it, Fareed."

"Very well." He gave a concierge smile. "Then please tell me how the GID can be of service."

"You can start by giving me everything you've got on Jalal Nasser."

"And then?"

"Stay away from him. Jalal belongs to me now."

"He's all yours. But no collateral damage." The Jordanian patted the back of Gabriel's hand. "His Majesty doesn't like collateral damage. And neither do I."

WHEN GABRIEL ARRIVED AT KING SAUL BOULEVARD, HE FOUND Uzi Navot alone in his office joylessly consuming a lunch of steamed white fish and wilted gray-green vegetables. He was using a pair of lacquered chopsticks rather than a knife and fork, which slowed his rate of intake and, theoretically, made the unappetizing meal more satisfying. It was Bella, his demanding wife, who had inflicted this indignity upon him. Bella kept track of every scrap of food that entered her husband's mouth and monitored his weight with the care of a geologist watching a rumbling volcano. Twice each day, when he rose and before he crawled exhausted into his bed, Navot was made to stand upon Bella's precise bathroom scale. She recorded the fluctuations in a leather-bound logbook and punished or rewarded him accordingly. When Navot had been good for an appropriate period of time, he was allowed a meal of stroganoff, goulash, schnitzel, or one of the other heavy Eastern European dishes he craved. And when he was bad, it was boiled fish and chopsticks. Clearly, thought Gabriel, watching him, Navot was paying the price for a dietary infidelity.

"It sounds to me as if you and Fareed really hit it off," he said after Gabriel described his visit to Amman. "The only thing Fareed ever gave me is candy and baklava. Bella can always tell when I've been to see him. It's rarely worth the trip."

"I tried to give back the pearls, but he wouldn't hear of it."

"Make sure you go on the record with Personnel. Heaven knows you're completely incorruptible, but we wouldn't want anyone to get the wrong idea about your newfound love affair with the GID."

Navot pushed away his plate. Nothing edible remained. Gabriel was surprised he hadn't eaten the chopsticks and the paper sleeve in which they had been presented.

"Do you really think that Fareed will back off Jalal Nasser?"

"Not in a million years."

"Which means Jordanian intelligence is going to have a front-row seat on your operation."

"With an obstructed view."

Navot smiled. "What are you going to do?"

"I'm going to penetrate Saladin's network. I'm going to find out who he really is and where he's operating. And then I'm going to drop a very large bomb on his head."

"That means sending an agent into Syria."

"Yes, Uzi, that's where ISIS is."

"The new caliphate is a forbidden kingdom. If you send an agent in there, he'll be lucky to come out again with his head still attached to his shoulders."

"*She*," said Gabriel. "Saladin clearly prefers women."

Navot shook his head gravely. "It's too dangerous."

"It's too dangerous not to, Uzi."

After a belligerent silence, Navot asked, "One of ours or one of theirs?"

"Ours."

"Languages?"

"French and Arabic. And I want someone who has something to offer. ISIS already has plenty of losers." Gabriel paused, then asked, "Do you know anyone like that, Uzi?"

"I might," said Navot.

One of the many improvements he had made to the director's suite was a high-tech video wall upon which the global news channels flickered day and night. At present, it was filled with images of human misery, much of it emanating from the shattered remnants of an ancient land called Syria. Navot watched the screen for a long moment before twirling the combination lock of his private safe. He removed two items, a file and an unopened box of Viennese butter cookies. He handed the file to Gabriel. The cookies he kept for himself. By the time Gabriel looked up again, they were gone.

"She's perfect."

"Yes," agreed Navot. "And if anything happens to her, it's on your head, not mine."

16

JERUSALEM

NO ONE COULD REALLY REMEMBER precisely when it all began. It might have been the Arab motorist who ran down three Jewish teenagers near a West Bank settlement south of Jerusalem. Or the Arab trader who stabbed two yeshiva students outside the Old City's Damascus Gate. Or the Arab worker at a luxury hotel who tried to poison a visiting congressman from Ohio. Inspired by the words and deeds of ISIS, frustrated by the broken promises of peace, many young Palestinians had quite literally taken matters into their own hands. The violence was low level, deeply personal, and difficult to stop. An Arab with a suicide vest was relatively easy to detect. An Arab armed with a kitchen knife, or an automobile, was a security nightmare, especially if the Arab was prepared to die. The random nature of the attacks had deeply unsettled the Israeli public. A recent poll had found that an overwhelming majority said they feared being attacked on the street. Many no longer frequented places where Arabs might be present, a difficult proposition in a city like Jerusalem.

Invariably, the wounded and the dying were rushed to Hadassah Medical Center, Israel's primary Level 1 trauma facility. Located in West Jerusalem, in the abandoned Arab village of Ein Kerem, the hospital's remarkable team of doctors and nurses routinely cared for the victims of the world's oldest conflict—the shattered survivors of suicide bombings, the IDF soldiers wounded in combat, the Arab demonstrators cut down by Israeli gunfire. They made no distinction between Arab and Jew, victim and perpetrator; they treated anyone who came through their door, including some of Israel's most dangerous enemies. It was not unusual to see a senior member of Hamas at Hadassah. Even the rulers of Syria, before the outbreak of the civil war, had sent their influential sick to the hills of Ein Kerem for care.

According to Christian tradition, Ein Kerem was the birthplace of John the Baptist. Church towers rose above the squat old limestone dwellings of the vanished Arabs, and the tolling of bells ushered one day into the next. Between the ancient village and the modern hospital was a parking lot reserved for senior physicians and administrators. Dr. Natalie Mizrahi was not yet permitted to park there; her space was located in a distant satellite lot at the edge of a deep ravine. She arrived at eight thirty and as usual had to wait several minutes for a shuttle bus. It dropped her a short walk from the entrance to the emergency room. For the moment, all appeared quiet. There were no ambulances in the courtyard, and the trauma center was darkened, with only a single nurse on duty in the event a team had to be assembled.

In the staff lounge, Natalie placed her handbag in a locker, pulled a white lab coat over her blue-green scrubs, and hung a stethoscope round her neck. Her shift commenced at nine a.m. and would terminate at nine the following morning. The face she examined in the bathroom mirror appeared reasonably rested and alert, much better than it would look in twenty-four hours. Her skin was olive complected, her eyes were nearly black. So was her hair. It was drawn into a tight bun and secured with a simple elastic band. A few escaped tendrils hung down the length of her neck. She wore no makeup and no fragrance; her nails were trimmed and covered in clear polish. The loose-fitting hospital attire concealed a body that was slender and taut, with narrow hips and the lightly muscled thighs and calves of a long-distance runner. These days, Natalie was confined to the treadmill at her health club. Like most Jerusalemites, she no longer felt safe alone in public.

She cleaned her hands with disinfectant and then leaned in to the mirror for a closer look at her face. She hated her nose and thought that her mouth, while sensuous, was slightly too large for her face. Her eyes, she had decided, were her most alluring asset, wide, dark, intelligent, beguiling, with a trace of treachery and perhaps some hidden reservoir of pain. After ten years of practicing medicine, she no longer considered herself beautiful, but she knew empirically that men found her attractive. As yet, she had stumbled upon no example of the species worth marrying. Her love life had consisted of a string of monogamous but ultimately unhappy relationships—in France, where she had lived until the age of twenty-six, and in Israel, where she had moved with her parents after they concluded that Marseilles was no longer a place for Jews. Her parents lived in Netanya, in an apartment overlooking the Mediterranean. Their assimilation into Israeli society was glancing at best. They watched French television, read French newspapers, shopped in French markets, passed their afternoons in French cafés, and spoke Hebrew only when necessary. Natalie's Hebrew, while fast and fluent, betrayed her Marseilles childhood. So, too, did her Arabic, which was flawless. In the markets of the Old City, she sometimes heard things that made her hair stand on end.

Leaving the staff room, she noticed two other doctors rushing into the trauma center. The emergency room was just down the hall. Only two of the bays were occupied. Dr. Ayelet Malkin, the shift supervisor, sat in the corral in the center of the room, glaring at the screen of a desktop computer.

"Just in time," she said without looking up.

"What's going on?"

"A Palestinian from East Jerusalem just stabbed two Haredim on Sultan Suleiman Street. One of them probably isn't going to make it. The other one is in bad shape, too."

"Another day, another attack."

"It gets worse, I'm afraid. A passerby jumped on the Arab and tried to disarm him. When the police arrived, they saw two men fighting over a knife, so they shot them both."

"How bad?"

"The hero got the worst of it. He's going into trauma."

"And the terrorist?"

"One shot, through and through. He's all yours."

Natalie hurried into the corridor in time to see the first patient being wheeled into the trauma center. He was wearing the dark suit, knee-length socks, and white shirt of an ultra-Orthodox Haredi Jew. The jacket was shredded and the white shirt was soaked with blood. His reddish-blond *payess* dangled from the edge of the gurney; his face was ashen. Natalie glimpsed him only briefly, a second or two, but her instincts told her that the man did not have long to live.

The next to arrive was a secular Israeli man, thirty-five or so, an oxygen mask over his face, a bullet in his chest, conscious, breathing, but just barely. He was followed a moment later by the second stabbing victim, a Haredi boy of fourteen or fifteen, with blood pouring from multiple wounds. Then, finally, came the cause of all the mayhem and bloodshed: the Palestinian from East Jerusalem who had awakened that morning and decided to kill two people because they were Israeli and Jewish. He was in his early twenties, Natalie reckoned, no more than twenty-five. He had a single bullet wound on the left side of his chest, between the base of the neck and the shoulder, and several cuts and abrasions to his face. Perhaps the hero had landed a blow or two while trying to disarm him. Or perhaps, thought Natalie, the police had given him a thrashing while taking him into custody. Four Israeli police officers, radios crackling, surrounded the gurney to which the Palestinian was handcuffed and strapped. There were also several men in plain clothes. Natalie suspected they were from Shabak, Israel's internal security service.

One of the Shabak officers approached Natalie and introduced himself as Yoav. His hair was shorn close to the scalp; wraparound sunglasses concealed his eyes. He seemed disappointed that the patient was still among the living.

"We'll need to stay while you work on him. He's dangerous."

"I can handle him."

"Not this one. He wants to die."

The ambulance attendants wheeled the young Palestinian down the corridor to the emergency room and with the help of the police officers moved him from the blood-soaked gurney to a clean treatment bed. The wounded man struggled briefly while the police officers secured his hands and feet to the aluminum railings with plastic flex cuffs. At Natalie's request, the officers withdrew from the bay. The Shabak man insisted on remaining behind.

"You're making him nervous," Natalie objected. "I need him to be calm so I can properly clean out that wound."

"Why should he be calm while the other three are fighting for their lives?"

"None of that matters in here, not now. I'll call you if I need you."

The Shabak man took a seat outside the bay. Natalie drew the curtain and, alone with the terrorist, examined the wound.

"What's your name?" she asked him in Hebrew, a language that many Arab residents of East Jerusalem spoke well, especially if they had jobs in the west. The wounded Palestinian hesitated, then said his name was Hamid.

"Well, Hamid, this is your lucky day. An inch or two lower, and you'd probably be dead."

"I want to be dead. I want to be a *shahid*."

"I'm afraid you've come to the wrong place for that."

Natalie lifted a pair of angled bandage scissors from her instrument tray. The Palestinian struggled against the restraints in fear.

"What's wrong?" asked Natalie. "You don't like sharp objects?"

The Palestinian recoiled but said nothing.

Switching to Arabic, Natalie said soothingly, "Don't worry, Hamid, I'm not going to hurt you."

He seemed surprised. "You speak Arabic very well."

"Why wouldn't I?"

"You're one of us?"

Natalie smiled and carefully cut the bloody shirt from his body.

THE INITIAL REPORT OF THE PATIENT'S CONDITION TURNED out to be incorrect. The wound was not through and through; the 9mm round was still lodged near the clavicle, which was fractured some eight centimeters from the breastbone. Natalie administered a local anesthetic, and when the drug had taken effect she went quickly to work. She flushed the wound with antibiotic and, using a pair of sterile tweezers, removed the bone fragments and several bits of imbedded fabric from Hamid's shirt. Then she removed the 9mm round, misshapen from the impact with the clavicle but still in one piece. Hamid asked to keep the bullet as a memento of his attack. Frowning, Natalie dropped the round into a bag of medical waste, closed the wound with four neat sutures, and covered it with a protective bandage. The left arm needed to be immobilized to allow the clavicle to heal, which would require removing the plastic flex-cuff restraint. Natalie decided it could wait. If the restraints were removed, she reckoned, Hamid would struggle and in the process cause further injury to the bone and the surrounding tissue.

The patient remained in the emergency room, resting, recovering, for another hour. In that time, two of his victims succumbed to their wounds down the hallway in the trauma center—the older of the Haredim, and the secular Israeli who had been mistakenly shot. When the police came for their prisoner, there was anger on their faces. Normally, Natalie would have kept a gunshot patient in the hospital overnight for observation, but she agreed to allow the police and Shabak men to take custody of Hamid immediately. When the restraints were removed, she hung his left arm in a sling and secured it tightly to his body. Then, without a soothing word in Arabic, she sent him on his way.

There was another attack later that afternoon, a young Arab from East Jerusalem, a kitchen knife, the busy Central Bus Station on the Jáffa Road. This time, the Arab did not survive. He was shot by an armed civilian, but not before stabbing two women, both septuagenarians. One expired on the way to Hadassah; the other, in the trauma center as Natalie was applying pressure to a chest wound. Afterward, on the television in the staff lounge, she watched the leader of the Palestinian Authority telling his people that it was their national duty to kill as many Jews as possible. "Slit their throats," he was saying, "stab them in their evil hearts. Every drop of blood shed for Jerusalem is holy."

Evening brought a respite of quiet. Natalie and Ayelet had dinner together in a restaurant in the hospital's gleaming shopping mall. They spoke of mundane subjects, men, movies, the sex life of a nymphomaniacal nurse from the childbirth center, anything but the horror they had witnessed that day. They were interrupted by yet another crisis; four victims of a head-on collision were on their way to the emergency room. Natalie saw to the youngest, a religious girl of fourteen, originally from Cape Town, who lived in an English-speaking community in Beit Shemesh. She had suffered numerous lacerations but no broken bones or internal injuries. Her father, however, was not so fortunate. Natalie was present when the child was told of his death.

Exhausted, she stretched out on a bed in the staff lounge for a few hours' sleep, and in her dreams she was chased by a mob of hooded men with knives. She woke with a start and squinted at her mobile phone. It was seven fifteen. Rising, she swallowed a cup of black coffee with sugar, made a halfhearted attempt to put her hair in order, and headed back to the emergency room to see what horror the last two hours of her shift would bring. It remained quiet until 8:55, when Ayelet was notified of another stabbing.

"How many?" asked Natalie.

Ayelet held up two fingers.

"Where?"

"Netanya."

"Netanya? You're sure it was Netanya?"

Ayelet nodded grimly. Natalie quickly dialed the number for her parents' apartment. Her father answered instantly, as though he were sitting next to the phone, waiting for her call.

"Papa," she said, closing her eyes with relief.

"Yes, of course. What's wrong, darling?"

She could hear the sound of a French morning television program in the background. She was about to tell him to switch to Channel 1 but stopped herself. Her parents didn't need to know that their little French sanctuary by the sea was no longer safe.

"And Mama?" asked Natalie. "She's well?"

"She's right here. Would you like to speak to her?"

"It's not necessary. I love you, Papa."

Natalie hung up the phone. It was nine o'clock exactly. Ayelet had given up her seat in the corral for the next shift supervisor, Dr. Marc Geller, a freckled, ginger-haired Scot.

"I want to stay," said Natalie.

Marc Geller pointed toward the door. "I'll see you in three days."

Natalie collected her belongings from the staff room and, numbed by fatigue, rode a shuttle to the satellite parking lot. An armed security guard wearing a khaki vest walked her to her car. So this is what it means to be Jewish in the twenty-first century, she thought as she slid behind the wheel. Chased from France by a rising tide of anti-Semitism, Natalie and her parents had come to the Jewish homeland, only to face a wave of brutal stabbings by young men bred and indoctrinated to hate. For the moment, Israel was not safe for the Jews. And if not Israel, where? We are, she thought, starting the engine, a people on the edge.

Her apartment was a short distance from the hospital in

Rehavia, a costly neighborhood in an increasingly costly city. She inched her way through the morning traffic along Ramban Street, turned left into Ibn Ezra Street, and eased into an empty space along the curb. Her apartment building was around the corner on Elkharizi Street, a tiny alleyway scarcely wide enough for cars. The air was cool and heavy with the scent of pine and bougainvillea. Natalie walked swiftly; even in Rehavia, an entirely Jewish neighborhood, she no longer felt safe. She passed through the gate, entered the foyer, and climbed the stairs to her flat. As she reached her door, her phone began to chime. She checked the caller ID before answering. It was her parents' number in Netanya.

"Is there something wrong?"

"Not at all," said a confident male voice in French.

Natalie checked the caller ID again. "Who is this?"

"Don't worry," said the voice. "Your parents are fine."

"Are you in their apartment?"

"No."

"Then how are you using their phone?"

"I'm not. It's just a little trick we use to make sure you didn't send us straight to voice mail."

"We?"

"My name is Uzi Navot. Perhaps you've heard of me. I'm the chief of something called the—"

"I know who you are."

"That's good. Because we know who you are, too, Natalie."

"Why are you calling?" she demanded.

"You sound like one of us," he said with a laugh.

"A spy?"

"An Israeli."

"I *am* an Israeli."

"Not anymore."

"What are you talking about?"

"Listen carefully, Natalie. I want you to hang up the phone and go inside your apartment. There's a woman waiting there. Don't be afraid, she works for me. She's taken the liberty of packing a bag for you."

"Why?"

The connection went dead. Natalie stood for a moment wondering what to do. Then she drew her keys from her handbag, opened the door, and went inside.

17

JEZREEL VALLEY, ISRAEL

THE WOMAN SEATED AT THE kitchen table didn't look much like a spy. She was small, smaller than Natalie, and wore an expression that fell somewhere between boredom and grief. She had helped herself to a cup of tea. Next to it was a mobile phone, and next to the phone was Natalie's passport, which had been hidden in a manila envelope in the bottom drawer of her bedside table. The envelope had also contained three letters of an intensely personal nature, written by a man Natalie had known at university in France. She had always regretted not burning them, never more so than at that moment.

"Open it," said the woman with a glance toward Natalie's stylish carry-on suitcase. It bore the bar-coded, stickered traces of her last trip to Paris, Air France instead of El Al, the preferred airline of French-Jewish exiles. Natalie tugged at the zipper and peered inside. It had been hastily and carelessly packed—a pair of trousers, two blouses, a cotton pullover sweater, a single pair of underwear. What kind of woman, she thought, packed one pair of panties?

"How long am I going to be away?"

"That depends."

"On what?"

The woman only sipped her tea.

"No makeup? No deodorant? No shampoo? Where am I going? Syria?"

There was a silence. Then the woman said, "Pack whatever you need. But don't take too long. He's very anxious to meet you. We mustn't keep him waiting."

"Who? Uzi Navot?"

"No," she answered, smiling for the first time. "The man you're going to meet is much more important than Uzi Navot."

"I have to be back at work in three days."

"Yes, we know. Nine o'clock." She held out her hand. "Your phone."

"But—"

"Please," the woman said, "you're wasting valuable time."

Natalie surrendered the phone and went into her bedroom. It looked as if it had been ransacked. The contents of the manila envelope lay scattered across the bed, everything but the letters, which seemed to have vanished. Natalie had a sudden vision of a roomful of people reading passages aloud and then bursting into uproarious laughter. She gathered up a few more items of clothing and packed a small toiletry kit, including her birth control pills and the prescription pain reliever she took for the headaches that sometimes swept over her like a storm. Then she returned to the kitchen.

"Where are my letters?"

"What letters?"

"The letters you took from my bedroom."

"I didn't take anything from you."

"Who did?"

"Let's go," was all the woman said.

Descending the stairs, suitcase in one hand, purse in the

other, Natalie noticed that the woman walked with a slight limp. Her car was parked in Ibn Ezra Street, directly in front of Natalie's. She drove calmly but very fast, down the Judean Hills toward Tel Aviv, then northward up the Coastal Plain along Highway 6. For a time they listened to the news on the radio, but it was all stabbings and death and predictions of a coming apocalyptic war between Jews and Muslims over the Temple Mount. The woman rebuffed all questions and attempts at conversation, leaving Natalie to stare out her window at the minarets rising above the West Bank towns just beyond the Separation Barrier. They were so close she imagined she could touch them. The proximity of the villages to such a vital road had left her dubious about the prospects of a two-state solution. French and Swiss villages existed side by side along a largely invisible border, but Switzerland did not wish to wipe France from the map. Nor did the Swiss beseech their sons to shed the blood of French infidels.

Gradually, the Coastal Plain fell away and the highway tilted toward the bluffs of Mount Carmel and the green-and-tan patchwork of the Galilee. They were headed vaguely toward Nazareth, but a few miles before reaching the city the woman turned onto a smaller road and followed it past the sporting fields of a school until a security barrier, metal and spiked, blocked their path. Automatically, the gate slid away, and they proceeded along a gently curving street lined with trees. Natalie had been expecting a secret installation of some sort. Instead, she found herself in a quiet little town. Its layout was circular. Bungalows fronted the road, and behind the bungalows, like the folds of a hand fan, lay pastures and cultivated cropland.

"Where are we?"

"Nahalal," replied the woman. "It's a moshav. Do you know this term? Moshav?"

"I'm an immigrant," answered Natalie coolly, "not an idiot. A moshav is a cooperative community of individual farms, which is different from a kibbutz."

"Very good."

"It's true, isn't it?"

"What's that?"

"You really do think we're idiots. You ask us to make aliyah and then you treat us as though we're not quite a member of the club. Why is that?"

"It's not such an easy life in Israel. We're innately mistrustful of people who *choose* to live here. Some of us had no choice. Some of us had nowhere else to go."

"And this makes you superior?"

"No. It makes me something of a cynic." The woman drove slowly past the shaded bungalows. "Not bad, eh?"

"No," said Natalie, "not bad at all."

"Nahalal is the oldest moshav in Israel. When the first Jews arrived here in 1921, this was marshland infested with Anopheles mosquitoes." She paused. "Do you know this type? The Anopheles spreads malaria."

"I'm a doctor," said Natalie wearily.

The woman appeared altogether unimpressed. "They drained the swamps and turned this place into productive farmland." She shook her head. "We think our lives are so difficult, but they came here with nothing and actually built a country."

"I suppose they didn't notice *that*," said Natalie, nodding toward the Arab village perched atop a hillock overlooking the valley.

The woman gave her a despairing sidelong glance. "You don't really believe all that drivel, do you?"

"What drivel is that?"

"That we stole their land."

"How would you describe it?"

"This land was purchased by the Jewish National Fund. No one *stole* anything. But if you're ashamed of our history, perhaps you should have stayed in France."

"That's no longer an option."

"You're from Marseilles, yes?"

"Yes."

"An interesting place, Marseilles. A bit seedy but nice."

"You've been?"

"Once," said the woman. "I was sent there to kill a terrorist."

She turned into the drive of a modern bungalow. On the covered veranda, his face obscured by shadow, stood a man clad in faded blue jeans and a leather jacket. The woman slid the car into park and switched off the engine.

"I envy you, Natalie. I'd give anything to be in your place right now, but I can't. I haven't your gifts."

"I'm only a doctor. How can I possibly help you?"

"I'll let him explain," the woman said with a glance toward the man on the porch.

"Who is he?"

The woman smiled and opened her door. "Don't worry about your bag. Someone will see to it."

THE FIRST THING NATALIE NOTICED AFTER STEPPING FROM THE car was the smell—the smell of rich earth and newly mown grass, the smell of blossom and pollen, the smell of animals and fresh dung. Her clothing, she thought suddenly, was wholly unsuited for such a place, especially her flat shoes, which were little more than ballet slippers. She was annoyed with the woman for having failed to tell her that their destination was a farm in the Jezreel Valley. Then, as they crossed the thick green lawn, Natalie again noticed the limp, and all sins were forgiven. The man on the veranda had yet to move. Despite the shadows, Natalie knew he was watching her with the intensity of a portrait artist studying his subject. At last, he came slowly down the three steps that led from the veranda to the lawn, moving from the shadow to the bright sunlight. "Natalie," he said, extending his hand. "I hope the drive wasn't too difficult. Welcome to Nahalal."

His temples were the color of ash, his eyes were an unnerving shade of green. Something about the handsome face was familiar. Then all at once Natalie realized where she had seen it before. She released his hand and took a step back.

"You're—"

"Yes, I'm him. And I'm obviously very much alive, which means you are in possession of an important state secret."

"Your obituary in *Haaretz* was quite moving."

"I thought so, too. But you mustn't believe everything you read in the newspapers. You're about to find out that about seventy percent of history is classified. And difficult things are almost always accomplished entirely in secret." His smile faded, the green eyes scanned her face. "I hear you had a long night."

"We've been having a lot of them lately."

"The doctors in Paris and Amsterdam had long nights recently, too." He tilted his head to one side. "I assume you followed the news of the bombing in the Marais quite carefully."

"Why would you assume that?"

"Because you're French."

"I'm Israeli now."

"But you retained your French passport after you made aliyah."

His question sounded like an accusation. She didn't respond.

"Don't worry, Natalie, I'm not being judgmental. In times

like these, it's best to have a lifeboat." He placed a hand to his chin. "Did you?" he asked suddenly.

"Did I what?"

"Follow the news from Paris?"

"I admired Madame Weinberg a great deal. In fact, I actually met her once when she came to Marseilles."

"Then you and I have something in common. I admired Hannah a great deal as well, and it was my pleasure to consider her a friend. She was very generous to our service. She helped us when we needed it, and a grave threat to our security was eliminated."

"Is that why she's dead?"

"Hannah Weinberg is dead," he said pointedly, "because of a man who calls himself Saladin." He removed his hand from his chin and leveled his gaze. "You are now a member of a very small club, Natalie. Not even the American CIA knows about this man. But we're getting ahead of ourselves." He smiled again and took her by the arm. "Come. We'll have some food. We'll get to know each other better."

He led her across the veranda and into a shaded garden, where a round table set for four people had been laid with a traditional Israeli lunch of salads and Middle Eastern dips. At one of the places sat a large, morose-looking man with closely cropped gray hair and small rimless spectacles. Natalie recognized him at once. She had seen him on television rushing into the prime minister's office in times of crisis.

"Natalie," said Uzi Navot, rising slowly to his feet. "So good of you to accept our invitation. I'm sorry about showing up on your doorstep unannounced like that, but that's how we've always done things, and I believe the old ways are the best."

A few paces from the garden stood a large barn of corrugated metal, and next to the barn were pens filled with cattle and horses. A pie slice of row crops stretched toward Mount

Tabor, which rose like a nipple from the tabletop flatlands of the valley.

"This farm belongs to a friend of our service," explained the one who was supposed to be dead, the one named Gabriel Allon. "I was born right over there"—he pointed toward a cluster of distant buildings to the right of Mount Tabor—"in Ramat David. It was established a few years after Nahalal. Many of the people who lived there were refugees from Germany."

"Like your mother and father."

"You obviously read my obituary quite carefully."

"It was fascinating. But very sad." She turned away and stared out at the land. "Why am I here?"

"First, we have lunch. Then we talk."

"And if I want to leave?"

"You leave."

"And if I stay?"

"I can promise you only one thing, Natalie. Your life will never be the same."

"And if the roles were reversed? What would you do?"

"I'd probably tell you to find someone else."

"Well," she said. "How can I possibly turn down an offer like that? Shall we eat? I'm absolutely famished."

18

THEY HAD PLUCKED HER FROM the overt world without a ripple and smuggled her to their pastoral secret citadel. Now came the hard bit—the vetting, the probing, the inquisition. The goal of this unpleasant exercise was to determine whether Dr. Natalie Mizrahi, formerly of Marseilles, lately of Rehavia in West Jerusalem, was temperamentally, intellectually, and politically suited for the job they had in mind. Unfortunately, thought Gabriel, it was a job no woman of sound mind would ever want.

Recruitments, said the great Ari Shamron, are like seductions. And most seductions, even those conducted by trained intelligence officers, involve a mutual unburdening of the soul. Usually, the recruiter cloaks himself in a cover identity, an invented persona that he wears like a suit and tie and changes at a whim. But on this occasion, in the valley of his childhood, the soul that Gabriel opened to Natalie Mizrahi was his own.

"For the record," he began after settling Natalie in her seat at the luncheon table, "the name you read in the newspapers after my alleged death is my real name. It is not a pseudonym or a work name, it is the name I was given at birth. Regrettably, many of the other details of my life were correct as well. I was a member of the unit that avenged the murder of our people in Munich. I killed the PLO's second-in-command in Tunis. My son was killed in a bombing in Vienna. My wife was gravely wounded." He did not mention the fact that he had remarried or that he was a father again. His commitment to truthfulness went only so far.

And, yes, he continued, pointing across the flat green-and-tan valley toward Mount Tabor, he was born in the agricultural settlement of Ramat David, a few years after the founding of the State of Israel. His mother arrived there in 1948 after staggering half-dead out of Auschwitz. She met a man from Munich, a writer, an intellectual, who had escaped to Palestine before the war. In Germany his name had been Greenberg, but in Israel he had taken the Hebrew name Allon. After marrying, they vowed to have six children, one for each million murdered, but one child was all her womb could bear. She named the child Gabriel, the messenger of God, the defender of Israel, the interpreter of Daniel's visions. And then she promptly turned her back on him.

The housing estates and settlements of early Israel were places of grief where the dead walked among the living, and the living did their best to find their way in an alien land. In the little breezeblock home where the Allons lived, candles burned next to photographs of loved ones lost to the fires of the Shoah. They had no other gravestone. They were smoke on the wind, ashes in a river.

The Allons did not particularly like Hebrew, so at home they spoke only German. Gabriel's father spoke with a Bavarian accent; his mother, with the distinct accent of a Berliner. She was prone to melancholia and mood swings, and nightmares disturbed her sleep. She rarely laughed or smiled, she could not show pleasure at festive occasions, she did not like rich food or drink. She wore long sleeves always, even in the furnace heat of summer, and placed a fresh bandage each morning over the numbers tattooed on her left forearm. She referred to them as her mark of Jewish weakness, her emblem of Jewish shame. As a child, Gabriel learned to be quiet around her, lest he awaken the demons. Only once did he dare to ask her about the war. After giving him a hurried, evasive account of her time at Auschwitz, she fell into a deep depression and was bedridden for many days. Never again was the war or the Holocaust spoken of in the Allon household. Gabriel turned inward, solitary. When he was not painting, he took long runs along the irrigation ditches of the valley. He became a natural keeper of secrets, a perfect spy.

"I wish my story was unique, Natalie, but it is not. Uzi's family was from Vienna. They are all gone. Dina's ancestors were from the Ukraine. They were murdered at Babi Yar. Her father was like my mother, the only survivor, the last child. When he arrived in Israel he took the name Sarid, which means remnant. And when his last child was born, his sixth, he named her Dina."

"Avenged."

Gabriel nodded.

"Until now," said Natalie, glancing at Dina across the table, "I was unaware she had a name."

"Sometimes our Dina reminds me of my mother, which is why I love her. You see, Natalie, Dina is grieving, too. And she is very serious about her work. We all are. We see it as our solemn duty to make certain it never happens again." He smiled in an attempt to lift the veil of death that had fallen over the luncheon table. "Forgive me, Natalie, but I'm afraid this valley has stirred many old memories. I hope your child-hood wasn't as difficult as mine."

It was an invitation to share something of herself, an inti-macy, some well of hidden pain. She did not accept it.

"Congratulations, Natalie. You just passed an important test. Never reveal anything about yourself to three intelli-gence officers unless one of them is holding a gun to your head."

"Are you?"

"Heavens, no. Besides, we already know a great deal about you. We know, for example, that your family was from Alge-ria. They fled in 1962 after the war had ended. Not that they had a choice. The new regime declared that only Muslims could be citizens of Algeria." He paused, then asked, "Can you imagine if we had done the same thing? What would they say about us then?"

Again, Natalie reserved judgment.

"More than a hundred thousand Jews were essentially driven into exile. Some came to Israel. The rest, like your family, chose France. They settled in Marseilles, where you were born in 1984. Your grandparents and parents all spoke the Algerian dialect of Arabic as well as French, and as a child you learned to speak Arabic, too." He looked across the valley toward the village perched atop the hillock. "This is another thing you and I have in common. I, too, learned to speak a bit of Arabic as a child. It was the only way I could communicate with our neighbors from the tribe of Ismael."

For many years, he continued, life was good for the Mizrahi clan and the rest of France's Jews. Shamed by the Holocaust, the French kept their traditional anti-Semitism in check. But then the demographics of the country began to change. France's Muslim population exploded in size, far eclipsing the small, vulnerable Jewish community, and the oldest hatred returned with a vengeance.

"Your mother and father had seen this movie before, as children in Algeria, and they weren't about to wait for the ending. And so for the second time in their lives they packed their bags and fled, this time to Israel. And you, after a period of prolonged indecision, decided to join them."

"Is there anything else you'd like to tell me about myself?"

"Forgive me, Natalie, but we've had our eye on you for some time. It is a habit of ours. Our service is constantly on the lookout for talented young immigrants and Jewish visitors to our country. The diaspora," he added with a smile, "has its advantages."

"How so?"

"Languages, for one. I was recruited because I spoke German. Not classroom German or audiotape German, but real German with the Berlin accent of my mother."

"I presume you also knew how to fire a gun."

"Not very well, actually. My IDF career was unremarkable, to say the least. I was much better with a paintbrush than I was with a gun. But this is unimportant," he added. "What I really want to know is why you were reluctant to come to Israel."

"I considered France my home. My career, my *life*," she added, "was in France."

"But you came here nonetheless."

"Yes."

"Why?"

"I didn't want to be separated from my parents."

"You are a good child?"

"I am an *only* child."

"Like me."

She was silent.

"We like people of good character, Natalie. We're not interested in people who desert their wives and children and don't look after their parents. We employ them as paid sources if we have to, but we don't like having them in our midst."

"How do you know I'm—"

"A person of good character? Because we've been watching you, quietly and from a distance. Don't worry, we're not voyeurs unless we have to be. We've allowed you a zone of privacy, and we've averted our eyes whenever possible."

"You had no right."

"Actually," he said, "we had every right. The rules that govern our conduct give us a certain room to maneuver."

"Do they allow you to read other people's mail?"

"That is our business."

"I want those letters back."

"What letters are those?"

"The letters you took from my bedroom."

Gabriel looked reproachfully at Uzi Navot, who shrugged his heavy shoulders, as if to say it was possible—in fact, it was doubtless true—that certain private letters had been pinched from Natalie's apartment.

"Your property," said Gabriel apologetically, "will be returned as soon as possible."

"How thoughtful of you." Her voice contained a knife's edge of resentment.

"Don't be angry, Natalie. It's all part of the process."

"But I never applied to work for—"

"The Office," said Gabriel. "We only call it the Office. And none of us ever asked to join. We are *asked* to join. That's how it works."

"Why me? I know nothing of your world or what you do."

"I'll let you in on another little secret, Natalie. None of us do. One doesn't earn a master's degree in how to be an intelligence officer. One is smart, one is innovative, one has certain skills and personality traits, and the rest one learns. Our training is very rigorous. No one, not even the British, trains their spies as well as we do. When we're finished with you, you'll no longer be one of us. You'll be one of *them*."

"Who?"

Gabriel lifted his gaze toward the Arab village again. "Tell me something, Natalie. What is the language of your dreams?"

"French."

"What about Hebrew?"

"Not yet."

"Never?"

"No, never."

"That's good," said Gabriel, still staring at the village. "Perhaps we should continue this conversation in French."

19

NAHALAL, ISRAEL

BUT FIRST, BEFORE GOING ANY FURTHER, Gabriel gave Natalie another chance to leave. She could go back to Jerusalem, back to her work at Hadassah, back to the overt world. Her file—yes, Gabriel admitted, she already had a file—would be shredded and burned. They would not blame her for turning her back on them; they would only blame themselves for having failed to close the deal. They would speak of her well, if at all. They would always think of her as the one who got away.

He said all this not in Hebrew but in French. And when she gave him her answer, after only a moment's deliberation, it was in the same language, the language of her dreams. She would stay, she said, but only if he told her why she was being asked to join their exclusive club.

"Shwaya, shwaya," said Gabriel. It was an Arabic expression that, in this context, meant little by little. Then, without providing Natalie an opening to object, he told her about the man called Saladin. Not the son of a Kurdish soldier of fortune who united the Arab world and reclaimed Jerusalem from the Crusaders, but the Saladin who in the span of a few days had shed infidel and apostate blood in Paris and Amsterdam. They did not know his real name, they did not know his nationality, though his nom de guerre surely was no accident. It suggested he was a man of ambition, a man of history who had visions of using mass murder as a means of unifying the Arab and Islamic world under the black flag of ISIS and the caliphate. His ultimate goals notwithstanding, he was clearly a terrorist mastermind of considerable skill. Under the noses of Western intelligence, he had built a network capable of delivering powerful vehicle-borne explosive devices to carefully chosen targets. Perhaps his tactics would remain the same, or perhaps he had bigger plans. Either way, they had to kill the network.

"And nothing kills a network faster," said Gabriel, "than to offer its leader a buyout."

"A buyout?" asked Natalie.

Gabriel was silent.

"Kill him? Is that what you mean?"

"Kill, eliminate, assassinate, liquidate—you choose the word. I'm afraid they've never mattered much to me. I'm in the business of saving innocent lives."

"I couldn't possibly—"

"Kill someone? Don't worry, we're not asking you to become a soldier or a special operative. We have plenty of men in black who are trained to do that sort of work."

"Like you."

"That was a long time ago. These days I wage war against our enemies from the comfort of a desk. I am a boardroom hero now."

"That's not what they wrote about you in *Haaretz*."

"Even the respectable *Haaretz* gets it wrong every now and then."

"So do the spies."

"You object to the business of espionage?"

"Only when spies do reprehensible things."

"Such as?"

"Torture," she answered.

"We don't torture anyone."

"What about the Americans?"

"Let's leave the Americans out of this for now. But I'm wondering," he added, "whether you would have any philosophical or moral objection to taking part in an operation that would result in someone's death."

"This might come as a shock to you, Mr. Allon, but I've never pondered that question before."

"You're a doctor, Natalie. You're trained to save lives. You swear an oath. Do no harm. Just yesterday, for example, you treated a young man who was responsible for the deaths of two people. Surely, that must have been difficult."

"Not at all."

"Why not?"

"Because it's my job."

"You still haven't answered my question."

"The answer is no," she said. "I would not have any philosophical or moral objection to taking part in an operation that results in the death of the man responsible for the attacks in Paris and Amsterdam, as long as no innocent lives are lost in the process."

"It sounds to me, Natalie, as though you're referring to the American drone program."

"Israel uses air strikes, too."

"And some of us disagree with that strategy. We prefer special operations to air power whenever possible. But our politicians have fallen in love with the idea of so-called *clean* warfare. Drones make that possible."

"Not for the people on the receiving end."

"That's true. Far too many innocent lives have been lost. But the best way to ensure that doesn't happen is good intelligence." He paused, then added, "Which is where you come in."

"What are you asking me to do?"

He smiled. *Shwaya, shwaya . . .*

SHE HAD NOT TOUCHED HER FOOD, NONE OF THEM HAD, SO before going any further Gabriel insisted they eat. He did not heed his own counsel, for truth be told he had never been much of a lunch person. And so while the others partook of the buffet, courtesy of an Office-approved caterer in Tel Aviv, he spoke of his childhood in the valley—of the Arab raids from the hills of the West Bank, of the Israeli reprisals, of the Six-Day War, which took his father, of the Yom Kippur War, which took his belief that Israel was invulnerable. The founding generation believed that a Jewish state in the historical land of Palestine would bring progress and stability to the Middle East. Yet all around Israel, in the frontline states and in the Arab periphery, anger and resentment burned long after the state came into existence, and societies stagnated under the thumbs of monarchs and dictators. While the rest of the world advanced, the Arabs, despite their massive petrowealth, went backward. Arab radio raged against the Jews while Arab children went barefoot and hungry. Arab newspapers printed blood libels that few Arabs could even read. Arab rulers grew rich while the Arab people had nothing but their humiliation and resentment—and Islam.

"Am I somehow to blame for their dysfunction?" asked Gabriel of no one in particular, and no one responded. "Did it happen because I lived here in this valley? Do they hate me because I drained it and killed the mosquitos and made it bloom? If I were not here, would the Arabs be free, prosperous, and stable?"

For a brief moment, he continued, it seemed peace might actually be possible. There was an historic handshake on the South Lawn of the White House. Arafat set up shop in Ramallah, Israelis were suddenly cool. And yet all the while the son of a Saudi construction billionaire was building an organization known as al-Qaeda, or the Base. For all its Islamic fervor, Osama bin Laden's creation was a highly bureaucratic enterprise. Its bylaws and workplace regulations resembled those of any modern company. They governed everything from vacation days to medical benefits to airline travel and furniture allowances. There were even rules for disability payments and a process by which a member's employment could be terminated. Those wishing to enter one of Bin Laden's Afghan training camps had to fill out a lengthy questionnaire. No corner of a potential recruit's life was spared scrutiny.

"But ISIS is different. Yes, it has its questionnaire, but it's nowhere near as thorough as al-Qaeda's. And with good reason. You see, Natalie, a caliphate without people is not a caliphate. It is a patch of empty desert between Aleppo and the Sunni Triangle of Iraq." He paused. Then for a second time he said, "Which is where you come in."

"You can't be serious."

His blank expression said that he was.

"You want me to join ISIS?" she asked, incredulous.

"No," he said. "You will be *asked* to join."

"By whom?"

"Saladin, of course."

A silence ensued. Natalie glanced from face to face—the mournful face of the avenged remnant, the familiar face of the chief of the Office, the face of a man who was supposed to be dead. It was to this face that she delivered her response.

"I can't do it."

"Why not?"

"Because I'm Jewish, and I can't pretend to be anything else just because I speak their language."

"You do it all the time, Natalie. At Hadassah they assign you Palestinian patients because they think you're one of them. So do the Arab traders in the Old City."

"The Arab traders aren't members of ISIS."

"Some of them are. But that's beside the point. You come to the table with certain natural attributes. You are, as we like to say, a gift from the intelligence gods. With our training, we'll complete the masterpiece. We've been doing this for a long time, Natalie, and we're very good at it. We can take a Jewish boy from a kibbutz and turn him into an Arab from Jenin. And we can surely turn someone like you into a Palestinian doctor from Paris who wishes to strike a blow against the West."

"Why would she want to do that?"

"Because like Dina, she is grieving. She craves vengeance. She is a black widow."

There was a long silence. When finally Natalie spoke, it was with a clinical detachment.

"She's French, this girl of yours?"

"She carries a French passport, she was educated and trained in France, but she is Palestinian by ethnicity."

"So the operation will take place in Paris?"

"It will begin there," he answered carefully, "but if the first phase is successful, it will necessarily migrate."

"Where?"

He said nothing.

"To Syria?"

"I'm afraid," said Gabriel, "that Syria is where ISIS is."

"And do you know what will happen to your doctor from Paris if ISIS finds out she's actually a Jew from Marseilles?"

"We are well aware of—"

"They'll saw her head off. And then they'll put the video on the Internet for the world to see."

"They'll never know."

"But I'll know," she said. "I'm not like you. I'm a terrible liar. I can't keep secrets. I have a guilty conscience. There's no way I can pull it off."

"You underestimate yourself."

"I'm sorry, Mr. Allon, but you've got the wrong girl." After a pause, she said, "Find someone else."

"You're sure?"

"I'm sure." She folded her napkin, rose, and extended her hand. "No hard feelings?"

"None whatsoever." Gabriel stood and reluctantly accepted her hand. "It was an honor almost working with you, Natalie. Please make no mention of this conversation to anyone, not even your parents."

"You have my word."

"Good." He released her. "Dina will take you back to Jerusalem."

20

NAHALAL, ISRAEL

NATALIE FOLLOWED HER ACROSS the shadowed garden and through a pair of French doors that led into the sitting room of the bungalow. It was sparsely furnished, more office than home, and upon its whitewashed walls hung several out-size black-and-white photographs of Palestinian suffering—the long dusty walk into exile, the wretched camps, the weathered faces of the old ones dreaming of paradise lost.

"This is where we would have trained you," explained Dina. "This is where we would have turned you into one of them."

"Where are my things?"

"Upstairs." Then Dina added, "In your room."

More photos lined the staircase and on the bedside table of a tidy little room rested a volume of verse by Mahmoud Darwish, the semi-official poet of Palestinian nationalism. Natalie's suitcase lay at the foot of the bed, empty.

"We took the liberty of unpacking for you," explained Dina.

"I guess no one ever turns him down."

"You're the first."

Natalie watched her limp across the room and open the top drawer of a wicker dresser.

You see, Natalie, Dina is grieving, too. And she is very serious about her work . . .

"What happened?" asked Natalie quietly.

"You said no, and now you're leaving."

"To your leg."

"It's not important."

"It is to me."

"Because you're a doctor?" Dina removed a handful of clothing from the drawer and placed it in the suitcase. "I am an employee of the secret intelligence service of the State of Israel. You don't get to know what happened to my leg. You aren't *allowed* to know. It's classified. *I'm* classified."

Natalie sat on the edge of the bed while Dina removed the rest of the clothing from the dresser.

"It was a bombing," said Dina finally. "Dizengoff Street in Tel Aviv. The Number Five bus." She closed the dresser drawer with more force than necessary. "Do you know this attack?"

Natalie nodded. The date was October 1994, long before she and her family had moved to Israel, but she had seen the small gray memorial at the base of a chinaberry tree along the pavement and, by chance, had once eaten in the quaint café directly adjacent.

"Were you *on* the bus?"

"No. I was standing on the pavement. But my mother and two of my sisters were. And I saw him before the bomb exploded."

"Who?"

"Abdel Rahim al-Souwi," Dina replied, as though reading the name from one of her thick files. "He was sitting on the left side behind the driver. There was a bag at his feet. It contained twenty kilos of military-grade TNT and bolts and nails soaked in rat poison. It was built by Yahya Ayyash, the one they called the Engineer. It was one of his best, or so he said. I didn't know that then, of course. I didn't know anything. I was just a girl. I was innocent."

"And when the bomb exploded?"

"The bus rose several feet into the air and then crashed to the street again. I was knocked to the ground. I could see people screaming all around me, but I couldn't hear anything— the blast wave had damaged my eardrums. I noticed a human leg lying next to me. I assumed it was mine, but then I saw that both my legs were still attached. The blood and the smell of burning flesh sickened the first police officers who arrived on the scene. There were limbs in the cafés and strips of flesh hanging from the trees. Blood dripped on me as I lay helpless on the pavement. It rained blood that morning on Dizengoff Street."

"And your mother and sisters?"

"They were killed instantly. I watched while the rabbis collected their remains with tweezers and placed them in plastic bags. That's what we buried. Scraps. *Remnants*."

Natalie said nothing, for there was nothing to say.

"And so you will forgive me," Dina continued after a moment, "if I find your behavior today puzzling. We don't do this because we *want* to. We do it because we *have* to. We do it because we have no other choice. It's the only way we're going to survive in this land."

"I wish I could help you, but I can't."

"Too bad," said Dina, "because you're perfect. And, yes," she added, "I would do anything to be in your place right now. I've listened to them, I've watched them, I've interrogated them. I know more about them than they know about themselves. But I've never been in the room with them when they plot and plan. It would be like being in the eye of a storm. I'd give anything for that one chance."

"You would go to Syria?"

"In an instant."

"What about your life? Would you give up your life for that chance?"

"We don't do suicide missions. We're not like them."

"But you can't guarantee I'll be safe."

"The only thing I can guarantee," said Dina pointedly, "is that Saladin is planning more attacks, and that more innocent people are going to die."

She dropped the last of the clothing into the suitcase and handed Natalie a flat, rectangular gift box. The lid was embossed with Arabic writing.

"A going-away present?"

"A tool to help with your transformation. Open it."

Natalie hesitantly removed the lid. Inside was a swath of silk, royal blue, about one meter by one meter. After a moment she realized it was a hijab.

"Arab clothing is very effective at altering appearances," explained Dina. "I'll show you." She took the hijab from Natalie's grasp, folded it into a triangle, and swiftly wrapped it around her own head and neck. "What do I look like?"

"Like an Ashkenazi girl wearing a Muslim headscarf."

Frowning, Dina removed the hijab and offered it to Natalie. "Now you."

"I don't want to."

"Let me help you."

Before Natalie could move away, the triangle of royal blue had been placed over her hair. Dina gathered the fabric beneath Natalie's chin and secured it with a safety pin. Then she took the two loose ends of fabric, one slightly longer than the other, and tied them at the base of Natalie's neck.

"There," said Dina, making a few final adjustments. "See for yourself."

Above the dresser hung an oval-shaped mirror. Natalie stared at her reflection for a long moment, entranced. At last, she asked, "What's my name?"

"Natalie," answered Dina. "Your name is Natalie."

"No," she said, staring at the veiled woman in the looking glass. "Not my name. *Her* name."

"Her name," said Dina, "is Leila."

"Leila," she repeated. "*Leila . . .*"

LEAVING NAHALAL, DINA NOTICED FOR THE FIRST TIME THAT Natalie was beautiful. Earlier, in Jerusalem and at lunch with the others, there had been no time for such an observation. Natalie was merely a target then. Natalie was a means to an end, and the end was Saladin. But now, alone with her in the car again, with the late-afternoon light golden and the warm air rushing through the open windows, Dina was free to contemplate Natalie at her leisure. The line of her jaw, the rich brown eyes, the long slender nose, the small upturned breasts, the bones of her delicate wrists and hands—hands that could save a life, thought Dina, or repair a leg ripped apart by a terrorist's bomb. Natalie's beauty was not the sort to turn heads or stop traffic. It was intelligent, dignified, pious even. It could be concealed, downgraded. And perhaps, thought Dina coldly, it could be used.

Not for the first time, she wondered why it was that Natalie was unmarried and without meaningful male attachment. The Office vetters had found nothing to suggest she was unsuited for work as an undercover field operative. She had no vices other than a taste for white wine, and no physical or emotional maladies except insomnia, which was brought on by the irregularity of her hours. Dina suffered the same affliction, though for different reasons. At night, when sleep finally claimed her, she saw blood dripping from chinaberry trees, and her mother, reassembled from her torn remnants, patched and sewn, calling to her from the open doorway of the Number 5 bus. And she saw Abdel Rahim al-Souwi, a bag at his feet, smiling to her from his seat behind the driver. *It was one of his best, or so he said* . . . Yes, thought Dina again, she would give anything to be in Natalie's place.

Natalie had taken nothing from the bungalow except for the hijab, which was wrapped around her neck like a scarf. She was gazing at the sun, low over Mount Carmel, and listening intently to the news on the radio. There had been another stabbing, another fatality, this time in the Roman ruins at Caesarea. The perpetrator was an Israeli Arab from a village located inside the heavily Palestinian corner of the country known as the Triangle. He would be receiving no urgent care from the doctors at Hadassah; an Israeli soldier had shot him dead. In Ramallah and Jericho there was jubilation. Another martyr, another dead Jew. God is great. Soon Palestine will be free again.

Ten miles south of Caesarea was Netanya. New apartment towers, white and balconied, rose from the dunes and cliff tops along the edge of the Mediterranean, conferring upon the city an outward air of Rivieran opulence. The interior quarters, however, retained the khaki Bauhaus grit of pioneer Israel. Dina found a space on the street outside the Park Hotel, where a Hamas suicide bomber murdered thirty people during Passover in 2002, and walked with Natalie to Independence Square. A squadron of young boys played a game of tag around the fountain, watched over by women in ankle-length skirts and headscarves. The women, like the children, were speaking French. So were the habitués of the cafés along the edge of the esplanade. Usually, they were overrun in late afternoon, but now, in the fading tawny light, there were plenty of tables to be had. Soldiers and police kept watch. The fear, thought Dina, was palpable.

"Do you see them?"

"There," replied Natalie, pointing across the square. "They're at their usual table at Chez Claude." It was one of several new establishments that catered to Netanya's growing French-Jewish community. "Would you like to meet them? They're really quite lovely."

"You go. I'll wait here."

Dina sat on a bench at the edge of the fountain and watched Natalie moving across the esplanade, the ends of the blue hijab dancing like pennants against her white blouse. Blue and white, observed Dina. How wonderfully Israeli. Unconsciously, she rubbed her damaged leg. It pained her at the damnedest times—when she was tired, when she was under stress, or, she thought, watching Natalie, when she regretted her behavior.

Natalie walked a straight line to the café. Her father, lean, gray, and very dark from the sea and the sun, looked up first, surprised to see his daughter coming toward him across the paving stones of the square, dressed as an Israeli flag. He placed a hand on his wife's arm and nodded in Natalie's direction, and a smile spread over the old woman's noble face. It was Natalie's face, thought Dina, Natalie in thirty years. Would Israel survive another thirty years? Would Natalie?

Natalie swerved from her path, but only to avoid a child, a girl of seven or eight, chasing down a stray ball. Then she kissed her parents in the French fashion, on each cheek, and sat down in one of the two empty chairs. It was the chair that, perhaps not coincidentally, presented Dina with her back. Dina watched the older woman's face. Her smile evaporated as Natalie recited the words Gabriel had composed for her. *I'm going to be away for a while. It's important you not try to contact me. If anyone asks, say I'm doing some important research and can't be disturbed. No, I can't tell you what it's about, but someone from the government will be coming around to check on you. Yes, I'll be safe.*

The stray ball was now bounding toward Dina. She captured it beneath her foot and with a flick of her ankle sent it back toward the girl of seven or eight, a small act of kindness that sent a stab of pain down her leg. She ignored it, for Natalie was again kissing the cheeks of her parents, this time in farewell. As she crossed the square, the setting sun on her face, the blue scarf fluttering in the breeze, a single tear streaked her face. Natalie was beautiful, observed Dina, even when she was crying. She rose and followed her back to the car, which was parked outside the crumbling hotel where thirty had died on a sacred night. It's what we do, Dina told herself as she shoved the key into the ignition. It's who we are. It's the only way we are going to survive in this land. It is our punishment for having survived.

PART TWO

ONE OF US

21

NAHALAL, ISRAEL

NEXT MORNING THE STAFF OF Hadassah Medical Center was informed via e-mail that Dr. Natalie Mizrahi would be taking an extended leave of absence. The announcement was thirty words in length and a masterpiece of bureaucratic murk. No reason was given for the sabbatical, no date of return was mentioned. This left the staff with no option but to speculate about the reasons for Natalie's sudden departure, a pursuit they engaged in freely, for it gave them something to talk about other than the stabbings. There were rumors of a serious illness, rumors of an emotional breakdown, rumors of a homesick return to France. After all, said one sage from cardiology, why in the world would anyone with a French passport actually *choose* to live in Israel at a time like this? Ayelet Malkin, who considered herself Natalie's closest friend at the hospital, found all these theories inadequate. She knew Natalie to be of sound mind and body and had heard her speak many times of her relief to be in Israel, where she could live as a Jew without fear of assault or rebuke. Moreover, she had worked a twenty-four-hour shift with Natalie that week, and the two women had shared a gossipy dinner during which Natalie made no mention of any pending leave of absence. She thought the entire thing reeked of official mischief. Like many Israelis, Ayelet had a relative, an uncle, who was involved in secret government work. He came and went without warning and never spoke of his job or his travels. Ayelet decided that Natalie, fluent in three languages, had been recruited as a spy. Or perhaps, she thought, she had always been one.

While Ayelet had stumbled upon something resembling the truth, she was not technically correct, as Natalie was to learn on her first full day in Nahalal. She was not going to be a spy. Spies, she was told, are human sources who are recruited to *spy* against their own intelligence service, government, terrorist organization, international body, or commercial enterprise. Sometimes they spied for money, sometimes for sex or respect, and sometimes they spied because they were coerced, owing to some blemish in their personal life. In Natalie's case, there was no coercion, only persuasion. She was from that point forward a special employee of the Office. As such, she would be governed by the same rules and strictures that applied to all those who worked directly for the service. She could not divulge secrets to foreign governments. She could not write a memoir about her work without approval. She could not discuss that work with anyone outside the Office, including members of her family. Her employment was to commence immediately and would terminate upon the completion of her mission. However, if Natalie wished to remain with the Office, suitable work would be found for her. A sum of five hundred thousand shekels was placed in a bank account bearing her real name. In addition, she would be paid the equivalent of her monthly salary from Hadassah. An Office courier would look after her apartment during her absence.

In the event of her death, two million shekels would be paid to her parents.

The paperwork, briefings, and stern warnings consumed the entire first day. On the second her formal education commenced. She felt rather like a graduate student in a private university of one. In the mornings, immediately following breakfast, she learned techniques for replacing her own identity with an assumed one—tradecraft, they called it. After a light lunch she embarked on Palestinian studies, followed by Islamic and jihadist studies. No one ever referred to her as Natalie. She was Leila, no family name, only Leila. The instructors spoke to her only in Arabic and referred to themselves as Abdul, Muhammad, or Ahmed. One two-person team of briefers called themselves Abdul and Abdul. Natalie called them Double-A for short.

The last hour of daylight was Natalie's exclusively. With her head spinning with Islam and jihad, she would set out for training runs along the dusty farm roads. She was never permitted to go alone; two armed security guards followed her always in a dark-green ATV. Often she returned to the house to find Gabriel waiting, and they would walk a mile or two through the perfumed twilight of the valley. His Arabic was not sufficiently fluent for prolonged conversation, so he addressed her in French. He spoke to her about her training and her studies but never about his childhood in the valley or its remarkable history. As far as Leila was concerned, the valley represented an act of colonial theft and dispossession. "Look at it," he would say, pointing toward the Arab village on the hillock. "Imagine how they must feel when they see the accomplishments of the Jews. Imagine their anger. Imagine their shame. It is your anger, Leila. It is your shame."

As her training progressed, she learned techniques for determining whether she was being followed. Or whether her flat or office was bugged. Or whether the person she assumed to be her best friend, or her lover, was in fact her worst enemy. The teaching team of Abdul and Abdul instructed her to assume she was being followed, observed, and listened to at all times. This was not a problem, they said, so long as she remained faithful to her cover. A proper cover was like a shield. The typical undercover Office field agent spent far more time maintaining his cover than actually gathering intelligence. Cover, they told her, was everything.

During the second week at the farm, her Palestinian studies took a decidedly harder turn. The entire Zionist enterprise, she was told, was based upon a myth—the myth that Palestine was a land without a people waiting for a people without a land. In fact, in 1881, the year before the first Zionist settlers arrived, the population of Palestine was 475,000. The vast majority were Muslim and were concentrated in the Judean Hills, the Galilee, and the other portions of the land that were then habitable. Roughly that same number of people were driven into exile during al-Nakba, the catastrophe of Israel's founding in 1948. And still another wave fled their villages in the West Bank after the Zionist conquest of 1967. They languished in the refugee camps—Khan Yunis, Shatila, Ein al-Hilweh, Yarmouk, Balata, Jenin, Tulkarm, and dozens more—and dreamed of their olive groves and lemon trees. Many kept the deeds to property and homes. Some even carried keys to front doors. This unhealed wound was the seedbed of the Arab world's grief. The wars, the suffering, the lack of economic progress, the despotism—all this was the fault of Israel.

"Spare me," groaned Natalie.

"Who said this?" demanded one of the Abduls, a cadaverous-looking creature, pale as milk, who was never without a cigarette or a cup of tea. "Was it Natalie or was it Leila? Because Leila does not question these assertions. Leila knows in her bones they are true. Leila drank it with her mother's milk. Leila heard it from the lips of her kin. Leila believes the Jews to be descendants of apes and pigs. She knows they use the blood of Palestinian children to make their matzo. She thinks they are an intrinsically evil people, children of the devil."

Her Islamic studies grew more rigid, too. After completing a crash course in the basics of ritual and belief, Natalie's instructors immersed her in the concepts of Islamism and jihad. She read Sayyid Qutb, the dissident Egyptian writer regarded as the founder of modern Islamism, and slogged her way through Ibn Taymiyyah, the thirteenth-century Islamic theologian who, according to many experts in the field, was the wellspring for it all. She read Bin Laden and Zawahiri and listened to hours of sermons by a Yemeni-American cleric who had been killed in a drone strike. She watched videos of roadside bombings of American forces in Iraq and surfed some of the more salacious Islamic Web sites, which her instructors referred to as jihadi porn. Before switching off her bedside lamp at night, she always read a few lines of Mahmoud Darwish. *My roots were entrenched before the birth of time* . . . In dreams she walked through an Eden of olive groves and lemon trees.

The technique was something akin to brainwashing, and slowly it began to work. Natalie packed away her old identity and life and became Leila. She did not know her family name; her legend, as they called it, would be given to her last, after a proper foundation had been poured and a frame constructed. In word and deed, she became more pious, more outwardly Islamic. In the evenings, when she ran along the dusty farm roads, she covered her arms and legs. And whenever her instructors were talking about Palestine or Islam, she wore her hijab. She experimented with several different ways of securing it but settled on a simple two-pin method that showed no hair. She thought she looked pretty in the hijab, but didn't like the way it focused attention on her nose and mouth. A partial facial veil would solve the problem, but it wasn't consistent with Leila's profile. Leila was an educated woman, a doctor, caught between East and West, present and past. She walked a tightrope that stretched between the House of Islam and the House of War, that part of the world where the faith was not yet dominant. Leila was conflicted. She was an impressionable girl.

They taught her the basics of martial arts but nothing of guns, for knowledge of weaponry didn't fit Leila's profile, either. Then, three weeks into her stay at the farm, they dressed her from head to toe as a Muslim woman and took her for a heavily guarded test drive in Tayibe, the largest Arab city in the so-called Triangle. Next she visited Ramallah, the seat of Palestinian authority in the West Bank, and a few days later, and on a warm Friday in mid-May, she attended Friday prayer services at the al-Aqsa Mosque in the Old City of Jerusalem. It was a tense day—the Israelis forbade young men from entering the Noble Sanctuary—and afterward there was a violent protest. Natalie briefly became separated from her undercover security guards. Eventually, they dragged her, choking on tear gas, into the back of a car and spirited her back to the farm.

"How did it make you feel?" asked Gabriel that evening, as they walked through the cool evening air of the valley. By then, Natalie was no longer running, for running didn't fit Leila's profile, either.

"It made me angry," she said without hesitation.

"At whom?"

"The Israelis, of course."

"Good," he replied. "That's why I did it."

"Did what?"

"Provoked a demonstration in the Old City for your benefit."

"You did that?"

"Trust me, Natalie. It really wasn't that difficult."

HE DIDN'T COME TO NAHALAL THE NEXT DAY OR FOR FIVE DAYS after that. Only later would Natalie learn that he had been in Paris and Amman preparing for her introduction into the field—operational spadework, he called it. When finally he returned to the farm it was at noon on a warm and breezy Thursday, as Natalie was becoming acquainted with some of the unique features of her new mobile phone. He informed her that they were going to take another field trip, just the two of them, and instructed her to dress as Leila. She chose a green hijab with embroidered edges, a white blouse that concealed the shape of her breasts and hips, and long pants that left only the insteps of her feet visible. Her pumps were Bruno Magli. Leila, it seemed, had a soft spot for Italian footwear.

"Where are we going?"

"North," was all he said.

"No bodyguards."

"Not today," he answered. "Today I am free."

The car was a rather ordinary Korean sedan, which he drove very fast and with an uncharacteristic abandon.

"You seem to be enjoying yourself," observed Natalie.

"It's been a long time since I've been behind the wheel of a car. The world looks different from the backseat of an armored SUV."

"How so?"

"I'm afraid that's classified."

"But I'm one of you now."

"Not quite," he answered, "but we're getting close."

They were the last words he spoke for several minutes. Natalie slipped on a pair of stylish sunglasses and watched a sepia-toned version of Acre slide past her window. A few miles to the north was Lohamei HaGeta'ot, a kibbutz founded by survivors of the Warsaw Ghetto uprising. It was a tidy little farming community of neat houses, green lawns, and regular streets lined with cypress. The sight of an obviously Israeli man driving a car in which a veiled woman was the sole passenger elicited glances of only mild curiosity.

"What's that?" asked Natalie, pointing toward a white conical structure rising above the rooftops of the kibbutz.

"It's called Yad Layeled. It's a memorial for the children killed in the Holocaust." There was a curious note of detachment in his voice. "But that's not why we're here. We're here to see something much more important."

"What's that?"

"Your home."

He drove to a shopping center just north of the kibbutz and parked in a distant corner of the lot.

"How charming," said Natalie.

"This isn't it." He pointed toward a patch of uncultivated land between the car park and Highway 4. "Your home is out there, Leila. The home that was stolen from you by the Jews."

He climbed out of the car without another word and led Natalie across a service road, into a field of weeds and prickly pear and broken blocks of limestone. "Welcome to Sumayriyya, Leila." He turned to face her. "Say it for me, please. Say it as though it is the most beautiful word you've ever heard. Say it as though it is the name of your mother."

"Sumayriyya," she repeated.

"Very good." He turned and watched the traffic rushing along the highway. "In May 1948 there were eight hundred people living here, all Muslims." He pointed toward the arches of an ancient aqueduct, largely intact, running along the edge of a field of soy. "That was theirs. It carried water from the springs and irrigated the fields that produced the sweetest melons and bananas in the Galilee. They buried their dead over there," he added, swinging his arm to the left. "And they prayed to Allah here"—he placed his hand on the ruins of an arched doorway—"in the mosque. They were your ancestors, Leila. This is who you are."

"'My roots were entrenched before the birth of time.'"

"You've been reading your Darwish." He walked deeper into the weeds and the ruins, closer to the highway. When he spoke again, he had to raise his voice to be heard over the whitewater rush of the traffic. "Your home was over there. Your ancestors were called Hadawi. This is your name, too. You are Leila Hadawi. You were born in France, educated in France, and you practice medicine in France. But whenever someone asks where you're from, you answer Sumayriyya."

"What happened here?"

"Al-Nakba happened here. Operation Ben-Ami happened here." He glanced at her over his shoulder. "Have your instructors mentioned Ben-Ami to you?"

"It was an operation undertaken by the Haganah in the spring of 1948 to secure the coast road between Acre and the Lebanese border, and to prepare the Western Galilee for the coming invasion by the regular Arab armies."

"Zionist lies!" he snapped. "Ben-Ami had one purpose and one purpose only, to capture the Arab villages of the Western Galilee and cast their inhabitants into exile."

"Is that the truth?"

"It doesn't matter whether it's true. It's what Leila believes. It's what she *knows*. You see, Leila, your grandfather, Daoud Hadawi, was there that night the Zionist forces of the Haganah came up the road from Acre in a convoy. The residents of Sumayriyya had heard what had happened in some of the other villages conquered by the Jews, so they immediately took flight. A few stayed behind but most fled to Lebanon, where they waited for the Arab armies to recapture Palestine from the Jews. And when the Arab armies were routed, the villagers of Sumayriyya became refugees, exiles. The Hadawi family lived in Ein al-Hilweh, the largest Palestinian refugee camp in Lebanon. Open sewers, cinderblock houses . . . hell on earth."

Gabriel led her past the rubble of the little houses—houses that were dynamited by the Haganah soon after Sumayriyya fell—and stopped at the edge of an orchard.

"It belonged to the people of Sumayriyya. Now it is the property of the kibbutz. Many years ago they were having trouble making the water flow through the irrigation tubes. A man appeared, an Arab who spoke a bit of Hebrew, and patiently explained how to do it. The kibbutzniks were amazed, and they asked the Arab how it was he knew how to make the water flow. And do you know what the Arab told them?"

"It was his orchard."

"No, Leila, it was *your* orchard."

He lapsed into silence. There was only the wind in the weeds and the rushing of the traffic along the highway. He was staring at the ruins of a house that lay scattered at his feet, the ruins of a life, the ruins of a people. He seemed angry; whether it was genuine or for Leila's benefit, Natalie could not tell.

"Why did you choose this place for me?" she asked.

"I didn't," he answered distantly. "It chose me."

"How?"

"I knew a woman from here, a woman like you."

"Was she like Natalie or Leila?"

"There is no Natalie," he said to the veiled woman standing next to him. "Not anymore."

22

NAHALAL, ISRAEL

WHEN NATALIE RETURNED TO NAHALAL, the volume of Darwish poetry had vanished from the bedside table in her room. In its place was a bound briefing book, thick as a manuscript and composed in French. It was the continuation of the story that Gabriel had begun amid the ruins of Sumayriyya, the story of an accomplished young woman, a doctor, who had been born in France of Palestinian lineage. Her father had lived an itinerant life typical of many stateless, educated Palestinians. After graduating from the University of Baghdad with a degree in engineering, he had worked in Iraq, Jordan, Libya, and Kuwait before finally settling in France, where he met a Palestinian woman, originally from Nablus, who worked part-time as a translator for a UN refugee agency and a small French publishing house. They had two children, a son who died in an auto accident in Switzerland at twenty-three, and a daughter whom they named after Leila Khaled, the famous freedom fighter from Black September who was the first woman to hijack an airplane. Leila's thirty-three-year existence had been rendered in the pages of the briefing book with the excruciating confessional detail of a modern memoir. Natalie had to admit it made for rather good reading. There were the slights she had suffered at school because she was an Arab and a Muslim. There was her brief experimentation with drugs. And there was an anatomically explicit description of her first sexual experience, at sixteen, with a French boy named Henri, who had broken poor Leila's heart. Next to the passage was a photograph of two teenagers, a French-looking boy and an Arab-looking girl, posed along the balustrade of the Pont Marie in Paris.

"Who are they?" Natalie asked the cadaverous Abdul.

"They're Leila and her boyfriend Henri, of course."

"But—"

"No buts, Leila. This is the story of your life. Everything you are reading in that book actually happened to you."

As a French Jew, Natalie found she had much in common with the Palestinian woman she would soon become. Both had suffered taunts at school because of their heritage and faith, both had unhappy early sexual experiences with French boys, and both had taken up the study of medicine in the autumn of 2003, Natalie at the Université de Montpellier, one of the oldest medical schools in the world, and Leila at Université Paris-Sud. It was a tense time in France and the Middle East. Earlier that year the Americans had invaded Iraq, inflaming the Arab world and Muslims across Western Europe. What's more, the Second Intifada was raging in the West Bank and Gaza. Everywhere it seemed Muslims were under siege. Leila was among the thousands who marched in Paris against the war in Iraq and the Israeli crackdown in the Occupied Terri-tories. As her interest in politics grew, so did her devotion to Islam. She decided to take the veil, which shocked her secular mother. Then, a few weeks later, her mother took the veil, too.

It was during her third year of medical school that Leila

met Ziad al-Masri, a Jordanian-Palestinian who was enrolled in the university's department of electronics. At first, he was a pleasant distraction from her mandatory curriculum of pharmacology, bacteriology, virology, and parasitology. But Leila soon realized she was desperately in love. Ziad was more politically active than Leila, and more religiously devout. He associated with radical Muslims, was a member of the extremist group Hizb ut-Tahrir, and attended a mosque where a cleric from Saudi Arabia regularly preached a message of jihad. Not surprisingly, Ziad's activities brought him to the attention of the French security service, which detained him twice for questioning. The interrogations only hardened Ziad's views, and against Leila's wishes he decided to travel to Iraq to join the Islamic resistance. He made it only as far as Jordan, where he was arrested and thrown into the notorious prison known as the Fingernail Factory. A month after his arrival he was dead. The dreaded Mukhabarat secret police never bothered to supply his family with an explanation.

The briefing book was not the work of a single author but the collaborative effort of three experienced intelligence officers from three capable services. Its plot was airtight, its characters well drawn. No reviewer would find fault with it, and not even the most jaded of readers would doubt its verisimilitude. Some might question the amount of extraneous detail concerning the subject's early life, but there was method in the authors' verbosity. They wanted to create in their subject a well of memory from which she could draw abundantly when the time came.

These seemingly inconsequential details—the names, the places, the schools she had attended, the layout of her family's apartment in Paris, the trips they had taken to the Alps and the sea—formed the core of Natalie's curriculum during her final days at the farm in Nahalal. And, of course, there was

Ziad, Leila's lover and deceased soldier of Allah. It meant that Natalie had to memorize the details of not one life but two, for Ziad had told Leila much about his upbringing and his life in Jordan. Dina served as her primary tutor and taskmaster. She spoke of Ziad's commitment to jihad and his hatred of Israel and America as though they were noble pursuits. His path in life was to be emulated, she said, not condemned. More than anything, though, his death required vengeance.

Natalie's training as a doctor served her well, for it allowed her to absorb and retain vast amounts of information, especially numbers. She was quizzed constantly, praised for her successes, and upbraided for even the smallest mistake or hesitation. Soon, warned Dina, others would be asking the questions.

She was visited during this time by a number of observers who sat in on her lessons but did not participate in any way. There was a tough-looking man with cropped dark hair and a pockmarked face. There was a bald, tweedy man who conducted himself with the air of an Oxford don. There was an elfin figure with thinning, flyaway hair whose face, try as she might, Natalie could never seem to recall. And, lastly, there was a tall, lanky man with pale bloodless skin and eyes the color of glacial ice. When Natalie asked Dina his name, she was met by a reproachful glare. "Leila would never be attracted to a non-Muslim," she admonished her pupil, "let alone a Jew. Leila is in love with the memory of Ziad. No one will ever take his place."

He came to Nahalal on two other occasions, both times accompanied by the wispy-haired man with an elusive face. They looked on judgmentally as Dina pressed Natalie on the small details of Leila's relationship with Ziad—the restaurant where they ate on their first date, the food they ordered, their first kiss, their final e-mail. Ziad had sent it from an Internet café in Amman while waiting for a courier to take him across the border into Iraq. The next morning he was arrested. They never spoke again.

"Do you remember what he wrote to you?" asked Dina.

"He was convinced he was being followed."

"And what did you say to him?"

"I told him I was concerned for his safety. I asked him to get on the next plane to Paris."

"No, Leila, your *exact* words. This is your final communication with a man you loved," Dina added, waving a piece of paper that purported to contain the text of the e-mail exchange. "Surely, you remember the last thing you said to Ziad before he was arrested."

"I said I was sick with worry. I begged him to leave."

"But that's not all you said. You told him he could stay with a relative of yours, is that not correct?"

"Yes."

"Who was this relative?"

"My aunt."

"Your mother's sister?"

"Correct."

"She lives in Amman?"

"In Zarqa."

"The camp or the town?"

"The town."

"Did you tell her that Ziad was coming to Jordan?"

"No."

"Did you tell your mother or father?"

"No."

"What about the French police?"

"No."

"And your contact in Jordanian intelligence? Did you tell him, Leila?"

"What?"

"Answer the question," snapped Dina.

"I don't have a contact in Jordanian intelligence."

"Did you betray Ziad to the Jordanians?"

"No."

"Are you responsible for his death?"

"No."

"And the night of your first date?" Dina asked, tacking suddenly. "Did you drink wine with dinner?"

"No."

"Why not?"

"It is haram," said Natalie.

That night, when she retired to her room, the volume of Darwish was back on her bedside table. She would be leaving soon, she thought. It was only a question of when.

THAT SAME QUESTION—THE QUESTION OF WHEN—WAS THE subject of a meeting between Gabriel and Uzi Navot at King Saul Boulevard later that evening. Between them, arrayed upon Navot's conference table, were the written conclusions of the various trainers, physicians, and psychiatric specialists assigned to the case. All stated that Natalie Mizrahi was of sound mind and body, and more than capable of carrying out the mission for which she had been recruited. None of the reports, however, were as important as the opinions of the chief of the Office and the man who would succeed him. Both were veteran field operatives who had spent much of their careers working under assumed identities. And they alone would suffer the consequences were anything to go wrong.

"It's only France," said Navot.

"Yes," said Gabriel darkly. "Nothing ever happens in France."

There was a silence.

"Well?" Navot asked finally.

"I'd like to give her one more test."

"She's been tested. And she's passed every one with flying colors."

"Let's get her out of her comfort zone."

"A murder board?"

"A peer review," offered Gabriel.

"How rough?"

"Rough enough to expose any flaws."

"Who do you want to handle it?"

"Yaakov."

"Yaakov would scare *me*."

"That's the point, Uzi."

"How soon do you want to do it?"

Gabriel looked at his wristwatch. Navot reached for the phone.

THEY CAME FOR HER IN THE HOUR BEFORE DAWN, WHEN SHE was dreaming of the lemon groves of Sumayriyya. There were three of them—or was it four? Natalie couldn't be sure; the room was in darkness, and her captors wore black. They pulled a hood over her, bound her hands with packing tape, and frog-marched her down the stairs. Outside, the grass of the garden was wet beneath her bare feet, and the air was cold and heavy with the smells of the land and the animals. They forced her into the back of a car. One sat to her left, another to her right, so that she was wedged tightly at the hips and shoulders. Frightened, she called Gabriel's name but received no reply. Nor did Dina respond to her cry for help. "Where are you taking me?" she asked, and to her surprise she addressed them in Arabic.

Like most physicians she had a good internal clock. The

drive, a nausea-inducing high-speed derby, lasted between twenty-five and thirty minutes. No one spoke a word to her, even when, in Arabic, she said she was about to be sick. Finally, the car lurched to a stop. Again, she was frog-marched, this time along a dirt pathway. The air was sweet with pine and colder than in the valley, and she could see a bit of light seeping through the fabric of her hood. She was led across a threshold, into a structure of some sort, and forced into a chair. Her hands were placed upon a tabletop. Lights warmed her.

She sat in silence, trembling slightly. She sensed a presence beyond the lamps. At last, a male voice said in Arabic, "Remove the hood."

It came off in a flourish, as though she were a prized object to be unveiled to a waiting audience. She blinked several times while growing accustomed to the harsh light. Then her eyes settled upon the man seated on the opposite side of the table. He was dressed entirely in black, and a black keffiyeh obscured everything of his face except his eyes, which were black, too. The figure to his right was identically attired, as was the one to his left.

"Tell me your name," commanded the figure opposite in Arabic.

"My name is Leila Hadawi."

"Not the name the Zionists gave you!" he snapped. "Your real name. Your Jewish name."

"It is my real name. I'm Leila Hadawi. I grew up in France, but I am from Sumayriyya."

BUT HE WOULD HAVE NONE OF IT—NOT HER NAME, NOT HER professed ethnicity, not her faith, not the story of her childhood in France, at least not all of it. He had in his possession a file, which he said had been prepared by the security department of his organization, though he did not say precisely what organization that was, only that its members emulated the original followers of Muhammad, peace be upon him. The file purported to prove that her real name was Natalie Mizrahi, that she was obviously Jewish, that she was an agent of the Israeli secret intelligence service who had been trained at a farmhouse in the Valley of Jezreel. She told him that she had never, nor would she *ever*, set foot in Israel—and the only training she had received was at the Université Paris-Sud, where she had studied medicine.

"Lies," said the man in black.

Which left no option, he added, but to start from the beginning. Under his relentless interrogation, Natalie's sense of time deserted her. For all she knew a week had passed since her sleep had been interrupted. Her head ached for want of caffeine, the bright lights were intolerable. Even so, her answers flowed from her effortlessly, as water flows downhill. She was not remembering something she had been taught, she was remembering something she already *knew*. She was Natalie no more. She was Leila. Leila from Sumayriyya. Leila who loved Ziad. Leila who wanted vengeance.

Finally, the man on the other side of the table closed his file. He looked toward the figure on his right, then the left. Then he unwound the headscarf to reveal his face. He was the one with pockmarked cheeks. The other two men removed their keffiyehs, too. The one on the left was the forgettable wispy-haired man. The one on the right was the one with pale bloodless skin and eyes like ice. All three of the men were smiling, but Natalie was suddenly weeping. Gabriel approached her quietly from behind and placed a hand on her shoulder as it convulsed. "It's all right, Leila," he said softly. "It's all over now."

But it wasn't over, she thought. It was only beginning.

———

THERE EXISTS IN TEL AVIV AND ITS SUBURBS A SERIES OF Office safe flats known as jump sites. They are places where, by doctrine and tradition, operatives spend their final night before departing Israel for missions abroad. Three days after Natalie's mock interrogation, she drove with Dina to a luxury apartment overlooking the sea in Tel Aviv. Her new clothing, all of it purchased in France, lay neatly folded atop the bed. Next to it was a French passport, a French driver's permit, French credit cards, bank cards, and various medical certificates and accreditations in the name of Leila Hadawi. There were also several photographs of the apartment she would inhabit in the heavily immigrant Paris banlieue of Aubervilliers.

"I was hoping for a cozy little garret on the Left Bank."

"I understand. But when one is fishing," said Dina, "it is best to go where the fish are."

Natalie made only one request; she wanted to spend the night with her mother and father. The request was denied. Much time and effort had been expended transforming her into Leila Hadawi. To expose her, even briefly, to her previous life was deemed far too risky. An experienced field officer could move freely between the thin membrane separating his real life from the life he led in service of his country. But newly trained recruits such as Natalie were often fragile flowers that wilted when exposed to direct sunlight.

And so she passed that evening, her last in Israel, with no company other than the melancholy woman who had wrenched her from the refuge of her old life. To occupy herself, she packed and repacked her suitcase three times. Then, after a carryout dinner of lamb and rice, she switched on the television and watched an episode of an Egyptian soap opera that she had grown fond of in Nahalal. Afterward, she sat on the balcony watching the pedestrians and the cyclists and the skateboarders flowing along the promenade in the cool windy night. It was a remarkable sight, the dream of the early Zionists fully realized, yet Natalie regarded the contented Jews beneath her with Leila's resentful eye. They were occupiers, children and grandchildren of colonialists who had stolen the land of a weaker people. They had to be defeated, driven out, just as they had driven Leila's ancestors from Sumayriyya on a May evening in 1948.

Her anger followed her to bed. If she slept that night, she did not remember it, and in the morning she was bleary-eyed and on edge. She dressed in Leila's clothing and covered her hair with Leila's favorite emerald-colored hijab. Downstairs, a taxi was waiting. Not a real taxi, but an Office taxi driven by one of the security agents who used to follow her on her runs in Nahalal. He took her directly to Ben Gurion Airport, where she was thoroughly searched and questioned at length before being allowed to proceed to her gate. Leila did not take offense at her treatment. As a veiled Muslim woman she was used to the special attention of security screeners.

Inside the terminal she made her way to the gate, oblivious to the hostile stares of the Israeli traveling public, and when her flight was called she filed dutifully onto the plane. Her seatmate was the gray-eyed man with bloodless skin, and across the aisle were her pockmarked interrogator and his wispy-haired accomplice. Not one of them dared to look at the veiled woman traveling alone. She was suddenly exhausted. She told the flight attendant, demurely, that she did not wish to be disturbed. Then, as Israel sank away beneath her, she closed her eyes and dreamed of Sumayriyya.

23

AUBERVILLIERS, FRANCE

TEN DAYS LATER THE Clinique Jacques Chirac opened to muted fanfare in the northern Paris banlieue of Aubervilliers. The minister of health attended the ceremony, as did a popular Ivory Coast–born footballer, who cut a tricolor ribbon to the rain-dampened applause of several community activists assembled for the occasion. French television ran a brief story about the opening on that evening's main newscast. *Le Monde*, in a short editorial, called it a promising start.

The goal of the clinic was to improve the lives of those who resided in a troubled suburb where crime and unemployment were high and government services scarce. Officially, the Ministry of Health oversaw the clinic's day-to-day operations, but in point of fact it was a classified joint undertaking by the ministry and Paul Rousseau's Alpha Group. The clinic's administrator, a man named Roland Girard, was an Alpha Group operative, as was the shapely receptionist. The six nurses and two of the three physicians, however, knew nothing of the clinic's split personality. All were employed by France's state-run hospital system, and all had been chosen for the project after a rigorous screening process. None had ever made the acquaintance of Dr. Leila Hadawi. Nor had they attended medical school with her or worked at her previous places of employment.

The clinic was located on the Avenue Victor Hugo, between an all-night laundry and a *tabac* frequented by members of a local Moroccan drug gang. Plane trees shaded the pavement outside the clinic's modest entrance, and above it rose three additional floors of a handsome old building with a tan exterior and shuttered windows. But behind the avenue soared the giant gray slabs of the *cités*, the public housing estates that warehoused the poor and the foreign born, mainly from Africa and the former French colonies of the Maghreb. This was the part of France where the poets and the travel writers rarely ventured, the France of crime, immigrant resentment, and, increasingly, radical Islam. Half the banlieue's residents had been born outside France, three-quarters of the young. Alienated, marginalized, they were ISIS recruits in waiting.

On the first day of the clinic's operation, it was the subject of mild, if skeptical, curiosity. But by the next morning it was receiving a steady stream of patients. For many, it was their first visit to a doctor in a long time. And for a few, especially the recent arrivals from the interior of Morocco and Algeria, it was their first visit to a physician ever. Not surprisingly, they felt most comfortable with the *médecine généraliste* who wore modest clothing and a hijab and could speak to them in their native language.

She tended to their sore throats and their chronic coughs and their assorted aches and pains and the illnesses they had carried from the third world to the first. And she told a mother of forty-four that the source of her severe headaches was a tumor of the brain, and a man of sixty that his lifetime of smoking had resulted in a case of untreatable lung cancer.

And when they were too sick to visit the clinic, she cared for them in their cramped flats in the housing estates. In the piss-scented stairwells and vile courts where trash swirled in tiny cyclones of wind, the boys and young men of Aubervilliers eyed her warily. On those rare occasions they spoke to her, they addressed her formally and with respect. The women and the teenage girls, however, were socially free to cross-examine her to their hearts' content. The housing estates were nothing if not gossipy, sexually segregated Arab villages, and Dr. Leila Hadawi was something new and interesting. They wanted to know where she was from, about her family, and about her medical studies. Mainly, they were curious as to why, at the advanced age of thirty-four, she was unmarried. At this, she would give a wistful smile. The impression she left was of unrequited love—or, perhaps, a love lost to the violence and chaos of the modern Middle East.

Unlike the other members of the staff, she actually resided in the community she served, not in the crime factories of the housing estates but in a comfortable little apartment in a *quartier* of the commune where the population was working class and native born. There was a quaint café across the street where, when not at the clinic, she was often seen drinking coffee at a sidewalk table. Never wine or beer, for wine and beer were haram. Her hijab clearly offended some of her fellow citizens; she could hear it in the edge of a waiter's remark and see it in the hostile stares of the passersby. She was the other, a stranger. It fed her resentment of the land of her birth and fueled her quiet rage. For Dr. Leila Hadawi, a servant of the French national medical bureaucracy, was not the woman she appeared to be. She had been radicalized by the wars in Iraq and Syria and by the occupation of Palestine by the Jews. And she had been radicalized, too, by the death of Ziad al-Masri, her only love, at the hands of the Jordanian Mukhabarat. She was a black widow, a ticking time bomb. She confessed this to no one, only to her computer. It was her secret sharer.

They had given her a list of Web sites during her final days at the farmhouse in Nahalal, a farmhouse that, try as she might, she could no longer quite conjure in her memory. Some of the sites were on the ordinary Internet; others, in the murky sewers of the dark net. All dealt with issues related to Islam and jihadism. She read blogs, dropped into chat rooms for Muslim women, listened to sermons from extremist preachers, and watched videos that no person, believer or unbeliever, should ever watch. Bombings, beheadings, burnings, crucifixions: a bloody day in the life of ISIS. Leila did not find the images objectionable, but several sent Natalie, who was used to the sight of blood, running into her bathroom to be violently sick. She used an onion routing application popular with jihadists that allowed her to wander the virtual caliphate without detection. She referred to herself as Umm Ziad. It was her nom de plume, her nom de guerre.

It did not take long for Dr. Hadawi to attract attention. She had no shortage of cybersuitors. There was the woman from Hamburg who had a cousin of marrying age. There was the Egyptian cleric who engaged her in a prolonged discussion on the subject of apostasy. And then there was the keeper of a particularly vile blog who knocked on her virtual door while she was watching the beheading of a captured Christian. The blogger was an ISIS recruiter. He asked her to travel to Syria to help build the caliphate.

I'D LOVE TO, Leila typed, BUT MY WORK IS HERE IN FRANCE. I'M CARING FOR OUR BROTHERS AND SISTERS IN THE LAND OF THE KUFAR. MY PATIENTS NEED ME.

YOU ARE A DOCTOR?

YES.

WE NEED DOCTORS IN THE CALIPHATE. WOMEN, TOO.

The exchange gave her an electrical charge, a lightness in her fingertips, a blurriness of her vision, that was akin to the first blush of desire. She did not report it; there was no need. They were monitoring her computer and her phone. They were watching her, too. She saw them sometimes on the streets of Aubervilliers—the pockmarked tough who had conducted her final interrogation in the land of the Jews, the man with the forgettable face, the man with eyes like winter. She ignored them, as she had been trained to do, and went about her business. She tended to her patients, she gossiped with the women of the housing estates, she averted her eyes piously in the presence of boys and young men, and at night, alone in her apartment, she wandered the rooms of the house of extremist Islam, hidden behind her protective software and her vague pen name. She was a black widow, a ticking time bomb.

APPROXIMATELY TWENTY MILES SEPARATE THE BANLIEUE OF Aubervilliers from the village of Seraincourt, but they are a world apart. There are no halal markets or mosques in Seraincourt, no looming housing blocks filled with immigrants from hostile lands, and French is the only language one hears on its narrow streets or in the brasserie next to the ancient stone church in the village square. It is a foreigner's idealized vision of France, France as it once was, France no more.

Just beyond the village, in a river valley of manicured farms and groomed woods, stood Château Treville. Shielded from prying eyes by twelve-foot walls, it had a heated swimming pool, two clay tennis courts, fourteen ornate bedrooms, and thirty-two acres of gardens where, if one were so inclined, one could pace with worry. Housekeeping, the Office division that acquired and maintained safe properties, was on good, if entirely deceptive, terms with the château's owner. The deal—

six months, with an option to extend—was concluded with a swift exchange of faxes and a wire transfer of several thousand well-disguised euros. The team moved in the same day that Dr. Leila Hadawi settled into her modest little flat in Aubervilliers. Most stayed only long enough to drop their bags and then headed straight into the field.

They had operated in France many times before, even in tranquil Seraincourt, but never with the knowledge and approval of the French security service. They assumed the DGSI was looking over their shoulders at all times and listening to their every word, and so they behaved accordingly. Inside the château they spoke a terse form of colloquial Office Hebrew that was beyond the reach of mere translators. And on the streets of Aubervilliers, where they kept a vigilant watch on Natalie, they did their best not to betray family secrets to their French allies, who were watching her, too. Rousseau acquired an apartment directly opposite Natalie's where rotating teams of operatives, one Israeli, the other French, maintained a constant presence. At first, the atmosphere in the flat was chilly. But gradually, as the two teams became better acquainted, the mood warmed. For better or worse, they were in this fight together now. All past sins were forgiven. Civility was the new order of the day.

The one member of the team who never set foot in the observation post or on the streets of Aubervilliers was its founder and guiding light. His movements were unpredictable, Paris one day, Brussels or London the next, Amman when he needed to consult with Fareed Barakat, Jerusalem when he needed the touch of his wife and children. Whenever he slipped into Château Treville, he would sit up late with Eli Lavon, his oldest friend in the world, his brother-in-arms from Operation Wrath of God, and scour the watch reports for signs of trouble. Natalie was his masterpiece. He had recruited her, trained her, and hung her in a gallery of religious madness for the monsters to see. The viewing period was nearing its end. Next would come the sale. The auction would be rigged, for Gabriel had no intention of selling her to anyone but Saladin.

And so it was that, two months to the day after the Clinique Jacques Chirac opened its doors, Gabriel found himself in Paul Rousseau's office on the rue de Grenelle. The first phase of the operation, declared Gabriel, batting away another on-slaught of pipe smoke, was over. It was time to put their asset into play. Under the rules of the Franco-Israeli operational accord, the decision to proceed was supposed to be a joint one. But the asset was Gabriel's, and therefore the decision was his, too. He spent that evening at the safe house in Seraincourt in the company of his team, and in the morning, with Mikhail at his side and Eli Lavon watching his back, he boarded a train at the Gare du Nord and headed for Brussels. Rousseau made no attempt to follow them. This was the part of the operation he didn't want to know about. This was the part where things would get rough.

24

RUE DU LOMBARD, BRUSSELS

DURING ONE OF HIS MANY visits to GID headquarters in Amman, Gabriel had taken possession of several portable hard drives. On them were the contents of Jalal Nasser's notebook computer, downloaded during his return visits to Jordan or during secret raids on his flat in the Bethnal Green section of East London. The GID had found nothing suspicious—no known jihadists in his contacts, no visits to jihadist Web sites in his browsing history—but Fareed Barakat had agreed to let the Office have a second look. It had taken the cybersleuths of King Saul Boulevard less than an hour to find a clever trapdoor concealed within an innocuous-looking gaming application. It led to a heavily encrypted cellar filled with names, numbers, e-mail addresses, and casing photographs, including several of the Weinberg Center in Paris. There was even a shot of Hannah Weinberg leaving her apartment on the rue Pavée. Gabriel broke the news to Fareed gently, so as not to bruise his valuable partner's enormous ego.

"Sometimes," said Gabriel, "it helps to have a fresh pair of eyes."

"Or a smart Jewish boy with a PhD from Caltech," said Fareed.

"That, too."

Among the names that featured most prominently in this hidden trove was Nabil Awad, originally from the northern Jordanian city of Irbid, lately of the Molenbeek district of Brussels. Separated from the elegant city center by an industrial canal, Molenbeek had once been occupied by Roman Catholic Walloons and Protestant Flemings who worked in the district's many factories and warehouses. The factories were a memory, as were Molenbeek's original inhabitants. It was now essentially a Muslim village of one hundred thousand people, where the call to prayer echoed five times each day from twenty-two different mosques. Nabil Awad lived on the rue Ransfort, a narrow street lined with terraces of flaking nineteenth-century brick houses that had been carved into crowded tenements. He worked part-time in a copy center in central Brussels, but like many young men who lived in Molenbeek, his primary occupation was radical Islam. Among security professionals, Molenbeek was known as the jihadi capital of Europe.

The neighborhood was not the sort of place for a man with the refined tastes of Fareed Barakat. Nor, for that matter, was the sixty-euro-a-night hotel on the rue du Lombard where he met Gabriel. He had toned down his clothing for the occasion—an Italian blazer, dove-gray trousers, a dress shirt with French cuffs, no tie. After being admitted to the cramped little room on the hotel's third floor, he contemplated the electric teakettle as though he had never laid eyes on such a contraption. Gabriel filled it with water from the bathroom tap and joined Fareed in the window. Directly opposite the hotel, on the ground floor of a modern seven-story office block, was XTC Printing and Copying.

"What time did he arrive?" asked the Jordanian.

"Promptly at ten."

"A model employee."

"So it would seem."

The Jordanian's dark eyes swept the street, a falcon looking for prey.

"Don't bother, Fareed. You'll never find them."

"Mind if I try?"

"Be my guest."

"The blue van, the two men in the parked car at the end of the block, the girl sitting alone in the window of the coffeehouse."

"Wrong, wrong, and wrong."

"Who are the two men in the car?"

"They're waiting for their friend to come out of the pharmacy."

"Or maybe they're from the Belgian security service."

"The last thing we need to worry about is the Sûreté. Unfortunately," added Gabriel gloomily, "neither do the terrorists who live in Molenbeek."

"Tell me about it," muttered Fareed. "They produce more terrorists here in Belgium than we do."

"Now that's saying something."

"You know," said Fareed, "we wouldn't have this problem if it wasn't for you Israelis. You upended the natural order of things in the Middle East, and now we are all paying the price."

Gabriel stared into the street. "Maybe this wasn't such a good idea, after all," he said quietly.

"You and I working together?"

Gabriel nodded.

"You need friends wherever you can find them, *habibi*. You should consider yourself lucky."

The water boiled, the kettle shut down with a click.

"Would you mind terribly?" asked the Jordanian. "I'm afraid I'm helpless in the kitchen."

"Sure, Fareed. It's not as if I have anything better to do."

"Sugar, please. Lots of sugar."

Gabriel poured water into a mug, dropped a stale teabag into it, and added three packets of sugar. The Jordanian blew on the tea furtively before raising the mug to his lips.

"How is it?" asked Gabriel.

"Ambrosia." Fareed started to light a cigarette but stopped when Gabriel pointed toward the NO SMOKING sign. "Couldn't you have booked a smoking room?"

"They were sold out."

Fareed returned the cigarette to his gold case and the case to the pocket of his blazer. "Maybe you're right," he said with a frown. "Maybe this wasn't such a good idea after all."

THEY SAW HIM AT ELEVEN THAT MORNING WHEN HE LEFT THE shop to collect four takeaway coffees for his colleagues, and again at one that afternoon when he took his lunch break at a café around the corner. Finally, at six, they watched as he left the shop for the last time, trailed by the meekest-looking soul in all of Brussels and by a couple—a tall tweedy man and a woman with childbearing hips—who could scarcely keep their hands off one another. Though he did not know it, his life as he knew it was almost at its end. Soon, thought Gabriel, he would exist only in cyberspace. He would be a virtual person, ones and zeros, digital dust. But only if they could get him cleanly, without the knowledge of his comrades or the Belgian police, without a trace. It would be no easy feat in a city like Brussels, a city of irregular streets and dense population. But as the great Ari Shamron once said, nothing worth doing is ever easy.

Six bridges span the wide industrial canal that separates the center of Brussels from Molenbeek. To cross any of them is to leave the West and enter the Islamic world. As usual, Nabil Awad made the passage over a graffiti-sprayed pedestrian footbridge upon which few native Belgians ever dared to set foot. On the Molenbeek side, parked along an unsightly quay, was a battered van, formerly white, with a sliding side door. Nabil Awad seemed not to notice it; he had eyes only for the lanky man, a non-Arab, walking along the pea-soup-green waters of the canal. It was rare to see a Western face in Molenbeek at night, and rarer still that the owner of the face did not have a friend or two for protection.

Nabil Awad, ever vigilant, paused next to the van to allow the man to pass, which was his mistake. For at that instant the side door slid open on well-greased runners, and two pairs of trained hands wrenched him inside. The man with the non-Arab face climbed into the front passenger seat, the van eased away from the curb. As it passed through the Muslim village known as Molenbeek, past sandaled men and veiled women, past halal markets and Turkish pizza stands, the man in back, now blindfolded and bound, struggled for his life. It was no use; his life as he knew it was over.

At half past six that evening, two men of late middle age, one an elegantly dressed Arab with a bird-of-prey face, the other vaguely Jewish in appearance, departed the hotel on the rue du Lombard and climbed into a car that seemed to materialize from thin air. The hotel's housekeeping staff entered the room a few minutes later, expecting the usual disaster after a brief stay by two men of suspect appearance. Instead, they found it in pristine condition, save for two dirty cups resting on the windowsill, one stained with tea, the other filled with cigarette butts, a clear violation of hotel policy. Management was furious, but not surprised. This was Brussels, after all, the crime capital of Western Europe. Management added one hundred euros to the bill for additional cleaning and spitefully tacked on a hefty room-service charge for food and drink that had never been ordered. Management was confident there would be no complaints.

25

NORTHERN FRANCE

PAUL ROUSSEAU'S PARTICIPATION IN WHAT came next was limited to the acquisition of a safe property near the Belgian border, the cost of which he buried deep within his operating budget. He warned Gabriel and Fareed Barakat to avoid using any tactic on their prisoner that might remotely be construed as torture. Even so, Rousseau was flying dangerously close to the sun. There was no provision in French law to allow for the extrajudicial capture of a Belgian resident from Belgian soil, even if the Belgian resident was suspected of involvement in an act of terror committed in France. Were the operation ever to become public, Rousseau would surely perish in the resulting scandal. It was a risk he was willing to take. He regarded his counterparts in the Belgian Sûreté as incompetent fools who had countenanced the establishment of an ISIS safe haven in the heart of Europe. On numerous occasions, the Sûreté had failed to pass along vital intelligence regarding threats against French targets. As far as Rousseau was concerned, he was merely returning the favor.

The safe property was a small isolated farmhouse near

Lille. Nabil Awad did not know this, for he had passed the journey blinded by a hood and deafened by earplugs. The cramped dining room had been prepared for his arrival—a metal table, two chairs, a lamp with a bulb like the sun, nothing more. Mikhail and Yaakov secured Nabil Awad to one of the chairs with duct tape, and on Fareed Bakarat's signal, a barely perceptible nod of his regal head, they removed the hood. Instantly, the young Jordanian recoiled in fear of the dreaded Mukhabarat man seated calmly on the opposite side of the table. For someone like Nabil Awad, a Jordanian from a modest family, it was the worst place in the world to be. It was the end of the line.

The ensuing silence was several minutes in length and unnerved even Gabriel, who was watching from the darkened corner of the room with Eli Lavon at his side. Nabil Awad was already trembling with fear. That was the thing about the Jordanians, thought Gabriel. They didn't have to torture; their reputation preceded them. It allowed them to think themselves superior to their kindred service in Egypt. The Egyptian version of the Mukhabarat hung its prisoners on hooks before bothering to say hello.

With another small nod, Fareed instructed Mikhail to return the hood to the prisoner's head. The Jordanians, Gabriel knew, were great believers in sensory deprivation. A man deprived of the ability to see and hear becomes disoriented very quickly, sometimes in mere minutes. He grows anxious and depressed, he hears voices and experiences hallucinations. Soon, he suffers from a kind of madness. With a whisper, he can be convinced of almost anything. His flesh is melting from his bones. His arm is missing. His father, long dead, is sitting beside him, watching his humiliation. And all of this can be accomplished without beatings, without electricity, without water. All that is required is a bit of time.

But time, thought Gabriel, was not necessarily on their side. Nabil Awad was at that moment on another bridge, a bridge separating his old life from the life he would soon be living on behalf of Fareed Barakat. He had to cross that bridge quickly, without the knowledge of the other members of the network. Otherwise, this phase of the operation—the phase that had the potential to derail all that had come before—would be a colossal waste of time, effort, and valuable resources. For now, Gabriel was reduced to the role of spectator. His operation was in the hands of his former enemy.

At last, Fareed spoke, a brief question, delivered in a rich baritone that seemed to shake the very walls of the little French dining room. There was no menace in the voice, for none was necessary. It said that he was powerful, privileged, and moneyed. It said that he was a relative of His Majesty and, as such, was a descendant of the Prophet Muhammad, peace be upon him. It said that *you*, Nabil Awad, are nothing. And if I should choose to take your life, I will do so without batting an eye. And then I will enjoy a nice cup of tea.

"Who is he?" was the question Fareed posed.

"Who?" came the weak and defeated voice from beneath the hood.

"Saladin," answered Fareed.

"He recaptured Jerusalem from the—"

"No, no," said Fareed, interrupting, "not *that* Saladin. I'm talking about the Saladin who ordered you to bomb the Jewish target in Paris and the market in Amsterdam."

"I had nothing to do with those attacks! Nothing! I swear it."

"That's not what Jalal told me."

"Who's Jalal?"

"Jalal Nasser, your friend from London."

"I don't know anyone by that name."

"Of course you do, *habibi*. Jalal has told me everything already. He said you were the operational planner for both Paris and Amsterdam. He said you are Saladin's trusted lieutenant in Western Europe."

"That's not true!"

"Which part?"

"I don't know anyone named Jalal Nasser, and I'm not an operational planner. I work in a print shop. I'm no one. Please, you have to believe me."

"Are you sure, *habibi*?" asked Fareed softly, as though disappointed. "Are you sure that's your answer?"

From beneath the hood there was only silence. With a glance, Fareed instructed Mikhail and Yaakov to remove the prisoner. Gabriel, from his post in the corner of the room, watched as his two trusted officers obeyed Fareed's command. For now, it was the Jordanian's operation. Gabriel was only a bystander.

A ROOM HAD BEEN PREPARED IN THE CELLAR. IT WAS SMALL AND cold and damp and stank of mildew. Mikhail and Yaakov chained Nabil Awad to the cot and locked the reinforced soundproof door. An overhead light, protected by a metal cage, burned brightly. It was no matter; the sun had set on Nabil Awad. With the opaque hood shielding his eyes, he lived in a world of permanent night.

It did not take long for the darkness and the silence and the fear to bore a hole in Nabil Awad's brain. Fareed monitored the feed from the camera inside the makeshift cell. He was looking for the telltale signs—the fidgeting, the squirming, the sudden starts—that signaled the onset of emotional distress and confusion. He had personally conducted countless interrogations in the bleak cellars of GID headquarters, and he knew when to ask questions and when to let the darkness and the silence do their work for him. Some of the terrorists Fareed had interrogated had refused to break, even under brutal questioning, but he judged Nabil Awad to be fashioned of weaker stuff. There was a reason he was in Europe instead of bombing and killing and cutting off heads in the caliphate. Awad was no action-figure jihadist. He was a cog, which is precisely what they needed.

After two hours Fareed requested that the prisoner be brought up from the cellar. He posed three questions. What was your precise role in the Paris and Amsterdam attacks? How do you communicate with Jalal Nasser? Who is Saladin? Again, the young Jordanian claimed to know nothing about terrorism or Jalal Nasser or the mysterious man who called himself Saladin. He was a loyal Jordanian subject. He did not believe in terrorism or jihad. He did not go to the mosque with any regularity. He liked girls, smoked cigarettes, and drank alcohol. He worked in a copy shop. He was a nothing man.

"Are you sure, *habibi*?" asked Fareed before returning Nabil Awad to his cell. "Are you sure that's your answer?"

And on it went, all through the long night, every two hours, sometimes a quarter-hour less, sometimes more, so that Nabil Awad could not set an internal clock and thus prepare himself for Fareed's quiet onslaught. With each appearance the young Jordanian was more skittish, more disoriented. Each time, he was asked the same three questions. What was your precise role in the Paris and Amsterdam attacks? How do you communicate with Jalal Nasser? Who is Saladin? His answers never varied. He was nothing. He was no one.

And all the while the jihadist's mobile phone pinged and flared with incoming traffic from a half-dozen different messaging and social media feeds. The phone was in the capable hands of Mordecai, a specialist in all things electronic, who was systematically mining its memory for valuable content. Two teams, one at GID headquarters, the other at King Saul Boulevard, were rapidly analyzing the intelligence haul. Together, they were drafting the responses that Mordecai sent from the phone itself, responses that would keep Nabil Awad alive in the minds of his friends, family, and fellow travelers in the global jihadist movement. One misstep, one stray word, could doom the entire operation.

It was high-wire work and a remarkable display of interservice cooperation. But then, the global war against Islamic extremism made for strange bedfellows, none stranger than Gabriel Allon and Fareed Barakat. In their youth they had been on opposite sides of the great Arab–Israeli divide, and their countries had fought a terrible conflict in which the goal of Fareed's side was to slaughter as many Jews as possible and drive the rest into the sea. Now they were allies in a new kind of war, a war against those who killed in the name of Fareed's ancient ancestor. It was a long war, perhaps a war without end.

On that night the war was being waged not in Yemen or Pakistan or Afghanistan but in a small isolated farmhouse near Lille, not far from the Belgian border. It was fought at two-hour intervals—sometimes two and a quarter, sometimes less—and three questions at a time. What was your precise role in the Paris and Amsterdam attacks? How do you communicate with Jalal Nasser? Who is Saladin?

"Are you sure, *habibi*? Are you sure that's your answer?"

"Yes, I'm sure."

But he was not sure, not at all, and with each hooded appearance before Fareed Barakat his confidence weakened. So, too, did his will to resist. By morning he was talking to a cellmate who did not exist, and by early afternoon he could no longer walk the flight of steep stairs leading from the cellar.

It was then Fareed removed the hood from his captive's head and laid before him a photograph of a round-faced, veiled woman. Other photos followed—a weathered man wearing a black-and-white keffiyeh, a boy of sixteen or so, a beautiful young girl. They were the ones who would pay the price for Nabil Awad's actions. The old ones would die in shame, the young ones had no future. That was the other thing about the Jordanians, thought Gabriel. They had the power to ruin lives. Not just the life of a terrorist but generations of lives. No one knew this better than Nabil Awad, who was soon sobbing in Fareed's powerful embrace. Fareed promised to make everything all right. But first, he said gently, they were going to have a little talk.

26

NORTHERN FRANCE

IT WAS AN ALL-TOO-FAMILIAR STORY—A story of disillusion and dissatisfaction, of needs unmet, of economic and marital hopes dashed, of rage against the Americans and Jews over their perceived mistreatment of Muslims. Half the jihadists in the world could have told the same sad tale; it was, thought Gabriel, well-trod territory. Yes, there were a few bright minds and young men from good families in the upper ranks of the global jihadist movement, but the foot soldiers and the cannon fodder were, for the most part, radical losers. Political Islam was their salvation, and ISIS was their paradise. ISIS gave purpose to lost souls and promised an afterlife of eternal copulation to those who perished for the cause. It was a powerful message for which the West had no antidote.

Nabil Awad's version of the story began in Irbid, where his father tended a stall in the central market. Nabil was a diligent student and upon graduation from secondary school was admitted to London's University College. The year was 2011; Syria was burning, British Muslims were seething. No longer under the thumb of the Jordanian Mukhabarat, Nabil quickly began associating with Islamists and radicals. He prayed at the East London Mosque and joined the London chapter of Hizb ut-Tahrir, the Sunni Islamic organization that supported the resurrection of the caliphate long before anyone had heard of a group called ISIS. The Hizb, as it was known colloquially, was active in more than fifty countries and counted more than a million followers. One was a Jordanian from Amman named Jalal Nasser, whom Nabil Awad met during a Hizb gathering in the East London borough of Tower Hamlets. Jalal Nasser had already crossed the line—the line between Islamism and jihadism, between politics and terror. In time, he took Nabil Awad with him.

"When exactly did you meet him?" asked Fareed.

"I don't remember."

"Of course you do, *habibi*."

"It was the spring of 2013."

"I knew you could do it," said Fareed with a paternal smile. He had removed the bindings from Nabil Awad's wrists, and had given him a cup of sugary tea to keep his energy up. Fareed was drinking tea, too—and smoking, which Nabil Awad, a Salafist, did not approve of. Gabriel was no longer present; he was watching a video feed of the interrogation on a laptop in the next room, along with the other members of his team. Two other teams were monitoring the interrogation as well, one at GID headquarters, the other at King Saul Boulevard.

With a nudge, Fareed encouraged Nabil Awad to expound on his relationship with Jalal Nasser, which he did. At first, he said, Jalal was guarded around his fellow Jordanian, wary. He was afraid he was an agent of the GID or MI5, the British security service. But gradually, after several conversations that bordered on interrogations, he took Nabil into his confidence. He said that he had been dispatched to Europe by ISIS to help build a network capable of striking targets in the West. He said he wanted Nabil to help him.

"How?"

"By looking for recruits."

"Recruits for ISIS?"

"For the network," said Nabil Awad.

"In London?"

"No. He wanted me to move to Belgium."

"Why Belgium?"

"Because Jalal could handle England on his own, and he thought Belgium was promising territory."

"Because there were many brothers there?"

"Many," answered Nabil Awad. "Especially in Brussels."

"Did you speak Flemish?"

"Of course not."

"French?"

"No."

"But you learned to speak French."

"Very quickly."

"You're a smart boy, aren't you, Nabil—too smart to be wasting your time with this jihad shit. You should have finished your education. Things might have turned out differently for you."

"In Jordan?" He shook his head. "Unless you are from a prominent family or connected to the king, you don't stand a chance. What was I going to do? Drive a taxi? Work as a waiter in a Western hotel serving alcohol to infidels?"

"Better to be a waiter than where you are now, Nabil."

The young Jordanian said nothing. Fareed opened a file.

"It's an interesting story," he said, "but I'm afraid Jalal tells it somewhat differently. He says that you approached *him*. He says that you were the one who built the network in Europe."

"That's not true!"

"But you see my problem, *habibi*. He tells me one thing, you tell me the complete opposite."

"I'm telling you the truth, Jalal is lying!"

"Prove it."

"How?"

"Tell me something that I don't already know about Jalal. Or better yet," Fareed added almost as an afterthought, "show me something on your phone or your computer."

"My computer is in my room in Molenbeek."

Fareed smiled sadly and patted the back of his prisoner's hand. "Not anymore, *habibi*."

SINCE THE BEGINNING OF THE WAR ON TERROR, AL-QAEDA AND its murderous offspring had proven remarkably adaptive. Chased from their original Afghan sanctuary, they had found new spaces to operate in Yemen, Iraq, Syria, Libya, the Sinai Peninsula of Egypt, and a district of Brussels called Molenbeek. They had also devised new methods of communication to avoid detection by the NSA and other Western eavesdropping services. One of the most innovative was an advanced 256-bit encryption program called Mujahideen Secrets. Once Nabil Awad settled in Belgium, he used it to communicate securely with Jalal Nasser. He simply wrote his messages on his laptop, encrypted them using Mujahideen Secrets, and then loaded them onto a flash drive, which would be carried by hand to London. The original messages Nabil shredded and deleted. Even so, Mordecai had little difficulty finding their digital remains on the hard drive of the laptop. Using Nabil's fourteen-character hard password, he raised the files from the dead, turning seemingly random pages of letters and numbers into clear text. One of the documents concerned a promising potential recruit, a Frenchwoman of Algerian descent named Safia Bourihane.

"You were the one who brought her into the network?" asked Fareed, when the interrogation resumed.

"No," answered the young Jordanian. "I was the one who found her. Jalal handled the actual recruitment."

"Where did you meet her?"

"Molenbeek."

"What was she doing there?"

"She has family there—cousins, I think. Her boyfriend had just been killed in Syria."

"She was grieving?"

"She was angry."

"At whom?"

"The Americans, of course, but mainly the French. Her boyfriend died in a French air strike."

"She wanted revenge?"

"Very badly."

"You spoke to her directly."

"Never."

"Where did you see her?"

"A party at a friend's apartment."

"What kind of party?"

"The kind that no good Muslim should ever attend."

"What were you doing there?"

"Working."

"You don't mind if your recruits drink alcohol?"

"Most do. Remember," Nabil Awad added, "Zarqawi was a drinker before he discovered the beauty of Islam."

"What happened after you sent your message to Jalal?"

"He instructed me to find out more about her. I went to Aulnay-sous-Bois to watch her for a few days."

"You're familiar with France?"

"France is part of my territory."

"And you liked what you saw?"

"Very much."

"And so you sent a second encrypted message to Jalal," said Fareed, waving a printout.

"Yes."

"How?"

"By courier."

"What's the courier's name?"

The young Jordanian managed a weak smile. "Ask Jalal," he said. "He can tell you."

Fareed held up a photograph of Nabil Awad's veiled mother. "What's the courier's name?"

"I don't know his name. We never met face-to-face."

"You use a dead drop system?"

"Yes."

"How do you summon him?"

"I post a message on Twitter."

"The courier monitors your feed?"

"Obviously."

"And the dead drop sites?"

"We have four."

"In Brussels?"

"Or nearby."

"How does the courier know which site to clean out?"

"The location is contained in the message."

In the adjoining room, Gabriel watched as Fareed Bakarat placed a yellow legal pad and a felt-tip pen before Nabil Awad. The broken young Jordanian reached for the pen quickly, as a drowning man reaches for a lifeline tossed upon a stormy sea. He wrote in Arabic, swiftly, without pause. He wrote for his parents and his siblings and for all those who would bear the Awad name. But mainly, thought Gabriel, he wrote for Fareed Barakat. Fareed had beaten him. Nabil Awad belonged to them now. They owned him.

When the task was complete, Fareed demanded one more name from his captive. It was the name of the man who was directing the network, approving the targets, training the operatives, and building the bombs. The name of the man who called himself Saladin. Nabil Awad tearfully claimed not to know it. And Fareed, perhaps because he was growing weary himself, chose to believe him.

"But you've heard of him?"

"Yes, of course."

"Is he Jordanian?"

"I doubt it."

"Syrian?"

"Could be."

"Iraqi?"

"I'd say so."

"Why?"

"Because he's very professional. Like you," Nabil Awad added quickly. "He's serious about his security. He doesn't want to be a star like Bin Laden. He just wants to kill infidels. Only the people at the top know his real name or where he comes from."

By then, night had fallen. They returned Nabil Awad hooded and bound to the formerly white van and drove him to Le Bourget Airport outside Paris, where a Gulfstream aircraft belonging to the Jordanian monarch waited. Nabil Awad boarded the plane without a struggle, and just six hours later was locked in a cell deep within GID headquarters in Amman. In the parallel universe of the World Wide Web, however, he was still very much a free man. He told friends, followers on social media, and the manager of the print shop where he worked that he had been compelled to return to Jordan suddenly because his father had taken ill. His father was not available to contradict the account, because he, like all the members of the extended Awad clan, was now in GID custody.

For the next seventy-two hours, Nabil Awad's mobile phone was besieged with expressions of concern. Two teams of analysts, one at GID headquarters, one at King Saul Boulevard, scrubbed each e-mail, text, and direct message for signs of trouble. They also drafted and posted several dire updates on Nabil Awad's Twitter feed. It seemed the patient had taken a turn for the worse. God willing, he would make a recovery, but for the moment it didn't look good.

To the uninitiated eyes, the words that flowed onto Nabil Awad's social media pages seemed entirely appropriate for the eldest son of a man who was gravely ill. But one message contained a somewhat peculiar syntax and choice of words that, to one reader, meant something quite specific. It meant that an empty can of Belgian beer had been hidden in a gorse bush at the edge of a small pasture not far from the city center of Brussels. Inside the can, wrapped in protective plastic, was a flash drive that contained a single encrypted document. Its subject was a Palestinian doctor named Leila Hadawi.

27

SERAINCOURT, FRANCE

AND THUS COMMENCED THE GREAT WAIT—or so it was referred to by all those who endured the appalling period, roughly seventy-two hours in length, during which the encrypted message sat untouched in its little aluminum sarcophagus, at the base of a power pole on the Kerselaarstraat, in the Brussels suburb of Dilbeek. The actors in this slow-moving drama were far-flung. They were spread from the Bethnal Green section of East London, to an immigrant banlieue north of Paris, to a room in the heart of a building in Amman known as the Fingernail Factory, where a jihadist was being kept on cyber life support. There was precedent for what they were doing; during World War II, British intelligence kept an entire network of captured German spies alive and functioning in the minds of their Abwehr controllers, feeding them false and deceptive intelligence in the process. The Israelis and Jordanians saw themselves as keepers of a sacred flame.

The one place where no members of the team were present was Dilbeek. Though scarcely a mile from the center of Brussels, it was a decidedly rural suburb ringed by small farms.

"In other words," declared Eli Lavon, who reconnoitered the drop site on the morning after Nabil Awad's interrogation, "it's a spy's nightmare." A fixed observation point was out of the question. Nor was it possible to surveil the target from a parked car or a café. Parking was not permitted on that stretch of the Kerselaarstraat, and the only cafés were in the center of the village.

The solution was to conceal a miniature camera in the patch of overgrown weeds on the opposite side of the road. Mordecai monitored its heavily encrypted transmission from a hotel room in central Brussels and routed the signal onto a secure network, which allowed the other members of the team to watch it, too. It was soon appointment viewing, a ratings bonanza. In London, Tel Aviv, Amman, and Paris, highly trained and motivated professional intelligence officers stood motionless before computer screens, staring at a tangle of gorse at the base of a concrete power pole. Occasionally, a vehicle would pass, or a cyclist, or a pensioner from the village out for a morning constitutional, but for the most part the image appeared to be a still photograph rather than a live video feed. Gabriel monitored it from the makeshift op center at Château Treville. He thought it the most unsightly thing he had ever produced. He referred to it as *Can by a Pole* and cursed himself inwardly for having chosen the Dilbeek drop site over the other three options. Not that they were any better. Clearly, Jalal Nasser had not selected the sites with aesthetics in mind.

The wait was not without its lighter moments. There was the Belgian shepherd, a colossal wolflike creature, which shat in the gorse bush daily. And the metal-detecting pensioner who unearthed the can and, after a careful inspection, dropped it where he had found it. And the biblical thunderstorm, four hours in duration, that threatened to wash away the can and its contents, not to mention the village itself. Gabriel ordered Mordecai to check on the condition of the flash drive, but Mordecai convinced him it wasn't necessary. He had placed it inside two watertight ziplock plastic baggies, Nabil Awad's usual technique. Besides, Mordecai argued, a check was far too risky. There was always the possibility that the courier might arrive at the very moment of the inspection. There was also the possibility, he added, that they were not the only ones watching the drop site.

The target of this undertaking, Jalal Nasser, Saladin's director of European operations, provided no clue as to his intentions. By then, it was early summer, and Jalal had been freed from his backbreaking course load at King's College—a single seminar having something to do with the impact of Western imperialism on the economies of the Arab world—which left him free to pursue jihad and terrorism to his heart's content. By all outward appearances, however, he was a man of taxpayer-financed leisure. He dawdled over his morning coffee at his favorite café on the Bethnal Green Road, he shopped in Oxford Street, he visited the National Gallery to view forbidden art, he watched an American action film at a theater in Leicester Square. He even took in a musical—*Jersey Boys*, of all things—which left the London teams wondering whether he planned to bomb the production. They saw no evidence that he was under British surveillance, but in Orwellian London looks could be deceiving. MI5 didn't have to rely solely on watchers to surveil suspected terrorists. The eyes of CCTV never blinked.

His bachelor flat in Chilton Street had been entered, searched, and compromised in every conceivable way. They watched him eat, they watched him sleep, they watched him pray, and they peered quietly over his shoulder with the silence of curious children while he toiled late into the night at his computer. He had not one laptop but two, one that was connected to the Internet and an identical model with no links to the cyber universe whatsoever, or so he believed. If he was communicating with elements of Saladin's network, it was not readily apparent. Jalal Nasser might have been a committed jihadist terrorist, but online he was a model resident of Great Britain and a loyal subject of the Hashemite Kingdom of Jordan.

But was he aware of the flash drive that lay at the base of a power pole in a pastoral suburb of Brussels called Dilbeek? And did he know that the man who had supposedly placed it there was now in Jordan tending to a gravely ill father? And did he find the confluence of events—the dead drop and the sudden travel of a trusted lieutenant—a bit too coincidental for comfort? Gabriel was certain it was so. And the proof, he declared, was the failure of the courier to clean out the drop site. Gabriel's mood darkened with each passing hour. He stalked the many rooms of Château Treville, he walked the footpaths of the gardens, he scoured the watch reports. Mainly, he stared at a computer screen, at an image of a concrete power pole rising from a tangle of gorse bush, quite possibly the most hideous image in the history of a proud service.

Late in the afternoon of the third day, the deluge that had flooded Dilbeek laid siege to the banlieues north of Paris. Eli Lavon had been caught on the streets of Aubervilliers, and when he returned to Château Treville he might have been mistaken for a lunatic who had decided to take a swim fully clothed. Gabriel was standing before his computer as though he had been bronzed. His green eyes, however, were burning brightly.

"Well?" asked Lavon.

Gabriel reached down, tapped a few keys on the keyboard,

and clicked on the play icon on the screen. A few seconds later a motorcyclist flashed across it, right to left, in a black blur.

"Do you know how many motorcyclists have passed by that spot today?" asked Lavon.

"Thirty-eight," answered Gabriel. "But only one did this."

He replayed the video in slow motion and then clicked on the pause icon. At the instant the image froze, the visor of the motorcyclist's helmet was pointed directly at the base of the power pole.

"Maybe he was distracted by something," said Lavon.

"Like what?"

"A beer can with a flash drive inside it."

Gabriel smiled for the first time in three days. He tapped a few keys on the computer, and the live image reappeared on the screen. *Can by a Pole*, he thought. It was suddenly the most beautiful thing he had ever seen.

THEY SAW HIM FOR A SECOND TIME AT SEVEN THAT EVENING and again at half past eight, as dusk was darkening the image like a painting being slowly devoured by surface grime and yellowed varnish. On both occasions he swept across the screen from left to right. And both times, upon slow-motion reexamination, his head turned almost imperceptibly toward the gorse bush at the base of the concrete power pole. When he returned for a third time it was long past dark, and the image was black as pitch. This time, he stopped and killed the bike's lights. Mordecai switched the camera from optical to infrared, and a moment later Gabriel and Eli Lavon watched as a yellow-and-red man-shaped blob slipped quickly in and out of the gorse at the edge of the Kerselaarstraat.

The USB flash drive was identical to the model used by Nabil Awad for previous communications, with one critical additional feature: its printed circuit board had been fitted with a tracking device that allowed the team to monitor its movements. From Dilbeek it moved to the city center of Brussels, where it spent a restful evening in a rather good hotel. Then, in the morning, it boarded the 8:52 Eurostar at Brussels Midi, and by ten o'clock it was moving along a platform at St. Pancras International in London. Yaakov Rossman managed to snap a photo of the courier as he crossed the arrivals hall. Later, they would identify him as an Egyptian national who lived off the Edgware Road and worked as a production assistant for Al Jazeera television.

The flash drive made the journey to East London on foot and at noon changed hands with admirable discretion on the pavements of Brick Lane. A few minutes later, in a bachelor flat in Chilton Street, it was inserted into a computer with no connection to the Internet, or so believed its owner. At which point a new wait commenced, the wait for Jalal Nasser, Saladin's man in Europe, to come to Paris to meet his new girl.

28

PARIS

NATALIE TOOK CONSCIOUS NOTE OF him for the first time on Saturday, at half past two o'clock, as she was crossing the Luxembourg Gardens. At that instant she realized she had seen him on several prior occasions, including the previous afternoon, at the café across the street from her flat in Aubervilliers. Shaded by a Pernod umbrella, he had nipped at a glass of white wine, feigned absorption in a worn paperback, and stared at her without reservation. She had mistaken his attentions for lust and had left the café earlier than intended. In retrospect, she supposed her actions had made a positive impression.

But it was not until that perfect sun-dappled Saturday that Natalie was certain the man was following her. She had intended to take the entire day off from work, but a pandemic of strep throat in the *cités* had compelled her to spend the morning at the clinic. She had left at noon and ridden an RER into the city center. And while pretending to window-shop in the rue Vavin she had seen him on the opposite side of the street, pretending to do the same. A few minutes later, on the footpaths of the Luxembourg Gardens, she had employed another one of the techniques she had learned at the farm in Nahalal—a sudden stop, a turn, a hasty retracing of her steps. And there he was again. She walked past him with her eyes averted. Even so, she could feel the weight of his gaze upon her face. A few paces behind him, dressed like an aging revolutionary poet, was the blurry-faced watcher from the Office, and behind him were two French surveillance men. Natalie returned quickly to the rue Vavin and entered a boutique she had visited a few minutes earlier. Instantly, her phone rang.

"Have you forgotten that we're having coffee today?"

Natalie recognized the voice. "Of course not," she answered quickly. "I'm just running a few minutes late. Where are you?"

"Café de Flore. It's on—"

"I know where it is," she interrupted with a flash of French superiority. "I'm on my way."

The connection went dead. Natalie dropped the phone into her bag and went into the street. Her pursuer was not there, but on the opposite pavement was one of the French surveillance men. He followed her through the Luxembourg Quarter to the boulevard Saint-Germain, where Dina Sarid was waving to her from a sidewalk table of one of Paris's most famous coffeehouses. She was brightly veiled and wearing a pair of large movie starlet sunglasses.

"Even with that getup," said Natalie softly as she kissed Dina's cheek, "you still look like an Ashkenazi Jew in a hijab."

"The maître d' doesn't agree. I was lucky to get a table."

Natalie laid a napkin across her lap. "I think I'm being followed."

"You are."

"When were you going to tell me?"

Dina only smiled.

"Is he the one we want?"

"Absolutely."

"How do you want me to play it?"

"Hard to get. And remember," added Dina, "no kissing on the first date."

Natalie opened her menu and sighed. "I need a drink."

29

AUBERVILLIERS, FRANCE

LEILA? IS THAT REALLY YOU? It's Jalal. Jalal Nasser from London. Remember me? We met a few weeks ago. May I join you? I was just going to have a coffee myself."

He blurted all this in classical Jordanian Arabic while hovering over Natalie's usual table at the café opposite her apartment. It was late the following morning, a Sunday, the air cool and soft, the sun adrift in a cloudless sky. The traffic in the street was light; consequently, Natalie had seen him walking along the pavement from a long way off. Passing her table, he had stopped abruptly—as Natalie had stopped on the footpaths of the Luxembourg Gardens—and spun around as though his shoulder had been tapped. He approached her slowly and established himself so that the sun was at his back and his long shadow fell upon Natalie's open newspaper. Looking up, she shaded her eyes and regarded him coolly, as if for the first time. His hair was tightly curled and neatly styled, his jawline was square and strong, his smile was restrained but warm. Women found him attractive, and he knew it.

"You're blocking the light," she said.

He grasped the back of an empty chair. "May I?"

Before Natalie could object, he pulled the chair away from the table and settled himself proprietarily into it. And there it was, she thought. All the preparation, all the training—and now he sat before her, the one they wanted, the one who would place her in the hands of Saladin. All at once she realized her heart was tolling like an iron bell. Her discomfort must have been apparent, because he placed a hand on the sleeve of her modest silk blouse. Met by her reproachful glare, he hastily removed it.

"Forgive me. I don't want you to be nervous."

But she wasn't nervous, she told herself. And why should she be? She was in her usual café across the street from her apartment. She was a respected member of the community, a healer who cared for the residents of the *cités* and spoke to them in their native language, though with a distinct Palestinian accent. She was Dr. Leila Hadawi, graduate of the Université Paris-Sud, fully accredited and licensed to practice medicine by the government of France. She was Leila from Sumayriyya, Leila who loved Ziad. And the handsome creature who had just intruded on her Sunday-morning coffee, who had dared to touch the hem of her sleeve, was of no consequence.

"I'm sorry," she said, folding her newspaper absently, "but I didn't catch your name."

"Jalal," he repeated. "Jalal Nasser."

"Jalal from London?"

"Yes."

"And you say we've met before?"

"Briefly."

"That would explain why I don't remember you."

"It might."

"And where exactly did we meet?"

"It was in the Place de la République, two months ago. Or maybe it was three. There was a demonstration against—"

"I remember it." She narrowed her eyes thoughtfully. "But I don't remember you."

"We spoke afterward. I told you that I admired your passion and commitment to the issue of Palestine. I said I wanted to discuss it with you further. I wrote down my contact information on the back of a leaflet and gave it to you."

"If you say so." Feigning boredom, she gazed into the street. "Do you use this tired approach on all the women you see sitting alone in cafés?"

"Are you accusing me of making this entire thing up?"

"I might be."

"How did I know you were at the demonstration in the Place de la République if I wasn't there?"

"I haven't figured that out yet."

"I know you were there," he said, "because I was there, too."

"So you say."

He flagged down the waiter and ordered a café crème. Natalie turned her head and smiled.

"What's so funny?"

"Your French is atrocious."

"I live in London."

"We've established that."

"I'm a student at King's College," he explained.

"Aren't you a bit old to still be a student?"

"My father tells me the same thing."

"Your father sounds like a wise man. Does he live in London, too?"

"Amman." He fell silent as the waiter placed a coffee before him. Then, casually, he asked, "Your mother is from Jordan, is she not?"

This time, the silence was Leila's. It was the silence of suspicion, the silence of an exile. "How do you know my mother is from Jordan?" she asked at last.

"You told me."

"When?"

"After the demonstration, of course. You told me your mother's family lived in Nablus. You said they fled to Jordan and were forced to live in the refugee camp at Zarqa. I know this camp, by the way. I have many friends from this camp. I used to pray in the mosque there. Do you know the mosque in Zarqa camp?"

"Are you referring to the al-Falah Mosque?"

"Yes, that's the one."

"I know it well," she said. "But I'm quite certain I never mentioned any of this to you."

"How could I know about your mother if you didn't tell me?"

Again, she was silent.

"You also told me about your father."

"Not possible."

He ignored her objection. "He wasn't from Nablus like your mother. He was from the Western Galilee." He paused, then added, "From Sumayriyya."

Her expression darkened and she engaged in a series of tiny gestures that interrogators refer to as displacement activity. She adjusted her hijab, she tapped a nail against the rim of her coffee cup, she glanced nervously around the quiet Sunday street—anywhere but into the face of the man seated on the other side of the table, the man who would place her in the hands of Saladin.

"I don't know who you are," she said finally, "but I've never told you anything about my parents. In fact, I'm quite certain I've never seen you until this moment."

"Never?"

"No."

"Then how do I know these things about you?"

"Maybe you're from the DGSI?"

"Me? French intelligence? My French is dreadful. You said so yourself."

"Then maybe you're American. Or Israeli," she added.

"You're paranoid."

"That's because I'm a Palestinian. And if you don't tell me who you really are and what you want, I'm leaving. And there's a very good chance I might find the nearest gendarme and tell him about the strange man who knows things about me he shouldn't."

"It's never a good idea for Muslims to get involved with the French police, Leila. There's a good chance they'll open an S file on you. And if they do, they'll learn things that could prove detrimental to someone in your position."

She placed a five-euro note next to her coffee and started to rise, but once again he placed his hand on her arm—not lightly but with a grip that was shockingly firm. And all the while he was smiling for the benefit of the waiter and the passersby, immigrants and native French, filing past through the soft sunlight.

"Who are you?" she murmured through clenched teeth.

"My name is Jalal Nasser."

"Jalal from London?"

"Correct."

"Have we ever met before?"

"No."

"You lied to me."

"I had to."

"Why are you here?"

"I was asked to come."

"By whom?"

"You, of course." He relaxed his grip. "Don't be nervous, Leila," he said calmly. "I'm not going to hurt you. I'm only here to help. I'm going to give you the chance you've been waiting for. I'm going to make your dreams come true."

PAUL ROUSSEAU'S OBSERVATION POST WAS LOCATED DIRECTLY above the café, and the sharp downward angle of the surveillance camera was such that Natalie and Jalal seemed like characters in an avant-garde French film. Audio coverage was supplied by Natalie's mobile phone, which meant that, when viewed live, there was a maddening two-second audio delay. But afterward, in the safe house at Seraincourt, Mordecai produced an edited version of the encounter in which sound and video were synchronized. With Eli Lavon at his side, Gabriel watched it three times from beginning to end. Then he adjusted the time code to 11:17:38 and clicked on the play icon.

"Why are you here?"

"I was asked to come."

"By whom?"

"You, of course."

Gabriel clicked PAUSE.

"Impressive performance," said Eli Lavon.

"His or hers?"

"Both, actually."

Gabriel clicked PLAY.

"I'm going to give you the chance you've been waiting for. I'm going to make your dreams come true."

"Who told you about these dreams of mine?"

"My friend Nabil. Perhaps you remember him."

"Very well."

"Nabil told me about the conversation you had after the demonstration in the Place de la République."

"*Why would he do that?*"

"*Because Nabil and I work for the same organization.*"

"*Which organization?*"

"*I'm not at liberty to say. Not here. Not now.*"

Gabriel clicked PAUSE and looked at Lavon. "Why *not* here?" he asked. "Why *not* now?"

"You didn't really think he would make his move in the café, did you?"

Gabriel frowned and pressed PLAY.

"*Perhaps we can meet somewhere more private to talk at length.*"

"*Perhaps.*"

"*Are you free this evening?*"

"*I might be.*"

"*Do you know La Courneuve?*"

"*Of course.*"

"*Can you make your way there?*"

"*It's not far. I can walk.*"

"*There's a large housing estate on the Avenue Leclerc.*"

"*I know it.*"

"*Be outside the pharmacy at nine. Don't bring your mobile phone or anything electronic. And dress warmly.*"

Gabriel paused the recording. "Sounds to me like they're going to be traveling by motorbike."

"Brilliant," said Lavon.

"Jalal or me?"

A silence fell between them. It was Lavon who finally broke it.

"What are you worried about?"

"I'm worried that he's going to drive her to a secluded location, brutally interrogate her, and then cut her head off. Other than that, I have no concerns at all."

Another silence, longer than the first.

"What are you going to do?" Lavon asked finally.

Gabriel stared at the computer screen, one hand to his chin, his head tilted slightly to one side. Then he reached down, reset the time code, and pressed PLAY.

"Leila? Is that really you? It's Jalal. Jalal Nasser from London . . ."

30

LA COURNEUVE, FRANCE

THE CLEAR SKIES WERE BY that evening a pleasant memory. A cold, damp wind plucked at Natalie's hijab as she made her way along the Avenue Leclerc, and above her head a blanket of thick clouds obscured the moon and stars. The raw weather was more typical of the northern banlieues; a trick of the prevailing southwesterly winds gave them a distinctly gloomier climate than the center of Paris. It only added to the air of dystopian misery that hung like a gray shroud over the looming concrete towers of the *cités*.

One of the largest housing estates in the entire department rose before Natalie now, two enormous slabs in the brutalist style, one tall and rectangular, like a giant deck of playing cards, the other lower and longer, as if to provide architectural balance. Between the two structures was a broad esplanade planted with many youthful trees in green leaf. A flock of veiled women, some wearing full facial veils, conversed quietly in Arabic while a few feet away a quartet of teenage boys openly passed a joint, knowing that a patrol by the French police was exceedingly unlikely. Natalie slipped past the women, returning their greeting of peace, and headed toward the parade of shops at the base of the tower. A supermarket, a hair salon, a small carryout restaurant, an optician, a pharmacy—all of life's needs met in one convenient location. That was the goal of the central planners, to create self-contained utopias for the working classes. Few residents of the banlieues ventured into the center of Paris unless they were lucky enough to have jobs there. Even then, they joked that the short journey, ten minutes on the RER, required a passport and proof of vaccination.

Natalie made her way to the entrance of the pharmacy. Outside was a pair of modular concrete benches, upon which sat several Africans in traditional flowing dress. She reckoned it was a few minutes before nine o'clock, but couldn't be sure; as instructed she had come without electronic devices, including her battery-powered wristwatch. One of the Africans, a tall thin man with skin like ebony, offered Natalie his seat, but with only a polite smile she indicated she preferred to stand. She watched the evening traffic moving in the avenue, and the hidden women chattering softly in Arabic, and the now-stoned teenage boys, who in turn were eyeing her malevolently, as though they could see the truth beneath her veil. She drew a deep breath to slow the beat of her heart. I'm in France, she told herself. Nothing can happen to me here.

Several minutes elapsed, long enough for Natalie to wonder whether Jalal Nasser had decided to abort the meeting. Behind her, the pharmacy door opened and from inside emerged a Frenchman who might have been mistaken for a North African. Natalie recognized him; he was one of her watchers from the French security service. He slipped past without a word and climbed into the backseat of a battered Renault. Approaching the car from behind was a motor scooter, black in color, large enough to accommodate two passengers. It stopped outside the pharmacy, a few feet from where Natalie stood. The driver lifted the visor of his helmet and smiled.

"You're late," said Natalie, annoyed.

"Actually," said Jalal Nasser, "you were early."

"How do you know?"

"Because I followed you."

He removed a second helmet from the rear storage compartment. Warily, Natalie accepted it. This was something they hadn't covered during her training at the farm in Nahalal, how to wear a helmet over a hijab. She slipped it on carefully, buckled the strap beneath her chin, and climbed onto the back of the bike. Instantly, it lurched forward into the traffic. As they shot through the canyons of the *cités* in a blur, Natalie wrapped her arms around Jalal Nasser's waist and held on for her life. I'm in France, she reassured herself. Nothing can happen to me here. Then she realized her mistake. She wasn't in France, not anymore.

EARLIER THAT AFTERNOON, IN THE ELEGANT SALON OF CHÂteau Treville, there had been an intense debate regarding the level of surveillance required for that evening's meeting. Gabriel, perhaps owing to the burden of pending command, had wanted as many eyes as possible on his agent, both human and electronic. Only Eli Lavon dared to offer a countervailing opinion. Lavon knew the possibilities of surveillance, and its pitfalls. Clearly, he argued, Jalal Nasser intended to take his potential recruit on a surveillance-detection run before baring his jihadist soul to her. And if he discovered they were being followed, the operation would be doomed before it left port. Nor was it possible, said Lavon, to conceal a tracking beacon on Natalie, because the technologically minded operatives of ISIS and al-Qaeda knew how to find them.

It was a brotherly row, but heated. There were voices raised, mild insults exchanged, and a piece of fruit, a banana of all things, hurled in frustration—though afterward Lavon insisted that Gabriel's lightning-fast duck, while impressive, had been wholly unnecessary, for it was only a warning shot across the bow. Lavon prevailed in the end, if only because Gabriel, in his operational heart, knew that his old friend was correct. He was magnanimous in defeat, but no less worried about sending his agent into the meeting entirely alone. Despite his unthreatening appearance, Jalal Nasser was a ruthless and committed jihadi killer who had served as a project manager for two devastating terror attacks. And Natalie, for all her training and intelligence, was a Jew who happened to speak Arabic very well.

And so, at two minutes past nine that evening, as Natalie swung her leg over the back of Jalal Nasser's Piaggio motorbike, only French eyes were watching, and only from a distance. The battered Renault followed for a time and was soon replaced by a Citroën. Then the Citroën dropped away too, and only the cameras watched over them. They tracked them northward, past Le Bourget Airport and Charles de Gaulle, and eastward through the villages of Thieux and Juilly. Then, at nine twenty, Paul Rousseau rang Gabriel to say that Natalie had vanished from their radar screens.

At which point Gabriel and his team settled in for another long wait. Mordecai and Oded engaged in a furious game of table tennis; Mikhail and Eli Lavon waged war over a chessboard, Yossi and Rimona watched an American film on television. Only Gabriel and Dina refused to distract themselves with trivial pursuits. Gabriel paced alone in the darkened garden, worrying himself to death, while Dina sat alone in the makeshift operations room, staring at a black computer screen. Dina was grieving. Dina would have given anything to be in Natalie's place.

AFTER PUTTING THE LAST OF THE PARIS SUBURBS BEHIND them, they rode for an hour through sleeping cropland and postcard villages, seemingly without aim or purpose or destination. Or was it two hours they journeyed? Natalie couldn't be sure. Her view of the world was limited. There were only Jalal's square shoulders, and the back of Jalal's helmet, and Jalal's narrow waist, to which she clung with guilt, for she was thinking of Ziad, whom she loved. For a time she tried to maintain a grasp of their whereabouts, noting the names of the villages they entered and exited, and the numbers of the roads along which they sped. Eventually, she surrendered and tilted her head heavenward. Stars shone in the black sky; a low luminous moon chased them across the landscape. She supposed she was back in France again.

At last, they arrived at the outskirts of a midsize town. Natalie knew it; it was Senlis, the ancient city of French kings located at the edge of the Forest of Chantilly. Jalal sped through the cobbled alleyways of the medieval center and parked in a small courtyard. On two sides were high walls of gray flint, and on the third, darkened and shuttered, was a two-story building that showed no sign of habitation. Somewhere a church bell tolled heavily, but otherwise the town was eerily quiet. Jalal dismounted and removed his helmet. Natalie did the same.

"Your hijab, too," he murmured in Arabic.

"Why?"

"Because this isn't the sort of place for people like us."

Natalie unpinned her hijab and tucked it into the helmet. In the darkness Jalal scrutinized her carefully.

"Is something wrong?"

"You're just . . ."

"Just what?"

"More beautiful than I imagined." He locked the two helmets in the bike's rear storage compartment. Then, from his coat pocket, he removed an object about the size of an old-fashioned pager. "Did you follow my instructions about phones and electronic devices?"

"Of course."

"And no credit cards?"

"None."

"Mind if I check?"

He moved the object methodically over her body, down her arms and legs, across her shoulders, her breasts, her hips, down the length of her spine.

"Did I pass?"

Wordlessly, he returned the device to his coat pocket.

"Is your name really Jalal Nasser?"

"Does it matter?"

"It matters to me."

"Yes, my name is Jalal."

"And your organization?"

"We seek to re-create the caliphate in the Muslim lands of the Middle East and establish Islamic dominance over the rest of the world."

"You're from ISIS."

Without responding he turned and led her along an empty street, toward the sound of the church bells.

"Take my arm," he said sotto voce. "Speak to me in French."

"About what?"

"Anything. It doesn't matter."

She threaded her arm through his and told him about her day at the clinic. He nodded occasionally, always at the wrong times, but made no attempt to address her in his dreadful French. Finally, in Arabic, he asked, "Who was the woman you had coffee with yesterday afternoon?"

"I'm sorry?"

"The woman at Café de Flore, the one with the veil. Who is she?"

"How long have you been watching me?"

"Answer my question, please."

"Her name is Mona."

"Mona what?"

"Mona el-Baz. We studied medicine together. She lives in Frankfurt now."

"She's a Palestinian, too?"

"Egyptian, actually."

"She didn't look Egyptian to me."

"She comes from an old family, very aristocratic."

"I'd like to meet her."

"Why?"

"Perhaps she could be helpful to our cause."

"Don't bother. Mona doesn't think the way we do."

He seemed shocked by this. "Why would you associate with such a person?"

"Why do you attend King's College and reside in the land of the *kufar*?"

The street brought them to the edge of a square. The tables of a small restaurant spilled onto the paving stones, and on the opposite side rose the Gothic towers and flying buttresses of Senlis Cathedral.

"And the clothing store on the rue Vavin?" he asked over the tolling of the bells. "Why did you return there?"

"I forgot my credit card."

"You were preoccupied?"

"Not necessarily."

"Nervous?"

"Why should I have been?"

"Did you know I was following you?"

"Were you?"

He was distracted by the sound of laughter rising from the tables of the restaurant. He took her hand and as the bells fell silent led her across the square.

"How well do you know the Koran and the Hadith?" he asked suddenly.

She was grateful for the change of subject, for it suggested he had no concerns as to her authenticity. Consequently, she did not confess that she had not cracked the Koran before settling into a farmhouse in the Valley of Jezreel. Instead, she explained that her parents were secular and that she did not discover the beauty of the Koran until she was at university.

"Do you know about the Mahdi?" he asked. "The one they call the Redeemer?"

"Yes, of course. The Hadith says he will appear as an ordinary man. 'His name will be my name,'" she said, quoting the relevant passage, "'and his father's name my father's name.' He will be one of us."

"Very good. Go on, please."

"The Mahdi will rule over the earth until the Day of Judgment and rid the world of evil. There will be no Christians after the Mahdi comes." She paused, then added, "And no Jews."

"And no Israel, either."

"Inshallah," Natalie heard herself say softly.

"Yes, God willing." He stopped in the center of the square and gazed disapprovingly at the darkened southern facade of the ancient cathedral. "Soon it will look like the Colosseum in Rome and the Parthenon in Athens. Our Muslim tour guides will explain what went on here. This is where the *kufar* worshiped, they will say. This is where they baptized their young. This is where their priests whispered the magic spells that turned bread and wine into the body and blood of Isa, our prophet. The end is near, Leila. The clock is ticking."

"You intend to destroy them?"

"We won't have to. They will destroy themselves by invading the lands of the caliphate. There will be a final battle between the armies of Rome and the armies of Islam in the Syrian village of Dabiq. The Hadith tells us the black flags will come from the east, led by mighty men with long hair and beards, their surnames taken from their hometowns. Men like Zarqawi and Baghdadi." He turned and looked at her for a moment in silence. Then he said, "And you, of course."

"I'm not a soldier. I can't fight."

"We don't allow our women to fight, Leila, not on the battlefield, at least. But that doesn't mean you can't be a soldier."

A squadron of rooks took noisy flight from the abutments of the cathedral. Natalie watched their black silhouettes flutter across the sky like the black flags of the mighty men from the east. Then she followed Jalal through a doorway, into the south transept. An attendant, a gray emaciated woman of perhaps seventy, informed them that the cathedral would be closing in ten minutes. Natalie accepted a brochure and then joined Jalal in the central crossing. He was staring westward down the nave. Natalie looked in the opposite direction, over the choir, toward the main altar. The stained-glass windows were invisible in the gloom. There was no one else in the cathedral, no one but the elderly attendant.

"The organization for which I work," Jalal explained, his Arabic echoing softly among the pillars of the arcades, "handles external affairs for the Islamic State. Our goal is to draw America and its European allies into a ground war in Syria through calculated acts of violence. The attacks in Paris and Amsterdam were carried out by our network. We have many more attacks planned, some in the coming days."

He said all this while gazing down the length of the cathedral. Natalie delivered her response to the apse.

"What does this have to do with me?"

"I would like you to work for us."

"I couldn't be involved with something like Paris or Amsterdam."

"That's not what you told my friend Nabil. You told Nabil that you wanted the *kufar* to know what it felt like to be afraid. You said you wanted to punish them for their support of Israel." He turned and looked directly into her eyes. "You said you wanted to pay them back for what happened to Ziad."

"I suppose Nabil told you about Ziad, too."

He took the brochure from her hand, consulted it briefly, and then led her down the center of the nave, toward the western facade. "You know," he was saying, "I think I actually met him once."

"Really? Where?"

"At a meeting of some brothers in Amman. For reasons of security we weren't using our real names." He stopped and craned his neck toward the ceiling. "You're afraid. I can see it."

"Yes," she replied. "I am afraid."

"Why?"

"Because I wasn't serious. It was only talk."

"You are a salon jihadist, Leila? You prefer to carry signs and shout slogans?"

"No. I just never imagined something like this might happen."

"This isn't the Internet, Leila. This is the real thing."

"That's what I'm afraid of."

From across the cathedral the old woman signaled that it

was time to leave. Jalal lowered his gaze from the ceiling to Natalie's face.

"And if I say yes?" she asked.

"You'll need to travel to the caliphate for training. We'll handle all the arrangements."

"I can't be away for long."

"A few weeks are all we need."

"What happens if the authorities find out?"

"Trust me, Leila, they'll know nothing. We have routes we use. False passports, too. Your time in Syria will be our little secret."

"And then?"

"You return to France and your job at the clinic. And you wait."

"For what?"

He placed his hands on her shoulders. "You know, Leila, you're lucky. You're going to do something incredibly important. I envy you."

She smiled in spite of herself. "My friend Mona told me the same thing."

"What was she talking about?"

"It was nothing," said Natalie. "Nothing at all."

31

AUBERVILLIERS, FRANCE

THAT NIGHT NATALIE COULD NOT sleep. For a time she lay awake in her bed, committing to memory every word Jalal Nasser had spoken. Afterward, she wrestled with her sheets while her mind raced with thoughts of what lay ahead. To distract herself she watched a tedious documentary on French television, and when that didn't work, she opened her laptop and surfed the Internet. Not the jihadist sites, though; Jalal had warned her to avoid those. Natalie was now a servant of two masters, a woman with two lovers. When sleep finally claimed her, it was Jalal who visited her in her dreams. He strapped a suicide vest to her nude body and kissed her softly. *You're lucky*, he said. *You're going to do something incredibly important.*

She awoke groggy and agitated and afflicted with a migraine that no amount of medication or caffeine would alleviate. A benevolent God might have seen fit to give her a quiet day at the clinic, but a parade of human malady kept her running from examination room to examination room until six that evening. As she was leaving work, Roland Girard, the clinic's ersatz administrative director, invited her for coffee. Outside, he helped her into the front seat of his Peugeot sedan, and for the next forty-five minutes he spoke not a word as he followed a meandering path toward the center of Paris. As they were passing the Musée d'Orsay, his mobile phone pinged with an incoming message. After reading it he drove across the Seine and made his way to the rue de Grenelle in the Seventh Arrondissement, where he nosed the car through the security gate of a handsome cream-colored building. Natalie glimpsed the brass plaque as it flashed past her window. It read SOCIÉTÉ INTERNATIONALE POUR LA LITTÉRATURE FRANÇAISE.

"An evening of Balzac?"

He switched off the engine and led her inside. In the foyer she glimpsed the Arab-looking Frenchman whom she had seen leaving the pharmacy in La Courneuve, and in the stairwell she passed a habitué of the café across the street from her apartment. The uppermost floor of the building felt like a bank after hours. A stern-looking woman sat behind an orderly desk, while in an adjacent office a sharp-suited man glared at his computer as though it were an uncooperative witness. Two men waited in a glass-enclosed conference room. One smoked a pipe and wore a crumpled blazer. The other was Gabriel.

"Leila," he said formally. "So nice to see you again. You're looking well. A bit tired, but well."

"It was a long night."

"For all of us. We were relieved when we saw that motorbike pull up outside your apartment building." Gabriel moved slowly from behind the table. "I trust your meeting with Jalal went well."

"It did."

"He has plans for you?"

"I think he does."

"Because of his security precautions, we weren't able to record the conversation. It is important you tell us everything he said last night, *exactly* the way he said it. Can you do that, Leila?"

She nodded.

"Good," said Gabriel, smiling for the first time. "Please have a seat and start from the beginning. What were the first words out of his mouth when he met you outside the pharmacy? Did he speak during the drive? Where did he take you? What was his route? Tell us everything you can. No detail is too small."

She lowered herself into her assigned seat, adjusted her hijab, and began to speak. After a moment or two, Gabriel reached across the table and placed a restraining hand upon hers.

"Did I do something wrong?" she asked.

"You're doing beautifully, Leila. But please start again from the beginning. And this time," he added, "it would be helpful if you spoke French instead of Arabic."

IT WAS AT THIS POINT THAT THEY WERE CONFRONTED WITH their first serious operational dilemma—for within the walls of the ancient cathedral of Senlis, Jalal Nasser, Saladin's man in Western Europe, had told his potential recruit that more attacks were coming, sooner rather than later. Paul Rousseau declared that they were compelled to inform his minister of the developments, and perhaps even the British. The goal of the operation, he said, had been to roll up the network. Working with MI5, they could arrest Jalal Nasser, interrogate him, learn his future plans, and scoop up his operatives.

"Call it a day?" asked Gabriel. "Job well done?"

"It happens to be true."

"And what if Nasser doesn't crack under the friendly interrogation he'll receive in London? What if he doesn't reveal his plans or the names of his operatives? What if there are parallel networks and cells, so that if one goes down the others survive?" He paused, then added, "And what about Saladin?"

Rousseau conceded the point. But on the question of bringing the threat to the attention of higher authority—namely, his chief and his minister—he was unyielding. And so it was that Gabriel Allon, the man who had operated on French soil with impunity and had left a trail of dead bodies stretching from Paris to Marseilles, entered the Interior Ministry at half past ten that evening, with Alpha Group's chief at his side. The minister was waiting in his ornate office, along with the chief of the DGSI and Alain Lambert, the minister's aide-de-camp, note taker, food taster, and general factotum. Lambert had come from a dinner party; the minister, from his bed. He shook Gabriel's hand as if he feared catching something. Lambert avoided Gabriel's eye.

"How serious is the threat of another attack?" the minister asked when Rousseau had completed his briefing.

"As serious as it gets," answered the Alpha Group chief.

"Will the next attack come in France?"

"We cannot say."

"What *can* you say?"

"Our agent has been recruited and invited to travel to Syria for training."

"Our agent?" The minister shook his head. "No, Paul, she is not *our* agent." He pointed to Gabriel and said, "She is his."

A silence fell over the room.

"Is she still willing to go through with it?" the minister asked after a moment.

"She is."

"And you, Monsieur Allon? Are you still willing to send her?"

"The best way to learn the time and place of the next attack is to insert an agent directly into the operation itself."

"I take it your answer is yes, then?"

Gabriel nodded gravely. The minister made a show of thought.

"How comprehensive is your surveillance of this man Nasser?" he asked.

"Physical and electronic."

"But he uses encrypted communications?"

"Correct."

"So he could issue an attack order and we would be completely in the dark."

"Conceivably," said Gabriel carefully.

"And the British? They are unaware of his activities?"

"It appears so."

"Far be it from me to tell you how to do your job, Monsieur Allon, but if I had an agent who was about to go into Syria, I wouldn't want the man who sent her there to be arrested by the British."

Gabriel did not disagree with the minister, largely because he had been thinking the same thing for some time. And so late the following morning he journeyed across the channel to inform Graham Seymour, the chief of Britain's Secret Intelligence Service, or MI6, that the Office had been covertly watching a high-ranking ISIS operative living in the Bethnal Green section of East London. Seymour was predictably appalled, as was Amanda Wallace, the chief of MI5, who heard the same confession an hour later across the river at Thames House. For his penance, Gabriel was forced to make the British services nonvoting partners in his operations. All he needed now was the Americans, he thought, and the disaster would be complete.

The woman now known as Dr. Leila Hadawi was unaware

of the interservice warfare raging around her. She tended to her patients at the clinic, she idled away her spare time at the café across the street from her apartment, she ventured occasionally into the center of Paris to shop or stroll. She no longer viewed extremist material on the Internet because she had been instructed not to. Nor did she ever discuss her political beliefs with friends or colleagues. Mainly, she spoke of her summer holiday, which she planned to spend in Greece with a friend from her university days. A packet containing her airline tickets and hotel accommodations arrived three days before she was due to depart. A travel agent in London named Farouk Ghazi handled the booking. Dr. Hadawi paid for nothing.

With the arrival of the packet, Gabriel and the rest of the team went on a war footing. They made travel accommodations of their own—in point of fact, King Saul Boulevard handled the arrangements for them—and by early the next morning the first operatives were moving quietly toward their failsafe points. Only Eli Lavon remained behind at Seraincourt with Gabriel, a decision he later came to regret because his old friend was distraught with worry. He watched over Natalie as a parent watches over an ailing child, looking for signs of distress, changes in mood and demeanor. If she was frightened, she gave no sign of it, even on the last night, when Gabriel spirited her into Paul Rousseau's lair on the rue de Grenelle for a final briefing. When he gave her a last chance to change her mind, she only smiled. Then she composed a letter to her parents, to be delivered in the event of her death. Tellingly, Gabriel did not refuse to accept it. He placed it in a sealed envelope and placed the envelope in the breast pocket of his jacket. And there it would remain until the day she came out of Syria again.

ISIS supplied most of its European recruits with a detailed list of items to pack for their trip. Dr. Leila Hadawi was no ordinary recruit, however, and so she packed with deception in mind—summer dresses of the kind worn by promiscuous Europeans, revealing swimwear, erotic undergarments. In the morning she dressed piously, pinned her hijab carefully into place, and wheeled her suitcase through the quiet streets of the banlieue to the Aubervilliers RER station. The ride to Charles de Gaulle Airport was ten minutes in length. She glided through unusually heavy security and onto an Air France jet bound for Athens. On the other side of the aisle, dressed for the boardroom of a Fortune 500 company, was the small man with an elusive face. Smiling, Natalie peered out her window as France disappeared beneath her. She was not alone. Not yet.

As it happened, the day of Natalie's departure was a particularly violent one in the Middle East, even by the region's bloody standards. There were beheadings and burnings in Syria, a string of simultaneous suicide bombings in Baghdad, a Taliban raid in Kabul, a new round of fighting in Yemen, several stabbings in Jerusalem and Tel Aviv, and a gun-and-grenade attack on Western tourists at a beach hotel in Tunisia. So it was understandable that a relatively minor skirmish between Islamic militants and Jordanian police went largely unnoticed. The incident occurred at ten fifteen in the morning outside the village of Ramtha, located just a few yards from the Syrian border. The militants were four in number; all perished during the brief firefight. One of the militants was later identified as Nabil Awad, a twenty-four-year-old Jordanian citizen who resided in the Molenbeek district of Brussels. In a statement released on social media, ISIS confirmed that Awad was a member of its organization who had played a major support role in the attacks in Paris and Amsterdam. It declared him a holy martyr and swore to avenge his death by unleashing "rivers of blood." The final battle, it said, would come in a place called Dabiq.

32

SANTORINI, GREECE

Dr. Leila Hadawi shed her veil in a public toilet at Athens International Airport ten minutes after clearing passport control. She shed her pious clothing, too, changing into a pair of white Capri-length pants, a sleeveless blouse, and a pair of gold flat-soled sandals that displayed her newly polished nails. While waiting for her next flight to be called, she repaired to an airport bar and consumed her first alcohol, two glasses of tart Greek white wine, since her recruitment. Boarding her next flight, the three-fifteen to Santorini, she was oblivious to fear. Syria was a troubled place on a map. Isis was the wife of Osiris, friend of slaves and sinners, protector of the dead.

Leila Hadawi had never visited Santorini, and neither for that matter had the woman who wore the good doctor's identity. Her first airborne glimpse of the island, with its sharp demonic peaks rising from the rim of a flooded caldera, was a revelation. And at the airport, as she stepped onto the bleached tarmac, the heat of the sun on her bare arms was like a lover's first kiss. She rode in a taxi to Thera and then made her way on foot along a pedestrian walkway to the Panorama Boutique Hotel. Entering the lobby, she saw a tall, sunburned Englishman shouting hysterically at the concierge while a woman with sandstone-colored hair and childbearing hips looked on in embarrassment. Natalie smiled. She was not alone. Not yet.

A young Greek woman stood watch behind the reception desk. Natalie walked over and stated her name. "We have you in a double for ten nights," said the woman after tapping a few keys on her computer keyboard. "According to our records, one other person will be joining you, a Miss Shirazi."

"I'm afraid she's been delayed."

"Problems with her flight?"

"A family emergency."

"Not serious, I hope."

"Not too."

"Passport, please."

Natalie slid her worn French passport across the counter while Yossi Gavish and Rimona Stern, using different names, flying false flags, stormed from the lobby in a rage. Even Natalie welcomed the sudden quiet.

"Their room isn't to their liking," explained the clerk.

"I gathered that."

"Yours is lovely, I assure you."

Natalie accepted the key and, after declining an offer of help with her bag, made her way alone to her room. It had two single beds and a small balcony overlooking the rim of the caldera, where a pair of gleaming white cruise ships floated like toys upon a flat perfect sea. One last fling, she thought, courtesy of the richest terrorist organization in history.

She unzipped her bag and unpacked her belongings as though she were settling in for a long stay. By the time she had finished, the sun was a few degrees above the horizon, flooding her room with fiery orange light. After locking her passport in the room safe, she headed downstairs to the terrace bar, which was crowded with other guests, mainly from the British Isles. Seated among them, in decidedly better spirits, were Yossi and Rimona.

Natalie seized an empty table and from a harried waitress ordered a glass of white wine. Slowly, the bar filled with other guests, including a lanky man with bloodless skin and eyes like glacial ice. She hoped he might join her but instead he sat at the bar, where he could keep watch over the terrace and pretend to flirt with a pretty girl from Bristol. Natalie was able to hear his voice for the first time and was surprised by the distinct Russian accent. Given the demographics of modern Israel, she suspected the accent was authentic.

Presently, the sun slipped behind the peaks of Therasia. The skies darkened, the sea turned to black. Natalie glanced at the man who spoke with a Russian accent but at that moment he was otherwise occupied, so she turned away again and stared into the emptiness. Someone will come for you, they had said. But at that instant, in this place, the only person Natalie wanted was the man at the bar.

For the next three days Dr. Leila Hadawi behaved as an ordinary, if solitary, tourist. She breakfasted alone in the Panorama's dining room, she roasted her skin on the black-pebble beach at Perissa, she hiked the rim of the caldera, she toured the island's archaeological and geological sites, she took her wine at sunset on the terrace. It was a small island, so it was understandable she might encounter other guests of the hotel far from its premises. She passed an unpleasant morning on the beach within earshot of the balding Englishman and his Rubenesque wife, and while touring the buried city of Akrotiri she bumped into the pale Russian, who pointedly ignored her. The next day, her fourth on the island, she saw the pretty girl from Bristol while shopping in Thera. Dr. Hadawi was coming out of a swimwear boutique. The pretty girl was standing outside in the narrow street.

"You're staying at my hotel," she said.

"Yes, I think I am."

"I'm Miranda Ward."

Dr. Leila Hadawi extended her hand and introduced herself.

"What a lovely name. Won't you join me for a drink?"

"I was just going back to the hotel."

"I can't bear the scene at our bar anymore. Too many bloody English! Especially that bald bloke and his curvy wife. God, what bores! If they complain about the service again, I'll open a vein."

"Let's go somewhere else then."

"Yes, let's."

"Where?"

"Have you been to the Tango?"

"I don't think so."

"It's this way."

She seized Natalie's arm as though she feared losing her and led her through the shadows of the street. She was thin and blond and freckled and smelled of cherry candy and coconut. Her sandals slapped the paving stones like the palm of a hand connecting to an unfaithful cheek.

"You're French," she said at once, her tone accusatory.

"Yes."

"*French* French?"

"My family is from Palestine."

"I see. A shame, that."

"How so?"

"The whole refugee thing. And those Israelis! Horrible creatures."

Dr. Hadawi smiled but said nothing.

"You're here alone?" asked Miranda Ward.

"That wasn't the plan, but it seems to have worked out that way."

"What happened?"

"My friend had to cancel at the last minute."

"Mine, too. He dumped me for another woman."

"Your friend is an idiot."

"He was gorgeous, though. Here we are."

The Tango generally didn't come alive until late. They passed through the deserted cavelike interior and went onto the terrace. Natalie ordered a glass of Santorini white; Miranda Ward, a vodka martini. She took a decorous sip, made a face, and returned the glass to the table.

"You don't like it?" asked Natalie.

"Actually, I never touch alcohol."

"Really? Then why did you invite me for a drink?"

"I needed to have a word with you in private." She gazed at the darkening sea. "It's lovely here, but dreadfully boring. What do you say we take a little trip, just the two of us? It will be an adventure, I promise."

"Where?"

Smiling, Miranda Ward raised the martini to her lips. "I used to love this stuff. Now it tastes like bloody nail polish to me."

TOGETHER THEY RETURNED TO THE PANORAMA AND INFORMED the clerk that they planned to travel to Turkey. No, they did not require assistance with ferry bookings; others had done that for them. Yes, they would like to keep their rooms; their stay in Turkey would be brief. Dr. Hadawi then returned to her room alone and packed her bags. Afterward, she dispatched a text message to her "father," telling him of her plans. Her father pleaded with her to be careful. A moment later he sent a second message.

ARE YOU WELL?

Natalie hesitated and then typed her answer.

LONELY BUT FINE.

DO YOU NEED COMPANY?

Another hesitation, then three taps on the screen.

YES.

No reply was forthcoming. Natalie went down to the terrace, expecting to see Miranda Ward, but there was no sign of her. The tall pale Russian was in his usual place at the bar, where he had found fresh prey. Natalie sat with her back to him and consumed the last wine she would taste for many weeks. When she had finished it, the waitress brought a second glass.

"I didn't order that."

"It's from him." The waitress glanced toward the bar. Then she handed Natalie a slip of paper, folded in half. "This is from him, too. Looks like this is your unlucky night."

When the waitress was gone, Natalie read the note. Smiling, she drank the second glass of wine, slipped the note into her handbag, and left without acknowledging the loathsome creature at the bar. In her room she showered quickly, hung the DO NOT DISTURB sign on the latch, and switched out the lights. Then she sat alone in the darkness and waited for the knock at her door. It came at twenty minutes past ten. When she unchained the door, he entered with the silence of a night thief. "Please," she said, collapsing into his arms. "Tell him I want to go home. Tell him I can't do it. Tell him I'm frightened to death."

33

SANTORINI, GREECE

WHAT'S YOUR REAL NAME?" asked Natalie.

"The management of the Panorama Hotel is under the impression it's Michael Danilov."

"Is it?"

"Close enough." He was standing before the door that gave onto the balcony. A pale moon illuminated his pale face. "And you, Dr. Hadawi, have no business inviting a man like me to your room."

"I did nothing of the sort, Mr. Danilov. I said I needed company. They could have sent the woman instead."

"Consider yourself lucky. Empathy isn't her strong suit." His head swiveled a few degrees, his eyes found hers in the darkness. "We all get nervous before a big operation, especially those of us who operate in places where there's no embassy if things go sideways. But we trust in our mission and our planning and we go. It's what we do."

"I'm not like you."

"Actually, you're more like me than you realize."

"What kind of work do you do?"

"The kind we never talk about."

"You kill people?"

"I eliminate threats to our security. And on the night before a big operation, I'm always afraid that I'm the one who's going to get eliminated."

"But you go."

He averted his gaze and changed the subject. "So the comely Miss Ward is going to take you to the other side."

"You don't sound surprised."

"I'm not. Did she give you the route?"

"Santorini to Kos, Kos to Bodrum."

"Two young women on holiday, very professional." He turned away and addressed his next words to the night. "He must think very highly of you."

"Who?"

"Saladin."

From beyond the door came the sound of voices in the corridor, Englishmen, drunk. When the silence returned, he looked at the luminous dial of his wristwatch.

"The Kos ferry leaves early. You should get some sleep."

"Sleep? You can't be serious."

"It's important. You have a long day tomorrow."

He drew the blinds, casting the room into pitch darkness, and started toward the door.

"Please don't go," whispered Natalie. "I don't want to be alone."

After a moment he eased onto the bed, propped his back against the headboard, and stretched his long legs before him. Natalie placed a pillow next to his hip and laid her head upon it. He covered her with a thin blanket and brushed her hair from her face.

"Close your eyes."

"They are closed."

"No, they're not."

"You can see in the dark?"

"Very well, actually."

"At least take off your shoes."

"I prefer to sleep with them on."

"You're joking."

With his silence he said that he wasn't. She laughed quietly and once again asked his name. This time, he answered truthfully. His name, he said, was Mikhail Abramov.

"When did you come to Israel?"

"When I was a teenager."

"Why did your family leave Russia?"

"The same reason yours left France."

"Maybe we're not so different after all."

"I told you."

"You're not married, are you? I would hate to think—"

"I'm not married."

"Serious girlfriend?"

"Not anymore."

"What happened?"

"It's not so easy to have a relationship in this business. You'll find out soon enough."

"I have no intention of staying with the Office when this is over."

"Whatever you say."

He placed his hand at the center of her back and worked his fingers gently along her spine.

"Has anyone ever told you that you're very good at that?"

"Close your eyes."

She did. But not because she was suddenly drowsy; his touch had sent an electrical charge straight to her abdomen. She draped an arm across his thighs. The fingers went still and then resumed their exploration of her spine.

"Do you think we could have a drink when this is over," she asked, "or is that not allowed?"

"Close your eyes," was all he said.

The fingers moved a few inches lower down her back. She laid her palm flat against his thigh and squeezed gently.

"Don't." Then he said, "Not now."

She removed her hand and placed it beneath her chin while his fingers strolled the length of her spine. Sleep stalked her. She kept it at bay.

"Tell him I can't go through with it," she said drowsily. "Tell him I want to go home."

"Sleep, Leila," was all he said, and she slept. And in the morning, when she awoke, he was gone.

THE SUGAR-CUBE DWELLINGS OF THERA WERE STILL PINK WITH the sunrise when Natalie and Miranda Ward stepped into the quiet street at seven fifteen. They walked to the nearest taxi stand, each towing a rolling suitcase, and hired a car to take them down the coast to the ferry terminal in Athinios. The eastward crossing to Kos was four and a half hours; they passed it on the sun-drenched observation deck or in the ship's café. Forsaking her training, Natalie actively searched for watchers among the faces of her fellow passengers, hoping Mikhail might be among them. She recognized no one. It seemed she was alone now.

At Kos they had to wait an hour for the next ferry to the Turkish port of Bodrum. It was a shorter journey, less than an hour, with strict passport control at both ends. Miranda Ward gave Natalie a Belgian passport and instructed her to hide her French passport deep within her luggage. The photograph in the Belgian passport was of a thirtysomething woman of

Moroccan ethnicity. Dark hair, dark eyes, not ideal but close enough.

"Who is she?" asked Natalie.

"She's you," answered Miranda Ward.

The Greek border policeman in Kos seemed to think so, too, as did his Turkish counterpart in Bodrum. He stamped the passport after a brief inspection and with a frown invited Natalie to enter Turkey. Miranda followed a few seconds later, and together they made their way to the bedlam of the car park, where a line of taxis smoked in the scalding midafternoon sun. Somewhere a horn sounded, and an arm gestured from the front window of a dusty cream-colored Mercedes. Natalie and Miranda Ward hoisted their bags into the boot and climbed in, Miranda in front, Natalie in the backseat. She opened her handbag, withdrew her favorite green hijab, and pinned it piously into place. She was Leila from Sumayriyya. Leila who loved Ziad. Leila who wanted vengeance.

CONTRARY TO HER ASSUMPTIONS, NATALIE HAD NOT MADE the crossing from Santorini to Bodrum alone. Yaakov Rossman had accompanied her on the first leg of the journey; Oded, the second. In fact, he had snapped a photo of her climbing into the back of the Mercedes, which he transmitted to King Saul Boulevard and the safe house in Seraincourt.

Within minutes of leaving the terminal, the car was headed east on the D330 motorway, watched over by an Ofek 10 Israeli spy satellite. Shortly after two the next morning, the car arrived at the border town of Kilis, where the satellite's infrared camera observed two figures, both women, entering a small house. They did not remain there long—two hours and twelve minutes, to be precise. Afterward, they crossed the porous border on foot, accompanied by four men, and slipped into another vehicle in the Syrian town of A'zaz. It bore them southward to Raqqa, the unofficial capital of the caliphate. There, cloaked in black, they entered an apartment building near al-Rasheed Park.

By then, it was approaching four a.m. in Paris. Sleepless, Gabriel slipped behind the wheel of a rented car and drove to Charles de Gaulle Airport, where he boarded a flight to Washington. It was time to have a word with Langley, and thus make the disaster complete.

34

N STREET, GEORGETOWN

"Raqqa? Are you out of your fucking mind?"

It was uncharacteristic of Adrian Carter to use profanity, especially of the Anglo-Saxon copulatory variety. He was the son of an Episcopal minister from New England. He regarded foul language as the refuge of lesser minds, and those who used it in his presence, even powerful politicians, were rarely invited back to his office on the seventh floor of the CIA's Langley headquarters. Carter was the chief of the Agency's Directorate of Operations, the longest serving in the Agency's history. For a brief period after 9/11, Carter's kingdom had been known as the National Clandestine Service. But his new director, his sixth in just ten years, had decided to call it by its old name. That's what the Agency did when it made mistakes; it swapped nameplates and moved desks. Carter's fingerprints were on many of the Agency's greatest failures, from the failure to predict the collapse of the Soviet Union to the botched National Intelligence Estimate regarding Iraq's weapons of mass destruction, and yet somehow he endured. He was the man who knew too much. He was untouchable.

Like Paul Rousseau, he did not look the role of spymaster. With his tousled hair, outdated mustache, and underpowered voice, he might have been mistaken for a therapist who passed his days listening to confessions of affairs and inadequacies. His unthreatening appearance, like his flair for languages, had been a valuable asset, both in the field, where he had served with distinction in several postings, and at headquarters. Adversaries and allies alike tended to underestimate Carter, a blunder Gabriel had never made. He had worked closely with Carter on several high-profile operations—including the one in which Hannah Weinberg had played a small role—but America's nuclear deal with Iran had altered the dynamics of their relationship. Where once Langley and the Office had worked hand-in-glove to sabotage Iran's nuclear ambitions, the United States, under the deal's provisions, was now sworn to protect what remained of Tehran's atomic infrastructure. Gabriel planned to spy the daylights out of Iran to make sure it was not violating the agreement's provisions. And if he saw any evidence that the mullahs were still enriching uranium or building delivery systems, he would advise his prime minister to strike militarily. And under no circumstances would he consult first with his good friend and ally Adrian Carter.

"Is he one of theirs," asked Carter now, "or one of yours?"

"*She*," said Gabriel. "And she's one of ours."

Carter swore softly. "Maybe you really have lost your mind."

From a pump-action thermos flask atop a credenza, he drew himself a cup of coffee. They were in the sitting room of a redbrick Federal house on N Street in Georgetown, the crown jewel of the CIA's vast network of safe houses in metropolitan Washington. Gabriel had been a frequent guest at the house during the salad days of the Office's post–9/11 relationship with Langley. He had planned operations there, recruited agents there, and once, early in the American president's first term, he had agreed to hunt down and kill a terrorist who happened to carry an American passport in his pocket. Such had been the nature of the relationship. Gabriel had willingly served as a black branch office of the CIA, carrying out operations that, for political reasons, Carter could not undertake himself. But soon Gabriel would be the chief of his service, which meant that, for protocol's sake, he would outrank Carter. Secretly, Gabriel suspected that Carter wanted nothing more than to be a chief himself. His past, however, would not allow it. In the months after 9/11, he had locked terrorists in secret black sites, rendered them to countries that tortured, and subjected them to interrogation methods of the sort that Gabriel had just countenanced in a farmhouse in the north of France. In short, Carter had done the dirty work necessary to prevent another al-Qaeda spectacular on the American homeland. And for his punishment he would be forever forced to knock politely on the doors of lesser men.

"I didn't realize the Office had any interest in going after ISIS," he was saying.

"Someone has to do it, Adrian. It might as well be us."

Carter frowned at Gabriel over his shoulder. Pointedly, he neglected to offer Gabriel any of the coffee.

"The last time I talked to Uzi about Syria, he was more than content to let the crazies fight it out. The enemy of my enemy is my friend—isn't that the golden rule in your charming little neighborhood? As long as the regime, the Iranians, Hezbollah, and the Sunni jihadists were all killing each other, the Office was content to sit in the orchestra section and enjoy the show. So don't stand there and lecture me about sitting on my hands and doing nothing about ISIS."

"Uzi isn't going to be the chief for long."

"That's the rumor," agreed Carter. "In fact, we were expecting the transition to occur several months ago and were quite surprised when Uzi let us know he would be staying on for an indefinite period of time. For a while we wondered whether the reports regarding the unfortunate death of Uzi's chosen successor were true. Now we know the real reason why Uzi is still the chief. His successor has decided to try to penetrate ISIS's global terror network with a live agent, a noble goal but incredibly dangerous."

Gabriel made no reply.

"For the record," said Carter, "I was very relieved to learn that the reports of your demise were premature. Maybe someday you'll tell me why you did it."

"Maybe someday. And, yes," Gabriel added, "I'd love a coffee."

Carter squeezed out a second cup. "I would have thought you'd had your fill of Syria after your last operation. How much did that one cost you? Eight billion dollars rings a bell."

"Eight point two," answered Gabriel. "But who's counting?"

"Rather steep for a single human life."

"It was the best deal I ever made. And you would have made the same one in my position."

"But I wasn't *in* your position," said Carter, "because you didn't tell us about that operation, either."

"And you didn't tell us that the administration was secretly negotiating with the Iranians, did you, Adrian? After all the work we did together to delay the program, you blindsided us."

"I didn't blindside you, my president did. I don't make policy, I steal secrets and produce analysis. Actually," Carter added after a thoughtful pause, "I don't do much of that anymore. Mainly, I kill terrorists."

"Not enough of them."

"I take it you're referring to our policy regarding ISIS."

"If that's what you want to call it. First, you failed to see the gathering storm. And then you refused to pack a raincoat and an umbrella."

"We weren't the only ones to miss the rise of ISIS. The Office missed it, too."

"We were preoccupied with Iran at the time. You remember Iran, don't you, Adrian?"

There was a silence. "Let's not do this," said Carter after a moment. "We accomplished too much together to allow a politician to come between us."

It was an olive branch. With a nod, Gabriel accepted it.

"It's true," said Carter. "We were late to the ISIS party. It is also true that even after arriving at the party we avoided the buffet and the punch bowl. You see, after many years of attending such parties, we've grown weary of them. Our president has made it clear that the last one, the one in Iraq, was a crashing bore. Expensive, too, in American blood and treasure. And he has no interest in throwing another one in Syria, especially when it conflicts with the narrative."

"What narrative is that?"

"The one about how we overreacted to nine-eleven. The one about how terrorism is a nuisance, not a threat. The one about how we can absorb another strike like the one that brought our economy and transportation system to its knees, and be stronger as a result. And let us not forget," Carter added, "the president's unfortunate remarks about ISIS being the jayvee team. Presidents don't like being proved wrong."

"Neither do spies, for that matter."

"I don't make policy," Carter repeated. "I produce intelligence. And at the moment, that intelligence is painting a dire picture of what we're up against. The attacks in Paris and Amsterdam were but a preview of coming attractions. The movie is coming to theaters everywhere, including here in America."

"If I had to guess," said Gabriel, "it's going to be a block-buster."

"The president's closest advisers agree. They're concerned an attack on the homeland so late in his second term will leave an indelible stain on his legacy. They've told the Agency in no uncertain terms to keep the beast at bay, at least until the president gets on Marine One for the last time."

"Then I suggest you get busy, Adrian, because the beast is already at the gates."

"We're aware of that. But unfortunately the beast is largely immune to our dominance in cyberspace, and we have no human assets in ISIS to speak of." Carter paused, then added, "Until now."

Gabriel was silent.

"Why didn't you tell us you were trying to get inside?"

"Because it's our operation."

"You're working alone?"

"We have partners."

"Where?"

"Western Europe and the region."

"The French and the Jordanians?"

"The British crashed the party, too."

"They're a lot of fun, the British." Carter paused, then asked, "So why are you coming to us now?"

"Because I'd like you to avoid dropping a bomb or firing a missile into an apartment building near al-Rasheed Park in downtown Raqqa."

"It'll cost you."

"How much?"

Carter smiled. "It's good to have you back in town, Gabriel. It's been too long since your last visit."

35

N STREET, GEORGETOWN

IT WAS DEEP SUMMER IN Washington, that inhospitable time of year when most well-heeled residents of Georgetown flee their little village for second homes in Maine or Martha's Vineyard or the mountains of Sun Valley and Aspen. With good reason, thought Gabriel; the heat was equatorial. As always, he wondered why America's founders had willingly placed their capital in the middle of a malarial swamp. Jerusalem had chosen the Jews. The Americans had only themselves to blame.

"Why are we walking, Adrian? Why can't we sit in the air conditioning and drink mint juleps like everyone else?"

"I needed to stretch my legs. Besides, I would have thought you'd be accustomed to the heat. This is nothing compared to the Jezreel Valley."

"There's a reason why I love Cornwall. It isn't hot there."

"It will be soon. Langley estimates that because of global warming, the south of England will one day be among the world's largest producers of premium wine."

"If Langley believes that," said Gabriel, "then I'm sure it won't happen."

They had reached the edge of Georgetown University, educator of future American diplomats, retirement home of many grounded spies. After leaving the safe house, Gabriel had told Carter about his unlikely partnership with Paul Rousseau and Fareed Barakat, and about an ISIS project manager in London named Jalal Nasser, and about an ISIS talent spotter in Brussels named Nabil Awad. Now, as they walked along Thirty-seventh Street, clinging to the thin shadows for cool, Gabriel told Carter the rest of it—that he and his team had made Nabil Awad disappear from the streets of Molenbeek without a trace, that they had kept him alive in the minds of ISIS in the tradition of the great wartime deceivers, that they had used him to feed Jalal Nasser the name of a promising recruit, a woman from a banlieue north of Paris. ISIS had sent her on an all-expenses-paid trip to Santorini and then spirited her to Turkey and across the border into Syria. Gabriel did not mention the woman's name—not her cover name and certainly not her real name—and Carter had the professional good manners not to ask.

"She's Jewish, this girl of yours?"

"Not so you'd know."

"God help you, Gabriel."

"He usually does."

Carter smiled. "I don't suppose this girl of yours referred to herself as Umm Ziad online, did she?"

Gabriel was silent.

"I'll take that as a yes."

"How do you know?"

"Turbulence," said Carter.

Gabriel knew the code name. Turbulence was an ultra-secret NSA computer surveillance program that constantly swept the Internet for militant Web sites and jihadist chat rooms.

"NSA identified her as a potential extremist not long after she popped up on the Web," Carter explained. "They tried to plant surveillance software inside her computer, but it proved resistant to all forms of assault. They couldn't even figure out where she was operating. Now we know why." With a sidelong glance at Gabriel, he asked, "Who's Ziad, by the way?"

"The dead boyfriend."

"She's a black widow, your girl?"

Gabriel nodded.

"Nice touch."

They rounded the corner into P Street and walked beside a high stone wall bordering a cloistered convent. The redbrick pavements were empty except for Carter's security detail. Two bodyguards walked before them, two behind.

"You'll be happy to know," said Carter, "that your new friend Fareed Barakat didn't breathe a word of this to me when we spoke last. He never mentioned anything about Saladin, either." He paused, then added, "I guess ten million dollars in a Swiss bank account only buys so much loyalty these days."

"Does he exist?"

"Saladin? Without question, or someone like him. And there's no way he's Syrian."

"Is he one of us?"

"A professional intelligence officer?"

"Yes."

"We think he might be ex-Iraqi Mukhabarat."

"So did Nabil Awad."

"May he rest in peace." Carter frowned. "Is he really dead, or was that shootout a ruse, too?"

With a shrug, Gabriel indicated it was the former.

"I'm glad someone still knows how to play rough. If I so

much as say an unkind word to a terrorist, I'll be indicted. Droning terrorists and their children is fine, though."

"You know, Adrian, sometimes a live terrorist is better than a dead one. A live terrorist can tell you things, such as where and when the next attack will occur."

"My president disagrees. He believes detaining terrorists only breeds more of them."

"Success breeds terrorists, Adrian. And nothing succeeds quite like an attack on the American homeland."

"Which brings us back to our original point," said Carter, wiping a trickle of sweat from the side of his neck. "I will prevail upon the Pentagon to take care with their air campaign in Syria. In exchange, you will share anything your girl picks up during her vacation in the caliphate."

"Agreed," said Gabriel.

"I assume the French military is on board?"

"And the British," said Gabriel.

"I'm not sure how I feel being the last to know about this."

"Welcome to the post-American world."

Carter said nothing.

"No air strikes on that building," said Gabriel quietly. "And lay off the training camps until she comes out again."

"When do you expect her?"

"The end of August, unless Saladin has other plans."

"We should be so lucky."

They had arrived back at the N Street safe house. Carter stopped at the foot of the curved front steps.

"How are the children?" he asked suddenly.

"I'm not sure."

"Don't blow it with them. You're too old to have any more."

Gabriel smiled.

"You know," said Carter, "for about twelve hours, I actually thought you were dead. That was a profoundly lousy thing to do."

"I had no other choice."

"I'm sure," said Carter. "But next time, don't keep me in the dark. I'm not the enemy. I'm here to help."

36

RAQQA, SYRIA

FROM THE OUTSET SHE MADE it clear to Jalal Nasser that she could remain in Syria for a limited period of time. She had to be back at the clinic no later than the thirtieth of August, the end of her summer holiday. If she were delayed, her colleagues and family would assume the worst. After all, she was politically active, she had left footprints on the Internet, she had lost her one and only love to the jihad. Undoubtedly, someone would go to the police, the police would go to the DGSI, and the DGSI would add her name to the long list of European Muslims who had joined the ranks of ISIS. There would be stories in the press, stories about an educated woman, a healer, who had been seduced by ISIS's cult of death. If that were to happen, she would have no choice but to remain in Syria, which was not her wish, at least not yet. First, she wanted to avenge Ziad's death by striking a blow against the West. Then, inshallah, she would make her way back to Syria, marry a fighter, and produce many children for the caliphate.

Jalal Nasser had said he wanted the same thing. Therefore, it came as a surprise to Natalie when, for three days and nights after her arrival in Raqqa, no one came for her. Miranda Ward, her travel companion, remained with her at the apartment near al-Rasheed Park to serve as her guide and minder. It was not Miranda's first visit to Raqqa. She was a Sherpa on the secret ratline that funneled British Muslims from East London and the Midlands to Syria and the Islamic caliphate. She was the decoy, the deception, the pretty clean face. She had escorted both men and women, posing as lovers and friends. She was, she joked, "bi-jihadi."

It was not really an apartment; it was a small bare room with a sink bolted to the wall and a few blankets on a bare floor. There was a single window, through which dust particles flowed freely, as if by osmosis. The blankets smelled of desert animals, of camels and goats. Sometimes a thread of water leaked from the sink tap, but usually there was none. They received water from an ISIS tanker truck in the street, and when the truck didn't come they carried water from the Euphrates. In Raqqa, time had receded. It was the seventh century, spiritually and materially.

There was no electricity—a few minutes a day, if that—and no gas for cooking. Not that there was much to eat. In a land where bread was a staple, bread was in short supply. Each day began with a quest to find a precious loaf or two. The ISIS dinar was the official currency of the caliphate, but in the markets most transactions were conducted in the old Syrian pound or in dollars. Even ISIS traded in the currency of its enemy. At Jalal Nasser's suggestion, Natalie had brought several hundred dollars with her from France. The money opened many doors, behind which were storerooms filled with rice, beans, olives, and even a bit of meat. For those willing to risk the wrath of the dreaded *husbah*, the sharia police, there were black-market cigarettes and liquor to be had, too. The punishment for smoking or drinking was severe—the lash, the cross, the chopping block. Natalie once saw a *husbah* whipping a man because the man had cursed. Cursing was haram.

To enter the streets of Raqqa was to enter a world gone mad. The traffic signals didn't work, not without electricity, so ISIS traffic police controlled the intersections. They carried pistols but no whistles because whistles were haram. Photographs of models in shop windows had been retouched to adhere to ISIS's strict decency codes. The faces were blacked out because it was haram to depict humans or animals, God's creations, and hang them on a wall. The statue of two peasants atop Raqqa's famous clock tower had been retouched, too—the heads had been removed. Na'eem Square, once beloved by Raqqa's children, was now filled with severed heads, not stone, but human. They stared mournfully down from the spikes of an iron fence, Syrian soldiers, Kurdish fighters, traitors, saboteurs, former hostages. The Syrian air force bombed the park frequently in retaliation. Such was life in the Islamic caliphate, bombs falling upon severed heads, in a park where children once played.

It was a black world, black in spirit, black in color. Black flags flew from every building and lamppost, men in black ninja suits paraded through the streets, women in black abayas moved like black ghosts through the markets. Natalie had been given her abaya shortly after she crossed the Turkish border. It was a heavy, scratchy garment that fit her like a sheet thrown over a piece of furniture. Beneath it she wore only black, for all other colors, even brown, were haram and could provoke a thrashing by the *husbah*. The facial veil rendered her features all but indistinguishable, and through it Natalie viewed a blurry world of murky charcoal gray. In the midday heat she felt as though she were trapped inside her own private oven, roasting slowly, an ISIS delicacy. There was danger in the abaya, the danger that she might believe herself to be invisible. She did not succumb to it. She knew they were watching her always.

ISIS was not alone in altering the cityscape of Raqqa. The Syrian air force and their Russian accomplices bombed by day, the Americans and their coalition partners by night. There was damage everywhere: shattered apartment buildings, burned-out cars and trucks, blackened tanks and armored personnel carriers. ISIS had responded to the air campaign by concealing its fighters and weaponry amid the civilian population. The ground floor of Natalie's building was filled with bullets, artillery shells, rocket-propelled grenades, and guns of every sort. Bearded black-clad ISIS fighters used the second and third floors as a barracks. A few were from Syria, but most were Saudis, Egyptians, Tunisians, or wild-eyed Islamic warriors from the Caucasus who were pleased to be fighting Russians again. There were many Europeans, including three Frenchmen. They were aware of Natalie's presence but made no attempt to communicate with her. She was off-limits. She was Saladin's girl.

The Syrians and the Russians did not hesitate to bomb civilian targets, but the Americans were more discriminating. Everyone agreed they were bombing less these days. No one knew why, but everyone had an opinion, especially the foreign fighters, who boasted that decadent, infidel America was losing the stomach for the fight. None suspected that the reason for the lull in American air activity was living among them, in a room with a single window looking onto al-Rasheed Park, with blankets that smelled of camel and goat.

Health care in Syria had been deplorable even before the uprising, and now, in the chaos of civil war, it was almost nonexistent. Raqqa's National Hospital was a ruin, emptied of medicine and supplies, filled with wounded ISIS fighters. The rest of the city's unfortunate residents received care, such as it was, from small clinics scattered amid the neighborhoods. Natalie happened upon one while searching for bread on her second day in Raqqa, and found it filled with civilian casualties from a Russian air strike, many dead, several others soon to be. There were no physicians present, only ambulance drivers and ISIS "nurses" who had been given only rudimentary training. Natalie announced that she was a doctor and immediately began treating the wounded with whatever supplies she could find. She did so while still clad in her clumsy, unsterilized abaya because a snarling *husbah* threatened to beat her if she removed it. That night, when she finally returned to the apartment, she washed the blood from the abaya in water from the Euphrates. In Raqqa, time had receded.

They did not wear their abayas in the apartment, only their hijabs. Miranda's flattered her, framing her delicate Celtic features, setting off her sea-green eyes. While preparing supper that evening she told Natalie of her conversion to Islam. Her childhood home had been a distinctly unhappy place—an alcoholic mother, an unemployed, sexually abusive lout of a father. At thirteen she began to drink heavily and use drugs. She became pregnant twice and aborted both. "I was a mess," she said. "I was going nowhere in flames."

Then one day, stoned, drunk, she found herself standing outside an Islamic bookstore in central Bristol. A Muslim man saw her staring through the shop window and invited her inside. She refused but accepted his offer of a free book.

"I was tempted to drop it in the nearest rubbish bin. I'm glad I didn't. It changed my life."

She stopped drinking and using drugs and having sex with boys she scarcely knew. Then she converted to Islam, took the veil, and began to pray five times a day. Her parents were lapsed Church of England, unbelievers, but they did not want a Muslim for a daughter. Ejected from her home with nothing but a suitcase and a hundred pounds in cash, she made her way to East London, where she was taken in by a group of Muslims in the Tower Hamlets section of London. There she met a Jordanian named Jalal Nasser who taught her about the beauty of jihad and martyrdom. She joined ISIS, traveled secretly to Syria for training, and returned undetected to Britain. She was in awe of Jalal and perhaps a little in love with him. "If he ever takes wives," she said, "I hope I will be one of them. At the moment, he's too busy for a bride. He's married to Saladin."

Natalie was familiar with the name, but Dr. Hadawi was not. She replied accordingly.

"Who?" she asked carefully.

"Saladin. He's the leader of the network."

"You've met him?"

"Saladin?" She smiled dreamily and shook her head. "I'm far too low on the food chain. Only the senior leaders know who he really is. But who knows? Maybe you'll get to meet him."

"Why would you say something like that?"

"Because they have big plans for you."

"Did Jalal tell you that?"

"He didn't have to."

But Natalie was not convinced. In fact, it seemed the opposite was true, that she had been forgotten. That night, and the next, she lay awake on her blanket, gazing at the square patch of sky framed by her single window. The city was entirely dark at night, the stars were incandescent. She imagined an Ofek 10 spy satellite peering down at her, following her as she moved through the streets of the black city.

Finally, shortly before dawn on the third night, not long after an American air strike in the north, she heard footfalls in the corridor outside her room. Four pile-driver blows shook the door; then it blew open, as if by the force of a car bomb. Natalie instantly covered herself with the abaya before a torch illuminated her face. They took only her, leaving Miranda behind. Outside in the street waited a dented and dusty SUV. They forced her into the backseat, these bearded, black-clad, wild-eyed warriors of Islam, and the SUV shot forward. She peered through the tinted window, through the tinted veil of her abaya, at the madness beyond—at the severed heads on iron skewers, at the bodies writhing on crosses, at the photos of faceless women in shop windows. I am Dr. Leila Hadawi, she told herself. I am Leila who loves Ziad, Leila from Sumayriyya. And I am about to die.

37

EASTERN SYRIA

THEY DROVE EASTWARD INTO THE rising sun, along a ruler-straight road black with oil. The traffic was light—a truck ferrying cargo from Anbar Province in Iraq, a peasant bringing produce to market in Raqqa, a flatbed spilling over with blood-drunk ninjas after a night of fighting in the north. The morning rush in the caliphate, thought Natalie. Occasionally, they came upon a burnt-out tank or troop carrier. In the empty landscape the wreckage looked like the corpses of insects fried by a child's magnifying glass. One Japanese-made pickup truck still burned as they passed, and in the back a charred fighter still clung to his .50-caliber machine gun, which was aimed skyward. "Allahu Akbar," murmured the driver of the SUV, and beneath her black abaya Natalie responded, "Allahu Akbar."

She had no guide other than the sun and the SUV's speedometer and dashboard clock. The sun told her they had maintained a steady easterly heading after leaving Raqqa. The speedometer and clock told her they had been barreling along at nearly ninety miles per hour for seventy-five minutes. Raqqa was approximately a hundred miles from the Iraqi border—the old border, she quickly reminded herself. There was no border anymore; the lines drawn on a map by infidel diplomats in London and Paris had been erased. Even the old Syrian road signs had been removed. "Allahu Akbar," said Natalie's driver as they passed another flaming wreck. And Natalie, smothering beneath her abaya, intoned, "Allahu Akbar."

They plunged eastward for another twenty minutes or so, the terrain growing drier and more desolate with each passing mile. It was still early—seven twenty, according to the clock—but already Natalie's window blazed to the touch. Finally, they came to a small village of bleached stone houses. The main street was wide enough for traffic, but behind it lay a labyrinth of passages through which a few villagers—veiled women, men in robes and keffiyehs, barefoot children— moved torpidly in the heat. There was a market in the main street and a small café where a few dried-out older men sat listening to a recorded sermon by Abu Bakr al-Baghdadi, the caliph himself. Natalie searched the street for evidence of the village's name, but found none. She feared she had crossed the invisible border into Iraq.

All at once the SUV turned through an archway and drew to a stop in the court of a large house. There were date palms in the court; in their shade reclined a half-dozen ISIS fighters. One, a young man of perhaps twenty-five whose reddish beard was a work in progress, opened Natalie's door and led her inside. It was cool in the house, and from somewhere came the soft reassuring chatter of women. In a room furnished with only carpets and pillows, the young man with the thin reddish beard invited Natalie to sit. He quickly withdrew and a veiled woman appeared with a glass of tea. Then the veiled woman took her leave, too, and Natalie had the room to herself.

She moved aside her veil and raised the glass tentatively to her lips. The sugary tea entered her bloodstream like drug from a needle. She drank it slowly, careful not to scald her mouth, and watched a shadow creeping toward her across the carpet. When the shadow reached her ankle, the woman reappeared to reclaim the glass. Then, a moment later, the room vibrated with the arrival of another vehicle in the court. Four doors opened and closed in near unison. Four men entered the house.

IT WAS INSTANTLY APPARENT WHICH OF THE FOUR WAS THE leader. He was a few years older than the others, more deliberative in movement, calmer in demeanor. The three younger men all carried large automatic combat rifles of a model Natalie could not identify, but the leader had only a pistol, which he wore holstered on his hip. He was attired in the manner of Abu Musab al-Zarqawi—a black jumpsuit, white trainers, a black keffiyeh tied tightly to his large head. His beard was unkempt, streaked with gray, and damp with sweat. His eyes were brown and oddly gentle, like the eyes of Bin Laden. His right hand was intact, but his left had only its thumb and forefinger, evidence of bomb making. For several minutes he stared down at the lump of black seated motionless on the carpet. When finally he addressed her, he did so in Arabic, with an Iraqi accent.

"Remove your veil."

Natalie did not stir. It was haram in the Islamic State for a woman to reveal her face to a male who was not a relative, even if the male was an important Iraqi from the network of Saladin.

"It's all right," he said at last. "It is necessary."

Slowly, carefully, Natalie raised her veil. She stared downward toward the carpet.

"Look at me," he commanded, and Natalie obediently raised her eyes. He regarded her for a long moment before taking her chin between the thumb and forefinger of his ruined hand and turning her face side to side to examine it in profile. His gaze was critical, as though he were examining the flesh of a horse.

"They tell me you are a Palestinian."

She nodded her assent.

"You look like a Jew, but I must admit all Palestinians look like Jews to me." He spoke these words with a desert Arab's disdain for those who lived in cities, marshes, and seacoasts. He was still holding her chin. "You've been to Palestine?"

"No, never."

"But you have a French passport. You could have gone very easily."

"It would have been too painful to see the land of my ancestors ruled by Zionists."

Her answer appeared to please him. With a nod he instructed her to veil her face. She was grateful for the garment's shelter, for it gave her a moment to compose herself. Hidden beneath her black tent, her face obscured, she prepared herself for the interrogation she knew lay ahead. The ease with which Leila's story flowed from her subconscious to her conscious surprised her. The intense training had succeeded. It was as if she were recalling events that had actually occurred. Natalie Mizrahi was lost to her; she was dead and buried. It was Leila Hadawi who had been brought to this village in the middle of the desert, and Leila Hadawi who confidently awaited the sternest test of her life.

Presently, the woman reappeared with tea for everyone. The Iraqi sat down opposite Natalie, and the three others sat behind him with their weapons lying across their thighs. An image flashed in Natalie's memory, a condemned man in an orange jumpsuit, a Westerner, pale as death, seated with his hands bound before a choir-like formation of faceless black-clad executioners. Beneath the shelter of her abaya, she deleted the dreadful picture from her thoughts. She realized then that she was sweating. It was trickling down the length of her spine and dripping between her breasts. She was allowed to sweat, she told herself. She was a pampered Parisian, unused to the heat of the desert, and the room was no longer cool. The house was warming beneath the assault of the late-morning sun.

"You are a doctor," the Iraqi said at last, holding his glass of tea between his thumb and forefinger, as a moment earlier he had held Natalie's face. Yes, she said, laboring with her own glass of tea beneath her veil, she was a doctor, trained at the Université Paris-Sud, employed at the Clinique Jacques Chirac in the Paris banlieue of Aubervilliers. She then elaborated that Aubervilliers was a largely Muslim suburb and that most of her patients were Arabs from North Africa.

"Yes, I know," said the Iraqi impatiently, making it abundantly clear he was familiar with her biography. "I'm told you spent a few hours caring for patients in a clinic in Raqqa yesterday."

"It was the day before," she corrected him. And obviously, she thought, gazing at the Iraqi through the black gauze of her veil, you and your friends were watching.

"You should have come here a long time ago," he continued. "We have a great need for doctors in the caliphate."

"My work is in Paris."

"And now you are here," he pointed out.

"I'm here," she said carefully, "because I was asked to come."

"By Jalal."

She made no response. The Iraqi sipped his tea thoughtfully.

"Jalal is very good at sending me enthusiastic Europeans, but I am the one who decides whether they are worthy of entering our camps." He made this sound like a threat, which Natalie supposed was his intention. "Do you wish to fight for the Islamic State?"

"Yes."

"Why not fight for Palestine?"

"I am."

"How?"

"By fighting for the Islamic State."

His eyes warmed. "Zarqawi always said the road to Palestine runs through Amman. First, we will take the rest of Iraq and Syria. Then Jordan. And then, inshallah, Jerusalem."

"Like Saladin," she replied. And not for the first time she wondered whether the man known as Saladin sat before her now.

"You've heard this name?" he asked. "Saladin?"

She nodded. The Iraqi looked over his shoulder and mumbled something to one of the three men seated behind him. The man handed him a sheaf of papers held together by a paper clip. Natalie reckoned it was her ISIS personnel file, a thought that almost made her smile beneath her abaya. The Iraqi leafed through the pages with an air of bureaucratic distraction. Natalie wondered what sort of work he had done before the American invasion overturned virtually every aspect of Iraqi life. Had he been a clerk in a ministry? Had he been a schoolteacher or a banker? Had he sold vegetables in a market? No, she thought, he was no poor trader. He was a former officer in the Iraqi army. Or perhaps, she thought as sweat dripped down her back, he had worked for Saddam's dreaded secret police.

"You are unmarried," he declared suddenly.

"Yes," answered Natalie truthfully.

"You were engaged once?"

"Almost."

"To Ziad al-Masri? A brother who died in Jordanian custody?"

She nodded slowly.

"Where did you meet him?"

"At Paris-Sud."

"And what was he studying?"

"Electronics."

"Yes, I know." He laid the pages of her file on the carpet. "We have many supporters in Jordan. Many of our brothers used to be Jordanian citizens. And none of them," he said, "have ever heard of anyone named Ziad al-Masri."

"Ziad was never politically active in Jordan," she answered with far more calm than she might have thought possible. "He became radicalized only after he moved to Europe."

"He was a member of Hizb ut-Tahrir?"

"Not formally."

"That would explain why none of our brothers from Hizb ut-Tahrir have heard of him, either." He regarded Natalie calmly while another waterfall of sweat sluiced down her back. "You're not drinking your tea," he pointed out.

"That's because you're making me nervous."

"That was my intention." His remark provoked restrained laughter among the three men seated behind him. He waited for it to subside before continuing. "For a long time the Americans and their friends in Europe did not take us seriously. They belittled us, called us silly names. But now they realize we are a threat to them, and they are trying very hard to penetrate us. The British are the worst. Every time they catch a British Muslim trying to travel to the caliphate, they try to turn him into a spy. We always find them very quickly. Some-times we play them back against the British. And sometimes," he said with a shrug, "we just kill them."

He allowed a silence to hang heavily over the sweltering room. It was Natalie who broke it.

"I didn't ask to join you," she said. "You asked me."

"No, Jalal asked you to come to Syria, not me. But I am the one who will determine whether you will stay." He gathered up the pages of the file. "I would like to hear your story from the beginning, Leila. I find that most helpful."

"I was born—"

"No," he said, cutting her off. "I said the beginning."

Confused, she said nothing. The Iraqi was looking down at her file again.

"It says here that your family was from a place called Sumayriyya."

"My father's family," she said.

"Where is it?"

"It *was* in the Western Galilee. It's not there anymore."

"Tell me about it," he said. "Tell me everything."

Beneath her veil, Natalie closed her eyes. She saw herself walking through a field of thorn bush and toppled stones, next to a man of medium height whose face and name she could no longer recall. He spoke to her now, as if from the bottom of a well, and his words became hers. They grew bananas and melons in Sumayriyya, the sweetest melons in all of Pales-tine. They irrigated their fields with water from an ancient aqueduct and buried their dead in a cemetery not far from the mosque. Sumayriyya was paradise on earth, Sumayriyya was an Eden. And then, on a night in May 1948, the Jews came up the coast road in a convoy with their headlamps blazing, and Sumayriyya ceased to exist.

IN THE OP CENTER OF KING SAUL BOULEVARD THERE IS A chair reserved for the chief. No one else is allowed to sit in it. No one else dares to even touch it. Throughout that long tense day it groaned and buckled beneath the bulk of Uzi Navot. Gabriel had remained constantly at his side, sometimes in a deputy's chair, sometimes nervously on his feet, a hand pressed to his chin, his head tilted slightly to one side.

Both men, like everyone else in the Op Center, had eyes only for the main video display screen. On it was an overhead satellite image of a large house in a village near the Syrian border. In the courtyard of the house, several men lounged in the shade of date palms. There were two other SUVs in the court. One had ferried a woman from central Raqqa; the other had brought four men from the Sunni Triangle of Iraq. Gabriel had sent along the coordinates of the house to Adrian Carter at CIA Headquarters, and Carter had dispatched a drone from a secret base in Turkey. Occasionally, the aircraft passed through the Ofek 10's image, circling lazily twelve thousand feet above the target, piloted by a kid in a trailer in another desert on the other side of the world.

Adrian Carter had brought additional resources to bear on the target as well. Specifically, he had instructed the NSA to gather as much cellular data from the house as possible. The NSA had identified no fewer than twelve phones present, one of which had been previously linked to a suspected senior ISIS commander named Abu Ahmed al-Tikriti, a former colonel from Iraq's military intelligence service. Gabriel suspected it was al-Tikriti who was questioning his agent. He felt sick to his stomach but took small comfort in the fact that he had prepared her well. Even so, he would have gladly taken her place. Perhaps, thought Gabriel, looking at Uzi Navot seated calmly in his designated chair, he was not cut out for the burden of command after all.

The day limped slowly past. The two SUVs remained in the courtyard, the jihadis sat in the shade of the date palms. Then the shade evaporated with the setting of the sun, and fires flared in the darkness. The Ofek 10 switched over to infrared mode. At nine that evening it detected several human heat signatures emerging from the house. Four of the signatures entered one of the SUVs. A fifth, a woman, entered the other. The drone tracked one of the vehicles to Mosul; the Ofek 10 watched the second as it made the return trip to Raqqa. There it stopped outside an apartment building near al-Rasheed Park, and a single heat signature, a woman, emerged from the back. She entered the apartment house shortly before midnight and disappeared from sight.

In a room on the second floor of the building, a thin, wizened Saudi cleric was lecturing several dozen spellbound fighters on the role they would play, inshallah, in bringing about the end of days. The time was drawing near, he declared, nearer than they might think. Drained by the arduous interrogation, blinded by exhaustion and her abaya, Natalie could think of no reason to doubt the old preacher's prophecy.

The stairwell, as usual, was in pitch darkness. She counted to herself softly in Arabic as she climbed, fourteen steps per flight, two flights per floor. Her room was on the sixth, twelve paces from the stairwell. Entering, she closed the door soundlessly behind her. A shaft of moonlight stretched from the single window to the female form that lay curled on the floor. Silently, Natalie removed her abaya and made a bed for herself. But as she pillowed her head, the female form on the other side of the room stirred and sat up. "Miranda?" asked Natalie, but there was no reply other than the striking of a match. Its flame touched the wick of an olive oil lamp. Warm light filled the room.

Natalie sat up, too, expecting to see a set of delicate Celtic features. Instead, she found herself staring into a pair of wide hypnotic eyes of hazel and copper. "Who are you?" she asked in Arabic, but her new roommate replied in French. "My name is Safia Bourihane," she said, extending her hand. "Welcome to the caliphate."

38

PALMYRA, SYRIA

THE CAMP WAS JUST OUTSIDE the ancient city of Palmyra, not far from the notorious Tadmor desert prison where the ruler's father had cast those who dared to oppose him. Before the civil war it was an outpost of the Syrian military in the Homs Governorate, but in the spring of 2015, ISIS had captured it largely intact, with scarcely a fight. The group had looted and destroyed many of Palmyra's astonishing ruins, as well as the prison, but the camp it had preserved. Surrounded by a twelve-foot wall topped with spirals of concertina wire, there were barracks for five hundred, a mess hall, recreation and meeting rooms, a gymnasium, and a diesel generator that provided air conditioning in the heat of the day and light at night. All the old Syrian military signs had been removed, and the black flag of ISIS billowed and snapped above the central courtyard. The installation's old name was never spoken. Graduates referred to it as Camp Saladin.

Natalie traveled there by SUV the next day, in the company of Safia Bourihane. Four months had passed since the attack on the Weinberg Center in Paris; in that time Safia had become a jihadist icon. Poems celebrated her, streets and squares bore her name, young girls sought to emulate her feats. In a world where death was celebrated, ISIS expended considerable effort to keep Safia alive. She moved constantly between a chain of safe houses in Syria and Iraq, always under armed escort. During her one and only appearance in an ISIS propaganda video, her face had been veiled. She did not use the telephone, she never touched a computer. Natalie took comfort in the fact she had been allowed into Safia's presence. It suggested she had come through her interrogation with no taint of suspicion. She was one of them now.

Safia had clearly grown accustomed to her exalted status. In France she had been a second-class citizen with limited career prospects, but in the upside-down world of the caliphate she was a celebrity. She was quite obviously wary of Natalie, for Natalie represented a potential threat to her standing. For her part, Natalie was content to play the role of terrorist upstart. Safia Bourihane was the charcoal sketch upon which Dr. Leila Hadawi was based. Leila Hadawi admired Safia, but Natalie Mizrahi felt sick being in her presence and, given the chance, would have gladly pumped a hypodermic full of poison into her veins. Inshallah, she thought as the SUV sped across the Syrian desert.

Safia's Arabic was rudimentary at best. Therefore, they passed the journey conversing quietly in French, each beneath the private tent of her abaya. They spoke of their upbringings and found they had little in common; as a child of educated Palestinians, Leila Hadawi had lived far differently than the child of Algerian laborers from the banlieues. Islam was their only bridge, but Safia had almost no understanding of the tenets of jihad or even the basics of Islamic practice. She admitted that she missed the taste of French wine. Mainly, she was curious about how she was remembered in the country she had attacked—not the France of the city centers and country villages, but the Arab France of the banlieues. Natalie told her, truthfully, that she was spoken of fondly in the *cités* of Aubervilliers. This pleased Safia. One day, she said, she hoped to return.

"To France?" asked Natalie incredulously.

"Yes, of course."

"You're the most wanted woman in the country. It isn't possible."

"That's because France is still ruled by the French, but Saladin says it will soon be part of the caliphate."

"You've met him?"

"Saladin? Yes, I've met him."

"Where?" asked Natalie casually.

"I'm not sure. They blindfolded me during the trip."

"How long ago was it?"

"It was a few weeks after my operation. He wanted to personally congratulate me."

"They say he's Iraqi."

"I'm not sure. My Arabic isn't good enough to tell the difference between a Syrian and an Iraqi."

"What's he like?"

"Very large, powerful, wonderful eyes. He is everything you would expect. Inshallah, you'll get to meet him someday."

Safia's arrival at the camp was an occasion for celebratory gunfire and cries of "Allahu Akbar!" Natalie, the new recruit, was an afterthought. She was assigned a private room—the former quarters of a junior Syrian officer—and that evening, after prayers, she took her first meal in the communal dining hall. The women ate apart from the men, behind a black curtain. The food was deplorable but plentiful: rice, bread, roasted fowl of some sort, a gray-brown stew of cartilaginous meat. Despite their segregation, the women were required to wear their abayas during mealtime, which made eating a challenge. Natalie ate ravenously of the bread and rice, but her training as a physician informed her decision to avoid the meat. The woman to her left was a silent Saudi called Bushra. To her right was Selma, a loquacious Tunisian. Selma had come to the caliphate for a husband, but her husband had been killed fighting the Kurds and now she wanted vengeance. It was her wish to be a suicide bomber. She was nineteen years old.

After dinner there was a program. A cleric preached, a fighter read a poem of his own composition. Afterward, Safia was "interviewed" on stage by a clever British Muslim who worked in ISIS's promotion and marketing department. That night the desert thundered with coalition air strikes. Alone in her room, Natalie prayed for deliverance.

Her terrorist education commenced after breakfast the next morning when she was driven into the desert for weapons training—assault rifles, pistols, rocket launchers, grenades. She returned to the desert each and every morning, even after her instructors declared her proficient. They were no wild-eyed jihadis, the instructors; they were exclusively Iraqi, all former soldiers and battle-hardened veterans of the Sunni insurgency. They had fought the Americans largely to a draw in Iraq and wanted nothing more than to fight them again, on the plains of northern Syria, in a place called Dabiq. The Americans and their allies—the armies of Rome, in the lexicon of ISIS—had to be poked and prodded and stirred into a rage. The men from Iraq had a plan to do just that, and the students at the camp were their stick.

During the heat of midday, Natalie repaired to the air-conditioned rooms of the camp for lessons in bomb assembly and secure communication. She also had to endure long lectures on the pleasures of the afterlife, lest she be chosen for a suicide mission. Time and again her Iraqi instructors asked whether she was willing to die for the caliphate, and without hesitation Natalie said she was. Soon, she was made to wear a heavy suicide vest during her weapons training, and she was taught how to arm the device and detonate it using a trigger concealed in her palm. The first time the instructor ordered her to press the detonator, Natalie's thumb hovered numb and frozen above the switch. "Yalla," he beseeched her. "It's not going to really explode." Natalie closed her eyes and squeezed the detonator. "Boom," whispered the instructor. "And now you are on your way to paradise."

With the camp director's permission, Natalie began seeing patients in the base's old infirmary. At first, the other students were reluctant to call upon her for fear of being regarded as soft by the Iraqi instructors. But soon she was receiving a steady stream of patients during her "office hours," which fell between the end of her bomb-making class and afternoon prayers. Their ailments ranged from infected battle wounds to whooping cough, diabetes, and sinusitis. Natalie had few supplies and little in the way of medicine, though she ministered patiently to each. In the process she learned a great deal about her fellow students—their names, their countries of origin, the circumstances of their travel to the caliphate, the status of their passports. Among those who came to see her was Safia Bourihane. She was several pounds underweight, mildly depressed, and required eyeglasses. Otherwise, she was in good health. Natalie resisted the impulse to give her an overdose of morphine.

"I'm leaving in the morning," Safia announced as she covered herself in her abaya.

"Where are you going?"

"They haven't told me. They *never* tell me. And you?" she asked.

Natalie shrugged. "I have to be back in France in a week."

"Lucky you." Safia slid childlike from Natalie's examination table and moved toward the door.

"What was it like?" Natalie asked suddenly.

Safia turned. Even through the mosquito netting of her abaya, her eyes were astonishingly beautiful. "What was *what* like?"

"The operation." Natalie hesitated, then said, "Killing the Jews."

"It was beautiful," said Safia. "It was a dream come true."

"And if it had been a suicide operation? Could you have done it?"

Safia smiled regretfully. "I wish it had been."

39

PALMYRA, SYRIA

THE CAMP DIRECTOR WAS AN Iraqi named Massoud from Anbar Province. He had lost his left eye fighting the Americans during the troop surge of 2006. The right he fixed suspiciously on Natalie when, after a thoroughly unappetizing supper in the dining hall, she requested permission to walk alone outside the camp.

"There's no need to deceive us," he said at length. "If you wish to leave the camp, Dr. Hadawi, you are free to do so."

"I have no wish to leave."

"Are you not happy here? Have we not treated you well?"

"Very well."

The one-eyed Massoud made a show of deliberation. "There's no phone service in town, if that's what you're thinking."

"It isn't."

"And no cellular or Internet service, either."

There was a short silence.

"I'll send someone with you," said Massoud.

"It isn't necessary."

"It is. You're far too valuable to go walking alone."

The escort Massoud selected to accompany Natalie was a handsome university-educated Cairene named Ismail who had joined ISIS in frustration not long after the coup that drove the Muslim Brotherhood from power in Egypt. They left the camp a few minutes after nine o'clock. The moon hung low over the northern Palmyrene mountain belt, a white sun in a black sky, and shone like a spotlight upon the mountains to the south. Natalie pursued her own shadow along a dusty path, Ismail trailing a few paces behind her, his black clothing luminous in the moonlight, a weapon across his chest. On both sides of the path, neat groves of date palms thrived in the rich soil along the Wadi al-Qubur, which was fed by the Efqa spring. It was the spring and the surrounding oasis that had first attracted humans to this place, perhaps as early as the seventh millennium BC. There arose a walled city of two hundred thousand where the inhabitants spoke the Palmyrene dialect of Aramaic and grew wealthy from the caravan traffic along the Silk Road. Empires came and went, and in the first century CE the Romans declared Palmyra a subject of the empire. The ancient city at the edge of an oasis would never be the same.

The date palms along the track moved in a cool desert wind. At last, the palms fell away and the Temple of Bel, the center of religious life in ancient Palmyra, appeared. Natalie slowed to a stop and stared, openmouthed, at the catastrophe that lay scattered across the desert floor. The temple's ruins, with their monumental gates and columns, were among the best preserved in Palmyra. Now the ruins were in ruins, with a portion of only a single wall remaining intact. Ismail the Egyptian was obviously unmoved by the damage. "Shirk," he said with a shrug, using the Arabic word for polytheism. "It had to be destroyed."

"You were here when it happened?"

"I helped to set the charges."

"Alhamdulillah," she heard herself whisper. *Praise be to God.*

The fallen stones glowed in the cold light of the moon. Natalie picked her way slowly through the wreckage, careful not to turn an ankle, and set out down the Great Colonnade, the ceremonial avenue that stretched from the Temple of Bel, to the Triumphal Arch, to the Tetrapylon, to the Funerary Temple. Here, too, ISIS had imposed an Islamic death sentence on the non-Islamic past. The colonnades had been toppled, the arches smashed. Whatever ISIS's ultimate fate, it had left an indelible mark on the Middle East. Palmyra, thought Natalie, would never be the same.

"You did this, too?"

"I helped," admitted Ismail, smiling.

"And the Great Pyramids of Giza?" she asked leadingly. "We will destroy them, too?"

"Inshallah," he whispered.

Natalie set out toward the Temple of Baalshamin, but soon her limbs grew heavy and tears blurred her vision, so she turned around and with Ismail in tow made her way back through the date palms, to the gates of Camp Saladin. In the main recreation room, a few trainees were watching a new ISIS recruiting video promoting the joys of life in the caliphate—a bearded young jihadi playing with a child in a leafy green park, no severed heads visible, of course. In the canteen, Natalie had tea with Selma, her friend from Tunisia, and told her wide-eyed of the wonders just beyond the camp's walls. Then she returned to her room and collapsed onto her bed. In her dreams she walked through ruins—a great Roman city, an Arab village in the Galilee. Her guide was a blood-drenched woman with eyes of hazel and copper. *He is every-*

thing you would expect, she said. *Inshallah, you'll get to meet him someday.*

In her last dream she was sleeping in her own bed. Not her bed in Jerusalem but her childhood bed in France. There was a hammering at the door and soon her room was filled with mighty men with long hair and beards, their surnames taken from their villages in the east. Natalie sat up with a start and realized she was no longer dreaming. The room was her room at the camp. And the men were real.

40

ANBAR PROVINCE, IRAQ

THIS TIME, SHE HAD NO sun or dashboard instruments by which to chart her course, for within minutes of leaving Palmyra she had been blindfolded. In her brief interlude of sight, she had managed to gather three small pieces of information. Her captors were four in number, she was in the backseat of another SUV, and the SUV was headed east on the Syrian highway that used to be called the M20. She asked her captors where they were taking her, but received no reply. She protested that she had done nothing wrong in Palmyra, that she had only wanted to see the destroyed temples of *shirk* with her own eyes, but again her captors were silent. Indeed, not a word passed between them throughout the entire journey. For entertainment they listened to a lengthy sermon by the caliph. And when the sermon ended they listened to a talk show on al-Bayan, ISIS's slick radio station. Al-Bayan was based in Mosul and transmitted on the FM broadcast band. The panelists were discussing a recent Islamic State fatwa regarding sexual relations between males and their female slaves. At first, the signal from Mosul was faint and filled with waves of static, but it grew stronger the longer they drove.

They stopped once to add fuel to the tank from a jerry can, and a second time to negotiate an ISIS checkpoint. The guard spoke with an Iraqi accent and was deferential toward the men in the SUV—fearful, almost. Through the open window, Natalie heard a great commotion in the distance, orders shouted, crying children, wailing women. "Yalla, yalla!" a voice was saying. "Keep moving! It's not far." An image formed in Natalie's mind—a thin line of ragged unbelievers, a trail of tears that led to an execution pit. Soon, she thought, she would be joining them.

Another half hour or so passed before the SUV stopped a third time. The engine died and the doors swung loudly open, admitting an unwelcome blast of dense wet heat. Instantly, Natalie felt water begin to flow beneath the heavy fabric of her abaya. A hand grasped her wrist and tugged, gently. She shimmied across the seat, swung her legs to the side, and allowed herself to slide until her feet touched the earth. All the while the hand maintained its hold on her wrist. There was no malice in its grip. It guided her only.

In the haste of her evacuation from the camp, she had been unable to put on her sandals. Beneath her bare feet the earth burned. A memory arose, as unwelcome as the heat. She is on a beach in the South of France. Her mother is telling her to remove the Star of David from her neck, lest others see it. She unclasps the pendant, surrenders it, and hurries toward the blue Mediterranean before the blazing sand can burn her feet.

"Careful," said a voice, the first to address her since leaving the camp. "There are steps ahead."

They were wide and smooth. When Natalie reached the top step, the hand pulled her forward, gently. She had the sensation of moving through a great house, through cool chambers, across sun-drowned courts. At last, she came to another flight of steps, longer than the first, twelve steps instead of six. At the summit she became aware of the presence of several men and heard the muted clatter of automatic weapons expertly held.

A few murmured words were exchanged, a door was opened. Natalie moved forward ten paces exactly. Then the hand squeezed her wrist and applied subtle downward pressure. Obediently, she lowered herself to the floor and sat cross-legged upon a carpet with her hands folded neatly in her lap. The blindfold was removed. Through the mosquito netting of her facial veil, she saw a man seated before her, identically posed. His face was instantly familiar; he was the senior Iraqi who had interrogated her before her transfer to Palmyra. He was lacking in his previous composure. His black clothing was covered in dust, his brown eyes were bloodshot and fatigued. The night, thought Natalie, had been unkind to him.

With a movement of his hand, he instructed her to lift her veil. She hesitated but complied. The brown eyes bored into her for a long moment while she studied the pattern of the carpet. Finally, he took her chin in the lobster claw of his ruined hand and raised her face toward his. "Dr. Hadawi," he said quietly. "Thank you so much for coming."

SHE PASSED THROUGH ONE MORE DOORWAY, ENTERED ONE MORE room. Its floor was bare and white, as were its walls. Above was a small round aperture through which poured a shaft of scalding sunlight. Otherwise, the shadows prevailed. In one corner, the farthest, four heavily armed ISIS fighters stood in a ragged circle, eyes lowered, like mourners at a graveside. Dust coated their black costumes. It was not the khaki-colored dust of the desert; it was pale and gray, concrete that had been smashed into powder by a sledgehammer from the sky. At the feet of the four men was a fifth. He lay supine upon a stretcher, one arm across his chest, the other, the left, at his side. There was blood on the left hand, and blood stained the bare floor around him. His face was pale as death. Or was it the gray dust? From across the room, Natalie could not tell.

The senior Iraqi nudged her forward. She passed through the cylinder of sun; its heat was molten. Before her there was movement, and a place was made for her among the mourners. She stopped and looked down at the man on the stretcher. There was no dust on his face. His ashen pallor was his own, the result of substantial loss of blood. He had suffered two visible wounds, one to the upper chest, the other to the thigh of the right leg—wounds, thought Natalie, that might have proven fatal to an ordinary man, but not him. He was quite large and powerfully built.

He is everything you would expect . . .

"Who is he?" she asked after a moment.

"It's not important," answered the Iraqi. "It is only important that he lives. You must not let him die."

Natalie gathered up her abaya, crouched beside the stretcher, and reached toward the chest wound. Instantly, one of the fighters seized her wrist. This time, the grip was not gentle; it felt as though her bones were about to crack. She glared at the fighter, silently chastising him for daring to touch her, a woman who was not a blood relative, and then fixed the Iraqi with the same stare. The Iraqi nodded once, the iron grip relaxed. Natalie savored her small victory. For the first time since her arrival in Syria, she felt a sense of power. For the moment, she thought, she owned them.

She reached toward the wound again, unmolested, and moved aside the shredded black garment. It was a large wound, about two inches at its widest, with ragged edges. Something hot and jagged had entered his body at extremely high speed and had left a trail of appalling damage—broken bone, shredded tissue, severed blood vessels. His respiration was shallow and faint. It was a miracle he was breathing at all.

"What happened?"

There was silence.

"I can't help him unless I know how he was injured."

"He was in a house that was bombed."

"Bombed?"

"It was an air strike."

"Drone?"

"Much larger than a drone." He spoke as if from personal experience. "We found him beneath the debris. He was unconscious but breathing."

"Has he ever stopped?"

"No."

"And has he ever regained consciousness?"

"Not for a moment."

She examined the skull, which was covered with thick dark hair. There were no lacerations or obvious contusions, but that meant nothing; serious brain trauma was still possible. She lifted the lid of the left eye, then the right. The pupils were responsive, a good sign. Or was it? She released the right eyelid.

"What time did this happen?"

"The bomb fell shortly after midnight."

"What time is it now?"

"Ten fifteen."

Natalie examined the gaping wound to the leg. A challenging case, to say the least, she thought dispassionately. The patient had been comatose for ten hours. He had suffered two serious penetration wounds, not to mention the likelihood of numerous additional fractures and crush injuries common to victims of building collapses. Internal bleeding was a given. Sepsis was just around the corner. If he were to have any hope of survival, he needed to be transported to a Level 1 trauma center immediately, a scenario she explained to the clawed Iraqi.

"Out of the question," he replied.

"He needs urgent critical care."

"This isn't Paris, Dr. Hadawi."

"Where are we?"

"I can't tell you that."

"Why not?"

"For security reasons," he explained.

"Are we in Iraq?"

"You ask too many questions."

"Are we?" she persisted.

With his silence he confirmed that they were.

"There's a hospital in Ramadi, is there not?"

"It's not safe for him there."

"What about Fallujah?" She couldn't believe the word had come out of her mouth. *Fallujah* . . .

"He's not going anywhere," the Iraqi said. "This is the only place that's safe."

"If he stays here, he dies."

"No, he won't," said the Iraqi. "Because you're going to save him."

"With what?"

One of the fighters handed her a cardboard box with a red cross on it.

"It's a first-aid kit."

"It is all we have."

"Is there a hospital or a clinic nearby?"

The Iraqi hesitated, then said, "Mosul is an hour's drive, but the Americans are attacking traffic along the roads."

"Someone has to try to get through."

"Give me a list of the things you need," he said, extracting a grubby notepad from the pocket of his black uniform. "I'll send one of the women. It could take a while."

Natalie accepted the notepad and a pen and wrote out her wish list of supplies: antibiotics, syringes, surgical instruments, gloves, suture material, a stethoscope, IV bags and solution, a chest tube, clamps, pain medication, sedatives, gauze, and plaster bandages and fiberglass casting tape for immobilizing fractured limbs.

"You don't happen to know his blood type, do you?"

"Blood type?"

"He needs blood. Otherwise, he's going to die."

The Iraqi shook his head. Natalie handed him the list of supplies. Then she opened the first-aid kit and looked inside. Bandages, ointment, a roll of gauze, aspirin—it was hopeless. She knelt beside the wounded man and raised an eyelid. Still responsive.

"I need to know his name," she said.

"Why?"

"I have to address him by his real name to bring him out of this coma."

"I'm afraid that's not possible, Dr. Hadawi."

"Then what shall I call him?"

The Iraqi looked down at the dying, helpless man at his feet. "If you must call him something," he said after a moment, "you may call him Saladin."

41

ANBAR PROVINCE, IRAQ

As a physician in the emergency room of Jerusalem's Hadassah Medical Center, Dr. Natalie Mizrahi had routinely confronted ethically fraught scenarios, sometimes on a daily basis. There were the gravely injured and the dying who received heroic treatment despite no chance of survival. And there were the murderers, the attempted suicide bombers, the knife-wielding butchers, upon whose damaged bodies Natalie labored with the tenderest of mercies.

The situation she faced now, however, was unlike anything she had faced before—or would again, she thought. The man in the bare room somewhere near Mosul was the leader of a terror network that had carried out devastating attacks in Paris and Amsterdam. Natalie had successfully penetrated that network as part of an operation to identify and decapitate its command structure. And now, owing to an American air strike, the life of the network's mastermind rested in her well-trained hands. As a doctor she was morally obligated to save his life. But as an inhabitant of the civilized world, she was inclined to let him die slowly and thus fulfill the mission for which she had been recruited.

But what would the men of ISIS do to the female physician who allowed the great Saladin to perish before his mission of uniting the Muslim world under the black banner of the caliphate was complete? Surely, she thought, they would not thank her for her efforts and send her peacefully on her way. The stone or the knife would likely be her fate. She had not come to Syria on a suicide mission and had no intention of dying in this wretched place, at the hands of these black-clad prophets of the apocalypse. What's more, Saladin's predicament provided her with an unprecedented opportunity—the opportunity to nurse him back to health, to befriend him, to earn his trust, and to steal the deadly secrets that resided in his head. *You must not let him die*, the Iraqi had said. But why? The answer, thought Natalie, was simple. The Iraqi did not know what Saladin knew. Saladin could not die because the network's ambitions would die with him.

As it turned out, the supplies were only ninety minutes in arriving. The woman, whoever she was, had managed to secure most of what Natalie needed. After pulling on gloves and a surgical mask, she quickly inserted an IV needle into Saladin's left arm and handed the bag of solution to the Iraqi, who was looking anxiously over her shoulder. Then, using a pair of surgical scissors, she cut away Saladin's soiled, blood-soaked clothing. The stethoscope was practically a museum piece, but it worked well. The left lung sounded normal but from the right there was only silence.

"He has a pneumohemothorax."

"What does that mean?"

"His right lung has stopped functioning because it's filled with air and blood. I need to move him."

The Iraqi motioned toward one of the fighters, who assisted

Natalie in easing Saladin onto his left side. Next she made a small incision between the sixth and seventh rib, inserted a hemostat clamp, and pushed a tube into the chest cavity. There was an audible rush of escaping air. Then the blood of Saladin flowed through the tube, onto the bare floor.

"He's bleeding to death!" cried the Iraqi.

"Be quiet," snapped Natalie, "or I'll have to ask you to leave."

A half-liter or more of blood spilled before the flow slowed to a trickle. Natalie clamped the tube to prevent outside air from entering. Then she eased Saladin carefully onto his back and went to work on the chest wound.

The piece of shrapnel had broken two ribs and caused significant damage to the pectoralis major muscle. Natalie flooded the wound with alcohol; then, using a pair of angled surgical tweezers, she removed the shrapnel. There was additional bleeding but it was not significant. She removed several bone fragments and threads of Saladin's black garment. After that, there was nothing more she could do. The ribs, if he survived, would heal, but the damaged pectoral muscle would likely never regain its original shape or strength. Natalie closed the deep tissue with sutures but left the skin open. Twelve hours had passed since the original wound. If she closed the skin now, she would be sealing infectious agents into the body, ensuring a case of sepsis and an agonizingly slow death. It was tempting, she thought, but medically reckless. She covered the wound with a gauze bandage and turned her attention to the leg.

Here again, Saladin had been fortunate. The lump of shrapnel had been discriminating in the havoc it had wreaked, damaging bone and tissue but sparing major blood vessels. Natalie's procedure was identical to the first wound—irrigation with alcohol, retrieval of bone fragments and clothing fibers, closure of deep tissue, a gauze bandage over the open skin. In all, the crude surgery had taken less than an hour. She added a heavy dose of antibiotic to the IV and covered the patient with a clean white sheet. The chest tube she left in place.

"It looks like a burial shroud," the Iraqi said darkly.

"Not yet," answered Natalie.

"What about something for the pain?"

"At this point," she said, "pain is our ally. It acts as a stimulus. It will help him regain consciousness."

"Will he?"

"Which answer do you want to hear?"

"The truth."

"The truth," said Natalie, "is that he's probably going to die."

"If he dies," said the Iraqi coldly, "then you will die soon after."

Natalie was silent. The Iraqi looked at the once-powerful man shrouded in white. "Do everything you can to revive him," he said. "Even for a moment or two. It is essential that I speak to him."

But why? thought Natalie as the Iraqi slipped from the room. Because the Iraqi did not know what Saladin knew. Because if Saladin died, the network would die with him.

WITH THE SURGERY COMPLETE, NATALIE DUTIFULLY COVERED herself with her abaya, lest the great Saladin awaken to find an unveiled woman in his court. She requested a timepiece to properly chart the patient's recovery and was given the Iraqi's personal Seiko digital. She checked Saladin's pulse and blood pressure every thirty minutes and recorded his intake of IV solution. His pulse was still rapid and weak, but his blood pressure was rising steadily, a positive development. It suggested there were no other sources of internal bleeding and that the IV was helping to increase his blood volume. Even so, he remained unconscious and unresponsive to mild stimulus. The likely culprit was the immense loss of blood and the shock he had suffered after being wounded, but Natalie could not rule out brain trauma. A CT scan would reveal evidence of brain bleeding and swelling, but the Iraqi had made it clear that Saladin could not be moved. Not that it mattered, thought Natalie. In a land where bread was scarce and women carried water from the Euphrates, the chances of finding a working scanner were almost zero.

.A pair of fighters remained in the room always, and the Iraqi appeared every hour or so to stare at the prostrate man on the floor, as if willing him to regain consciousness. During his third visit, Natalie pulled at Saladin's earlobe and tugged the thick hair of his beard, but there was no response.

"Must you?" asked the Iraqi.

"Yes," said Natalie, "I must."

She pinched the back of his hand. Nothing.

"Try talking to him," she suggested. "A familiar voice is helpful."

The Iraqi crouched next to the stretcher and murmured something into Saladin's ear that Natalie could not discern.

"It might help if you say it so he can actually hear it. Shout at him, in fact."

"Shout at Saladin?" The Iraqi shook his head. "One does not even raise one's voice to Saladin."

By then, it was late afternoon. The shaft of light from the oculus had traveled slowly across the room, and now it heated the patch of bare floor where Natalie sat. She imagined that God was watching her through the oculus, judging her. She imagined that Gabriel was watching her, too. In his wildest operational dreams, surely he had not contemplated a scenario such as this. She pictured her homecoming, a meeting in a safe house, a tense debriefing, during which she would be forced to defend her attempt to save the life of the most dangerous terrorist in the world. She pushed the thought from her mind, for such thoughts were perilous. She had never met a man named Gabriel Allon, she reminded herself, and she had no interest in the opinion of her God. Only Allah's judgment mattered to Leila Hadawi, and surely Allah would have approved.

There was no electricity in the house, and with nightfall it plunged into darkness. The fighters lit old-fashioned hurricane lamps and placed them around the room. The Iraqi joined Natalie for supper. The fare was far better than at the camp in Palmyra, a couscous worthy of a Left Bank café. She did not share this insight with her dinner companion. He was in a dark mood, and not particularly good company.

"I don't suppose you can tell me your name," said Natalie.

"No," he answered through a mouthful of food. "I don't suppose I can."

"You don't trust me? Even now?"

"Trust has nothing to do with it. If you are arrested when you return to Paris next week, French intelligence will ask you who you met during your vacation in the caliphate. And you will give them my name."

"I would never talk to French intelligence."

"Everyone talks." Again, it seemed the Iraqi spoke from personal experience. "Besides," he added after a moment, "we have plans for you."

"What sort of plans?"

"Your operation."

"When will I be told?"

He said nothing.

"And if he dies?" she asked with a glance at Saladin. "Will the operation go forward?"

"That is none of your affair." He scooped up a portion of the couscous.

"Were you there when it happened?"

"Why do you ask?"

"I'm making conversation."

"In the caliphate, conversation can be dangerous."

"Forget I asked."

He didn't. "I arrived soon after," he said. "I was the one who pulled him out of the rubble. I thought he was dead."

"Were there other casualties?"

"Many."

"Is there anything I can—"

"You have one patient and one patient only." The Iraqi fixed his dark eyes on Saladin. "How long can he go on like this?"

"He's a large man, strong, otherwise healthy. It could go on a very long time."

"Is there anything more you can do to revive him? A shot of something?"

"The best thing you can do is talk to him. Say his name loudly. Not his nom de guerre," she said. "His real name. The name his mother called him."

"He didn't have a mother."

With those words the Iraqi departed. A woman cleared away the couscous and brought tea and baklava, an unheard of delicacy in the Syrian portion of the caliphate. Natalie checked Saladin's pulse, blood pressure, and lung function every thirty minutes. All showed signs of improvement. His heartbeat was slowing and growing stronger, his blood pressure was rising, the right lung was clearing. She checked his eyes, too, by the light of a butane cigarette lighter—the right eye first, then the left. The pupils were still responsive. His brain, regardless of its state, was alive.

At midnight, some twenty-four hours after the American air strike, Natalie was in desperate need of a few hours' sleep. Moonlight shone through the oculus, cold and white, the same moon that had illuminated the ruins of Palmyra. She checked the pulse, blood pressure, and lungs. All were progressing nicely. Then she checked the eyes by the blue glow of the butane lighter. The right eye, then the left.

Both remained open after the examination.

"Who are you?" asked a voice of shocking strength and resonance.

Startled, Natalie had to compose herself before answering. "My name is Dr. Leila Hadawi. I'm taking care of you."

"What happened?"

"You were injured in an air strike."

"Where am I now?"

"I'm not sure."

He was momentarily confused. Then he understood. Fatigued, he asked, "Where is Abu Ahmed?"

"Who?"

Wearily, he raised his left hand and made a lobster claw of his thumb and forefinger. Natalie smiled in spite of herself.

"He's right outside. He's very anxious to talk to you."

Saladin closed his eyes. "I can imagine."

42

ANBAR PROVINCE, IRAQ

"YOU ARE MY MAIMONIDES."

"Who?"

"Maimonides. The Jew who looked after Saladin whenever he was in Cairo."

Natalie was silent.

"I meant it as a compliment. I owe you my life."

Saladin closed his eyes. It was late morning. The circle of light from the oculus had only just begun its slow journey across the bare floor, and the room was still pleasantly cool. After regaining consciousness, he had passed a restful night, thanks in part to the dose of morphine that Natalie had added to his IV drip. At first, he had objected to the drug, but Natalie had convinced him it was necessary. "You cannot heal properly if you are in pain," she had scolded him. "For the sake of the caliphate, you must." Once again, she could not fathom that such words had passed her lips.

She placed the stethoscope to his chest. He recoiled slightly from the cold.

"Am I still alive?" he asked.

"Be quiet, please. I can't hear properly if you speak."

He said nothing more. His right lung sounded as though it had regained normal function; his heartbeat was steady and strong. She wrapped the blood pressure cuff around the upper portion of his left arm and inflated it with several quick squeezes of the bulb. He winced.

"What's wrong?"

"Nothing," he said through gritted teeth.

"Do you have more pain?"

"Not at all."

"Tell me the truth."

"The arm," he said after a moment.

Natalie released the air pressure, removed the cuff, and tenderly probed the arm with her fingertips. She had noticed the swelling last night and had suspected a fracture. Now, with the assistance of a conscious patient, she all but confirmed it.

"The only thing I can do is immobilize it."

"Perhaps we should."

Natalie applied the cuff to the right arm.

"Pain?"

"No."

His blood pressure was at the low end of normal. Natalie removed the cuff and changed the dressings on his chest and leg. There was no visible sign of infection in either wound. Miraculously, it appeared as though he had come through surgery in an unsterile environment with no sepsis. Unless he took a sudden turn for the worse, Saladin would survive.

She opened a package of fiberglass casting tape and commenced work on the arm. Saladin watched her intently.

"It's not necessary for you to conceal your face in my presence. After all," he said, fingering the white sheet that covered his otherwise nude body, "we are well acquainted, you and I. A hijab is sufficient."

Natalie hesitated, then removed the heavy black garment. Saladin stared hard at her face.

"You're very beautiful. But Abu Ahmed is right. You look like a Jew."

"Is that supposed to be a compliment, too?"

"I've known many beautiful Jewesses. And everyone knows that the best doctors are always Jewish."

"As an Arab doctor," said Natalie, "I take exception to that."

"You're not an Arab, you're a Palestinian. There's a difference."

"I take exception to that, too."

Silently, she bound his arm with the fiberglass tape. Orthopedics was hardly her specialty, but then she was not a surgeon, either.

"It was a mistake," he said, watching her work, "for me to mention Abu Ahmed's name in front of you. Names have a way of getting people killed. You will do your best to forget you ever heard it."

"I already have."

"He tells me you're French."

"Who?" she asked playfully, but Saladin did not rise to the bait. "Yes," she said, "I am French."

"You approved of our attack on the Weinberg Center?"

"I wept with joy."

"The Western press said it was a soft target. I can assure you it was not. Hannah Weinberg was an associate of an Israeli intelligence officer named Gabriel Allon, and her so-called center for the study of anti-Semitism was a front for the Israeli service. Which is why I targeted it." He fell silent. Natalie could feel the weight of his gaze on her while she worked on the arm. "Perhaps you've heard of this man Gabriel Allon," he said at last. "He is an enemy of the Palestinian people."

"I think I read about him in the papers a few months ago," she answered. "He's the one who died in London, is he not?"

"Gabriel Allon? Dead?" He shook his head slowly. "I don't believe it."

"Be quiet for a moment," Natalie instructed him. "It's important that I immobilize your arm properly. If I don't, you'll have problems with it later."

"And my leg?"

"You need surgery—proper surgery in a proper hospital. Otherwise, I'm afraid your leg will be badly damaged."

"I'll be a cripple, is that what you're saying?"

"You'll have restricted movement, you'll require a cane to walk, you'll have chronic pain."

"I already have restricted movement." He smiled at his own joke. "They say Saladin walked with a limp, the *real* Saladin. It didn't stop him, and it won't stop me, either."

"I believe you," she said. "A normal man would never have survived wounds as serious as yours. Surely, Allah is watching over you. He has plans for you."

"And I," said Saladin, "have plans for *you*."

She finished the cast in silence. She was pleased with her work. So, too, was Saladin.

"Perhaps when your operation is complete, you can return to the caliphate to serve as my personal physician."

"Your Maimonides?"

"Exactly."

"It would be an honor," she heard herself say.

"But we won't be in Cairo. Like Saladin, I've always preferred Damascus."

"What about Baghdad?"

"Baghdad is a city of *rafida*."

It was a bigoted Sunni slur for Shia Muslims. Natalie wordlessly prepared a new IV bag.

"What's that you're putting in the solution?" he asked.

"Something for your pain. It will help you sleep through the heat of the afternoon."

"I'm not in pain. And I don't want to sleep."

Natalie attached the bag to the IV tube and squeezed it to start the flow of fluid. Within a few seconds, Saladin's eyes dulled. He fought to keep them open.

"Abu Ahmed is right," he said, watching her. "You do look like a Jew."

"And you," said Natalie, "need to rest."

The eyelids dropped like window blinds and Saladin slipped helplessly into unconsciousness.

43

ANBAR PROVINCE, IRAQ

HER DAYS MOVED TO THE rhythm of Saladin. She slept when he slept and woke whenever he stirred on his sickbed. She monitored his vital signs, she changed his dressings, she gave him morphine against his wishes for the pain. For a few seconds after the drug entered his blood, he would hover in a hallucinatory state where words escaped his mouth, like the air that had rushed from his damaged lung. Natalie could have prolonged his talkative mood by giving him a smaller measure of the drug; conversely, she could have ushered him to death's door with a larger dose. But she was never alone with her patient. Two fighters stood over him always, and Abu Ahmed—he of the lobster claw and overcast disposition—was never far. He consulted with Saladin frequently, about what Natalie was not privy. When matters of state or terror were discussed, she was banished from the room.

She was not permitted to go far—the next room, the toilet, a sun-blasted court where Abu Ahmed encouraged her to take exercise in order to stay fit for her operation. She was never allowed to see the rest of the great house or told where she was, though when she listened to al-Bayan on the ancient transistor radio they gave her, the signal was without interference. All other radio was forbidden, lest she be exposed to un-Islamic ideas or, heaven forbid, music. The absence of music was harder to bear than she imagined. She longed to hear a few notes of a melody, a child sawing away at a major scale, even the thud of hip-hop from a passing car. Her rooms became a prison. The camp at Palmyra seemed a paradise in comparison. Even Raqqa was better, for at least in Raqqa she had been allowed to roam the streets. Never mind the severed heads and the men on crosses, at least there was some semblance of life. The caliphate, she thought grimly, had a way of reducing one's expectations.

And all the while she watched an imaginary clock in her head and turned the pages of an imaginary calendar. She was scheduled to fly from Athens to Paris on Sunday evening, and to return to work at the clinic in Aubervilliers Monday morning. But first, she had to get from the caliphate to Turkey and from Turkey to Santorini. For all their talk of an important role in an upcoming operation, she wondered whether Saladin and Abu Ahmed had other plans for her. Saladin would require constant medical care for months. And who better to care for him than the woman who had saved his life?

He referred to her as Maimonides and she, having no other name for him, called him Saladin. They did not become friends or confidants, far from it, but a bond was forged between them. She played the same game she had played with Abu Ahmed, the game of guessing what he had been before the American invasion upended Iraq. He was obviously of high intelligence and a student of history. During one of their conversations, he told her that he had been to Paris many times—for what reason he did not say—and he spoke French badly but with great enthusiasm. He spoke English, too, much better than he spoke French. Perhaps, thought Natalie, he had attended an English preparatory school or military academy. She tried to imagine him without his wild hair and beard. She dressed him in a Western suit and tie, but he didn't wear it well. Then she clothed him in olive drab, and the fit was better. When she added a thick mustache of the sort worn by Saddam loyalists, the picture was complete. Saladin, she decided, was a secret policeman or a spy. For that reason she was always fearful in his presence.

He was no fire-breathing jihadist, Saladin. His Islam was political rather than spiritual, a tool by which he intended to redraw the map of the Middle East. It would be dominated by a massive Sunni state that would stretch from Baghdad to the Arabian Peninsula and across the Levant and North Africa. He did not rant or spew venom or recite Koranic verses or the sayings of the Prophet. He was entirely reasonable, which made him all the more terrifying. The liberation of Jerusalem, he said, was high on his agenda. It was his wish to pray in the Noble Sanctuary at least once before his death.

"You've been, Maimonides?"

"To Jerusalem? No, never."

"Yes, I know. Abu Ahmed told me that."

"Who?"

Eventually, he told her he had been raised in a small, poor village in the Sunni Triangle of Iraq, though he pointedly did not say the village's name. He had joined the Iraqi army, hardly surprising in a land of mass conscription, and had fought in the long war against Iranians, though he referred to them always as Persians and *rafida*. The years between the war with Iran and the first Gulf War were a blank; he mentioned something about government work but did not elaborate. But when he spoke of the second war with the Americans, the war that destroyed Iraq as he knew it, his eyes flashed with anger. When the Americans disbanded the Iraqi army and removed all Baath Party members from their government posts, he was put on the streets along with thousands of other mainly Sunni Iraqi men. He joined the secular resistance and, later, al-Qaeda in Iraq, where he met and befriended Abu Musab al-Zarqawi. Unlike Zarqawi, who relished his Bin Laden–like role as a terror superstar, Saladin preferred to keep a lower profile. It was Saladin, not Zarqawi, who masterminded many of al-Qaeda in Iraq's most spectacular and deadly attacks. And yet even now, he said, the Americans and the Jordanians did not know his real name.

"You, Maimonides, will not be so fortunate. Soon you will be the most wanted woman on the planet. Everyone will know your name, especially the Americans."

She asked again about the target of her attack. Annoyed, he refused to say. For reasons of operational security, he explained, recruits were not given their targets until the last possible minute.

"Your friend Safia Bourihane wasn't told her target until the night before the operation. But your target will be much bigger than hers. One day they will write books about you."

"Is it a suicide operation?"

"Maimonides, please."

"I must know."

"Did I not tell you that you were going to be my personal physician? Did I not say that we would live together in Damascus?"

Suddenly fatigued, he closed his eyes. His words, thought Natalie, were without conviction. She knew at that moment that Dr. Leila Hadawi would not be returning to the caliphate. She had saved Saladin's life, and yet Saladin, with no trace of misgivings or guilt, would soon send her to her death.

"How is your pain?" she asked.

"I feel nothing."

She placed her forefinger in the center of his chest and pressed. His eyes shot open.

"It seems you have pain, after all."

"A little," he confessed.

She prepared his dose of morphine.

"Wait, Maimonides. There's something I must tell you."

She stopped.

"You'll be leaving here in a few hours to begin your journey back to France. In time, someone will contact you and tell you how to proceed."

Natalie finished preparing his dose of morphine.

"Perhaps," she said, "we shall meet again in paradise."

"Inshallah, Maimonides."

She fed the morphine through his IV tube into his veins. His eyes blurred and grew vacant; he was in a vulnerable state. Natalie wanted to double his dose and shove him through death's door, but she hadn't the courage. If he died, the knife or the stone would be her fate.

Finally, he slipped into unconsciousness and his eyes closed. Natalie checked his vital signs one last time and while he was sleeping removed the chest tube and sutured the incision. That night, after supper, she was blindfolded and placed in the backseat of another SUV. She was too tired to be afraid. She plunged into a dreamless sleep, and when she woke they were near the Turkish border. A pair of smugglers took her across and drove her to the ferry terminal in Bodrun, where Miranda Ward was waiting. They traveled together on the ferry to Santorini and shared a room that night at the Panorama Hotel. It was not until late the following morning, when they arrived in Athens, that Miranda returned Natalie's phone. She sent a text message to her "father" saying that her trip had gone well and that she was safe. Then, alone, she boarded an Air France flight bound for Paris.

PART THREE

THE END OF DAYS

44

CHARLES DE GAULLE AIRPORT, PARIS

THE NAME ON THE RECTANGULAR paper sign read MORESBY. Christian Bouchard had chosen it himself. It came from a book he had read once about wealthy, naive Americans wandering among the Arabs of North Africa. The story ended badly for the Americans; someone had died. Bouchard hadn't cared for the novel, but then Bouchard was the first to admit he wasn't much of a reader. This shortcoming had not endeared him initially to Paul Rousseau, who famously read while brushing his teeth. Rousseau was forever foisting dense volumes of prose and poetry upon his ill-read deputy. Bouchard displayed the books on the coffee table in his apartment to impress his wife's friends.

He clutched the paper sign in his damp right hand. In his left he held a mobile phone, which for the past several hours had pinged with a steady stream of messages regarding a certain Dr. Leila Hadawi, a French citizen of Palestinian Arab extraction. Dr. Hadawi had boarded Air France Flight 1533 in Athens earlier that afternoon, following a month's holiday in Greece. She had been granted reentry into France with no questions about her travel itinerary and was now making her way to the arrivals hall of Terminal 2F, or so said the last message Bouchard had received. He would believe it when he saw her with his own eyes. The Israeli standing next to him seemed to feel the same way. He was the lanky one with gray eyes, the one the French members of the team knew as Michel. There was something about him that made Bouchard uneasy. It was not difficult to picture him with a gun in his hand, pointed at a man who was about to die.

"There she is," murmured the Israeli, as though addressing his footwear, but Bouchard didn't see her. A flight from Cairo had arrived at the same time as the flight from Athens; there were hijabs aplenty. "What color?" asked Bouchard, and the Israeli replied, "Burgundy." It was one of the few French words he knew.

Bouchard's gaze swept over the arriving passengers, and then at once he saw her, a turning leaf afloat a rushing stream. She walked within a few feet of where they were standing, her eyes straight ahead, her chin raised slightly, pulling her little rolling suitcase. Then she slipped through the outer doors and was gone again.

Bouchard looked at the Israeli, who was suddenly smiling. His sense of relief was palpable, but Bouchard detected something else. As a Frenchman, he knew a thing or two about matters of the heart. The Israeli was in love with the woman who had just returned from Syria. Of that, Bouchard was certain.

SHE SETTLED QUIETLY INTO HER APARTMENT IN THE BANLIEUE of Aubervilliers and resumed her old life. She was Leila before Jalal Nasser had approached her at the café across the street,

Leila before a pretty girl from Bristol had spirited her secretly to Syria. She had never witnessed the horrors of Raqqa or the tragedy of Palmyra, she had never dug shrapnel from the body of a man called Saladin. She had been to Greece, to the enchanted isle of Santorini. Yes, it had been as lovely as she imagined. No, she would probably not return. Once was quite enough.

She was surprisingly thin for a woman who had been on holiday, and her face was stained with evidence of strain and fatigue. The fatigue would not abate, for even after her return, sleep eluded her. Nor did she regain her appetite. She forced herself to eat croissants and baguettes and Camembert and pasta, and quickly she regained a lost kilo or two. It did little for her appearance. She looked like a cyclist who had just completed the Tour de France—or a jihadist who had just spent a month training in Syria and Iraq.

Roland Girard, the clinic's ersatz administrator, tried to lighten her patient load, but she wouldn't hear of it. After a month in the upside-down world of the caliphate, she longed for some semblance of normality, even if it was Leila's and not her own. She discovered that she missed her patients, the inhabitants of the *cités*, the citizens of the other France. And for the first time, she saw the Arab world as they undoubtedly saw it, as a cruel and unforgiving place, a place with no future, a place to be fled. The vast majority of them wanted nothing more than to live in peace and care for their families. But a small minority—small in percentage, but large in number—had fallen victim to the siren song of radical Islam. Some were prepared to slaughter their fellow Frenchmen in the name of the caliphate. And some would surely have slit Dr. Hadawi's throat if they knew the secret she was hiding beneath her hijab.

Still, she was pleased to be back in their presence, and back in France. Mainly, she was curious as to why she had not been summoned for the debriefing she was secretly dreading. They were watching her; she could see them in the streets of the banlieue and in the window of the apartment opposite. She supposed they were just being cautious, for surely they were not the only ones watching. Surely, she thought, Saladin was watching her, too.

Finally, on the first Friday evening after her return, Roland Girard again invited her for an after-work coffee. Instead of heading to the center of Paris, as he had before her departure for Syria, he drove her northward into the countryside.

"Aren't you going to blindfold me?" she asked.

"I beg your pardon?"

Silent, she watched the clock and the speedometer and thought of a ruler-straight road stained with oil, stretching eastward into the desert. At the end of the road was a great house of many rooms and courts. And in one of the rooms, bandaged and infirm, was Saladin.

"Can you do me a favor, Roland?"

"Of course."

"Turn on some music."

"What kind?"

"It doesn't matter. Any kind will do."

THE GATE WAS IMPOSING, THE DRIVE WAS LONG AND GRAVEL. AT the end of it, ivied and stately, stood a large manor house. Roland Girard stopped a few meters from the front entrance. He left the engine running.

"This is as far as I'm allowed to go. I'm disappointed. I want to know what it was like."

She gave no answer.

"You're a very brave woman to go to that place."

"You would have done the same thing."

"Not in a million years."

An exterior light bloomed in the dusk, the front door opened.

"Go," said Roland Girard. "They've waited a long time to see you."

Mikhail was now standing in the entrance of the house. Natalie climbed out of the car and approached him slowly.

"I was beginning to think you'd forgotten about me." She looked past him, into the interior of the grand house. "How lovely. Much better than my little place in Aubervilliers."

"Or that dump near al-Rasheed Park."

"You were watching me?"

"As much as we could. We know that you were taken to a village near the Iraqi border, where you were undoubtedly interrogated by a man named Abu Ahmed al-Tikriti. And we know that you spent several days at a training camp in Palmyra, where you managed to find time to tour the ruins by moonlight." He hesitated before continuing. "And we know," he said, "that you were taken to a village near Mosul, where you spent several days in a large house. We saw you pacing in a courtyard."

"You should have bombed that house."

Mikhail gave her a quizzical look. Then he stepped aside and with a movement of his hand invited her to enter. She remained frozen in place.

"What's wrong?"

"I'm afraid he's going to be disappointed with me."

"Not possible."

"We'll see about that," she said, and went inside.

THEY EMBRACED HER, THEY KISSED HER CHEEKS, THEY CLUNG to her limbs as though they feared she might drift away from them and never return. Dina removed the hijab from Natalie's head; Gabriel pressed a glass of chilled white wine into her hand. It was a sauvignon blanc from the Western Galilee that Natalie adored.

"I couldn't possibly," she laughed. "It is haram."

"Not tonight," he said. "Tonight you are one of us again."

There was food and there was music, and there were a thousand questions no one dared ask; there would be time for that later. They had sent an agent into the belly of the beast, and the agent had come back to them. They were going to savor their achievement. They were going to celebrate life.

Only Gabriel seemed to withhold himself from the revelry. He did not partake of the food or wine, only coffee. Mainly, he watched Natalie with an unnerving intensity. She remembered the things he had told her about his mother on that first day at the farm in the Jezreel Valley, how she rarely laughed or smiled, how she could not show pleasure on festive occasions. Perhaps he had inherited her affliction. Or perhaps, thought Natalie, he knew that tonight was not an occasion for celebration.

At last, as if by some imperceptible signal, the party came to an end. The dishes were cleared away, the wine was removed. In one of the sitting rooms a wing chair had been reserved for Natalie. There were no cameras or microphones visible, but surely, she thought, the proceedings were being recorded. Gabriel chose to remain standing.

"Usually," he said, "I prefer to start debriefings from the beginning. But perhaps tonight we should start at the end."

"Yes," she agreed. "Perhaps we should."

"Who was staying in the large house near Mosul?"

"Saladin," she answered without hesitation.

"Why were you brought there?"

"He required medical attention."

"And you gave it to him?"

"Yes."

"Why?"

"Because," replied Natalie, "he was going to die."

45

SERAINCOURT, FRANCE

ONE DAY," said GABRIEL, "they're going to write a book about you."

"It's funny," replied Natalie, "but Saladin told me the same thing."

They were walking along a footpath in the garden of the château. A bit of light leaked from the French doors of the sitting room, but otherwise it was dark. A storm had come and gone during the many hours of her debriefing, and the gravel was wet beneath their feet. Natalie shivered. The air was chill with the promise of autumn.

"You're cold," said Gabriel. "We should go back inside."

"Not yet. There's something I wanted to tell you in private."

Gabriel stopped and turned to face her.

"He knows who you are."

"Saladin?" He smiled. "I'm flattered but not surprised. I have quite a following in the Arab world."

"There's more, I'm afraid. He knows about your connection to Hannah Weinberg. And he suspects that you are very much alive."

This time, he did not dismiss her words with a smile.

"What does it mean?" asked Natalie.

"It means that our suspicions about Saladin being a former Iraqi intelligence officer are almost certainly correct. It also means he's probably connected to certain elements in Saudi Arabia. Who knows? Perhaps he's receiving support from them."

"But ISIS wants to destroy the House of Saud and incorporate the Arabian Peninsula into the caliphate."

"In theory."

"So why would the Saudis support ISIS?"

"You are now our foremost expert on ISIS. You tell me."

"Saudi Arabia is a classic straddling state. It combats Sunni extremism while at the same time nurturing it. They're like a man holding a tiger by the ears. If the man lets go of the tiger, it will devour him."

"You were obviously paying attention during those long lectures at the farm. But you left out one other important factor, and that's Iran. The Saudis are more afraid of Iran than they are of ISIS. Iran is Shiite. And ISIS, for all its evil, is Sunni."

"And from the Saudi perspective," continued Natalie, "a Sunni caliphate is far preferable to a Shiite Crescent that stretches from Iran to Lebanon."

"Exactly." Again, he smiled. "You're going to make a fine intelligence officer. Actually," he corrected himself, "you already are."

"A fine intelligence officer wouldn't have saved the life of a monster like Saladin."

"You did the right thing."

"Did I?"

"We're not like them, Natalie. If they want to die for Allah, we will help them in any way we can. But we will not sacrifice ourselves in the process. Besides," he added after a moment, "if you had killed Saladin, Abu Ahmed al-Tikriti would have taken his place."

"So why bother to kill any of them if another will rise?"

"It is a question with which we wrestle all the time."

"And the answer?"

"What choice do we have?"

"Maybe we should bomb that house."

"Bad idea."

"Why?"

"You tell me."

She considered the question carefully before answering. "Because they would suspect that the woman who saved Saladin—the woman he called Maimonides—was a spy who had revealed the location of the house to her handlers."

"Very good. And you can be certain they moved him the minute you crossed into Turkey."

"Were you watching?"

"Our satellite had been retasked to follow you."

"I saw al-Tikriti use a phone several times."

"That phone is now off the air. I'll ask the Americans to review their satellite and cellular data. It's possible they'll be able to retrace Saladin's movements, but unlikely. They've been looking for al-Baghdadi for a long time without success. In a case like this we need to know where Saladin is *going* to be, not where he's been." With a sidelong glance he asked, "Is there any chance he might have already died of his wounds?"

"There's always a chance. But I'm afraid he had a very good doctor."

"That's because she was Jewish. Everyone knows that all the best doctors are Jewish."

She smiled.

"You dispute this?"

"No. It's just that Saladin said the same thing."

"Even a stopped clock is right twice a day."

They walked in silence for a moment, the gravel of the pathway crunching beneath their feet, watched over by Greek and Roman statuary. Apollo emerged spectrally from the darkness. For an instant Natalie was once more in Palmyra.

"What now?" she asked at last.

"We wait for Saladin to summon you. And we stop the next attack."

"What if they don't choose me for the team?"

"They've invested a great deal of time and effort in you. Almost as much as we have," he added.

"How long will we have to wait?"

"A week, a month . . ." He shrugged. "Saladin has been at this for a long time, a thousand years in fact. He's obviously a patient man."

"I can't keep living as Leila Hadawi."

He said nothing.

"How are my parents?"

"Worried, but fine."

"Do they know I went to Syria?"

"No. But they know you're safe."

"I wish to make one demand."

"Anything," he said. "Within reason, of course."

"I wish to see my parents."

"Impossible," he said with a dismissive wave of his hand.

"Please," she pleaded. "Just for a few minutes."

"A few minutes?"

"Yes, that's all. I just want to hear the sound of my mother's voice. I want my father to hold me."

He made a show of thought. "I think that can be arranged."

"Really? How soon?"

"Now," he said.

"What are you talking about?"

He pointed toward the facade of the house, toward the light spilling from the French doors. Natalie turned and scampered childlike down the darkened garden path. She was beautiful, thought Gabriel, even when she was crying.

46

PARIS—TIBERIAS, ISRAEL

THE REMAINDER OF SEPTEMBER PASSED without a nibble, and so did the entire month of October, which in Paris was drenched with sun and warmer than usual, much to the delight of the surveillance artists, the operation's unsung heroes. By the first week of November, the team was beset by something approaching abject panic. Even the normally placid Paul Rousseau was beside himself, but then Rousseau was to be forgiven. He had a chief and a minister breathing down his neck, and a president who was too politically weak to survive another attack on French soil. The president would soon be leaving for Washington for a meeting with his American counterpart, and for that Rousseau was eternally grateful.

Natalie soldiered on, but clearly she was growing weary of her double life in the dreary banlieue. There were no more team gatherings; they communicated with her only by text. Status checks invariably elicited a terse response. She was fine. She was well. She was bored. She was lonely. On her days off from the clinic, she escaped the banlieue by RER train and ran the watchers ragged on the streets of central Paris.

During one such visit she was accosted by a Frenchwoman of National Front persuasion who took exception to her hijab. Natalie returned fire and instantly the two women were nose to nose on a busy street corner. Were it not for the gendarme who pulled them apart, they might very well have come to blows.

"An admirable performance," Paul Rousseau told Gabriel that evening at Alpha Group's headquarters on the rue de Grenelle. "Let us hope Saladin was watching."

"Yes," said Gabriel. "Let us hope."

But was he even alive? And if he was, had he lost faith in the woman who had saved him? This was their greatest fear, that Saladin's operational train had left the station and Dr. Leila Hadawi had not been issued a ticket. In the meantime, the system was blinking red. European capitals, including Paris, were on high alert, and in Washington the Department of Homeland Security reluctantly raised its threat level, though publicly the president continued to play down the danger. The fact that warnings came and went with no attack seemed to bolster his case that the group did not possess the capability to carry out a major terror spectacular on the American homeland. A climate change accord was signed, a famous pop star released a long-awaited album, China's stock market collapsed, and soon the world forgot. But the world did not know what Gabriel and Natalie and the rest of the team knew. Somewhere in Iraq or Syria was a man called Saladin. He was not a raving lunatic; he was a man of reason, a Sunni nationalist, quite possibly a former spy. He had suffered two serious shrapnel wounds to the right side of his body, one in the chest, the other to the thigh. If he was ambulatory, he would almost certainly require a cane or crutches to walk. The scars would make him easily identifiable. So, too, would his ambition. He planned to carry out an attack of such severity that the West would have no choice but to invade the Islamic caliphate. The armies of Rome and the men with black flags and long hair and beards would clash in a place called Dabiq, on the plains of northern Syria. The men who flew black flags would prevail, thus unleashing a chain of apocalyptic events that would bring about the appearance of the Mahdi and the end of days.

But even in the sacred city of Jerusalem, Saladin's ultimate target, attention wandered. Several months had passed since Gabriel was to have assumed control of the Office, and even the prime minister, who had been complicit in the delay, was losing patience. He had an ally in Ari Shamron, who never supported the delay in the first place. Frustrated, Shamron rang a compliant journalist and told him—anonymously, of course—that a change in leadership at the Office was imminent, days rather than weeks. He also suggested that the prime minister's choice for a new chief would be surprising, to say the least. There followed a round of intense media speculation. Many names were floated, though the name Gabriel Allon was mentioned only in passing and with sadness. Gabriel was the chief who never was. Gabriel was dead.

But he was not dead, of course. He was jetlagged, he was anxious, he was worried that his meticulously planned and executed operation had been in vain, but he was very much alive. On a Friday afternoon in mid-November he returned to Jerusalem after several days in Paris, hoping to spend a quiet weekend with his wife and children. But within minutes of his arrival, Chiara informed him that they were all expected for dinner that evening at Shamron's villa in Tiberias.

"Not a chance," said Gabriel.

"It's Shabbat," replied Chiara. She said nothing more. She was the daughter of the chief rabbi of Venice. In Chiara's world, Shabbat was the ultimate trump card. No further argument was necessary. The case was closed.

"I'm too tired. Call Gilah and tell her we'll do it another night."

"*You* call her."

Which he did. The conversation was brief, less than a minute.

"What did she say?"

"She said it's Shabbat."

"Is that all?"

"No. She said Ari isn't doing well."

"He's been sick all autumn. You've been too busy to notice, and Gilah didn't want to worry you."

"What is it this time?"

She shrugged. "Your *abba* is getting old, Gabriel."

To move the Allon family was no easy feat. The children's car seats had to be buckled into the back of Gabriel's SUV, and an additional vehicle added to the motorcade. It barreled down the Bab al-Wad at rush hour, sped northward up the Coastal Plain, and then raced westward across the Galilee. Shamron's honey-colored villa stood atop a rocky bluff overlooking the lake. At the base of the drive was a small guardhouse where a security detail kept watch behind a metal gate. It was like entering a forward military base in a hostile land.

It was precisely three minutes before sunset when the motorcade rumbled to a stop outside the entrance of the villa. Gilah Shamron was standing on the steps, tapping her wristwatch to indicate that time was running short if they were going to light the candles in time. Gabriel carried the children inside while Chiara saw to the food she had spent the afternoon preparing. Gilah, too, had spent the day cooking. There was enough to feed a multitude.

Chiara's description of Shamron's failing health had left Gabriel expecting the worst, and he was deeply relieved to find Shamron looking rather well. Indeed, if anything, his appearance had improved since Gabriel saw him last. He was dressed, as usual, in a white oxford cloth shirt and pressed khaki trousers, though tonight he had added a navy cardigan against the November chill. Little remained of his hair and his skin was pale and translucent, but his blue eyes shone brightly behind his ugly steel spectacles when Gabriel entered with a child in each arm. Shamron raised his liver-spotted hands—hands that were far too large for so small a man—and without apprehension Gabriel entrusted them with Raphael. Shamron held the child as though he were a live grenade and whispered nonsense into his ear in his murderous Polish accent. When Raphael emitted a peal of laughter, Gabriel was instantly glad he had come.

He had been raised in a home without religion, but as always, when Gilah drew the light of the Sabbath candles to her eyes while reciting the blessing, he thought it the most beautiful thing he had ever seen. Shamron then recited the blessings of the bread and the wine in the Yiddish intonations of his youth, and the meal commenced. Gabriel had yet to take his first bite when Shamron attempted to quiz him on the operation, but Gilah adroitly changed the subject to the children. Chiara briefed them on the latest developments—the dietary changes, the growth and weight gain, the attempts at speech and movement. Gabriel had caught only passing glimpses of the changes during the many months of the operation. In a few weeks' time they would gather again in Tiberias to celebrate the children's first birthday. He wondered whether Saladin would allow him to attend the party.

For the most part, though, he tried to forget the operation long enough to enjoy a quiet evening in the company of his family. He didn't dare turn off his phone, but he didn't check for updates from Paris, either. It wasn't necessary. He knew that in a few minutes Natalie would be leaving the clinic on the Avenue Victor Hugo, in the banlieue of Aubervilliers. Perhaps she would go to her café for something to eat or drink, or perhaps she would repair directly to her flat for another evening alone. Gabriel felt a stab of guilt—Natalie, he thought, should be passing the Sabbath in the company of her family, too. He wondered how much longer she could go on. Long enough, he hoped, for Saladin to come calling.

Shamron was quiet at dinner, for small talk had never been his strong suit. After finishing his coffee, he pulled on his old leather bomber jacket and led Gabriel outside to the terrace. It looked east toward the silvery surface of the lake and the looming black mass of the Golan Heights. Behind them was Mount Arbel, with its ancient synagogue and cave fortresses, and on the southeastern slope was a small town by the same name. The town had once been an Arab village called Hittin, and long before that, a thousand years ago, it had been known as Hattin. It was there, a stone's throw from the spot where Gabriel and Shamron now stood, that Saladin, the *real* Saladin, had laid waste to the armies of Rome.

Shamron ignited a pair of gas heaters to take the sharp chill off the air. Then, after fending off a halfhearted attack by Gabriel, he ignited one of his Turkish cigarettes, too. They sat in a pair of chairs at the edge of the terrace, Gabriel at Shamron's right hand, his phone resting on the small table between them. A minaret moon floated above the Golan Heights, shining its benevolent light on the lands of the caliphate. From behind them, through an open door, came the voices of Gilah and Chiara and the chirp and laughter of the children.

"Have you noticed," asked Shamron, "how much your son looks like Daniel?"

"It's difficult not to."

"It's shocking."

"Yes," said Gabriel, his eyes on the moon.

"You're a lucky man."

"Am I really?"

"It's not often we are given a second chance at happiness."

"But with happiness," said Gabriel, "comes guilt."

"You have nothing to feel guilty about. I was the one who recruited you. And I was the one who allowed you to take your wife and child with you to Vienna. If there's anyone who should feel guilty," said Shamron gravely, "it's me. And I'm reminded of my guilt each time I gaze into your son's face."

"And every time you put on that old jacket."

Shamron had torn the left shoulder of the jacket while hastily climbing into the back of his car on the night of the bombing in Vienna. He had never repaired it—it was Daniel's tear. From behind them came the soft voices of women and the laughter of a child, which one Gabriel could not tell. Yes, he thought, he was happy. But not an hour of a day went by when he did not hold the lifeless body of his son, or pull his wife from behind the wheel of a burning car. Happiness was his punishment for having survived.

"I enjoyed the article about the coming change in leadership at the Office."

"Did you?" Even Shamron seemed pleased by the change in subject. "I'm glad."

"That was low, Ari, even by your standards."

"I've never believed in fighting cleanly. That's why I'm a spy instead of a soldier."

"It was disruptive," said Gabriel.

"That's why I did it."

"Does the prime minister know you were behind it?"

"Who do you think asked me to do it in the first place?" Shamron raised his cigarette to his lips with a tremulous hand. "This situation," he said disdainfully, "has gone on long enough."

"I'm running an operation."

"You can walk and chew gum at the same time."

"Your point?"

"I was an operational chief," answered Shamron, "and I expect you to be an operational chief, too."

"The minute Saladin's network makes contact with Natalie, we'll have to go on a war footing. I can't be worrying about personnel matters and parking privileges while trying to stop the next attack."

"*If* he makes contact with her." Shamron slowly crushed out his cigarette. "Two and a half months is a long time."

"Two and a half months is nothing, and you know it. Besides, it fits the network's profile. Safia Bourihane was dormant for many months after her return from Syria. So dormant, in fact, that the French lost interest in her, which is exactly what Saladin wanted to happen."

"I'm afraid the prime minister isn't prepared to wait much longer. And neither am I."

"Really? It's good to know you still have the prime minister's ear."

"What makes you think I ever lost it?" Shamron's old Zippo lighter flared. He touched the end of another cigarette to the flame.

"How long?" asked Gabriel.

"If Saladin's network hasn't made contact with Natalie by next Friday, the prime minister will announce your appointment live on television. And next Sunday you will attend your first cabinet meeting as chief of the Office."

"When was the prime minister planning to tell me this?"

"He's telling you now," said Shamron.

"Why now? Why the sudden rush to get me into the job?"

"Politics," said Shamron. "The prime minister's coalition is in danger of fracturing. He needs a boost, and he's confident you'll give him one."

"I have no interest in coming to the prime minister's political rescue, now or ever."

"May I give you a piece of advice, my son?"

"If you must."

"One day soon you're going to make a mistake. There will be a scandal or an operational disaster. And you'll need the prime minister to save you. Don't alienate him."

"I hope to keep the disasters and scandals to a minimum."

"Please don't. Remember, a career without scandal—"

"Is not a proper career at all."

"You were listening after all."

"To every word."

Shamron lifted his rheumy gaze toward the Golan Heights. "Where do you suppose he is?"

"Saladin?"

Shamron nodded.

"The Americans think he's somewhere near Mosul."

"I wasn't asking the Americans, I was asking you."

"I haven't a clue."

"I'd avoid using phrases like that when you're briefing the prime minister."

"I'll keep that in mind."

There was a brief silence.

"Is it true she saved his life?" asked Shamron.

"I'm afraid so."

"And for her reward, Saladin will send her to her death."

"We should be so lucky."

Just then, Gabriel's phone flared. The screen lit his face as he read the message. Shamron could see he was smiling.

"Good news?" he asked.

"Very."

"What is it?"

"It looks as though I've been granted another reprieve."

"By the prime minister?"

"No," said Gabriel, switching off the phone. "By Saladin."

47

AMMAN, JORDAN

GABRIEL RETURNED TO NARKISS STREET long enough to throw a few items of clothing into a suitcase. Then he crawled into the backseat of his SUV for a high-speed drive across the West Bank to Amman's Queen Alia Airport, where one of His Majesty's Gulfstreams was fueled and ready for takeoff. Fareed Barakat was stretched out on one of the leather seats, his necktie loosened, looking like a busy executive at the end of a long but lucrative day. The plane was taxiing before Gabriel had settled into his own seat, and a moment later it was airborne. It was still climbing as it passed over Jerusalem.

"Look at the settlements," said Fareed, pointing toward the orderly yellow streetlamps spilling down the ancient hills into the West Bank. "Every year, more and more. At the rate you're building, Amman will soon be a suburb of Jerusalem."

Gabriel's gaze was elsewhere, on the old limestone apartment house near the end of Narkiss Street where his wife and children slept peacefully because of people like him.

"Maybe this was a mistake," he said quietly.

"Would you rather fly El Al?"

"I can get a kosher meal, and I don't have to listen to a lecture about the evils of Israel."

"I'm afraid we don't have any kosher food on board."

"Don't worry, Fareed, I already ate."

"Something to drink? How about a film? His Majesty gets all the new American movies from his friends in Hollywood."

"I think I'll just sleep."

"Wise decision."

Fareed switched off his light as the Gulfstream departed Israeli airspace, and soon he was sleeping soundly. Gabriel had never been able to sleep on airplanes, an affliction that not even the fully reclining seat of the Gulfstream could cure. He ordered coffee from the cabin crew and stared distractedly at the inane film that flickered on his private screen. His phone provided him no company. The plane had Wi-Fi, but Gabriel had powered off and dismantled his phone before crossing the Jordanian border. As a rule, it was better not to allow one's mobile phone to attach itself to the wireless network of a monarch—or an Israeli network, for that matter.

An hour from the eastern seaboard of the United States, Fareed woke gently, as though an invisible butler had tapped him lightly on the shoulder. Rising, he repaired to His Majesty's private quarters, where he shaved and showered and changed into a fresh suit and tie. The cabin crew brought him a lavish English breakfast. He lifted the lid of the teapot and sniffed. The Earl Grey had been brewed to his requested strength.

"Nothing for you?" asked the Jordanian as he poured.

"I had a snack while you were sleeping," lied Gabriel.

"Feel free to use His Majesty's facilities."

"I'll just steal a towel as a souvenir."

The plane touched down at Dulles Airport in a steel morning rain and taxied to a distant hangar. Three black SUVs waited there, along with a large all-American detail of security men. Gabriel and Fareed climbed into one of the vehicles and were whisked eastward along the Dulles Access Road toward the Capital Beltway. The Liberty Crossing Intelligence Campus, ground zero of Washington's post–9/11 national security sprawl, occupied several acres of land adjacent to the giant highway interchange. Their destination, however, was located a few miles farther to the east along Route 123. It was the George Bush Center for Intelligence, otherwise known as CIA Headquarters.

After clearing the massive security checkpoint, they proceeded to an underground parking garage and boarded a restricted elevator that bore them to the seventh floor of the Original Headquarters Building. A security detail waited in the wood-paneled foyer to relieve them of their mobile phones. Fareed dutifully surrendered his device, but Gabriel refused. A brief standoff ensued before he was allowed to proceed.

"Why didn't I ever think of that?" murmured Fareed as they padded silently down a densely carpeted hall.

"What do they think I'm going to do? Bug myself?"

They were led to a conference room with windows overlooking the woods along the Potomac. Adrian Carter waited there alone. He was wearing a blue blazer and a pair of wrinkled chinos, a spymaster's Saturday-morning attire. He looked decidedly displeased to see his two closest Middle East allies.

"I don't suppose this is a social call."

"I'm afraid not," answered Gabriel.

"What have you got?"

"An airline ticket, a hotel reservation, and a rental car."

"What does it mean?"

"It means the jayvee team is about to launch a major terrorist attack on the American homeland."

Carter's face turned ashen. He said nothing.

"Am I forgiven, Adrian?"

"That depends."

"On what?"

"On whether you can help me stop it."

"WHICH FLIGHT IS SHE COMING IN ON?"

"Air France Fifty-four."

"When?"

"Tuesday."

"A few hours before the French president arrives," Carter pointed out.

"I doubt it's a coincidence."

"Which hotel?"

"Key Bridge Marriott."

"Rental car?"

"Hertz."

"I don't suppose they gave her a target, too."

"Sorry, Adrian, but that's not Saladin's style."

"It was worth asking. After all, she *did* save his life."

Gabriel frowned but said nothing.

"I assume," said Carter, "that you intend to let her get on that plane."

"With your approval," said Gabriel. "And you would be wise to let her into the country."

"Put her under watch—is that what you're suggesting? Wait for the other members of the attack cell to make contact? Roll them up before they can strike?"

"Do you have a better idea?"

"What if she's not the only operational asset? What if there are other teams? Other targets?"

"You should assume there *are* other teams and targets, Adrian. A lot of them, in fact. Saladin told Natalie that she was going to be involved in something big—big enough to leave the United States with no choice but to put boots on the ground in Syria."

"What if they don't make contact with her? Or what if she's part of a second wave of attacks?"

"Forgive me for not bringing you the entire plot gift wrapped, Adrian, but that's not the way it works in the real world."

Fareed Barakat smiled. It wasn't often he was given a front-row seat to a spat between the Americans and the Israelis.

"How much does Jalal Nasser know?" asked Carter.

"Should I call and ask him? I'm sure he'd love to help us."

"Maybe it's time to pull him in for a little chat."

Fareed shook his head gravely. "Bad idea."

"Why?"

"Because in all likelihood he doesn't know the entire picture. Furthermore," added Fareed, "if we arrest Jalal, it will send a signal to Saladin that his network has been compromised."

"Maybe that's exactly the signal we should send him."

"He'll lash out, Adrian. He'll hit you any way he can."

Carter exhaled slowly. "Who's handling the surveillance in London?"

"We're working jointly with the British."

"I need in on that, too."

"Three's a crowd, Adrian."

"I don't give a shit." Carter frowned at his wristwatch. It was half past eight on a Saturday morning. "Why do these things always seem to break on the weekend?" Greeted by silence, he looked at Gabriel. "In a few minutes, several hundred employees of my government are going to learn that the Office has an agent deep inside ISIS. Are you prepared for that?"

"I wouldn't be here otherwise."

"Once she gets off that plane, she's no longer your agent. She'll be our agent, and it will be *our* operation. Are we clear?"

"Perfectly," said Gabriel. "But whatever you do, make damn sure nothing happens to her."

Carter reached for the phone and dialed. "I need to speak to the director. *Now.*"

48

ARLINGTON, VIRGINIA

Q ASSAM EL-BANNA WOKE TO THE call to prayer. He had
been dreaming, about what he could not recall—his dreams,
like contentment, eluded him. From an early age, while still
a boy in the Nile Delta of Egypt, he believed he was destined
for greatness. He had studied hard in school, won admission
to a mildly prestigious university in the eastern United States,
and after a lengthy struggle had convinced the Americans to
let him remain in the country to work. And for all his efforts
he had been rewarded with a life of uninterrupted tedium. It
was a distinctly American tedium of traffic jams, credit card
debt, fast food, and weekend trips to the Tysons Corner mall
to push his son past shop windows hung with photographs
of unveiled, half-naked women. For a long time he blamed
Allah for his plight. Why had he given him visions of greatness, only to make him ordinary? What's more, Qassam was
now forced by the folly of his ambition to reside in the House
of War, in the land of the unbelievers. After much reflection
he had come to the conclusion that Allah had placed him in
America for a reason. Allah had provided Qassam el-Banna

with a path to greatness. And with greatness would come immortality.

Qassam lifted his Samsung from the bedside table and silenced the muezzin's tinny nasally wail. Amina had slept through it. Amina, he had discovered, could sleep through anything—the cry of a child, thunder, fire alarms, the tap of his fingers on the keyboard of his laptop. Amina, too, was disappointed, not with Allah but with Qassam. She had come to America with reality-TV visions of a life in Bel Air, only to find herself living around the corner from a 7-Eleven off Carlin Springs Road. She berated Qassam daily for failing to earn more money and consoled herself by driving them deeper into debt. Her latest acquisition was a new luxury car. The dealership had approved the sale despite their abysmal credit rating. Only in America, thought Qassam.

He slipped soundlessly from bed, unfurled a small mat, and prayed for the first time that day. He pressed his forehead only lightly to the floor to avoid giving himself a dark callused prayer mark—it was known as a *zabiba*, the Arabic word for raisin—like the marks on the religious men from his village. Islam had left no visible marks on Qassam. He did not pray in any of the Northern Virginia mosques and avoided other Muslims as much as possible. He even tried to play down his Arabic name. At his last place of employment, a small IT consulting firm, he had been known as Q or Q-Ban, which he liked because of its vaguely Hispanic and hip-hop sensibilities. He was not one of those Muslims with his face on the ground and his ass in the air, he would say to his colleagues over beers in his faintly accented English. He came to America because he wanted to escape all that. Yes, his wife wore a hijab, but that had more to do with tradition and fashion than faith. And, yes, he had named his son Mohamed, but it had nothing to do with the Prophet. That much, at least, was true.

Qassam el-Banna had named his son after Mohamed Atta, the operational leader of the 9/11 plot. Atta, like Qassam, was a son of the Nile Delta. It was not the only trait they had in common.

His prayers complete, Qassam rose and went quietly downstairs to the kitchen, where he popped a capsule of French roast into the Keurig. Then, in the living room, he performed two hundred push-ups and five hundred abdominal crunches. His twice-daily workouts had reshaped his body. He was no longer the skinny kid from the Delta; he had the body of a cage fighter. In addition to his exercises, he had become a master of both karate and Brazilian jujitsu. Qassam el-Banna, Q-Ban, was a killing machine.

He finished the workout with a few lethal movements of each discipline and then headed back upstairs. Amina was still sleeping, as was Mohamed. Qassam used the third bedroom of the little duplex as his office. It was a hacker's paradise. Entering, he sat down at one of the three computers and quickly surfed a dozen e-mail accounts and social media pages. A few more keystrokes took him to a doorway of the dark net, the murky Internet world hidden beneath the surface Web that can be accessed only if the user has the proper protocol, ports, passwords, and software applications. Qassam, an IT professional, had everything he needed—and more.

Qassam passed easily through the door and soon found himself standing before another. The proper password admitted him, a line of text wished him peace and inquired as to his business. He typed his answer into the designated box and after a brief delay was presented with a waiting message.

"Alhamdulillah," he said softly.

His heart beat faster—faster than during his rigorous workout. Twice, he had to reenter the password because in his haste he had typed it incorrectly. At first, the message appeared as gibberish—lines, letters, and numbers, with no apparent purpose—but the proper password instantly turned the gibberish into clear text. Qassam read it slowly, for the message could not be printed, saved, copied, or retrieved. The words themselves were coded, too, though he knew precisely what they meant. Allah had finally put him on the path to greatness. And with greatness, he thought, would come immortality.

GABRIEL DECLINED CARTER'S INVITATION TO ACCOMPANY HIM to the White House. His only previous meeting with the president had been a tense affair, and his presence in the West Wing now would only be an unhelpful distraction. It was far better to let Adrian tell the administration that the American homeland was about to be attacked by a group that the president had once written off as weak and ineffectual. To hear such news from the mouth of an Israeli would only invite skepticism, something they could not afford.

Gabriel did, however, accept Carter's offer of the N Street safe house and an Agency SUV and security detail. After leaving Langley, he headed to the Israeli Embassy in far Northwest Washington. There, in the Office's secure communications crypt, he checked in with his teams in Paris and London before ringing Paul Rousseau at his office on the rue de Grenelle. Rousseau had just returned from the Élysée Palace, where he had delivered the same message that Adrian Carter was conveying to the White House. ISIS was planning an attack on American soil, in all likelihood while the French president was in town.

"What else has he got on his schedule other than the White House meeting with the president and the state dinner?"

"A cocktail reception at the French Embassy."

"Cancel it."

"He refuses to make any changes in his schedule."

"How courageous of him."

"He seems to think so."

"How soon can you get here?"

"I arrive Monday night with the advance team. We're staying at the Four Seasons."

"Dinner?"

"Done."

From the embassy Gabriel headed to the safe house for a few hours of badly needed sleep. Carter woke him in late afternoon.

"We're on," was all he said.

"Did you speak to Mr. Big?"

"For a minute or two."

"How did he take the news?"

"As well as you might expect."

"Did my name come up?"

"Oh, yes."

"And?"

"He says hello."

"Is that all?"

"At least he knows your name. He still calls me Andrew."

Gabriel tried to sleep again but it was no good, so he showered and changed and with an Agency security team in tow slipped from the safe house in the last minutes of daylight. The air was heavy with a coming storm; leaves of copper and gold littered the redbrick pavements. He drank a café crème in a patisserie on Wisconsin Avenue and then wandered through the East Village of Georgetown to M Street, with its parade of shops, restaurants, and hotels. Yes, he thought, there would be other teams and other targets. And even if they managed to stop Dr. Leila Hadawi's attack, it was likely that in a few days' time Americans would once again die in their own country because of an ideology, and a faith, born of a region that most could not find on a map. The enemy could not be reasoned with or dismissed; it could not be appeased by an American withdrawal from the Islamic world. America could leave the Middle East, thought Gabriel, but the Middle East would follow it home.

At once, the skies erupted and a downpour sent the pedestrians along M Street scurrying for cover. Gabriel watched them for a moment, but in his thoughts they were running from something else—men with long hair and beards, their surnames taken from their hometowns. The appearance of an SUV curbside wrenched him back to the present. He climbed inside, his leather jacket sodden, and rode back to N Street through the rain.

49

ALEXANDRIA, VIRGINIA

THE SAME RAIN THAT DRENCHED Georgetown beat down upon Qassam el-Banna's modest Korean sedan as he drove along a tree-lined section of Route 7. He had told Amina that he had to make a work call. It was an untruth, but only a small one.

It had been more than a year since Qassam had left his old IT consulting firm. He had told his colleagues and his wife that he was striking out on his own, a risky move in Northern Virginia's crowded tech world. The real reasons for his career change, however, lay elsewhere. Qassam had left his previous place of employment because he needed something more precious than money. He needed time. He could not be at the beck and call of Larry Blackburn, his old supervisor— Larry of the sewer breath, the secret addiction to painkillers, and the taste for cheap Salvadoran hookers. Qassam was now beholden to a man of far greater ambitions. He did not know the man's real name, only his nom de guerre. He was the one from Iraq, the one they called Saladin.

Not surprisingly, Qassam's journey had begun in cyber-

space, where, his identity carefully shielded, he had indulged
in his unquenchable appetite for the blood and bombs of jihadist porn—an appetite he had developed during the American occupation of Iraq, when he was still at university. One
evening, after a miserable day at work and a nightmarish
commute home, he had knocked on the cyberdoor of an ISIS
recruiter and inquired about traveling to Syria to become a
fighter. The ISIS recruiter had made inquiries of his own and
had convinced Qassam to remain in suburban Washington.
Not long after, a month or so, he realized he was being followed. At first, he feared it was the FBI, but it soon became
clear he was seeing the same man again and again. The man
finally approached Qassam in a Starbucks near Seven Corners
and introduced himself. He was a Jordanian who lived in London. His name was Jalal Nasser.

The rain was coming down in torrents, more like a summer thunderstorm than a slow and steady autumn soaker. Perhaps the doomsday scenarios were true after all, he thought.
Perhaps the earth was irrevocably broken. He continued
along Route 7 into the center of Alexandria and made his
way to an industrial park on Eisenhower Avenue. Wedged
between a transmission repair shop and a shooting range
were the offices of Dominion Movers. Two of the company's
American-made Freightliner trucks were parked outside. Two
more were parked on the floor of the warehouse, where they
had been for the past six months. Qassam el-Banna was the
moving company's nominal owner. He had twelve employees.
Seven were recent arrivals in America, five were citizens. All
were members of ISIS.

Qassam el-Banna did not enter the premises of his moving
enterprise. Instead, he engaged the stopwatch function on his
mobile and headed back to Eisenhower Avenue. His Korean
sedan was quick and nimble, but now he drove it at the slow,

lumbering pace of a fully loaded moving truck. He followed the Eisenhower Avenue Connector to the Capital Beltway and the Beltway in a clockwise direction to Route 123 in Tysons. As he was approaching Anderson Road, the traffic light turned to amber. Normally, Qassam would have put his foot to the floor. But now, imagining he were behind the wheel of a laden truck, he slowed to a stop.

When the light turned green, Qassam accelerated so slowly that the driver behind him flashed his headlamps and sounded his horn. Undeterred, he proceeded at five miles below the speed limit to Lewinsville Road, where he made a left. It was less than a quarter mile to the intersection of Tysons McLean Drive. To the left, the road rose gently into what appeared to be the campus of a high-tech firm. Qassam turned to the right and stopped next to a bright yellow road sign that read WATCH FOR CHILDREN. Qassam watched his phone instead: *24:23:45 . . . 24:23:46 . . . 24:23:47 . . . 24:23:48 . . .*

When it reached twenty-five minutes exactly, he smiled and whispered, "Boom."

50

GEORGETOWN

THE RAIN POURED STEADILY DOWN for the remainder of the weekend, returning Washington to the swamp it had once been. Gabriel was largely a prisoner of the N Street safe house. Once each day he journeyed to the Israeli Embassy to check in with his field teams and with King Saul Boulevard, and once each day Adrian Carter rang him with an update. The FBI and the other agencies of American homeland security were closely monitoring more than a thousand known or suspected members of ISIS. "And not one of them," said Carter, "appears to be in the final preparations for an attack."

"There's just one problem, Adrian."

"What's that?"

"The FBI is watching the wrong people."

By Monday afternoon the rains began to slow, and by that evening a few stars were visible through the thinning clouds. Gabriel wanted to walk to the Four Seasons for his dinner with Paul Rousseau, but his CIA security detail prevailed upon him to take the SUV instead. It dropped him outside the hotel's covered entrance and, trailed by a single bodyguard, he entered the lobby. Several bleary-eyed French officials, their suits wrinkled by transatlantic travel, waited at reception, behind a tall, broad-shouldered man, Arab in appearance, who looked as though he had borrowed Fareed Barakat's London tailor. Only the Arab-looking man took note of the thin Israeli who was accompanied by an American security guard. Their eyes met briefly. Then the tall Arab-looking man turned his gaze once more toward the woman behind the desk. Gabriel inspected his back as he passed. He appeared to be unarmed. A leather attaché case stood upright next to his right shoe. And leaning against the front of the reception desk, black and polished, was an elegant walking stick.

Gabriel continued across the lobby and entered the restaurant. It seemed the bar had been commandeered by a convention of the hard of hearing. He gave the maître d' a name not his own and was shown to a table overlooking Rock Creek Parkway. Better still, it had an unobstructed view of the lobby, where the tall, impeccably clad Arab was now limping slowly toward the elevators.

HE HAD REQUESTED A SUITE ON THE UPPERMOST FLOOR OF THE hotel. His request had been granted, in no small part because the hotel's management believed him to be a distant relative of the king of Saudi Arabia. A moment after he entered the room, there was a discreet knock at the door. It was the porter with his luggage. The tall Arab admired the vista from his window while the porter, an African, hung his garment bag in the closet and placed his suitcase on a stand in the bedroom. The usual pre-tip banter ensued, with its many offers of additional assistance, but a crisp twenty-dollar bill sent the porter gratefully toward the door. It closed softly and once again the tall Arab was alone.

His eyes were fixed on the traffic rushing along Rock Creek Parkway. His thoughts, however, were on the man whom he had seen downstairs in the lobby—the man with gray temples and distinctive green eyes. He was almost certain he had seen the man before, not in person but in photographs and news accounts. It was possible he was mistaken. In fact, he thought, it was likely the case. Even so, he had learned long ago to trust his instincts. They had been sharpened to a razor's edge during the many years he served the Arab world's cruelest dictator. And they had helped him to survive the long fight against the Americans, when many other men like him had been vaporized by weapons that struck from the sky with the suddenness of lightning.

He removed a laptop computer from his attaché case and connected it to the hotel's wireless Internet system. Because the Four Seasons was popular with visiting dignitaries, the NSA had undoubtedly penetrated its network. It was no matter; the hard drive of his computer was a blank page. He opened the Internet browser and typed a name into the search box. Several photos appeared on the screen, including one from London's *Telegraph* newspaper that showed a man running along a footpath outside Westminster Abbey, a gun in his hand. Linked to the photo was an article by a reporter named Samantha Cooke concerning the man's violent death. It seemed the reporter was mistaken, because the subject of her article had just crossed the lobby of the Four Seasons Hotel in Washington.

There was another knock at the door, soft, almost apologetic—the obligatory fruit plate, along with a note addressed to Mr. Omar al-Farouk, promising to fulfill his every wish. At the moment he wanted only a few minutes of uninterrupted solitude. He typed an address for the dark net, picked the lock of a password-protected door, and entered a virtual room where all was encrypted. An old friend was waiting there for him.

The old friend asked, HOW WAS YOUR TRIP?

He typed, FINE BUT YOU WILL NEVER GUESS WHO I JUST SAW.

WHO?

He typed the first and last name—the name of an archangel followed by a rather common Israeli surname. The response was a few seconds longer in coming.

YOU SHOULDN'T JOKE ABOUT THINGS LIKE THAT.

I'M NOT.

WHAT DO YOU THINK IT MEANS?

A very good question indeed. He logged off the Internet, shut down the computer, and limped slowly to the window. He felt as though a dagger were lodged in the thigh of his right leg, his chest throbbed. He watched the traffic moving along the parkway, and for a few seconds the pain seemed to diminish. Then the traffic blurred and in his thoughts he was astride a mighty Arabian horse on a mountaintop near the Sea of Galilee, gazing down at a sunbaked place called Hattin. The vision was not new to him; it came often. Usually, two mighty armies—one Muslim, the other Crusader, the army of Rome—were arrayed for battle. But now only two men were present. One was an Israeli named Gabriel Allon. And the other was Saladin.

PAUL ROUSSEAU WAS STILL ON PARIS TIME, AND SO THEY DID not linger long over dinner. Gabriel bade him good night at the elevators and, trailed by his bodyguard, headed across the lobby. The same woman was behind the reception desk.

"May I help you?" she asked as Gabriel approached.

"I certainly hope so. Earlier this evening I saw a gentleman checking in. Tall, very well dressed, walked with a cane."

"Mr. al-Farouk?"

"Yes, that's him. We used to work together a long time ago."

"I see."

"Do you know how long he's staying?"

"I'm sorry, but I'm not—"

He held up a hand. "Don't apologize. I understand your rules."

"I'd be happy to give him a message."

"That's not necessary. I'll ring him in the morning. But don't mention any of this to him," Gabriel added conspiratorially. "I want to surprise him."

Gabriel went outside into the chill night. He waited until he was in the back of his Suburban before ringing Adrian Carter. Carter was still at his office in Langley.

"I want you to have a look at someone named al-Farouk. He's about forty-five years old, maybe fifty. I don't know his first name or the color of his passport."

"What *do* you know about him?"

"He's staying at the Four Seasons."

"Am I missing something?"

"I got a funny feeling at the back of my neck, Adrian. Find out who he is."

The connection went dead. Gabriel returned the phone to his coat pocket.

"Back to N Street?" asked the driver.

"No," answered Gabriel. "Take me to the embassy."

51

AUBERVILLIERS, FRANCE

THE ALARM ON NATALIE'S MOBILE phone sounded at seven fifteen, which was odd, because she didn't remember setting it. In fact, she was quite certain she hadn't. She silenced the phone with an annoyed tap of her finger and tried to sleep a little longer, but five minutes later it rang a second time. "All right," she said to the spot in the ceiling where she imagined the camera to be hidden. "You win. I'll get up."

She threw aside the bedding and swung her feet to the floor. In the kitchen she brewed a pot of oily black Carte Noire in the Mocha stovetop maker and poured it into a bowl of steaming milk. Outside, the night was draining slowly from her drab street. In all likelihood, it was the last Paris morning that Dr. Leila Hadawi would ever see, for if Saladin had his way, she would not be returning to France from her sudden, unexpected trip to America. Natalie's return was uncertain, too. Standing in her sooty little window, her hands wrapped around the café au lait, she realized she would not miss it. Her life in the banlieues had only reinforced her conviction that there was no future in France for the Jews. Israel was her home—Israel and the Office. Gabriel was right. She was one of them now.

Neither ISIS nor the Office had given her packing instructions, and so instinctively she packed lightly. Her flight was scheduled to depart Charles de Gaulle at 1:45 p.m. She journeyed to the airport on the RER and at half past eleven joined the long line at the economy check-in counter. After a wait of thirty minutes a disagreeable Frenchwoman informed her that she had been upgraded to business class.

"Why?"

"Would you rather stay in economy?"

The woman handed Natalie her boarding pass and returned her passport. She loitered for several minutes in the shops of duty-free, observed by the watchers of the DGSI, before making her way to the departure gate. Because Flight 54 was bound for America, there were special security measures. Her hijab and Arabic name earned her several minutes of additional preflight screening, but eventually she was admitted into the departure lounge. She searched for familiar faces but found none. In a complimentary copy of *Le Monde* she read about the French president's upcoming visit to America and, on an inside page, about a new wave of stabbings in Israel. She burned with rage. She rejoiced.

Presently, the crackle of a boarding call brought her to her feet. She had been given a seat on the right side of the aircraft against the window. The seat next to her remained empty long after the economy passengers had boarded, instilling in her the hope she might not have to spend the next seven and a half hours with a complete stranger. That hope died when a business-suited man with coal-black hair and matching eyeglasses lowered himself into the seat next to her. He didn't appear pleased to be sitting next to an Arab woman in a hijab. He stared at his mobile phone, Natalie stared at hers.

After a few seconds a message appeared on her screen.

LONELY?

She typed, YES.

WANT SOME COMPANY?

LOVE SOME.

LOOK TO YOUR LEFT.

She did. The man with coal-black hair and matching eye-wear was still staring at his phone, but now he was smiling.

"Is this a good idea?" she asked.

"What's that?" asked Mikhail.

"You and me together?"

"I'll tell you after we land."

"What happens then?"

Before he could answer, an announcement instructed passengers to switch off their mobile devices. Natalie and her seatmate complied. As the plane thundered down the runway, she placed her hand on his.

"Not yet," he whispered.

"When?" she asked, pulling away her hand.

"Soon," he said. "Very soon."

52

HUME, VIRGINIA

IN WASHINGTON THE RAINS HAD finally ended, and a blast of cold, clear air had scrubbed the last remaining clouds from the sky. The great marble monuments glowed white as bone in the sharp sunlight; a brisk wind chased fallen leaves through the streets of Georgetown. Only the Potomac River bore the scars of the deluge. Swollen by runoff, clogged with tree limbs and debris, it flowed brown and heavy beneath Key Bridge as Saladin drove toward Virginia. He was dressed for a weekend in the English countryside—corduroy trousers, a woolen crewneck sweater, a dark-green Barbour jacket. He turned right onto the George Washington Memorial Parkway and headed west.

The roadway ran along the bank of the river for about a quarter mile before climbing to the top of the gorge. Trees in autumn leaf blazed in the bright sunlight, and across the muddy river traffic flowed along a parallel parkway. Even Saladin had to admit it was a welcome change from the harsh world of western Iraq and the caliphate. The comfortable leather seat of the luxury German sedan held him with the tenderness of a cupped hand. A member of the network had left it for him in a small parking lot at the corner of M Street and Wisconsin Avenue, a painful walk of several blocks from the Four Seasons Hotel. Saladin was tempted to put the machine through its paces and test his skills on the smooth, winding road. Instead, he kept assiduously to the posted speed limit while other drivers rode his rear bumper and made obscene gestures as they roared past on his left. Americans, he thought—always in a hurry. It was both their greatest strength and their undoing. How foolish they were to think they could snap their fingers and alter the political landscape of the Middle East. Men like Saladin did not measure time in four-year election cycles. As a child he had lived on the banks of one of the four rivers that flowed out of the Garden of Eden. His civilization had flourished for thousands of years in the harsh and unforgiving land of Mesopotamia before anyone had ever heard of a place called America. And it would survive long after the great American experiment receded into history. Of this, Saladin was certain. All great empires eventually collapsed. Only Islam was forever.

The car's navigation system guided Saladin onto the Capital Beltway. He drove south, across the Dulles Access Road, past the shopping malls of Tysons Corner, to Interstate 66, where he once again headed west, toward the foothills of the Shenandoah Mountains. The eastbound lanes were still clogged with morning commuter traffic, but before Saladin stretched several car-lengths of empty asphalt, a rarity for the metropolitan Washington motorist. Again, he kept diligently to the speed limit while other traffic overtook him. The last thing he needed now was a traffic stop; it would put at risk an elaborate plot that had taken months of meticulous planning. Paris and Amsterdam had been dress rehearsals. Washington was Saladin's ultimate target, for only the Americans had the power to unleash the chain of events he was attempting to bring about. A final review of the plan with his primary Washington operative was all that remained. It was dangerous—there was always the possibility the operative had been compromised—but Saladin wanted to hear from the man's lips that everything was in place.

He passed the exit for a town with the quintessentially American-sounding name of Gainesville. The traffic thinned, the terrain turned hilly, the blue peaks of the Shenandoah seemed within reach. He had been driving for three-quarters of an hour, and his right leg was beginning to throb from the effort of controlling his speed. To distract himself from the pain, he allowed his mind to drift. It settled quickly on the man he had seen in the lobby of the Four Seasons Hotel the previous evening.

Gabriel Allon . . .

It was possible Allon's presence in Washington was entirely coincidental—after all, the Israeli had worked closely with the Americans for many years—but Saladin doubted that was the case. Several Israeli citizens had died in the Paris attack, along with Hannah Weinberg, a woman who was a personal friend of Allon's and an asset of Israeli intelligence. It was entirely possible that Allon had taken part in the post-attack investigation. Perhaps he had learned of the existence of Saladin's network. And perhaps he had learned, too, that the network was about to carry out an attack in America. *But how?* The answer to that question was quite simple. Saladin had to assume that Allon had managed to penetrate his network—it was, thought the Iraqi, Allon's special talent. And if Allon knew about the network, the Americans knew about it, too. Most of Saladin's operatives had infiltrated the country from abroad through the porous American visa and immigration system. But several operatives, including the man Saladin was about to meet, were American based, and therefore more vulnerable to U.S. counterterrorism efforts. They were critical to the operation's success, but they were the weak link in the network's long chain.

The navigation system advised Saladin to leave Interstate 66 at Exit 18. He followed the instructions and found himself in a town called Markham. No, he thought, it was not a town, it was a tiny collection of houses with covered porches looking out upon overgrown lawns. He headed south along Leeds Manor Road, past fenced pastures and barns, until he came to a town called Hume. It was slightly larger than the first. Still, there were no shops or markets, only an auto repair shop, a country inn, and a couple of churches where the infidels worshiped their blasphemous version of God.

The navigation system was now essentially useless; the address of Saladin's destination was far too remote. He turned right onto Hume Road and followed it six-tenths of a mile, until he came to an unpaved track. It bore him across a pasture, over a ridge of wooded hills, and into a small dell. There was a black pond, its surface smooth as glass, and a timbered A-frame cottage. Saladin switched off the engine; the silence was like the silence of the desert. He opened the trunk. Concealed inside were a 9mm Glock 19 and a high-performance sound and flash suppressor, both of which had been purchased legally in Virginia by a member of Saladin's network.

The gun in his left hand, his cane in the right, Saladin cautiously entered the cottage. Its furnishings were rustic and sparse. In the kitchen he boiled a pot of water—it smelled as though it came unfiltered from the pond—and coaxed a cup of weak tea from an elderly bag of Twinings. Returning to the sitting room, he lowered himself onto the couch and gazed through the triangular picture window, toward the ridge of hills he had just crossed. After a few minutes a little Korean sedan appeared, trailing a cloud of dust. Saladin concealed the gun beneath an embroidered pillow that read GOD BLESS THIS HOUSE. Then he blew on his tea and waited.

SALADIN HAD NEVER MET THE OPERATIVE IN PERSON, THOUGH he knew him to be a green-carded Egyptian citizen named Qassam el-Banna, five foot nine inches in height, 165 pounds, tightly curled hair, light brown eyes. The man who entered the cottage matched that description. He appeared nervous. With a nod, Saladin instructed him to sit. Then in Arabic he said, "Peace be upon you, Brother Qassam."

The young Egyptian was clearly flattered. Softly, he repeated the traditional Islamic greeting of peace, though without the name of the man he was addressing.

"Do you know who I am?" asked Saladin.

"No," answered the Egyptian quickly. "We've never met."

"But surely you've heard of me."

It was obvious the young Egyptian did not know how to answer the question, so he proceeded with caution. "I received a message instructing me to come to this location for a meeting. I was not told who would be here or why he wanted to see me."

"Were you followed?"

"No."

"Are you sure?"

The young Egyptian vigorously nodded his head.

"And the moving company?" asked Saladin. "I trust there are no problems?"

There was a brief pause. "Moving company?"

Saladin gave him a reassuring smile. It was surprisingly charming, the smile of a professional.

"Your caution is admirable, Qassam. But I can assure you it's not necessary."

The Egyptian was silent.

"Do you know who I am?" Saladin asked again.

"Yes, I believe I do."

"Then answer my question."

"There are no problems at the moving company. Everything is in place."

Again, Saladin smiled. "I'll be the judge of that."

HE DEBRIEFED THE YOUNG EGYPTIAN WITH THE PATIENCE OF A skilled professional. Saladin's professionalism, however, was twofold. He was an intelligence officer turned master terrorist. He had honed his skills in the badlands of Anbar Province, where he had plotted countless car bombings and suicide attacks, all while sleeping in a different bed every night and evading the drones and the F-16s. Now he was about to lay siege to the American capital from the comfort of the Four Seasons Hotel. The irony, he thought, was exquisite. Saladin was prepared for this moment like no other terrorist in history. He was America's creation. He was America's nightmare.

No detail of the operation was too small to evade Saladin's scrutiny—the primary targets, the backup targets, the weapons, the vehicle-borne bombs, the suicide vests. The young Egyptian answered each question fully and without hesitation. Jalal Nasser and Abu Ahmed al-Tikriti had been wise to choose him; he had a brain like a computer hard drive. The individual operatives knew portions of the plot, but Qassam el-Banna knew almost everything. If he happened to fall into the hands of the FBI while driving back to Arlington, it would be a disaster. For that reason alone, he would not be leaving the isolated cottage outside Hume alive.

"Have all the operatives been told their targets?" asked Saladin.

"Everyone but the Palestinian doctor."

"When does she arrive?"

"Her flight is scheduled to land at four thirty, but it's running a few minutes ahead of schedule."

"You checked?"

He nodded. He was good, thought Saladin, as good as Mohamed Atta. Too bad he would never achieve the same fame. Mohamed Atta was spoken of with reverence in jihadi circles, but only a handful of people in the movement would ever know the name Qassam el-Banna.

"I'm afraid," said Saladin, "there's been a slight change in the plan."

"Regarding?"

"You."

"What about me?"

"I want you to leave the country tonight and make your way to the caliphate."

"But if I make a reservation at the last minute, the Americans—"

"Will suspect nothing," Saladin said firmly. "It's too dangerous for you to stay here, Brother Qassam. You know too much."

The Egyptian made no reply.

"You've cleaned out your computers?" asked Saladin.

"Yes, of course."

"And your wife knows nothing of your work?"

"Nothing."

"Will she join you?"

"I doubt it."

"A shame," said Saladin. "But I can assure you there's no shortage of beautiful young women in the caliphate."

"So I've heard."

The young Egyptian was smiling for the first time. When Saladin lifted the embroidered pillow, exposing the silenced Glock, the smile evaporated.

"Don't worry, my brother," said Saladin. "It was just a precaution in case the FBI came through the door instead of you." He held out his hand. "Help me up. I'll see you out."

Gun in one hand, walking stick in the other, Saladin followed Qassam el-Banna outside to his car.

"If for some reason you are arrested on the way to the airport . . ."

"I won't tell them a thing," said the young Egyptian bravely, "even if they waterboard me."

"Haven't you heard, Brother Qassam? The Americans don't do that sort of thing anymore."

Qassam el-Banna climbed behind the wheel of his car, closed the door, and started the engine. Saladin rapped lightly on the window with the grip of his cane. The window slid down. The young Egyptian looked up inquisitively.

"There's just one more thing," said Saladin.

"Yes?"

Saladin pointed the silenced Glock through the open window and fired four shots in rapid succession. Then he reached into the interior, careful not to stain his jacket in blood, and eased the car into drive. A moment later it disappeared into the black pond. Saladin waited until the bubbling had stopped and the surface of the pond was once again as smooth as glass. Then he climbed into his own car and headed back to Washington.

53

LIBERTY CROSSING, VIRGINIA

Unlike Saladin, Gabriel passed a quiet if restless morning at the N Street safe house, watching a tiny mouthwash-green airplane creeping slowly across the screen of his Samsung mobile. Finally, at half past two in the afternoon, he climbed into the back of a black Suburban and was driven across Chain Bridge to the wealthy Virginia enclave of McLean. On Route 123 he saw a sign for the George Bush Center for Intelligence. The driver blew past the entrance without slowing.

"You missed your turn," said Gabriel.

The driver smiled but said nothing. He continued along Route 123, past the low-slung shopping centers and business parks of downtown McLean, before finally turning onto Lewinsville Road. He turned again after a quarter mile onto Tysons McLean Drive and followed it up the slope of a gentle rise. The road bent to the left, then to the right, before delivering them to a large checkpoint manned by a dozen uniformed guards, all heavily armed. A clipboard was consulted, a dog sniffed for bombs. Then the Suburban proceeded slowly to the forecourt of a large office building, the headquarters of the National Counterterrorism Center. On the opposite side of the court, connected by a convenient sky bridge, was the Office of the Director of National Intelligence. The complex, thought Gabriel, was a monument to failure. The American intelligence community, the largest and most advanced the world had ever known, had failed to prevent the attacks of 9/11. And for its sins it had been reorganized and rewarded with money, real estate, and pretty buildings.

An employee of the center—a pantsuited, ponytailed woman of perhaps thirty—awaited Gabriel in the lobby. She gave him a guest pass, which he clipped to the pocket of his suit jacket, and led him to the Operations Floor, the NCTC's nerve center. The giant video screens and kidney-shaped desks gave it the appearance of a television newsroom. The desks were an optimistic shade of pale pine, like something from an IKEA catalog. At one sat Adrian Carter, Fareed Barakat, and Paul Rousseau. As Gabriel took his assigned seat, Carter handed him a photograph of a dark-haired man in his mid-forties.

"Is this the fellow you saw at the Four Seasons?"

"A reasonable facsimile. Who is he?"

"Omar al-Farouk, Saudi national, not quite a member of the royal family, but close enough."

"Says who?"

"Says our man in Riyadh. He checked him out. He's clean."

"Checked him out how? Checked him with whom?"

"The Saudis."

"Well," said Gabriel cynically, "that settles it then."

Carter said nothing.

"Put him under watch, Adrian."

"Perhaps you didn't hear me the first time. Not quite a member of the royal family, but close enough. Besides, Saudi Arabia is our ally in the fight against ISIS. Every month," Carter added with a glance toward Fareed Barakat, "the Saudis write a big fat check to the king of Jordan to finance his efforts against ISIS. And if the check is one day late, the king calls Riyadh to complain. Isn't that right, Fareed?"

"And every month," Fareed replied, "certain wealthy Saudis funnel money and other support to ISIS. The Saudis aren't alone. Qataris and Emiratis are doing it, too."

Carter was unconvinced. He looked at Gabriel and said, "The FBI doesn't have the resources to watch everyone who gives you a funny feeling at the back of your neck."

"Then let us watch him for you."

"I'll pretend I didn't hear that." Carter's mobile chirped. He looked at the screen and frowned. "It's the White House. I need to take this in private."

He entered one of the fishbowl conference rooms at the edge of the Operations Floor and closed the door. Gabriel looked up at one of the video screens and saw a mouthwash-green airplane approaching the American coastline.

"How good are your sources inside Saudi Arabia?" he asked Fareed Barakat quietly.

"Better than yours, my friend."

"Do me a favor then." Gabriel handed Fareed the photograph. "Find out who this asshole really is."

Fareed snapped a photo of the photo with his mobile phone and forwarded it to the GID headquarters in Amman. At the same time, Gabriel sent a message to King Saul Boulevard ordering surveillance of a guest at the Four Seasons Hotel named Omar al-Farouk.

"You realize," murmured Fareed, "that we are totally busted."

"I'll send Adrian a nice fruit basket when this is all over."

"He's not allowed to accept gifts. Believe me, my friend, I've tried."

Gabriel smiled in spite of himself and looked at the video screen. The mouthwash-green airplane had just entered American airspace.

54

DULLES INTERNATIONAL AIRPORT

IT TOOK AN HOUR FOR Dr. Leila Hadawi to navigate the frozen welcome mat at Dulles Airport's passport control—forty minutes in the long, mazelike line, and another twenty minutes standing before the dais of a Customs and Border Protection officer. The officer was clearly not part of the operation. He questioned Dr. Hadawi at length about her recent travels—Greece was of particular interest—and about the purpose of her visit to the United States. Her response, that she had come to visit friends, was one he had heard many times before.

"Where do the friends live?"

"Falls Church."

"What are their names?"

She gave him two Arabic names.

"Are you staying with them?"

"No."

"Where *are* you staying?"

And on it went until finally she was invited to smile for a camera and place her fingers on the cool glass of a digital scanner. Returning her passport, the customs officer hollowly wished her a pleasant stay in the United States. She made her way to baggage claim, where her suitcase was circling slowly on an otherwise empty carousel. In the arrivals hall she searched for a man with coal-black hair and matching eyewear, but he was nowhere in sight. She was not surprised. While crossing the Atlantic, he had told her that the Office would be relegated to a secondary role, that the Americans were now in charge and would be taking the operational lead.

"And when I'm given my target?" she had asked.

"Send us a text through the usual channel."

"And if they take my phone away from me?"

"Take a walk. Handbag over the left shoulder."

"What if they don't let me take a walk?"

She wheeled her bag outside and, assisted by a well-built American with a military-style haircut, boarded a Hertz shuttle bus. Her car, a bright red Chevrolet Impala, was in its assigned space. She placed her bag in the trunk, climbed behind the wheel, and hesitantly started the engine. The nobs and dials of the instrument panel seemed entirely alien to her. Then she realized she had not driven an automobile since the morning she had returned to her apartment in Jerusalem to find Dina Sarid sitting at her kitchen table. What a disaster it would be, she thought, if she were to kill or seriously injure herself in an accident. She punched a destination into her mobile phone and was informed that her drive of twenty-four miles would take well over an hour because of unusually heavy traffic. She smiled; she was glad for the delay. She removed her hijab and tucked it carefully into her handbag. Then she slipped the car into gear and headed slowly toward the exit.

IT WAS NO ACCIDENT THE IMPALA WAS BRIGHT RED; THE FBI had quietly intervened in the booking. In addition, the Bureau's technicians had fitted the car with a beacon and bugged its interior. As a result, the analysts on duty on the Operations Floor at the National Counterterrorism Center heard Natalie singing softly to herself in French as she drove along the Dulles Access Road toward Washington. On one of the giant video screens, the traffic cameras tracked her every move. On another blinked the blue light of the beacon. Her mobile phone was emitting a signal of its own. Her French phone number appeared in a shaded rectangular box, next to the blinking blue light. The Office had real-time access to her voice calls, texts, and e-mails. And now that the phone was on American soil, connected to an American cellular network, the NCTC had access to them, too.

The bright red car passed within a few hundred feet of the Liberty Crossing campus and continued along Interstate 66 to the Rosslyn section of Arlington, Virginia, where it turned into the surface parking lot of the Key Bridge Marriott. There the blinking blue light of the beacon came to a stop. But after an interval of thirty seconds—long enough for a woman to adjust her hair and retrieve a suitcase from the trunk of a car—the shaded rectangular box of the mobile phone moved toward the hotel's entrance. It paused briefly at the reception desk, where the device's owner, an Arab woman in her early thirties, veiled, French passport, stated her name for the clerk. There was no need to present a credit card; ISIS had already paid for her room charges and incidentals. Weary from a long day of travel, she gratefully accepted an electronic key card and wheeled her suitcase slowly across the lobby toward the elevators.

AFTER PRESSING THE CALL BUTTON, NATALIE BECAME AWARE OF the attractive woman, late twenties, shoulder-length blond hair, knock-off Vuitton luggage, watching her from a barstool in the chrome-and-laminate lounge. Natalie assumed the woman to be an American intelligence officer and boarded the first available elevator without making eye contact. She pressed the button for the eighth floor and moved to the corner of the carriage, but as the doors were closing a hand appeared in the breach. The hand belonged to the attractive blonde from the lounge. She stood on the opposite side of the carriage and stared straight ahead. Her heavy lilac fragrance was intoxicating.

"What floor?" asked Natalie in English.

"Eight is fine." The accent was French, the voice vaguely familiar.

They said nothing more to one another as the elevator climbed slowly upward. When the doors opened on the eighth floor, Natalie exited first. She paused briefly to take her bearings and then set off along the corridor. The attractive blond woman walked in the same direction. And when Natalie stopped outside Room 822, the woman stopped, too. It was then Natalie looked into her eyes for the first time. Somehow, she managed to smile.

They were the eyes of Safia Bourihane.

IN PREPARATION FOR NATALIE'S ARRIVAL, THE FBI HAD STA-tioned a pair of agents, a man and a woman, in the same lounge of the Key Bridge Marriott. It had also hacked into the hotel's security system, giving the NCTC unfettered access to some three hundred cameras. Both the agents and the cameras had noticed the attractive blond woman who joined Natalie in the elevator. The agents had made no attempt to follow the two women, but the cameras had shown no such restraint. They tracked their movement down the half-lit corridor, to the door of Room 822. It, too, had been penetrated by the FBI. There were four microphones and four cameras. All watched and listened as the women entered. In French, the blond woman murmured something the microphones couldn't quite catch. Then, ten seconds later, the shaded rectangular box vanished from the giant display at the NCTC.

"Looks like the network just made contact with her," said Carter, watching as the two women settled into the room. "Too bad about the phone going dark."

"But not unexpected."

"No," agreed Carter. "It would have been too much to hope for."

Gabriel asked to see a replay of the elevator video. Carter gave the order, and a few seconds later it appeared on the screen.

"Pretty girl," said Carter.

"Natalie or the blond?"

"Both, actually, but I was referring to the blond. Think she's a natural?"

"Not a chance," replied Gabriel. He asked to see a close-up of the blond woman's face. Again, Carter gave the order.

"Recognize her?"

"Yes," said Gabriel with a glance toward Paul Rousseau, "I'm afraid I do."

"Who is she?"

"She's someone who has no business being in this country," said Gabriel ominously. "And if she's here, it means there are many more just like her."

55

ARLINGTON, VIRGINIA

THE FRENCH PRESIDENT AND HIS glamorous ex–fashion model of a wife arrived at Joint Base Andrews at seven that evening. The motorcade that bore the couple from suburban Maryland to Blair House—the Federal-style guest mansion located across Pennsylvania Avenue from the White House—was the largest anyone could recall. The many street closures snarled the Potomac River crossings and turned downtown Washington into a parking lot for thousands of commuters. Unfortunately, the disruption to life in the capital was only going to get worse. Earlier that morning, the *Washington Post* had reported that the security operation surrounding the Franco-American summit was the most extensive since the last inauguration. The primary threat, the newspaper said, was an attack by ISIS. But even the venerable *Post*, with its many sources inside the U.S. intelligence community, was unaware of the true nature of the peril hanging over the city.

By that evening, the intense efforts to prevent an attack were centered on a hotel at the foot of Key Bridge in Arlington, Virginia. In a room on the eighth floor were two women, one an agent of Israeli intelligence, the other an agent of a man called Saladin. The presence of the second woman on American soil had set off alarm bells inside the NCTC and throughout the rest of the U.S. homeland security apparatus. A dozen different government agencies were trying desperately to discover how she had managed to get into the country and how long she had been there. The White House had been advised of the situation. The president was said to be livid.

At half past eight that evening, the two women decided to leave the hotel for dinner. The concierge advised them to avoid Georgetown—"It's a zoo because of the traffic"—and directed them instead to a chain bar-and-grill in the Clarendon section of Arlington. Natalie drove there in the bright red Impala and parked in a public lot off Wilson Boulevard. The bar-and-grill was a no-reservations establishment, infamous for the size of its portions and the length of its lines. The wait for a table was thirty minutes, but there was a small round high-top available in the bar. The menu was ten pages of spiral-bound plastic laminate. Safia Bourihane leafed desultorily through it, mystified.

"Who can eat so much food?" she asked in French, turning another page.

"Americans," said Natalie, glancing at the well-fed clientele around her. The room was high-ceilinged and impossibly loud. As a result, it was the perfect place to talk.

"I think I've lost my appetite," Safia was saying.

"You should eat something."

"I ate on the train."

"What train?"

"The train from New York."

"How long were you in New York?"

"Just a day. I flew there from Paris."

"You can't be serious."

"I told you I would go back to France one day."

Safia smiled. With her blond hair and snug-fitting dress, she looked very French. Natalie imagined the woman Safia might have become were it not for radical Islam and ISIS.

A waitress came and took their drink orders. They both asked for tea. Natalie was annoyed by the interruption. Safia, it seemed, was in a talkative mood.

"How did you manage to get back to France?"

"How do you think?"

"On a borrowed passport?"

Safia nodded.

"Who did it belong to?"

"A new girl. She was the right height and weight, and her face was close enough."

"How did you travel?"

"By bus and train mostly. Once I was back in the EU, no one even looked at my passport."

"How long were you in France?"

"About ten days."

"Paris?"

"Only at the end."

"And before Paris?"

"I was hidden by a cell in Vaulx-en-Velin."

"Did you use the same passport to come here?"

She nodded.

"No problems?"

"None at all. The American customs agents were quite nice to me, actually."

"Were you wearing that dress?"

The tea arrived before Safia could answer. Natalie opened her menu for the first time.

"What's the name on the passport?"

"Why do you ask?"

"What happens if we're detained? What if they ask me your name and I can't tell them?"

Safia appeared to give the questions serious thought. "It's Asma," she said finally. "Asma Doumaz."

"Where's Asma from?"

Safia pulled her lips down and said, "Clichy-sous-Bois."

"I'm sorry to hear that."

"What are you going to have to eat?"

"An omelet."

"Do you think they can make a proper omelet?"

"We'll find out."

"Are you going to have anything to start?"

"I was thinking about the soup."

"It sounds terrible. Have a salad instead."

"They look enormous."

"I'll share it with you. But don't get any of those horrible dressings. Just ask for oil and vinegar."

The waitress reappeared, Natalie did the ordering.

"You speak English very well," said Safia resentfully.

"My parents both speak English, and I studied it at school."

"I didn't learn anything at my school." Safia glanced at the television over the bar. It was tuned to CNN. "What are they talking about?"

"The threat of an ISIS attack during the French president's visit."

Safia was silent.

"Have you been given your target?" asked Natalie quietly.

"Yes."

"Is it a suicide operation?"

Safia, her eyes on the television screen, nodded slowly.

"What about me?"

"You'll be given yours soon."

"By whom?"

Safia gave a noncommittal shrug.

"Do you know what it is?"

"No."

Natalie looked at the television.

"What are they saying now?" asked Safia.

"The same thing."

"They always say the same thing."

Natalie slid off her barstool.

"Where are you going?"

Natalie nodded toward the passageway leading to the restrooms.

"You went before we left the hotel."

"It's the tea."

"Don't be long."

Natalie placed her handbag over her shoulder, her left, and wove her way slowly across the bar, through the maze of high-top tables. The women's lounge was unoccupied. She entered one of the stalls, locked the door, and began counting slowly to herself. When she reached forty-five, she heard the restroom door open and close, followed by the hiss of water rushing into a basin and the blast of a hand dryer. To this symphony of bathroom sounds Natalie added the thunderous flush of an industrial toilet. Stepping from the stall, she saw a woman standing before the mirror applying makeup to her face. The woman was in her early thirties. She wore tight stretch jeans and a sleeveless pullover that did not flatter her powerful physique. She had the broad shoulders and muscular arms of an Olympic skier. Her skin was dry and porous. It was the skin of a woman who had lived in the desert or at altitude.

Natalie went to the second sink and opened the tap. When she looked up into the mirror, the woman was staring at her in the glass.

"How are you, Leila?"

"Who are you?"

"It doesn't matter who I am."

"Unless you're one of them. Then it matters a great deal to me."

The woman applied powder to the rough skin of her face. "I'm Megan," she said to her reflection. "Megan from the FBI. And you're wasting valuable time."

"Do you know who that woman is?"

Nodding, the woman put away the powder and went to work on her lips. "How did she get into the country?"

"On a false passport."

"Where did she come in?"

Natalie answered.

"Kennedy or Newark?"

"I don't know."

"How did she get down to Washington?"

"The train."

"What's the name on the passport?"

"Asma Doumaz."

"Have you been given a target?"

"No. But she's been given hers. It's a suicide operation."

"Do you know her target?"

"No."

"Have you met any other members of the attack cells?"

"No."

"Where's your phone?"

"She took it from me. Don't try to send me any messages."

"Get out of here."

Natalie switched off the tap and went out. Warily, Safia watched her approach the table. Then her eyes moved to the athletic-looking woman with open-air skin who reclaimed her seat at the bar.

"Did that woman try to talk to you?"

"What woman?"

Safia nodded toward the bar.

"Her?" Natalie shook her head. "She was on the phone the whole time."

"Really?" Safia expertly dressed the salad with the oil and the vinegar. "Bon appétit."

56

KEY BRIDGE MARRIOTT, ARLINGTON

THE ROOM WAS A SINGLE, the bed scarcely large enough for two. Safia slept rather well for a woman who knew she would soon be dead, though once during the night she sat bolt upright and engaged in a somniloquous explanation about how to properly wear a suicide vest. Natalie listened carefully to Safia's mumbled words, searching for clues about her target, but soon Safia was asleep again. Eventually, sometime after three in the morning, Natalie slept, too. She woke to find Safia clinging marsupial-like to her back. Outside, the weather was gray and wet, and the overnight change of pressure had left Natalie with a throbbing headache. She swallowed two tablets of pain reliever and drifted into a pleasant half-sleep until the scream of a jetliner woke her a second time. It seemed to pass within a few feet of their window. Then it banked low over the Potomac and disappeared into the clouds before reaching the end of the runway at Reagan National Airport.

Natalie rolled over and saw Safia sitting up in bed, staring at her mobile phone.

"How did you sleep?" Safia asked, her eyes still on the screen.

"Well. You?"

"Not bad." Safia switched off the phone. "Get dressed. We have work to do."

AFTER SHOWERING AND DRESSING, THEY HEADED DOWNSTAIRS to the lobby to partake of the complimentary breakfast. Safia had no appetite. Neither for that matter did Natalie. She drank three cups of coffee for the sake of her headache and forced down a container of Greek yogurt. The restaurant was full of tourists and two clean-cut men who looked as though they were in town for business. One of the men couldn't keep his eyes off Safia. The other was watching the news on the overhead television. A network icon in the bottom-right corner of the screen read LIVE. The American and French presidents were seated before the fireplace in the Oval Office. The American president was speaking. The French president didn't look happy.

"What's he saying?" asked Safia.

"Something about working with our friends and allies in the Middle East to defeat ISIS."

"Is he serious?"

"Our president doesn't seem to think so."

Safia's eyes met the eyes of her not-so-secret admirer on the other side of the restaurant. She looked quickly away.

"Why does that man keep looking at me?"

"He finds you attractive."

"Are you sure that's all it is?"

Natalie nodded.

"It's annoying."

"I know."

"I wish I could put on my hijab."

"It wouldn't help."

"Why not?"

"Because you'd still be beautiful." Natalie scraped the last of the yogurt from the bottom of the plastic container. "You really should eat something."

"Why?"

Natalie had no answer. "Where are we going this morning?" she asked.

"Shopping."

"What do we need?"

"Clothes."

"I have clothes."

"*Nice* clothes."

Safia glanced at the television screen, where the White House press secretary was herding the reporters from the Oval Office. Then she stood without another word and walked out of the restaurant. Natalie followed a few paces behind, her handbag over her right shoulder. Outside, the rain had subsided to a cold drizzle. They hurried across the parking lot and climbed into the Impala. Natalie shoved the key into the ignition and started the engine while Safia pulled her mobile from her purse and thumbed TYSONS CORNER into Google Maps. When the blue route line appeared on the screen, she pointed toward Lee Highway. "Make a right."

ON THE OPERATIONS FLOOR AT THE NCTC, GABRIEL AND Adrian Carter watched as the bright red Impala eased into a westbound lane of I-66, followed by a Ford Explorer containing two officers from the FBI's Special Surveillance Group. On the neighboring video screen, the blue light of the beacon flashed on a giant digital map of metropolitan Washington.

"What are you going to do?" asked Gabriel.

"It's not my call. Not even close."

"Whose call is it?"

"His," said Carter, nodding toward a CNN live shot from the Oval Office. "He's on his way down to the Situation Room. All the national security principals are there."

Just then, the phone in front of Carter rang. It was a decidedly one-sided conversation. "Understood," was all Carter said. Then he hung up and stared at the winking blue light moving west along I-66.

"What's the decision?" asked Gabriel.

"We're going to let them run."

"Good call."

"Maybe," said Carter. "Or maybe not."

NATALIE FOLLOWED I-66 TO THE BELTWAY AND THE BELTWAY to the Tysons Corner Center shopping mall. There were several spaces available on the coveted first level of Lot B, but Safia directed Natalie to the second level instead. "There," she said, pointing to a deserted distant corner of the lot. "Park over there."

"Why so far from the mall?"

"Just do what I tell you," Safia hissed.

Natalie pulled into the space and killed the engine. Safia scrutinized the instrument panel as a Ford Explorer passed behind them. It parked at the end of the same row, and two all-American males in their early thirties climbed out and headed toward the mall. Safia didn't seem to notice them. She was looking at the instrument panel again.

"Does this car have an internal trunk release?"

"There," said Natalie, pointing toward the button near the center of the dash.

"Leave the doors unlocked."

"Why?"

"Because I told you to."

Safia climbed out without another word. Together, they made their way to the stairwell and descended to the Bloomingdale's entrance of the mall. The all-Americans were pretending to shop for winter coats. Safia followed the signs to the women's department and spent the next thirty minutes moving from boutique to boutique, rack to rack. Natalie explained to the saleswoman that her friend was looking for something appropriate for a business dinner—a skirt and jacket, but the jacket couldn't be too tight. Safia tried on several of the saleswoman's suggestions but rejected all of them.

"Too tight," she said in labored English, running her hands over her shapely hips and flat stomach. "Looser."

"If I had a body like yours," the saleswoman said, "I'd want it as tight as possible."

"She wants to make a good impression," explained Natalie.

"Tell her to try Macy's. She might have more luck there."

She did. Within a few minutes she found a five-button car-length jacket by Tahari that she declared suitable. She selected two—one red, the other gray, both size six.

"They're much too big for her," said the saleswoman. "She's a four at most."

Natalie wordlessly swiped her credit card through the scanner and scribbled her signature on the touch screen. The saleswoman covered the two jackets in a white plastic bag emblazoned with the Macy's logo and handed them over. Natalie accepted the garment bag and followed Safia from the store.

"Why did you buy two jackets?"

"One is for you."

Natalie felt suddenly ill. "Which one?"

"The red one, of course."

"I've never looked good in red."

"Don't be silly."

Outside in the mall, Safia checked her phone.

"Do you need anything?" she asked.

"Like what?"

"Makeup? Some jewelry?"

"You tell me."

"How about some coffee?"

Natalie didn't feel much like drinking coffee, but she didn't want to earn another reproach from Safia, either. They went next door to Starbucks, ordered two lattes, and sat in the seating area outside in the mall. Several Muslim women, all veiled, were conversing softly in Arabic, and many other women in hijabs, some middle-aged, some mere girls, were strolling the arcades. Natalie felt as though she were back in her banlieue. She looked at Safia, who was staring vacantly into the middle distance. She held her mobile phone tightly in her hand. Her coffee stood on the table next to her, untouched.

"I need to use the restroom," said Natalie.

"You can't."

"Why not?"

"It's not allowed."

Safia's phone pulsed. She read the message and stood abruptly.

"We can go now."

They returned to Lot B and climbed the stairs to the second level. The distant corner was now filled with other cars. As they approached the red Impala, Natalie popped the trunk with her fob, but Safia quickly closed it again.

"Hang the clothes in the back."

Natalie did as instructed. Then she slid behind the wheel and started the engine while Safia thumbed KEY BRIDGE MAR-

RIOTT into Google Maps. "Follow the signs to the exit," she said. "And then make a left."

THE BULLET-POINT REPORTS FROM THE FBI SURVEILLANCE teams flashed onto the video screens at the NCTC like up-dates on an airport departure board. *SUBJECTS PURCHAS-ING GARMENTS AT MACY'S . . . SUBJECTS HAVING COFFEE AT STARBUCKS . . . SUBJECTS DEPARTING MALL . . . ADVISE . . .* Huddled in the White House Situation Room, the president and his national security team had delivered their verdict. Listen, watch, wait. Let them run.

"Good call," said Gabriel.

"Maybe," said Adrian Carter. "Or maybe not."

At twelve fifteen the red Impala turned into the parking lot of the Key Bridge Marriott and slid into the same space it had abandoned two hours earlier. The hotel security cam-eras told part of the story. The terse dispatches from the FBI watchers told the rest. The subjects were exiting the vehicle. Subject one, the Israeli agent, collected the Macy's bag from the backseat. Subject two, the Frenchwoman, lifted two large paper bags from the trunk.

"What two bags in the trunk?" asked Gabriel.

Carter was silent.

"Where are the bags from?"

Carter shouted the question to the Operations Floor. The answer appeared on the screen a few seconds later.

The bags were from L.L.Bean.

"Shit," said Gabriel and Carter in unison.

Natalie and Safia had never gone to L.L.Bean.

57

THE WHITE HOUSE

MUCH LATER, THE MEETING BETWEEN the American and French leaders would be recalled as the most interrupted ever. Three times, the American president was summoned to the Situation Room. Twice, he went alone, leaving the French president and his closest aides behind in the Oval Office. The third time, the French president went, too. After all, the two women in Room 822 of the Key Bridge Marriott both held French passports, though both documents were fraudulent. Eventually, the two leaders managed to spend an hour together without disruption before repairing to the East Room for a joint news conference. The American president was grim-faced throughout, and his answers were uncharacteristically rambling and unfocused. One reporter said the president appeared annoyed with his French colleague. Nothing could have been further from the truth.

The French president departed the White House at three p.m. and returned to Blair House. At that same moment, the Department of Homeland Security issued a vaguely worded warning of a possible terrorist attack on U.S. soil, perhaps in metropolitan Washington. When the bulletin failed to attract sufficient attention—only one cable news outlet bothered to report it—the DHS secretary hastily called a press conference to repeat the warning for the cameras. His tense demeanor made it clear that this was no cover-your-backside statement. The threat was real.

"Will there be any changes to the president's schedule?" asked a reporter.

"Not at this time," replied the secretary cryptically.

The secretary then listed several steps the federal government had taken to prevent or disrupt a potential attack, though he made no mention of the situation unfolding across the Potomac River, where, at 12:18 p.m., two women—subjects one and two, as they were known—had returned to their hotel room after a brief shopping excursion to Tysons Corner Center. Subject one had hung a Macy's bag in the closet while subject two had placed two suspect parcels—L.L.Bean shopping bags—on the floor near the window. Three times, the microphones heard subject one asking about the contents of the bags. Three times, subject two refused to answer.

The entire national security apparatus of the United States was desperately asking the same question. How the bags had found their way into the trunk of the Impala, however, had been established rather quickly with the help of Tysons Corner's massive array of security cameras. The delivery had occurred at 11:37 a.m., on the second level of Lot B. A hatted, coated man of indeterminate age and ethnicity had entered the parking garage on foot, an L.L.Bean bag in each hand, and had placed them in the Impala's trunk, which he opened after gaining access to the car's interior through an unlocked door. He then left the garage, once again on foot, and made his way to Route 7, where traffic cameras saw him climbing into a Nissan Altima with Delaware plates. It had been rented

Friday afternoon at the Hertz outlet at Union Station. Hertz records identified the customer as a Frenchwoman named Asma Doumaz. The name was unfamiliar to the FBI.

All of which said nothing about the actual contents of the bags, though the highly professional method of delivery suggested the worst. At least one senior FBI official, not to mention a top political aide to the president, recommended an immediate raid on the room. But calmer heads, including the president's, had prevailed. The cameras and the microphones would alert the FBI the instant the two subjects were preparing to go operational. In the meantime, the surveillance devices had the potential to supply invaluable intelligence, such as the targets and identities of other members of the attack cells. As a precaution, FBI SWAT and hostage rescue teams had quietly moved into position around the hotel. For now, the Marriott's management knew nothing.

The signal from the cameras and microphones inside Room 822 flowed through the NCTC to the White House and beyond. The primary camera was concealed inside the entertainment console; it peered out at its subjects like a tele-screen keeping watch over Winston Smith in his flat at the Victory Mansions. Subject two was lying seminude on the bed, smoking in violation of hotel rules and the laws of ISIS. Subject one, a devout nonsmoker, had requested permission to leave the room to get some fresh air, but subject two had denied it. It was, she said, haram to leave.

"Says who?" asked subject one.

"Says Saladin."

The mention of the mastermind's name raised hopes at the NCTC and the White House that critical intelligence would soon flow from the mouth of subject two. Instead, she lit a fresh cigarette and with the remote switched on the television. The secretary of homeland security was at the podium.

"What's he saying?"

"He says there's going to be an attack."

"How does he know?"

"He won't say."

Subject two, still smoking, checked her phone—a phone that the FBI and NSA had been unable to penetrate. Then she squinted at the television. The secretary of homeland security had concluded his news conference. A panel of terrorism experts was analyzing what had just transpired.

"What are they saying?"

"The same thing," said subject one. "There's going to be an attack."

"Do they know about us?"

"They would have arrested us if they knew."

Subject two didn't appear convinced. She checked her phone, checked it again fifteen seconds later, and checked it again ten seconds after that. Clearly, she was expecting an imminent communication from the network. It came at 4:47 p.m.

"Alhamdulillah," whispered subject two.

"What is it?"

Subject two crushed out her cigarette and switched off the television. On the Operations Floor of the National Counterterrorism Center, several dozen analysts and officers watched and waited. Also present was the leader of an elite French counterterrorism organization, the chief of the Jordanian GID, and the future chief of Israel's secret intelligence service. Only the Israeli could not watch what unfolded next. He sat in his assigned seat at the kidney-shaped desk, elbows resting on the pale blond wood, hands over his eyes, and listened.

"In the name of God, the most gracious, the most merciful . . ."

Natalie was making her suicide video.

58

ALEXANDRIA, VIRGINIA

IT WAS AN UNUSUALLY QUIET day for Dominion Movers of Alexandria, Virginia—just one small job, a single woman who was trading her rented wreck on Capitol Hill for a cramped cottage in North Arlington, a steal at $700,000. The job had required only one truck and two employees. One of the men was a Jordanian national, the other was from Tunisia. Both were members of ISIS and had fought and trained in Syria. The woman, who worked as an aide to a prominent Republican senator, knew none of this, of course. She served the men coffee and cookies and on completion of the job tipped them well.

The two men left North Arlington at five thirty and started back to the company's headquarters on Eisenhower Avenue in Alexandria. Owing to the heavy rush-hour traffic, they did not arrive until six fifteen, a few minutes later than they hoped. They parked the truck, a 2011 Freightliner model, outside the warehouse and entered the business office through a glass doorway. Fatimah, the young woman who answered the company's phones, was absent and her desk was bare. She had flown to Frankfurt the previous evening and was now in Istanbul. By morning, she would be in the caliphate.

Another doorway led to the warehouse floor. There were two additional Freightliners, both painted with the Dominion logo, and three white Honda Pilots. Inside the Hondas was an arsenal of AR-15 assault rifles and .45-caliber Glock pistols, along with a backpack bomb and a suicide vest. Each Freightliner had been fitted with a thousand-pound ammonium nitrate/fuel oil bomb. The devices were exact replicas of the massive bomb that had devastated London's Canary Wharf in February 1996. It was no coincidence. The man who built the Canary Wharf bomb, a former Irish Republican Army terrorist named Eamon Quinn, had sold his design to ISIS for $2 million.

The other members of the attack cell were already present. Two wore ordinary Western clothing, but the others, eleven in all, wore black tactical suits and white athletic shoes, a sartorial homage to Abu Musab al-Zarqawi. For operational reasons, the Tunisian and the Jordanian remained in their blue Dominion coveralls. They had one last delivery to make.

At seven o'clock all fifteen men prayed together one last time. The other members of the attack cell departed shortly thereafter, leaving only the Tunisian and the Jordanian behind. At half past the hour, they climbed into the cabs of the Freightliners. The Tunisian had been selected to drive the lead truck. In many respects, it was the more important assignment, for if he failed, the second truck could not reach its target. He had named the truck Buraq, the heavenly steed that had carried the Prophet Muhammad from Mecca to Jerusalem during the Night Journey. The Tunisian would take a similar journey tonight, a journey that would end, inshallah, in paradise.

It began, however, on an unsightly industrial section of Eisenhower Avenue. He followed it to the connector and followed the connector to the Beltway. The traffic was heavy but moving just below the speed limit. The Tunisian eased into the right travel lane and then glanced into his side-view mirror. The second Freightliner was about a quarter mile behind, exactly where it was supposed to be. The Tunisian stared straight ahead and began to pray.

"In the name of Allah, the most gracious, the most merciful . . ."

SALADIN OBSERVED THE OBLIGATORY EVENING PRAYER AS WELL, though with far less fervor than the men in the warehouse, for he had no intention of achieving martyrdom this night. Afterward, he dressed in a dark gray suit, a white shirt, and a solid navy-blue tie. His suitcase was packed. He wheeled it into the corridor and, using his cane for support, limped to the elevator. Downstairs, he collected a printed receipt at the front desk before going outside to the motor court. The car was waiting. He instructed the valet to place his suitcase in the trunk and then climbed behind the wheel.

DIRECTLY ACROSS THE STREET FROM THE FOUR SEASONS, outside the entrance of a CVS drugstore, was a rented Buick Regal. Eli Lavon sat in the front passenger seat, Mikhail Abramov behind the wheel. They had passed that long day watching the front of the hotel, sometimes from the comfort of the car, sometimes from the pavement or a café, and, briefly, from inside the hotel itself. Of their target, the alleged Saudi national Omar al-Farouk, they had caught not a glimpse. A call to the hotel operator had confirmed, however, that Mr. al-Farouk, whoever he was, was indeed a guest of the establishment. He had instructed the switchboard to hold his calls. A walk past his door had revealed a DO NOT DISTURB sign hanging from his latch.

Mikhail, a man of action rather than observation, was drumming his fingers anxiously on the center console, but Lavon, a battle-scarred veteran of many such vigils, sat with the stillness of a stone Buddha. His brown eyes were fixed on the exit of the hotel, where a black BMW sedan was waiting to turn into M Street.

"There's our boy," he said.

"You sure that's him?"

"Positive."

The BMW rounded a traffic island of small trees and shrubs and sped off down M Street.

"That's definitely him," agreed Mikhail.

"I've been doing this a long time."

"Where do you think he's going?"

"Maybe you should follow him and find out."

SALADIN TURNED RIGHT ONTO WISCONSIN AVENUE AND THEN made a quick left into Prospect Street. On the north side was Café Milano, one of Georgetown's most popular restaurants. Directly opposite was one of Washington's costliest parking lots. Saladin left the car with an attendant and entered the restaurant. The maître d' and two hostesses stood behind a pulpit-like counter in the foyer.

"Al-Farouk," said Saladin. "I have a reservation for two."

One of the hostesses checked the computer. "Eight o'clock?"

"Yes," he said, his eyes averted.

"You're early."

"I hope that's not a problem."

"Not at all. Is the rest of your party here?"

"Not yet."

"I can seat you now, or if you prefer you can wait at the bar."

"I prefer to sit."

The hostess led Saladin to a coveted table near the front of the restaurant, a few paces from the bar.

"I'm dining with a young lady. She should be arriving in a few minutes."

The hostess smiled and withdrew. Saladin sat down and surveyed the interior of the restaurant. Its patrons were money-eyed, comfortable, and powerful. He was surprised to find he recognized a few, including the man seated at the next table. He was a columnist for the *New York Times* who had supported—no, thought Saladin, that was too weak a word—*campaigned* for the American invasion of Iraq. Saladin smiled. Qassam el-Banna had chosen well. It was a shame he would not see the results of his hard work.

A waiter appeared and offered Saladin a cocktail. With practiced confidence, he ordered a vodka martini, specifying the brand of alcohol he preferred. It arrived a few minutes later and with great ceremony was poured from its silver shaker. It stood untouched before him, beads of condensation clouding the glass. At the bar a trio of half-naked women were screaming with laughter, and at the next table the columnist was holding forth on the subject of Syria. Apparently, he did not think the band of murderous thugs known as ISIS posed much of a threat to the United States. Saladin smiled and checked his watch.

THERE WERE NO PARKING SPACES TO BE HAD ON PROSPECT Street, so Mikhail made a U-turn at the end of the block and parked illegally opposite a sandwich shop that catered to students from Georgetown University. Café Milano was more than a hundred yards away, a smudge in the distance.

"This won't do," said Eli Lavon, pointing out the obvious. "One of us has to go in there and keep an eye on him."

"You go. I'll stay with the car."

"It's not really my kind of place," replied Lavon.

Mikhail climbed out and started back toward Café Milano on foot. It was not the only restaurant on the street. Besides the sandwich shop, there was a Thai restaurant and an upscale bistro. Mikhail walked past them and descended the two steps to Café Milano's entrance. The maître d' smiled at Mikhail as though he were expected.

"I'm meeting a friend at the bar."

The maître d' pointed the way. Only one stool was available, a few paces from where a well-dressed man, Arab in appearance, sat alone. There was a second place setting opposite, which meant that in all likelihood the well-dressed man would not be dining alone. Mikhail settled onto the empty stool. It was far too close to the target, though it had the advantage of an unobstructed view of the entrance. He ordered a glass of wine and dug his phone from his pocket.

MIKHAIL'S MESSAGE LANDED ON GABRIEL'S PHONE THIRTY SEConds later. He now had a choice to make: keep the information to himself or confess to Adrian Carter that he had deceived him. Given the circumstances, he chose the latter. Carter took the news surprisingly well.

"You're wasting your time," he said. "And mine."

"Then you won't mind if we stick around a little longer and see who he's having dinner with."

"Don't bother. We have more important things to worry about than a rich Saudi having dinner with the beautiful people at Café Milano."

"Like what?"

"Like *that*."

Carter nodded toward the video screen, where subject number two, otherwise known as Safia Bourihane, was placing the L.L.Bean bags upon the bed. From one, she carefully removed a black nylon vest fitted with wires and explosives and held it to her torso. Then, smiling, she examined her appearance in the mirror while the entire counterterrorism apparatus of the United States looked on in horror.

"Game over," said Gabriel. "Get my girl out of there."

59

KEY BRIDGE MARRIOTT

THERE WAS A MOMENT'S CONFUSION regarding who would wear which suicide vest. It seemed peculiar to Natalie—the vests appeared identical in every way—but Safia was insistent. She wanted Natalie to wear the vest with the small stitch of red thread along the inside of the zipper. Natalie accepted it without argument and carried it into the bathroom, warily, as though it were a cup brimming over with scalding liquid. She had treated the victims of weapons like these, the poor souls like Dina Sarid whose limbs and vital organs had been shredded by nails and ball bearings or ravaged by the unseen destructive power of the blast wave. And she had heard the macabre stories about the damage done to those who had been seduced into strapping bombs to their bodies. Ayelet Malkin, her friend from Hadassah Medical Center, had been sitting in her apartment one afternoon in Jerusalem when the head of a suicide bomber landed like a fallen coconut on her balcony. The thing had lain there for more than an hour, glaring at Ayelet reproachfully, until finally a policewoman zipped it into a plastic evidence bag and carted it off.

Natalie sniffed the explosive; it smelled of marzipan. She held the detonator lightly in her right hand and then threaded her arm carefully through the sleeve of the red Tahari jacket. The left arm was even more of a challenge. She didn't dare use her right hand for fear of accidentally hitting the detonator button and blowing herself and a portion of the eighth floor to bits. Next she fastened the jacket's five decorative buttons using only her left hand, smoothed the front, and straightened the shoulders. Examining her appearance in the mirror, she thought Safia had chosen well. The cut of the jacket concealed the bomb perfectly. Even Natalie, whose back was aching beneath the weight of the ball bearings, could see no visible evidence of it. There was only the smell, the faint smell of almonds and sugar.

She looked around the interior of the bathroom, around the edges of the mirror, at the overhead light fixture. Surely, the Americans were watching and listening. And surely, she thought, Gabriel was watching, too. She wondered what they were waiting for. She had come to Washington in an attempt to identify targets and other members of the attack cells. Thus far, she had learned almost nothing because Safia had very deliberately withheld even the most basic information about the operation. But why? And why had Safia insisted that Natalie wear the suicide vest with the red stitch in the zipper? Again, she glanced around the bathroom. *Are you watching? Do you see what's going on in here?* Obviously, they intended to let it play out a little longer. But not too long, she thought. The Americans wouldn't allow a proven terrorist like Safia, a black widow with blood on her hands, to walk around the streets of Washington wearing a suicide vest. As an Israeli, Natalie knew that such operations were inherently dangerous and unpredictable. Safia would have to be shot cleanly through the brain stem with a large-caliber weapon to ensure that she did not retain the capacity to squeeze her detonator with a dying spasm. If she did, anyone close to her would be cut to pieces.

Natalie scrutinized her face one last time in the mirror, as if committing her own features to memory—the nose she detested, the mouth she thought too large for her face, the dark alluring eyes. Then, quite unexpectedly, she saw someone standing beside her, a man with pale skin and eyes the color of glacial ice. He was dressed for a special occasion, a wedding, perhaps a funeral, and was holding a gun in one hand.

Actually, you're more like me than you realize . . .

She switched out the light and went into the next room. Safia was sitting at the end of the bed, dressed in her suicide vest and her gray jacket. She was staring blankly at the television. Her skin was pale as milk, her hair lay heavy and limp against the side of her neck. The young woman who had carried out a massacre of innocents in the name of Islam was obviously frightened.

"Are you ready?" asked Natalie.

"I can't." Safia spoke as though a hand were squeezing her throat.

"Of course you can. There's nothing to be afraid of."

Safia held a cigarette between the trembling fingers of her left hand. With her right she was clutching her detonator—too tightly, thought Natalie.

"Maybe I should drink a little vodka or whisky," Safia was saying. "They say it helps."

"Do you really want to meet Allah smelling of alcohol?"

"I suppose not." Her eyes moved from the television to Natalie's face. "Aren't you afraid?"

"A little."

"You don't look afraid. In fact, you look happy."

"I've been waiting for this for a long time."

"For death?"

"For vengeance," said Natalie.

"I thought I wanted vengeance, too. I thought I wanted to die . . ."

The invisible hand had closed around her throat again. She appeared incapable of speech. Natalie removed the cigarette from Safia's fingertips, crushed it out, and laid the butt next to the twelve others she had smoked that afternoon.

"Shouldn't we be leaving?"

"In a minute."

"Where are we going?"

She didn't answer.

"You have to tell me the target, Safia."

"You'll know soon enough."

Her voice was as brittle as dead leaves. She had the pallor of a corpse.

"Do you think it's true?" she asked. "Do you think we'll go to paradise after our bombs explode?"

I don't know where you'll go, thought Natalie, but it won't be into the loving arms of God.

"Why wouldn't it be true?" she asked.

"I sometimes wonder whether it's just . . ." Again, her voice faltered.

"Just what?"

"Something men like Jalal and Saladin say to women like us to turn us into martyrs."

"Saladin would put on the vest if he were here."

"Would he really?"

"I met him after you left the camp in Palmyra."

"I know. He's very fond of you." An edge of jealousy crept into her voice. It seemed she was still capable of at least one emotion other than fear. "He told me you saved his life."

"I did."

"And now he's sending you out to die."

Natalie said nothing.

"And what about the people we kill tonight?" Safia asked. "Or the people I killed in Paris?"

"They were unbelievers."

The detonator suddenly felt hot in Natalie's hand, as though she were clutching a live ember. She wanted nothing more than to rip the suicide vest from her body. She glanced around the interior of the room.

Are you watching? What are you waiting for?

"I killed the woman in France," Safia was saying. "The Weinberg woman, the Jew. She was going to die of her injuries, but I shot her anyway. I'm afraid—" She cut herself off.

"Afraid of what?"

"That I'm going to meet her again in paradise."

Natalie could summon no response from the well of lies within her. She placed a hand on Safia's shoulder, lightly, so as not to startle her. "Shouldn't we be going?"

Safia stared dully at her mobile phone, drugged by the opiate of fear, and then rose unsteadily to her feet—so unsteadily, in fact, that Natalie was afraid she might inadvertently press her detonator trying to maintain her balance.

"How do I look?" she asked.

Like a woman who knows she has only minutes to live, thought Natalie.

"You look beautiful, Safia. You always look beautiful."

With that, Safia moved to the doorway and opened it without hesitation, but Natalie was searching for something amid the twisted sheets and blankets of the bed. She had hoped to hear the sound of a large-caliber weapon dispatching Safia on her journey to paradise. Instead, she heard Safia's voice. The fear had evaporated. She sounded faintly annoyed.

"What are you waiting for?" she demanded. "It's time."

60

THE WHITE HOUSE

THE STATE DINNER WAS SCHEDULED to begin at eight o'clock that evening. The French president and his wife arrived punctually at the North Portico, having made the crossing from Blair House in record time, under the tightest security anyone had ever seen. They hurried inside, as if trying to escape a sudden deluge, and found the president and the first lady, both formally attired, waiting in the Entrance Hall. The president's smile was dazzling, but his handshake was damp and full of tension.

"We have a problem," he said sotto voce as the cameras flashed.

"Problem?"

"I'll explain in a minute."

The photo opportunity was much shorter than usual, fifteen seconds exactly. Then the president led the party to the Cross Hall. The first lady and her French counterpart turned to the left, toward the East Room. The two leaders headed to the right, toward the West Wing. Downstairs in the Situation Room it was standing room only—principals in their assigned seats, deputies and aides lining the walls. On one of the display screens, two women, one blond, the other dark-haired, were walking along a hotel corridor. The president quickly brought the French leader up to date. A few minutes earlier, Safia Bourihane had produced a pair of suicide vests. A hasty evacuation of the hotel had been rejected as too time-consuming and too risky. A direct assault on the room had been ruled out as well.

"So what are we left with?" asked the French president.

"Undercover SWAT and hostage rescue teams are standing by outside the front of the hotel and in the lobby. If they're afforded an opportunity to kill Safia Bourihane with no collateral loss of innocent life, they will request permission to take the shot."

"Who gives the approval?"

"Me and me alone." The president looked at his French counterpart soberly. "I don't need your permission to do this, but I'd like your approval."

"You have it, Mr. President." The French leader watched as the two women entered the elevators. "But may I offer one small piece of advice?"

"Of course."

"Tell your snipers not to miss."

BY THE TIME THE TUNISIAN REACHED THE EXIT FOR ROUTE 123, the second Freightliner was directly behind him, exactly where it was supposed to be. He checked the clock. It was five minutes past eight. They were a minute ahead of schedule, better than the alternative but not ideal. The clock was Saladin's trademark. He believed that in terror, as in life, timing was everything.

Six times the Tunisian had performed dry runs, and six

times the traffic signal at Lewinsville Road had temporarily halted his advance, as it did now. When the light changed to green he meandered up the suburban lane at a leisurely pace, followed by the second Freightliner. Directly ahead was the intersection of Tysons McLean Drive. Again, the Tunisian checked the clock. They were back on schedule. He turned to the left and the overloaded truck labored up the slope of the gentle hill.

This was the portion of the approach the Tunisian had never driven, though he and the Jordanian had practiced it on a sophisticated computer simulator. The road bent gradually to the left, then, at the top of a hill, sharply to the right, where it led to an elaborate security checkpoint. By now, the highly trained and heavily armed guards were already aware of his presence. The Americans had been attacked by vehicle-borne bombs before—at the Marine barracks in Beirut in 1983 and Khobar Towers in Saudi Arabia in 1996—and they were no doubt prepared for just such an attack on this critical facility, the nerve center of their counterterrorism apparatus. But unfortunately for the Americans, Saladin had prepared, too. The engine blocks of the trucks were encased in pig iron, the windshields and tires were bulletproof. Short of a direct hit by an antitank missile, the trucks were unstoppable.

The Tunisian waited until he had made the first slight left turn before slamming the accelerator to the floor. On the right a line of neon-orange pylons funneled inbound traffic into one lane. The Tunisian made no effort to avoid them, thus signaling to the Americans that his intentions were far from innocent.

He rounded the sharp right turn without slowing, and for an instant he feared the top-heavy truck would overturn. Before him several American security guards were gesturing wildly for him to stop. Several others already had their weapons trained on him. All at once he was blinded by a searing white light—arc lights, perhaps a laser. Then came the first gunshots. They bounced off the windshield like hail. The Tunisian gripped the wheel with his left hand and the detonator switch with his right.

"In the name of Allah, the most gracious, the most merciful . . ."

THE MEN AND WOMEN ON THE OPERATIONS FLOOR OF THE National Counterterrorism Center were unaware of the situation at the facility's front gate. They had eyes only for the giant video screen at the front of the room, where two women—one blond, the other dark-haired: subjects one and two, as they were known—had just boarded a hotel elevator in nearby Arlington. The shot was from above and at a slight angle. The blond woman, subject two, appeared catatonic with fear, but the dark-haired woman seemed curiously serene. She was staring directly into the lens of the camera, as though posing for a final portrait. Gabriel stared back at her. He was on his feet, a hand pressed to his chin, his head tilted slightly to one side. Adrian Carter stood next to him, a phone to each ear. Fareed Barakat was twirling an unlit cigarette nervously between his manicured fingers, his onyx-black eyes fastened to the video screen. Only Paul Rousseau, who had no taste for blood, could not watch. He was staring at the carpet as if searching for lost valuables.

Outside the hotel, the bright red Impala was parked in the surface lot, watched over clandestinely by the agents of the FBI's Critical Incident Response Group. The blue light of the beacon winked on the NCTC's screens like a channel marker. The car's hidden microphones captured the faint drone of traffic moving along North Fort Myer Drive.

Two undercover SWAT agents were chatting amiably just outside the hotel's entrance. Two more waited near the taxi stand. In addition, there were SWAT agents inside the hotel, two in the chrome-and-laminate lobby lounge, and two at the concierge stand. Each SWAT agent carried a concealed Springfield .45-caliber semiautomatic pistol with an eight-round magazine and an additional round in the chamber. One of the agents at the concierge stand, a veteran of the Iraq surge, was the designated shooter. He planned to approach the target, subject number two, from behind. If ordered by the president—and if no innocent lives would be lost—he would employ lethal force.

All eight members of the SWAT team tensed as the elevator doors opened and the two women, subjects one and two, stepped out. A new camera followed them across the foyer to the edge of the lobby. There the blond woman stopped abruptly and placed a restraining hand on the arm of the dark-haired woman. Words were exchanged, inaudible inside the NCTC, and the blond woman pondered her mobile phone. Then something happened that no one was expecting—not the FBI teams inside and outside the hotel, not the president and his closest aides in the Situation Room, and surely not the four spymasters watching from the Operations Floor at the NCTC. Without warning, the two women turned away from the lobby and set out along a ground-floor corridor, toward the back of the hotel.

"They're going the wrong way," said Carter.

"No, they're not," replied Gabriel. "They're going the way Saladin told them to go."

Carter was silent.

"Tell the SWAT teams to follow them. Tell them to take the shot."

"They can't," snapped Carter. "Not inside the hotel."

"Take it now, Adrian, because we're not going to get another chance."

Just then, the Operations Floor flashed with an intense burst of white light. An instant later there came a sound like a sonic boom that shook the building violently. Carter and Paul Rousseau were momentarily confused; Gabriel and Fareed Barakat, men of the Middle East, were not. Gabriel rushed to the window as a mushroom cloud of fire rose over the facility's main security checkpoint. A few seconds later he saw a large cargo truck careening at high speed into the forecourt separating the NCTC from the Office of the Director of National Intelligence.

Gabriel whirled around and shouted like a madman at those closest to the windows to move to safety. He glanced briefly at the giant video screen and saw the two women, subjects one and two, entering the parking garage of the Key Bridge Marriott. Then there was a second explosion, and the video screen, like everything else, turned to black.

IN THE SITUATION ROOM OF THE WHITE HOUSE, THE SCREENS went black, too. So did the videoconference link with the director of the NCTC.

"What just happened?" asked the president.

It was the secretary of homeland security who answered.

"Obviously, there's some sort of problem with the feed."

"I can't order the SWAT teams to move unless I can see what's going on."

"We're checking, Mr. President."

So was every other principal, deputy, and aide in the room. It was the director of the CIA, thirty seconds later, who informed the president that two loud sounds, possibly explosions, had been heard in the McLean–Tysons Corner area, near the intersection of Route 123 and the Beltway.

"Heard by whom?" asked the president.

"They could hear the explosions at CIA Headquarters, sir."

"A mile away?"

"More like two, sir."

The president stared at the blank video screen. "What just happened?" he asked again, but this time there was no answer in the room, only the concussive thump of another explosion, close enough to rattle the White House. "What the hell was that?"

"Checking, sir."

"Check faster."

Fifteen seconds later the president had his answer. It came not from the senior officials gathered inside the Situation Room but from the Secret Service agents stationed atop the Executive Mansion. Smoke was pouring from the Lincoln Memorial.

America was under attack.

61

THE LINCOLN MEMORIAL

H E HAD ARRIVED ON FOOT, a single man, dark hair, about five eight, wearing a bulky woolen coat against the evening chill and carrying a backpack over one shoulder. Later, the FBI would determine that a Honda Pilot SUV, Virginia plates, had dropped him at the corner of Twenty-third Street and Constitution Avenue. The Honda Pilot had continued north on Twenty-third Street to Virginia Avenue, where it made a left turn. The man with the heavy woolen coat and backpack had headed south, across the far western end of the Washington Mall, to the Lincoln Memorial. Several U.S. Park Police officers stood watch at the base of the steps. They did not challenge or even seem to notice the man with the backpack and the oversize coat.

The monument, built in the form of a Greek Doric temple, was aglow with a warm golden light that seemed to radiate from within. The man with the backpack paused for several seconds on the spot where Dr. Martin Luther King had delivered his "I Have a Dream" speech, then proceeded up the final steps, into the memorial's central chamber. About twenty tourists were gathered before the nineteen-foot statue of a seated Lincoln. Equal numbers were in the two side chambers, before the towering engravings of the Gettysburg Address and the Second Inaugural Address. The man with the oversize coat placed his backpack near the base of one of the ionic columns and, drawing a mobile phone from his pocket, began taking photographs of the statue. Curiously, his lips were moving.

In the name of Allah, the most gracious, the most merciful . . .

A young couple, in broken English, asked the man whether he would take their photograph in front of the statue. He declined and, turning abruptly, hurried down the steps toward the Reflecting Pool. Too late, a female Park Police officer, twenty-eight years old, a mother of two, noticed the unattended bag and ordered the tourists to evacuate the memorial. An instant later the policewoman was decapitated by the circular saw of ball bearings that flew from the bag at detonation, as were the man and woman who had asked to have their photo taken. The bomber was blown from his feet by the force of the explosion. A tourist from Oklahoma, sixty-nine years old, a Vietnam veteran, unwittingly helped the murderer to his feet, and for this benevolent act was shot through the heart with the Glock 19 pistol that the man pulled from beneath his coat. The man managed to kill six more people before being shot by the Park Police officers at the base of the steps. In all, twenty-eight would die.

By the time the bomb exploded, the Honda Pilot was braking to a stop outside the main entrance of the John F. Kennedy Center for the Performing Arts. One man climbed out and entered the Hall of States. His coat was identical to the one worn by the man who attacked the Lincoln Memorial, though he carried no backpack; his bomb was strapped to his body. He made his way past the visitor center to the main box office, where he detonated his device. Three more men then emerged from the Honda, including the driver. All were armed with AR-15 semiautomatic assault rifles. They slaughtered the wounded and the dying in the Hall of States and then moved methodically from the Eisenhower Theater to the Opera House to the Concert Hall, killing indiscriminately. In all, more than three hundred would die.

By the time the first units of the Metropolitan Police had arrived, the three surviving terrorists had crossed the Rock Creek and Potomac Parkway on foot and were entering Washington Harbor. There they moved from restaurant to restaurant, killing without mercy. Fiola Mare, Nick's Riverside Grill, Sequoia: all were raked with gunfire. Once again, they encountered no resistance from the Metropolitan Police; the Americans, it seemed, had been caught flat-footed. Or perhaps, thought the leader of the attack cell, Saladin had deceived them. The three men reloaded their weapons and headed into the heart of Georgetown in search of other prey.

It was into this chaos that the two women—one dark-haired, the other blond: subjects one and two, as they were known—entered the rear parking garage of the Key Bridge Marriott. A second car, a rented Toyota Corolla, was waiting. Much later, it would be established that the car had been left in the garage earlier that day by the same man who had delivered the suicide vests at Tysons Corner Center.

Usually, it was subject one, the Israeli agent, who handled the driving, but this time subject two, the Frenchwoman, slid behind the wheel. Leaving the garage, she careened past the little blockhouse of the parking attendant, smashing the barrier gate in the process, and headed for the hotel's Lee Highway exit. The undercover SWAT teams stationed in the surface parking lot did not deploy lethal force against subject one, the Frenchwoman, because they had received no authorization from the president or the director of the FBI. Even the FBI surveillance teams were momentarily paralyzed because they were receiving no guidance from the NCTC. A moment earlier the watchers had heard something over their radios that sounded like an explosion. Now, from the NCTC, there was only silence.

The Lee Highway exit of the hotel was a right turn only. The Frenchwoman turned left instead. She evaded the oncoming cars, turned left onto North Lynn Street, and a few seconds later was racing across Key Bridge toward Georgetown. The FBI undercover SWAT and surveillance teams had no choice but to repeat the Frenchwoman's reckless moves. Two vehicles spilled from the Lee Highway exit, two more into North Fort Myer Drive. By the time they reached Key Bridge, the Corolla was already turning onto M Street. It had no tracking beacon and no interior microphones. From the heights of the bridge, the FBI teams could see flashing red-and-blue lights streaking toward Georgetown.

62

LIBERTY CROSSING, VIRGINIA

GABRIEL OPENED ONE EYE, then, slowly, painfully, the other. He had lost consciousness, for how long he did not know—a few seconds, a few minutes, an hour or more. Nor could he fathom the attitude of his own body. He was submerged in a sea of debris, that much he knew, but he could not discern whether he was prone or supine, upright or topsy-turvy. He felt no undue pressure in his head, which he took as a good sign, though he was afraid he had lost the ability to hear. The last sound he could recall was the roar of the detonation and the *whoosh-thump* of the vacuum effect. The supersonic blast wave seemed to have scrambled his internal organs. He hurt everywhere—his lungs, his heart, his liver, *everywhere*.

He pushed with his hands, and the debris yielded. Through a fog of dust he glimpsed the exposed steel skeleton of the building and the severed arteries of network cables and electric wiring. Sparks rained down, as if from a Roman candle, and through a rip in the ceiling he could make out the handle of the Big Dipper. A cold November wind chilled him. A finch landed within his grasp, studied him dispassionately, and was gone again.

Gabriel swept aside more of the debris and, wincing, sat up. One of the kidney-shaped tables had come to rest across his legs. Lying next to him, motionless, dredged in dust, was a woman. Her face was pristine, save for a few small cuts from the flying glass. Her eyes were open and fixed in the thousand-yard stare of death. Gabriel recognized her; she was an analyst who worked at a pod near his. Jill was her name— or was it Jen? Her job was to scour the manifests of incoming flights for potential bad actors. She was a bright young woman, barely out of college, probably from a wholesome town some- where in Iowa or Utah. She had come to Washington to help keep her country safe, thought Gabriel, and now she was dead.

He placed his hand lightly on her face and closed her eyes. Then he pushed away the table and rose unsteadily to his feet. Instantly, the shattered world of the Operations Floor began to spin. Gabriel placed his hands on his knees until the merry- go-round stopped. The right side of his head was warm and wet. Blood flowed into his eyes.

He wiped it away and returned to the window where he had seen the approaching truck. There were no bodies and very little debris on this side of the building; everything had been blown inward. Nor were there any windows or outer walls. The entire southern facade of the National Counterterrorism Center had been shorn away. Gabriel moved cautiously toward the edge of the precipice and looked down. In the forecourt was a deep crater, far deeper than the one that had been left outside the Weinberg Center in Paris, a meteor strike. The skyway connecting the NCTC to the Office of the Director of National Intelligence was gone. So was the entire northern face of the building. Inside its shattered conference rooms and offices not a single light burned. A survivor waved to Gabriel from the cliff's edge of an upper floor. Gabriel, not knowing what else to do, waved back.

The traffic on the Beltway had ground to a halt, white headlights on the inner loop, red taillights on the outer. Gabriel patted the front of his jacket and discovered he was still in possession of his mobile phone. He removed it and thumbed it into life. He still had service. He dialed Mikhail's number and raised the phone to his ear, but there was only silence. Or maybe Mikhail was speaking and Gabriel couldn't hear. He realized he had heard nothing since regaining consciousness—not a siren, not a groan of pain or cry for help, not his footfalls through the rubble. He was in a silent world. He wondered if the condition were permanent and thought about all the sounds he would never hear again. He would never hear the nonsensical chatter of his children or thrill to the arias of *La Bohème*. Nor would he hear the soft bristly tap of a Winsor & Newton Series 7 paintbrush against a Caravaggio. But it was the sound of Chiara singing he would miss the most. Gabriel always joked that he had fallen in love with Chiara the first time she made him fettuccini and mushrooms, but it wasn't true. He lost his heart to her the first time he heard her singing a silly Italian love song when she thought no one was listening.

Gabriel killed the connection to Mikhail and picked his way through the debris of what a moment ago had been the Operations Floor. He had to give Saladin credit; it was a masterstroke. Honor was due. The dead were everywhere. The astonished survivors, the lucky ones, were hauling themselves laboriously from the rubble. Gabriel located the spot where he had been standing when he heard the first explosion. Paul Rousseau was bleeding heavily from numerous lacerations and cradling an obviously broken arm. Fareed Barakat, the ultimate survivor, seemed to have come through it unscathed. Looking only mildly annoyed, he was brushing the dust from his handmade English suit. Adrian Carter was still holding a phone to his ear. He didn't seem to realize the receiver was no longer connected to its base.

Gabriel gently removed the phone from Carter's grasp and asked whether Safia Bourihane was dead. He could not hear the sound of his own voice, nor could he hear Carter's response. It was as if someone had pressed the mute button. He looked toward the giant video screen, but the screen was gone. And then he realized that Natalie was gone, too.

63

GEORGETOWN

SAFIA CLEARLY KNEW WHERE SHE was going. After making the right turn onto M Street, she blew through the red light at the base of Thirty-fourth and then swerved hard into Bank Street, a cobbled alley that climbed the gentle hill up to Prospect. Ignoring the stop sign, she made a right, and then another left onto Thirty-third. It was a one-way street running south-to-north up the length of Georgetown's West Village, with four-way stops at every block. Safia flashed across N Street without slowing. She was holding the steering wheel tightly with her left hand. Her right, the one with the detonator, was clutching the grip of the shift.

"Are they still behind us?"

"Who?"

"The Americans!" Safia shouted.

"What Americans?"

"The ones who've been watching us at the hotel. The ones who followed us to the shopping mall."

"No one followed us."

"Of course they did! And they were waiting for us just now in the parking lot of the hotel. But he tricked them."

"Who tricked them?"

"Saladin, of course. Can't you hear the sirens? The attack has begun."

Natalie could hear them. There were sirens everywhere.

"Alhamdulillah," she said softly.

Ahead, an elderly man entered the crosswalk at O Street, trailed by a basset hound on a leash. Safia slammed on the horn with her detonator hand, and both man and canine moved out of the car's path. Natalie glanced over her shoulder. The man and the dog appeared uninjured. Far behind them, a car rounded the corner at Prospect Street at high speed.

"Where did we attack them?" asked Natalie.

"I don't know."

"What's my target?"

"In a minute."

"What's yours?"

"It doesn't matter." Alarm flashed on Safia's face. "They're coming!"

"Who?"

"The Americans."

Safia put her foot to the floor and raced across P Street. Then, at Volta Place, she made another right turn.

"There's a French restaurant on Wisconsin Avenue called Bistrot Lepic. It's about a kilometer up the street, on the left side. Some diplomats from the French Embassy are having a private dinner there tonight with people from the Foreign Ministry from Paris. It will be very crowded. Walk as far into the restaurant as you can and hit your detonator. If they try to stop you at the door, do it there."

"Is it just me, or are there others?"

"Just you. We're part of the second wave of attacks."

"What's your target?"

"I told you once already, it doesn't matter."

Safia braked hard at Wisconsin Avenue.

"Get out."

"But—"

"Get out!" Safia waved her clenched right fist in Natalie's face, the fist that held the detonator. "Get out or I'll kill us both right now!"

Natalie climbed out and watched the Toyota speed south on Wisconsin Avenue. Then she looked up the length of Volta Place. No traffic moved in the street. It seemed Safia had managed to elude their pursuers. Once again, Natalie was alone.

She stood frozen with indecision for a moment, listening to the screaming of the sirens. They all seemed to be converging at the southern end of Georgetown, near the Potomac. Finally, she headed in the opposite direction, toward her target, and started looking for a telephone. And all the while she was wondering why Safia had insisted she wear the suicide vest with the red stitch in the zipper.

FIVE CRITICAL MINUTES WOULD ELAPSE BEFORE THE FBI managed to find the car. It was parked at the corner of Wisconsin and Prospect, illegally and very badly. The right-front wheel was on the curb, the driver's-side door was ajar, the headlights were on, the engine was running. More important, the two female occupants, one dark-haired, one blond, subjects one and two, had vanished.

64

CAFÉ MILANO, GEORGETOWN

SAFIA WAS SLIGHTLY OUT OF breath when she entered Café Milano. With a martyr's serenity, she walked across the foyer to the maître d' stand.

"Al-Farouk," she said.

"Mr. al-Farouk has already arrived. Right this way, please."

Safia followed the maître d' into the main dining room, and then to the table where Saladin sat alone. He rose slowly on his wounded leg and kissed her lightly on each cheek.

"Asma, my love," he said in perfect English. "You look absolutely lovely."

She didn't understand what he was saying, and so she merely smiled and sat down. While reclaiming his own seat, Saladin shot a glance toward the man sitting at the end of the bar. The man with dark hair and eyeglasses who had entered the restaurant a few minutes after Saladin. The man, thought Saladin, who had taken great interest in Safia's arrival and who was holding a mobile phone tightly to his ear. It could mean only one thing: Saladin's presence in Washington had not gone unnoticed.

He raised his eyes toward the television over the bar. It was tuned to CNN. The network was only just beginning to grasp the scope of the calamity that had befallen Washington. There had been attacks at the National Counterterrorism Center, the Lincoln Memorial, and the Kennedy Center. The network was also hearing reports, unconfirmed, of attacks on a number of restaurants in the Washington Harbor complex. The patrons of Café Milano were clearly on edge. Most were staring at their mobiles, and about a dozen were gathered around the bar, watching the television. But not the man with dark hair and glasses. He was trying his best not to stare at Safia. It was time, thought Saladin, to be leaving.

He placed his hand lightly on Safia's and stared into her hypnotic eyes. In Arabic, he asked, "You dropped her where I told you?"

She nodded.

"The Americans followed you?"

"They tried. They seemed confused."

"With good reason," he said with a glance toward the television.

"It went well?"

"Better than expected."

A waiter approached. Saladin waved him away.

"Do you see the man at the end of the bar?" he asked quietly.

"The one who's talking on the phone?"

Saladin nodded. "Have you ever seen him before?"

"I don't think so."

"He's going to try to stop you. Don't let him."

There was a moment's silence. Saladin granted himself the luxury of one last look around the room. This was the reason he had made the risky journey to Washington, to see with his own eyes fear on American faces. For too long, only Muslims had been afraid. Now the Americans would know what it was

like to taste fear. They had destroyed Saladin's country. Tonight, Saladin had begun the process of destroying theirs.

He looked at Safia. "You're ready?"

"Yes," she answered.

"After I leave, wait one minute exactly." He gave her hand
a soft squeeze of encouragement and then smiled. "Don't be
afraid, my love. You won't feel a thing. And then you'll see the
face of Allah."

"Peace be with you," she said.

"And with you."

With that, Saladin rose and, taking up his cane, limped
past the man with dark hair and glasses, into the foyer.

"Is everything all right, Mr. al-Farouk?" asked the maître d'.

"I have to make a phone call, and I don't want to disturb
your other guests."

"I'm afraid they're already disturbed."

"So it would seem."

Saladin went into the night. On the redbrick pavement, he
paused for a moment to savor the wail of sirens. A black Lincoln Town Car waited curbside. Saladin lowered himself into
the backseat and instructed the driver, a member of his network, to move forward a few yards. Inside the restaurant, surrounded by more than a hundred people, a woman sat alone,
staring at her wristwatch. And though she did not realize it,
her lips were moving.

65

WISCONSIN AVENUE, GEORGETOWN

AFTER CROSSING Q STREET, NATALIE encountered two Georgetown students, both women, both terrified. Over the scream of a passing ambulance, she explained that she had been robbed and needed to call her boyfriend for help. The women said that the university had sent out an alert ordering all students to return to their dorms and residences and to shelter in place. But when Natalie made a second appeal, one of the women, the taller of the two, handed over an iPhone. Natalie held the device in the palm of her left hand, and with her right, the one that held the detonator switch, entered the number she was supposed to use only in an extreme emergency. It rang on the Operations Desk at King Saul Boulevard in Tel Aviv. A male voice answered in terse Hebrew.

"I need to speak to Gabriel right away," Natalie said in the same language.

"Who is this?"

She hesitated and then spoke her given name for the first time in many months.

"Where are you?"

"Wisconsin Avenue in Georgetown."

"Are you safe?"

"Yes, I think so, but I'm wearing a suicide vest."

"It might be booby-trapped. Don't try to take it off."

"I won't."

"Stand by."

Twice the man on the Operations Desk in Tel Aviv tried to transfer the call to Gabriel's mobile. Twice there was no answer.

"There seems to be a problem."

"Where is he?"

"The National Counterterrorism Center in Virginia."

"Try again."

A police cruiser flashed past, siren screaming. The two Georgetown students were growing impatient.

"Just a minute," Natalie said to them in English.

"Please hurry," replied the owner of the phone.

The man in Tel Aviv tried Gabriel's phone again. It rang several times before a male voice answered in English.

"Who is this?" asked Natalie.

"My name is Adrian Carter. I work for the CIA."

"Where's Gabriel?"

"He's here with me."

"I need to speak to him."

"I'm afraid that's not possible."

"Why not?"

"Is this Natalie?"

"Yes."

"Where are you?"

She answered.

"Are you still wearing your vest?"

"Yes."

"Don't touch it."

"I won't."

"Can you keep this phone?"

"No."

"We're going to bring you in. Walk north on Wisconsin Avenue. Stay on the west side of the street."

"There's going to be another attack. Safia is somewhere close."

"We know exactly where she is. Get moving."

The connection went dead. Natalie returned the phone and headed north up Wisconsin Avenue.

IN THE RUINS OF THE NATIONAL COUNTERTERRORISM CENTER, Carter managed to communicate to Gabriel that Natalie was safe and would momentarily be in FBI custody. Deafened, bleeding, Gabriel had no time for celebration. Mikhail was still inside Café Milano, not twenty feet from the table where Safia Bourihane sat alone, her thumb on her detonator, her eyes on her watch. Carter raised the phone to his ear and again ordered Mikhail to leave the restaurant at once. Gabriel still couldn't hear what Carter was saying. He only hoped that Mikhail was listening.

LIKE SALADIN, MIKHAIL SURVEYED THE INTERIOR OF CAFÉ Milano's elegant dining room before rising. He, too, saw fear on the faces around him, and like Saladin he knew that in a moment many people would die. Saladin had had the power to stop the attack. Mikhail did not. Even if he was armed, which he was not, the chances of stopping the attack were slim. Safia's thumb was atop the detonator switch, and when she was not staring at her watch, she was staring at Mikhail.

Nor was it possible to issue any sort of warning. A warning would only cause a panicked rush to the door, and more would die. Better to let the vest explode with the patrons as they were. The lucky ones at the outer tables might survive. The ones closest to Safia, the ones who had been granted the coveted tables, would be spared the awful knowledge that they were about to die.

Slowly, Mikhail slid from the barstool and stood. He didn't dare try to leave the restaurant through the front entrance; his path would take him far too close to Safia's table. Instead, he moved calmly down the length of the bar toward the toilets. The door to the men's room was locked. He twisted the flimsy latch until it snapped and went inside. A thirtysomething man with gelled hair was admiring himself in the mirror.

"What's your problem, man?"

"You'll know in a minute."

The man tried to leave, but Mikhail seized his arm.

"Don't go. You'll thank me later."

Mikhail closed the door and pulled the man to the ground.

FROM HIS VANTAGE POINT ON PROSPECT STREET, ELI LAVON had witnessed a series of increasingly unsettling developments. The first was the arrival at Café Milano of Safia Bourihane, followed a few minutes later by the departure of the large Arab known as Omar al-Farouk. The large Arab was now in the backseat of a Lincoln Town Car, which was parked about fifty yards from Café Milano's entrance, behind a white Honda Pilot. What's more, Lavon had called Gabriel several times at the NCTC without success. Subsequently, he had learned, from King Saul Boulevard and the car radio, that the NCTC had been attacked by a pair of truck bombs.

Lavon now feared that his oldest friend in the world might be dead, this time for real. And he feared that, in a few seconds, Mikhail might be dead, too.

Just then, Lavon received a message from King Saul Boulevard reporting that Gabriel had been slightly injured in the attack at the NCTC but was still very much alive. Lavon's relief was short-lived, however, for at that same instant the thunderclap of an explosion shook Prospect Street. The Lincoln Town Car eased sedately from the curb and slid past Lavon's window. Then four armed men spilled from the Honda Pilot and started running toward the wreckage of Café Milano.

66

WISCONSIN AVENUE, GEORGETOWN

NATALIE HEARD THE EXPLOSION AS she was approaching R Street and knew at once it was Safia. She turned and gazed down the length of Wisconsin Avenue, with its graceful rightward bend toward M Street, and saw hundreds of panicked people walking north. It reminded her of the scenes in Washington after 9/11, the tens of thousands of people who had simply left their offices in the world's most powerful city and started walking. Once again, Washington was under siege. This time, the terrorists weren't armed with airplanes, only explosives and guns. But the result, it seemed, was far more terrifying.

Natalie turned and joined the exodus moving north. She was growing weary beneath the dead weight of the suicide vest, and the weight of her own failure. She had saved the life of the very monster who had conceived and plotted this carnage, and after her arrival in America she had been unable to uncover a single piece of intelligence about the targets, the other terrorists, or the timing of the attack. She had been kept in the dark for a reason, she was certain of it.

All at once there was a burst of gunfire from the same direction as the explosion. Natalie hurried across R Street and continued north, keeping to the west side of the street as the man named Adrian Carter had instructed. *We're going to bring you in*, he had said. But he had not told her how. Suddenly, she was pleased to be wearing the red jacket. She might not be able to see them, but they would see her.

North of R Street, Wisconsin Avenue sank for a block or two before rising into the neighborhoods of Burleith and Glover Park. Ahead, Natalie saw a blue-and-yellow awning that read BISTROT LEPIC & WINE BAR. It was the restaurant Safia had ordered her to bomb. She stopped and peered through the window. It was a charming place—small, warm, inviting, very Parisian. Safia had said it would be crowded, but that wasn't the case. Nor did the people sitting at the tables look like French diplomats or officials from the Foreign Ministry in Paris. They looked like Americans. And, like everyone else in Washington, they looked frightened.

Just then, Natalie heard someone calling her name—not her own name but the name of the woman she had become in order to prevent a night like this. She turned sharply and saw that a car had pulled up at the curb behind her. At the wheel was a woman with open-air skin. It was Megan, the woman from the FBI.

Natalie crawled into the front seat as though she were crawling into the arms of her mother. The weight of the suicide vest pinned her to the seat; the detonator felt like a live animal in her palm. The car swung a U-turn and joined the northward exodus from Georgetown, as all around the sirens wailed. Natalie covered her ears, but it was no use.

"Please turn on some music," she begged.

The woman switched on the car radio, but there was no music to be found, only the terrible news. The National

Counterterrorism Center, the Lincoln Memorial, the Kennedy Center, Harbor Place: the death toll, it was feared, could approach one thousand. Natalie was able to bear it for only a minute or two. She reached for the radio's power button but stopped when she felt a sharp pain in her upper arm, like the bite of a viper. Then she looked at the woman and saw that she, too, was holding something in her right hand. But it was not a detonator switch upon which her thumb rested. It was the plunger of a syringe.

Instantly, Natalie's vision blurred. The woman's weather-beaten face receded; a passing police cruiser left time-lapse streaks of red and blue on the night. Natalie called out a name, the only name she could recall, before a darkness descended upon her. It was like the blackness of her abaya. She saw herself walking through a great Arabian house of many rooms and courts. And in the last room, standing in the molten light of an oculus, was Saladin.

67

CAFÉ MILANO, GEORGETOWN

FOR A FEW SECONDS AFTER the explosion there was only silence. It was like the silence of the crypt, thought Mikhail, the silence of death. Finally, there was a moan, and then a cough, and then the first screams of agony and terror. Soon there were others, many others—the limbless, the blind, the ones who would never be able to gaze into a mirror again. A few more would surely die tonight, but many would survive. They would see their children again, they would dance at weddings and weep at funerals. And perhaps one day they would be able to eat in a restaurant again without the nagging fear that the woman at the next table was wearing a suicide vest. It was the fear that all Israelis had lived with during the dark days of the Second Intifada. And now, thanks to a man called Saladin, that same fear had come to America.

Mikhail reached for the door latch but stopped when he heard the first gunshot. He realized then that his phone was vibrating in his coat pocket. He checked the screen. It was Eli Lavon.

"Where the hell are you?"

In a whisper, Mikhail told him.

"Four men with guns just entered the restaurant."

"I can hear them."

"You've got to get out of there."

"Where's Natalie?"

"The FBI is about to pick her up."

Mikhail returned the phone to his pocket. From beyond the lavatory's thin door came another gunshot—large caliber, military grade. Then there were two more: *crack, crack* . . . With each shot, another scream went silent. Clearly, the terrorists were determined to see that no one left Café Milano alive. These were no video-game jihadis. They were well trained, disciplined. They were moving methodically through the ruins of the restaurant in search of survivors. And eventually, thought Mikhail, their search would bring them to the lavatory door.

The American man with gelled hair was shaking with fear. Mikhail looked around for something he might use as a weapon but saw nothing suitable. Then, with a sideways nod of his head, he instructed the American to conceal himself in the stall. Somehow, the restaurant still had power. Mikhail killed the lights, muffling the snap of the switch, and pressed his back against the wall next to the door. In the sudden darkness, he vowed that he would not die this night in a toilet in Georgetown, with a man he did not know. It would be an ignoble way for a soldier to depart this world, he thought, even a soldier of the secret variety.

From beyond the door there was the sharp crack of another gunshot, closer than the last, and another scream went silent. Then there were footsteps outside in the corridor. Mikhail flexed the fingers of his lethal right hand. Open the door, you bastard, he thought. Open the fucking door.

IT WAS AT THAT SAME INSTANT THAT GABRIEL REALIZED HIS hearing loss was not permanent. The first sound he heard was the same sound that many Washingtonians would associate with that night, the sound of sirens. The first responders were rolling up Tysons McLean Drive toward what had once been the security checkpoint of the National Counterterrorism Center and the Office of the Director of National Intelligence. Inside the ruined buildings, the less seriously injured were tending to the gravely wounded in a desperate attempt to stem bleeding and save lives. Fareed Barakat was looking after Paul Rousseau, and Adrian Carter was looking after what remained of Gabriel's operation. With borrowed mobile phones he had reestablished contact with Langley, FBI Headquarters, and the White House Situation Room. Washington was in chaos, and the federal government was struggling to keep pace with events. Thus far, there had been confirmed attacks at Liberty Crossing, the Lincoln Memorial, the Kennedy Center, Washington Harbor, and Café Milano. In addition, there were reports of more attacks along M Street. It was feared that hundreds of people, perhaps as many as a thousand, had been killed.

At that moment, however, Gabriel was focused on only two people: Mikhail Abramov and Natalie Mizrahi. Mikhail was trapped in the men's room at Café Milano. Natalie was walking north on the west side of Wisconsin Avenue.

"Why hasn't the FBI brought her in?" he snapped at Carter.

"They can't seem to find her."

"How hard can it be to find a woman wearing a suicide vest and a red jacket?"

"They're looking."

"Tell them to look harder."

THE DOOR CRASHED OPEN, THE GUN ENTERED FIRST. MIKHAIL recognized the silhouette. It was an AR-15, no scope. He seized the warm barrel with his left hand and pulled, and a man came with it. In the ruined dining room, he had been a jihadist holy warrior, but in the darkened confines of the men's room, he was now helpless. With the edge of his right hand, Mikhail hit him twice in the side of the neck. The first blow caught a bit of jawbone, but the second was a direct hit that caused something to crack and snap. The man went down without a sound. Mikhail lifted the AR-15 from the limp hands, shot him through the head, and spun into the corridor.

Directly in front of him, in the back corner of the dining room, one of the terrorists was about to execute a woman whose arm had been shorn off at the shoulder. Hidden in the darkened corridor, Mikhail put the terrorist down with a head shot and then moved cautiously forward. There were no other terrorists in the main dining room, but in a smaller room at the back of the restaurant, a terrorist was executing survivors huddled against a wall, one by one, like an SS man moving along the edge of a burial pit. Mikhail shot the terrorist cleanly through the chest, saving a dozen lives.

Just then, Mikhail heard another gunshot from an adjoining room—the private dining room he had seen when he entered the restaurant. He moved past the toppled barstool where he had been seated a moment earlier, past the upended table splattered with the viscera of Safia Bourihane, and entered the foyer. The maître d' and the two hostesses were all dead. It appeared as though they had survived the bombing, only to be shot to death.

Mikhail crept silently past the corpses and peered into the private dining room, where the fourth terrorist was in the process of executing twenty well-dressed men and women. Too late, the terrorist realized that the man standing in the doorway of the private dining room was not a friend. Mikhail shot him through the chest. Then he fired a second shot, a head shot, to make certain he was dead.

It had all taken less than a minute, and Mikhail's mobile phone had been vibrating intermittently the entire time. Now he snatched it from his pocket and peered at the screen. It was a voice call from Gabriel.

"Please tell me you're alive."

"I'm just fine, but four members of ISIS are now in paradise."

"Grab their cell phones and as much hardware as you can carry and get out of there."

"What's going on?"

The connection went dead. Mikhail searched the pockets of the dead terrorist lying at his feet and found a Samsung Galaxy disposable phone. He found identical Samsungs on the dead terrorists in the main dining room and the room in the back, but the one in the toilet apparently preferred Apple products. Mikhail had all four phones in his possession when he slipped from the restaurant's rear service door. He also had two AR-15s and four additional magazines of ammunition, for what reason he did not know. He hurried down a darkened alleyway, praying that he did not encounter a SWAT team, and emerged onto Potomac Street. He followed it south to Prospect, where Eli Lavon was sitting behind the wheel of a Buick.

"What took you so long?" he asked as Mikhail fell into the front passenger seat.

"Gabriel gave me a shopping list." Mikhail laid the AR-15s and the magazines on the floor of the backseat. "What the fuck is going on?"

"The FBI can't find Natalie."

"She's wearing a red jacket and a suicide vest."

Lavon swung a U-turn and headed west across George-town.

"You're going the wrong way," said Mikhail. "Wisconsin Avenue is behind us."

"We're not going to Wisconsin Avenue."

"Why not?"

"She's gone, Mikhail. *Gone* gone."

68

KING SAUL BOULEVARD, TEL AVIV

THE UNIT THAT TOILED IN Room 414C of King Saul Boulevard had no official name because, officially, it did not exist. Those who had been briefed on its work referred to it only as the Minyan, for the unit was ten in number and exclusively male in gender. With but a few keystrokes, they could darken a city, blind an air traffic control network, or make the centrifuges of an Iranian nuclear-enrichment plant spin wildly out of control. Three Samsungs and an iPhone weren't going to be much of a challenge.

Mikhail and Eli Lavon uploaded the contents of the four phones from the Israeli Embassy at 8:42 p.m. local time. By nine o'clock Washington time, the Minyan had determined that the four phones had spent a great deal of time during the past few months at the same address on Eisenhower Avenue in Alexandria, Virginia. In fact, they had been there at the same time earlier that evening and had traveled into Washington at the same speed, along the same route. Furthermore, all the phones had placed numerous calls to a local moving company based at the address. The Minyan delivered the intelligence to Uzi Navot, who in turn forwarded it to Gabriel. By then, he and Adrian Carter had left the bombed-out NCTC and were in the CIA's Global Ops Center at Langley. Of Carter, Gabriel asked a single question.

"Who owns Dominion Movers in Alexandria?"

Fifteen precious minutes elapsed before Carter had an answer. He gave Gabriel a name and an address and told him to do whatever it took to find Natalie alive. Carter's words meant little; as deputy director of the Central Intelligence Agency, he had no power to let a foreign intelligence service operate with impunity on American soil. Only the president could grant such authority, and at that moment the president had bigger things to worry about than a missing Israeli spy. America was under attack. And like it or not, Gabriel Allon was going to be the first to retaliate.

At twenty minutes past nine, Carter dropped Gabriel at the Agency's main security gate and departed quickly, as though fleeing the scene of a crime, or of a crime soon to be committed. Gabriel stood alone in the darkness, watching the ambulances and rescue vehicles hurtling along Route 123 toward Liberty Crossing, waiting. It was a fitting way for his career in the field to end, he thought. *The waiting . . . Always the waiting . . .* Waiting for a plane or a train. Waiting for a source. Waiting for the sun to rise after a night of killing. Waiting for Mikhail and Eli Lavon at the entrance of the CIA so that he could begin his search for a woman he had asked to penetrate the world's most dangerous terrorist group. She had done it. Or had she? Perhaps Saladin had been suspicious of her from the beginning. Perhaps he had granted her entrée into his court in order to penetrate and mislead Western intelligence. And perhaps he had dispatched her to America to act as a decoy, a shiny object that would occupy the Americans' attention while the real terrorists—the men who worked for a moving company in Alexandria, Virginia—engaged in their final preparations unmolested. How else to explain the fact that Safia had withheld Natalie's target until the final minute? Natalie had no target. Natalie was the target.

He thought of the man he had seen in the lobby of the Four Seasons Hotel. The large Arab named Omar al-Farouk who walked with a limp. The large Arab who had left Café Milano a few minutes before Safia detonated her suicide vest. Was he truly Saladin? It didn't matter. Whoever he was, he would soon be dead. So would everyone else associated with Natalie's disappearance. Gabriel would make it his life's work to hunt them all down and destroy ISIS before ISIS could destroy the Middle East and what remained of the civilized world. He suspected he would have a willing accomplice in the American president. ISIS was now two hours from Indiana.

Just then, Gabriel's mobile phone pulsed. He read the message, returned the phone to his pocket, and walked to the edge of Route 123. A few seconds later a Buick Regal appeared. It stopped only long enough for Gabriel to slide into the backseat. On the floor were two AR-15s and several magazines of ammunition. The Second Amendment, thought Gabriel, definitely had its advantages. He looked into the rearview mirror and saw Mikhail's frozen eyes looking back at him.

"Which way, boss?"

"Take the GW Parkway back toward Key Bridge," said Gabriel. "The Beltway is a fucking mess."

69

HUME, VIRGINIA

NATALIE AWOKE WITH THE SENSATION of having slept an eternity. Her mouth seemed to be stuffed with cotton, her head had lolled sideways against the cool of the window. Here and there, over front porches and in lace-curtained windows, a light faintly burned, but otherwise the atmosphere was one of sudden abandonment. It was as if the inhabitants of this place, having learned of the attacks in Washington, had packed their belongings and taken to the hills.

Her head throbbed with a hangover's dull ache. She tried to raise it, but could not. Casting her eyes to the left, she watched the woman drive, the woman she had mistakenly believed to be Megan from the FBI. She was holding the wheel with her right hand; in her left was a gun. The time, according to the dashboard clock, was 9:22. Natalie, through the fog of the drug, tried to reconstruct the evening's events—the second car in the parking garage, the wild ride into Georgetown, the quaint little French restaurant that was supposed to be her target, the bomb vest with the red stitch in the zipper. The detonator was still in her right hand. Lightly, she ran the tip of her forefinger over the switch.

Boom, she thought, recalling her bomb training in Palmyra. *And now you are on your way to paradise . . .*

A church appeared on Natalie's right. Soon after, they came to a deserted intersection. The woman came to a complete stop before turning, as instructed by the navigation system, onto a road with a philosopher's name. It was very narrow, with no yellow centerline. The darkness was absolute; there seemed to be no world at all beyond the patch of asphalt illuminated by the car's headlights. The navigation system grew suddenly confused. It advised the woman to make a U-turn if possible, and when no turn was forthcoming it fell into a reproachful sulk.

The woman followed the road for another half mile before turning into a dirt-and-gravel track. It bore them across a pasture, over a ridge of wooded hills, and into a small dell, where a timbered A-frame cottage overlooked a black pond. Lights burned within the cottage, and parked outside were three vehicles—a Lincoln Town Car, a Honda Pilot, and a BMW sedan. The woman pulled up behind the BMW and switched off the engine. Natalie, her head against the glass, feigned a coma.

"Can you walk?" asked the woman.

Natalie was silent.

"I saw your eyes moving. I know you're awake."

"What did you give me?"

"Propofol."

"Where did you get it?"

"I'm a nurse." The woman climbed out of the car and opened Natalie's door. "Get out."

"I can't."

"Propofol is a short-duration anesthetic," lectured the

woman pedantically. "Patients who are given it can typically walk on their own a few minutes after awakening."

When Natalie did not move, the woman pointed the gun at her head. Natalie raised her right hand and placed her thumb lightly atop the detonator switch.

"You haven't got the guts," said the woman. Then she seized Natalie's wrist and dragged her from the car.

The door of the cottage was a walk of perhaps twenty yards, but the leaden weight of the suicide vest, and the lingering effects of the propofol, made it seem more like a mile. The room Natalie entered was rustic and quaint. Consequently, its male occupants looked obscenely out of place. Four wore black tactical suits and were armed with combat assault rifles. The fifth wore an elegant business suit and was warming his hands before a wood-burning stove. His back was turned to Natalie. He was well over six feet tall and his shoulders were broad. Still, he looked vaguely infirm, as though he were recovering from a recent injury.

At length, the man in the elegant business suit turned. His hair was neatly groomed and combed, his face was clean-shaven. His dark brown eyes, however, were exactly as Natalie remembered them. So, too, was his confident smile. He took a step toward her, favoring the damaged leg, and stopped.

"Maimonides," he said pleasantly. "So good to see you again."

Natalie clutched the detonator tightly in her hand. Beneath her feet the earth burned.

70

ARLINGTON, VIRGINIA

IT WAS A SMALL DUPLEX, two floors, aluminum siding. The unit on the left was painted granite gray. The one on the right, Qassam el-Banna's, was the color of a shirt that had been dried too many times on a radiator. Each unit had a single window on the ground floor and a single window on the second. A chain-link fence divided the front yard into separate plots. The one on the left was a showpiece, but Qassam's looked as though it had been chewed bare by goats.

"Obviously," observed Eli Lavon darkly from the backseat of the Buick, "he hasn't had much time for gardening."

They were parked on the opposite side of the street, outside a duplex of identical construction and upkeep. In the space in front of the gray-white duplex was an Acura sedan. It still had dealer plates.

"Nice car," said Lavon. "What's the husband drive?"

"A Kia," said Gabriel.

"I don't see a Kia."

"Neither do I."

"Wife drives an Acura, husband drives a Kia—what's wrong with this picture?"

Gabriel offered no explanation.

"What's the wife's name?" asked Lavon.

"Amina."

"Egyptian?"

"Apparently so."

"Kid?"

"Boy."

"How old?"

"Two and a half."

"So he won't remember what's about to happen."

"No," agreed Gabriel. "He won't remember."

A car moved past in the street. The driver had the look of an indigenous South American—a Bolivian, maybe Peruvian. He seemed not to notice the three Israeli intelligence operatives sitting in the parked Buick Regal across the street from the house owned by an Egyptian jihadi who had slipped through the cracks of America's vast post–9/11 security structure.

"What did Qassam do before he got into the moving business?"

"IT."

"Why are so many of them in IT?"

"Because they don't have to study un-Islamic subjects like English literature or Italian Renaissance painting."

"All the things that make life interesting."

"They aren't interested in life, Eli. Only death."

"Think he left his computers behind?"

"I certainly hope so."

"What if he smashed his hard drives?"

Gabriel was silent. Another car moved past in the street,

another South American behind the wheel. America, he thought, had its banlieues, too.

"How are you going to play it?" asked Lavon.

"I'm not going to knock on the door and invite myself in for a cup of tea."

"But no rough stuff, though."

"No," said Gabriel. "No rough stuff."

"You always say that."

"And?"

"There's always rough stuff."

Gabriel picked up one of the AR-15s and checked to make sure it was properly loaded.

"Front door or back?" asked Lavon.

"I don't do back doors."

"What if they have a dog?"

"Bad swing thought, Eli."

"What do you want me to do?"

"Stay in the car."

Without another word, Gabriel climbed out and started swiftly across the street, gun in one hand, Mikhail at his side. It was funny, thought Lavon, watching him, but even after all these years he still moved like the boy of twenty-two who had served as Israel's angel of vengeance after Munich. He scaled the chain-link fence with a straddling sidestep and then hurled himself toward the el-Bannas' front door. There was a sharp splintering of wood, followed by a female scream, abruptly smothered. Then the door slammed shut and the lights of the house went dark. Lavon slid behind the wheel and surveyed the quiet street. So much for no rough stuff, he thought. There was always rough stuff.

71

HUME, VIRGINIA

NATALIE'S BODY SEEMED TO LIQUEFY with fear. She clutched the detonator tightly in her hand, lest it slip from her grasp and sink like a coin to the bottom of a wishing well. Inwardly, she reviewed the elements of her fabricated curriculum vitae. She was Leila from Sumayriyya, Leila who loved Ziad. At a rally in the Place de la République, she had told a young Jordanian named Nabil that she wanted to punish the West for its support of Israel. Nabil had given her name to Jalal Nasser, and Jalal had given her to Saladin. Inside the global jihadist movement, a story such as hers was commonplace. But it was just that, a story, and somehow Saladin knew it.

But how long had he known? From the beginning? No, thought Natalie, it wasn't possible. Saladin's lieutenants would never have allowed her to be in the same room with him if they suspected her loyalty. Nor would they have placed his fate in her hands. But they *had* entrusted her with Saladin's life, and to her shame she had preserved it. And now she stood before him with a bomb strapped to her body and a detonator in her right hand. *We don't do suicide missions*, Gabriel had said after her return from the caliphate. *We don't trade our lives for theirs.* She placed her thumb atop the trigger switch and, testing the resistance, pressed it lightly. Saladin, watching her, smiled.

"You are very brave, Maimonides," he said to her in Arabic. "But then I always knew that."

He reached into the breast pocket of his suit jacket. Natalie, fearing he was reaching for a gun, pressed harder on the switch. But it was not a gun, it was a phone. He tapped the screen a few times, and the device emitted a sharp hissing sound. Natalie realized after a few seconds that the sound was water rushing into a basin. The first voice she heard was her own.

"Do you know who that woman is?"

"How did she get into the country?"

"On a false passport."

"Where did she come in?"

"New York."

"Kennedy or Newark?"

"I don't know."

"How did she get down to Washington?"

"The train."

"What's the name of the passport?"

"Asma Doumaz."

"Have you been given a target?"

"No. But she's been given hers. It's a suicide operation."

"Do you know her target?"

"No."

"Have you met any other members of the attack cells?"

"No."

"Where's your phone?"

"She took it from me. Don't try to send me any messages."

"Get out of here."

Saladin, with a tap on the screen, silenced the recording. Then he regarded Natalie for several unbearable seconds. There was no reproach or anger in his expression. It was the gaze of a professional.

"Who do you work for?" he asked at last, again addressing her in Arabic.

"I work for you." She did not know from what reservoir of pointless courage she drew this response, but it seemed to amuse Saladin. "You are very brave, Maimonides," he said again. "Too brave for your own good."

She noticed for the first time that there was a television in the room. It was tuned to CNN. Three hundred invited guests in evening gowns and tuxedos were streaming from the White House East Room under Secret Service escort.

"A night to remember, don't you think? All the attacks were successful except for one. The target was a French restaurant where many prominent Washingtonians are known to eat. For some reason, the operative chose not to carry out her assignment. Instead, she climbed into a car driven by a woman she believed to be an agent of the FBI."

He paused to allow Natalie a response, but she remained silent.

"Her treachery posed no threat to the operation," he continued. "In fact, it proved quite valuable because it allowed us to distract the Americans during the critical final days of the operation. The end game," he added ominously. "You and Safia were a feint, a deception. I am a soldier of Allah, but a great admirer of Winston Churchill. And it was Churchill who said that in wartime, truth is so precious that she should always be attended by a bodyguard of lies."

He had addressed these remarks to the television screen. Now he turned once more toward Natalie.

"But there was one question we were never able to answer satisfactorily," he continued. "Whom, exactly, were you working for? Abu Ahmed assumed you were an American, but it didn't feel like an American operation to me. Quite honestly, I assumed you were British, because as we all know, the British are the very best when it comes to running live agents. But that also turned out not to be the case. You weren't working for the Americans *or* the British. You were working for someone else. And tonight you finally told me his name."

Again, he tapped the screen of his mobile phone, and again Natalie heard a sound like water running into a basin. But it wasn't water, it was the drone of a car fleeing the chaos of Washington. This time, the only voice she heard was her own. She was speaking Hebrew, and her voice was heavy with sedative.

"Gabriel . . . Please help me . . . I don't want to die . . ."

Saladin silenced the phone and returned it to the breast pocket of his magnificent suit jacket. Case closed, thought Natalie. Still, there was no anger in his expression, only pity.

"You were a fool to come to the caliphate."

"No," said Natalie, "I was a fool to save your life."

"Why did you?"

"Because you would have died if I hadn't."

"And now," said Saladin, "it is *you* who will die. The question is, will you die alone, or will you press your detonator and take me with you? I'm wagering you don't have the courage or the faith to push the button. Only we, the Muslims, have such faith. We are prepared to die for our religion, but not you Jews. You believe in life, but we believe in death. And in any fight, it is those who are prepared to die who will win." He paused briefly, then said, "Go ahead, Maimonides, make a liar of me. Prove me wrong. Push your button."

Natalie raised the detonator to her face and stared directly into Saladin's dark eyes. The trigger button yielded to a slight increase in pressure.

"Don't you remember your training in Palmyra? We deliberately use a firm trigger to avoid accidents. You have to push it harder."

She did. There was a click, then silence. Saladin smiled.

"Obviously," he said, "a malfunction."

72

ARLINGTON, VIRGINIA

AMINA EL-BANNA HAD BEEN A legal resident of the United States for more than five years, but her grasp of English was limited. As a result, Gabriel questioned her in his Arabic, which was limited, too. He did so at the tiny kitchen table with Mikhail hovering in the doorway, and in a voice that was not loud enough to wake the child sleeping upstairs. He did not fly a false flag and claim to be an American, for such a pretense was not possible. Amina el-Banna, an Egyptian from the Nile Delta, knew very well that he was an Israeli, and consequently she feared him. He did nothing to put her mind at ease. Fear was his calling card, and at a time like this, with an agent in the hands of the most violent terrorist group the world had ever known, fear was his only asset.

He explained to Amina el-Banna the facts as he knew them. Her husband was a member of the ISIS terror cell that had just laid waste to Washington. He was no bit player; he was a major operational asset, a planner who had patiently moved the pieces into place and provided cover for the attack cells. In all likelihood, Amina would be charged as an accomplice and spend the rest of her life in jail. Unless, of course, she cooperated.

"How can I help you? I know nothing."

"Did you know Qassam owned a moving company?"

"Qassam? A moving company?" She shook her head incredulously. "Qassam works in IT."

"When was the last time you saw him?"

"Yesterday morning."

"Where is he?"

"I don't know."

"Have you tried to call him?"

"Of course."

"And?"

"His phone goes straight to voice mail."

"Why didn't you call the police?"

She gave no answer. Gabriel didn't need one. She didn't call the police, he thought, because she thought her husband was an ISIS terrorist.

"Did he make arrangements for you and the child to go to Syria?"

She hesitated, then said, "I told him I wouldn't go."

"Wise decision. Are his computers still here?"

She nodded.

"Where?"

She glanced toward the ceiling.

"How many?"

"Two. But they're locked, and I don't have the password."

"Of course you do. Every wife knows her husband's password, even if her husband is an ISIS terrorist."

She said nothing more.

"What's the password?"

"The Shahada."

"English or Arabic transliteration?"

"English."

"Spaces or no spaces?"

"No spaces."

"Let's go."

She led him up the narrow stairs, quietly, so as not to wake the child, and opened the door to Qassam el-Banna's office. It was a counterterrorism officer's nightmare. Gabriel sat down at one of the computers, awakened it with a small movement of the mouse, and placed his fingers lightly on the keyboard. He typed THEREISNOGODBUTGOD and pressed the return button.

"Shit," he said softly.

The hard drive had been wiped clean.

HE WAS VERY GOOD, QASSAM, BUT THE TEN HACKERS OF THE Minyan were much better. Within minutes of Gabriel's upload, they had discovered the digital traces of Qassam's documents folder. Inside the folder was another folder, locked and encrypted, filled with documents related to Dominion Movers of Alexandria—and among those documents was a one-year lease agreement for a small property near a town called Hume.

"It's not far from that old CIA safe house in The Plains," explained Uzi Navot by telephone. "It's about an hour from your current location, maybe more. If you drive all that way and she's not there . . ."

Gabriel rang off and dialed Adrian Carter at Langley.

"I need an aircraft with thermal-imaging capability to make a pass over a cottage off Hume Road in Fauquier County. And don't try to tell me you don't have one."

"I don't. But the FBI does."

"Can they spare a plane?"

"I'll find out."

They could. In fact, the FBI already had one airborne over Liberty Crossing—a Cessna 182T Skylane, owned by a Bureau front company called LCT Research of Reston, Virginia. It took the single-engine aircraft ten minutes to reach Fauquier County and to locate the small A-frame house in a vale north of Hume Road. Inside were the heat signatures of seven individuals. One of the signatures, the smallest, appeared immobile. There were three vehicles parked outside the cottage. All had been recently driven.

"Are there any other heat signatures in that valley?" asked Gabriel.

"Only wildlife," explained Carter.

"What kind of wildlife?"

"Several deer and a couple of bear."

"Perfect," said Gabriel.

"Where are you now?"

Gabriel told him. They were heading west on I-66. They had just passed the Beltway.

"Where's the closest FBI SWAT or hostage rescue team?" he asked.

"All the available teams have been sent to Washington to deal with the attacks."

"How long can we keep the Cessna up top?"

"Not long. The Bureau wants it back."

"Ask them to make one more pass. But not too low. The men inside that house know the sound of a surveillance aircraft when they hear it."

Gabriel killed the connection and watched the images of American suburbia flashing past his window. In his head, however, there were only numbers, and the numbers did not look good. Seven heat signatures, two AR-15 assault rifles, one veteran of the IDF's most elite special forces unit, one former assassin who would soon be the chief of Israeli intelligence, one surveillance specialist who never cared for rough stuff, two bears. He looked down at his mobile phone. Distance to destination: fifty-one miles. Time to destination: one hour and seven minutes.

"Faster, Mikhail. You have to drive faster."

73

HUME, VIRGINIA

SHE WAS TO BE GIVEN no trial, for none was necessary; with a press of her detonator button she had admitted her guilt. There was only the matter of her confession, which would be recorded for dissemination on ISIS's myriad propaganda platforms, and her execution, which would be by beheading. It might all have been handled quite swiftly were it not for Saladin himself. The brief delay was by no means an act of mercy. Saladin was still a spy at heart. And what a spy craved most was not blood but information.

The success of the attacks on Washington, and the prospect of Natalie's imminent death, had the effect of loosening his tongue. He acknowledged that, yes, he had served in the Iraqi Mukhabarat under Saddam Hussein. His primary duty, he claimed, was to provide material and logistical support to Palestinian terrorist groups, especially those that rejected absolutely the existence of a Jewish state in the Middle East. During the Second Intifada he had overseen the payment of lucrative death benefits to the families of Palestinian suicide bombers. Abu Nidal, he boasted, was a close friend. Indeed, it was Abu Nidal, the most vicious of the so-called rejectionist terrorists, who had given Saladin his code name.

His work required him to become something of an expert on the Israeli secret intelligence service. He developed a grudging admiration for the Office and for Ari Shamron, the master spy who guided it, on and off, for the better part of thirty years. He also came to admire the accomplishments of Shamron's famous protégé, the legendary assassin and operative named Gabriel Allon.

"And so you can imagine my surprise," he told Natalie, "to see him walking across the lobby of the Four Seasons Hotel in Washington, and to hear you speak his name."

After completing his opening remarks, he commenced questioning Natalie on every aspect of the operation—her life prior to joining Israeli intelligence, her recruitment, her training, her insertion into the field. Having been told she would soon face beheading, Natalie had no reason to cooperate other than to delay by a few minutes her inevitable death. It was motive enough, for she knew that her disappearance had not gone unnoticed. Saladin, with his spy's curiosity, had given her the opportunity to run a little sand through the hourglass. He began by asking her real name. She resisted for several precious minutes, until in a rage he threatened to carve the flesh from her bones with the same knife he would use to take her head.

"Amit," she said at last. "My name is Amit."

"Amit what?"

"Meridor."

"Where are you from?"

"Jaffa."

"How did you learn to speak Arabic so well?"

"There are many Arabs in Jaffa."

"And your French?"

"I lived in Paris for several years as a child."

"Why?"

"My parents worked for the Foreign Ministry."

"Are you a doctor?"

"A very good one."

"Who recruited you?"

"No one. I applied to join the Office."

"Why?"

"I wanted to serve my country."

"Is this your first operation?"

"No, of course not."

"Were the French involved in this operation?"

"We never work with other services. We prefer to work alone."

"Blue and white?" asked Saladin, using one of the slogans of the Israeli military and security establishment.

"Yes," said Natalie, nodding slowly. "Blue and white."

Despite the exigencies of the situation, Saladin insisted that her face be properly veiled during her questioning. There was no abaya to be had in the cottage, so they covered her with a sheet stripped from one of the beds. She could only imagine how she looked to them, a faintly comic figure draped in white, but the cloak did have the advantage of privacy. She lied with the full confidence that Saladin could see no telltale trace of deception in her eyes. And she managed to convey a sense of inward calm, even peace, when in truth she was thinking only of the pain she would feel when the blade of the knife bit into her neck. With her vision obscured, her sense of hearing grew acute. She was able to track Saladin's labored movements around the sitting room of the cottage and to discern the placement of the four armed ISIS terrorists. And she could hear, high above the cottage, the slow lazy circling of a single-engine aircraft. Saladin, she sensed, could hear it, too.

He fell silent for a moment until the plane was gone and then resumed his interrogation.

"How were you able to transform yourself so convincingly into a Palestinian?"

"We have a special school."

"Where?"

"In the Negev."

"Are there other Office agents who have infiltrated ISIS?"

"Yes, many."

"What are their names?"

She gave him six—four men, two other women. She said that she did not know the nature of their assignments. She knew only that, high above the little A-frame cottage, the plane had returned. Saladin, she thought, knew it, too. He had one final question. Why? he asked. Why had she saved his life in the house of many rooms and courts near Mosul?

"I wanted to gain your trust," she answered truthfully.

"You did," he admitted. "And then you betrayed it. And for that, Maimonides, you will die tonight."

There was a silence in the room, but not in the sky above. From beneath her death shroud, Natalie asked one final question of her own. How had Saladin known that she was not real? He gave her no answer, for he was listening once again to the drone of the aircraft. She followed the tap and scrape of his slow journey across the room to the front door of the cottage. It was the last she ever heard of him.

HE STOOD FOR SEVERAL MOMENTS OUTSIDE IN THE DRIVE, HIS face tilted toward the sky. There was no moon but the night was bright with stars and very quiet except for the plane. It took some time for him to locate it, for its wingtip navigation lights were dimmed. Only the beat of its single propeller betrayed its location. It was flying a steady orbit around the little valley, at an altitude of about ten thousand feet. Finally, when it reached the northernmost point, it turned due east, toward Washington, and then disappeared. Instinctively, Saladin believed the plane was trouble. They had failed him only once, his instincts. They had told him that a woman named Leila, a gifted doctor who claimed to be a Palestinian, could be trusted, even loved. Soon, the woman would be given the death she deserved.

His face was still lifted toward the heavens. Yes, the stars were bright this night, but not as bright as the stars of the desert. If he hoped to see them again, he had to leave now. Soon there would be another war—a war that would end with the defeat of the armies of Rome, in a town called Dabiq. There was no way the American president could avoid this war, he thought. Not after tonight.

He climbed into the BMW, started the engine, and entered his destination into the navigation system. It advised him to proceed to a road it recognized. Saladin did so, like the surveillance aircraft, with his lights doused, following the dirt-and-gravel road over the rim of the little valley and across the pasture to Hume Road. The navigation system instructed him to turn to the left and make his way back to I-66. Saladin, trusting his instincts, turned right instead. After a moment he switched on the radio. He smiled. It wasn't over, he thought. It was only beginning.

74

HUME, VIRGINIA

THE LAST REPORT FROM THE FBI Cessna was the same as the first—seven individuals inside the cottage, three vehicles outside. One of the individuals was entirely stationary, one appeared to be pacing slowly. There were no other human heat signatures in the little valley, only the bears. They were about fifty yards to the north of the cottage. For that reason, among others, Gabriel and Mikhail approached from the south.

A single road led into the valley, the private track leading from Hume Road to the cottage itself. They used it only as a point of reference. They kept to the pastureland, Mikhail leading the way, Gabriel a step behind. The earth was sodden and treacherous with the holes of burrowing animals. Occasionally, Mikhail illuminated their path with the light of his mobile phone, but mainly they moved in darkness.

At the edge of the pasture was a steep hill thick with oak and maple. Fallen tree limbs littered the ground, slowing their pace. Finally, after breasting the ridgeline of the valley, they glimpsed the cottage for the first time. One thing had changed since the departure of the FBI Cessna. There were two vehicles instead of three. Mikhail started down the slope of the hill, Gabriel a step behind.

AFTER SALADIN'S ABRUPT DEPARTURE, THE PREPARATIONS FOR Natalie's execution began in earnest. The white sheet was removed from her head, her hands were bound behind her back. A brief argument ensued among the four men over who would have the honor of removing her head. The tallest of the four prevailed. By his accent, Natalie could tell that he was a Yemeni. Something about his demeanor was vaguely familiar. All at once she realized that she and the Yemeni had been at the camp in Palmyra at the same time. He had worn his hair and beard long then. Now he was clean-shaven and neatly groomed. Were it not for his black tactical suit, he might have been mistaken for a sales associate at the Apple store.

The four men covered their faces, leaving only their pitiless eyes exposed. They made no attempt to alter the striking Americana of the setting—indeed, they seemed to revel in it. Natalie was made to kneel before the camera, which was held by the woman she knew as Megan. It was a real camera, not a cell phone; ISIS was second to none when it came to production value. They ordered Natalie to stare directly into the lens, but she refused, even after the Yemeni struck her viciously across the face. She stared straight ahead, toward the window over the woman's right shoulder, and tried to think of something, anything, other than the steel blade of the hunting knife in the Yemeni's right hand.

He stood directly behind her, with the other three men arrayed to his right, and read from a prepared statement, first in Arabic, then in a language that Natalie, after a moment, realized was broken English. It was no matter; the team at ISIS media productions would surely add subtitles. Natalie tried not to listen, focusing her attention instead on the window. Because it was dark outside, the glass was acting as a mirror. She could see the tableau of her execution roughly as it was being framed by the camera—one helpless woman kneeling, three masked men cradling automatic rifles, a Yemeni with a knife speaking no known language. But there was something else in the window, something less distinct than the reflection of Natalie and her four murderers. It was a face. Instantly, she realized it was Mikhail's. It was odd, she thought. Of all the faces she might conjure from her memory in the moments before her death, his was not the one she had expected.

The Yemeni's voice rose with an oratorical flourish as he concluded his statement. Natalie took one last look at her reflection in the window, and at the face of the man she might have loved. *Are you watching?* she thought. *What are you waiting for?*

SHE BECAME AWARE OF A SILENCE. IT LASTED A SECOND OR TWO, it lasted an hour or more—she could not tell. Then the Yemeni set upon her like a wild animal and she toppled sideways. When his hand seized her throat, she prepared herself for the pain of the knife's first bite. *Relax*, she told herself. It would hurt less if her muscles and tendons were not constricted. But then there was a sharp crack, which she mistook for the severing of her own neck, and the Yemeni fell beside her. The other three jihadists fell next, one by one, like targets in a shooting gallery. The woman was the last to die. Shot through the head, she collapsed as if a trapdoor had opened beneath her. The camera slipped from her grasp and clattered to the floor. Benevolently, the lens averted its gaze from Natalie's face. She was beautiful, thought Gabriel, as he cut the binds from her wrists. Even when she was screaming.

PART FOUR

THE ONE IN CHARGE

75

WASHINGTON—JERUSALEM

THE RECRIMINATIONS BEGAN EVEN BEFORE the sun had risen. One party blamed the president for the calamity that had befallen America, the other blamed his predecessor. That was the only thing Washington was good at these days—recriminations and apportionment of blame. There was once a time, during the darkest days of the Cold War, when American foreign policy was characterized by consensus and steadfastness. Now the two parties could not agree on what to call the enemy, let alone how to combat him. It was little wonder, then, that an attack on the nation's capital was yet another occasion for partisan bickering.

In the meantime—at the National Counterterrorism Center, the Lincoln Memorial, the John F. Kennedy Center for the Performing Arts, Harbor Place, a string of restaurants along M Street, and at Café Milano—they counted the dead. One hundred and sixteen at the NCTC and the Office of the Director of National Intelligence, 28 at the Lincoln Memorial, 312 at the Kennedy Center, 147 at Harbor Place, 62 along M Street, and 49 at Café Milano. Among those killed at the renowned Georgetown eatery were the four ISIS gunmen. All had been shot to death. But in the immediate aftermath, there was confusion over precisely *who* had done the shooting. The Metropolitan Police said it had been the FBI. The FBI said it had been the Metropolitan Police.

The suicide bomber was identified as a woman, late twenties, blond. In short order, it would be established that she had flown from Paris to New York on a French passport and had spent a single night at the Key Bridge Marriott in Arlington, in a room registered to a Dr. Leila Hadawi, also a French citizen. The French government was then forced to acknowledge that the suicide bomber, identified by her passport as Asma Doumaz, was in fact Safia Bourihane, the woman who had attacked the Weinberg Center in Paris. But how had the most wanted woman in the world, a jihadist icon, managed to slip back into France, board an international flight, and enter the United States? On Capitol Hill, members of both political parties called for the secretary of homeland security to resign, along with the commissioner of customs and border protection. Recriminations and apportionment of blame: Washington's favorite pastime.

But who was Dr. Leila Hadawi? The French government claimed she had been born in France of Palestinian parentage and was an employee of the state-run health care system. According to passport records, she had spent the month of August in Greece, though French security and intelligence officials now suspected she had traveled clandestinely to Syria for training. Curiously, ISIS seemed not to know her. Indeed, her name appeared in none of the celebratory videos or social media postings that flooded the Internet in the hours after the attack. As for her current whereabouts, they were unknown.

Media on both sides of the Atlantic began calling it the "French Connection"—the uncomfortable links between the attack on Washington and citizens of America's oldest ally. *Le Monde* revealed an additional "connection" when it reported that a senior DGSI officer named Paul Rousseau, the hero of the secret campaign against Direct Action, had been wounded in the bombing of the National Counterterrorism Center. But why was Rousseau there? The DGSI claimed that he was involved in the routine security measures surrounding the French president's visit to Washington. *Le Monde*, however, politely disagreed. Rousseau, said the newspaper, was the chief of something called Alpha Group, an ultra-secret counterterrorism unit known for deception and dirty tricks. The interior minister denied Alpha Group's existence, as did the chief of the DGSI. No one in France believed them.

Nor did anyone really care at that point, at least not in America, where blood vengeance was the first order of business. The president immediately ordered massive air strikes against all known ISIS targets in Syria, Iraq, and Libya, though he went out of his way to assure the Islamic world that America was not at war with them. He also rejected calls for a full-scale U.S. invasion of the caliphate. The American response, said the president, would be limited to air strikes and special operations to kill or capture senior ISIS leaders, like the man, still unidentified, who had planned and executed the attack. The president's critics were livid. So, too, was ISIS, which wanted nothing more than a final apocalyptic battle with the armies of Rome, in a place called Dabiq. The president refused to grant ISIS its wish. He had been elected to end the endless wars in the Middle East, not start another one. This time, America would not overreact. It would survive the attack on Washington, he said, and be stronger as a result.

Among the first targets of the U.S. military response was an apartment building near al-Rasheed Park in Raqqa and a large house of many rooms and courts west of Mosul. At home, however, the American media was focused on a house of a far different sort, a timbered A-frame cottage near the town of Hume, Virginia. The cottage had been rented to a Northern Virginia–based shell entity owned by an Egyptian national named Qassam el-Banna. The very same Qassam el-Banna had been discovered in a small pond on the property, in the front seat of his Kia sedan, having been shot four times at close range. Five additional bodies were discovered inside the cottage, four ISIS fighters in black tactical suits and a woman who would later be identified as Megan Taylor, a convert to Islam originally from Valparaiso, Indiana. The FBI concluded that all five had been shot with 5.56x45mm rounds fired by two AR-15 assault rifles. Later, through ballistics analysis, it would be determined that those same AR-15s had been involved in the attack on Café Milano in Georgetown. But exactly *who* had done the shooting? The FBI director said he did not know the answer. No one believed him.

Not long after the discovery in rural Virginia, the FBI detained Amina el-Banna, the wife of the man found in the pond, for questioning. And it was at this point that the story took an intriguing turn. For immediately after her release, Mrs. el-Banna retained the services of a lawyer from a civil rights organization with well-established ties to the Muslim Brotherhood. A press conference soon followed, conducted on the front lawn of the el-Bannas' small duplex on Eighth Place in Arlington. Speaking in Arabic, with the lawyer acting as her translator, Mrs. el-Banna denied that her husband was a member of ISIS or had played any role in the attack on Washington. Furthermore, she claimed that, on the night of the attack, two men had broken into her house and brutally interrogated her. She described one of the men as tall and lanky. The other was of medium height and build, with gray temples and the greenest eyes she had ever seen. Both were quite obviously Israeli. She claimed that they had threatened to kill her and her son—she never mentioned that he was named for Mohamed Atta—unless she gave them the passwords for her husband's computers. After uploading the contents of the devices, they left quickly. No, she admitted, she did not report the incident to the police. She was frightened, she claimed, because she was a Muslim.

Mrs. el-Banna's claims might well have been dismissed were it not for her description of one of the men who had entered her house—the man of medium height and build, with gray temples and vivid green eyes. Former inhabitants of the secret world recognized him as the noted Israeli operative named Gabriel Allon, and a few said so on television. They were quick to point out, however, that Allon could not possibly have been present in Mrs. el-Banna's house because he had been killed in a bombing in London's Brompton Road almost a year earlier. Or had he? Israel's ambassador to Washington inadvertently muddied the waters when he refused to state categorically and without equivocation that Gabriel Allon was indeed no longer among the living. "What do you want me to say?" he snapped during an interview. "That he's *still* dead?" Then, hiding behind Israel's long-standing policy of refusing to comment on intelligence matters, the ambassador asked the interviewer to change the subject. And thus commenced the slow resurrection of a legend.

There quickly appeared in the press accounts of many Washington sightings, all of dubious provenance and reliability. He had been seen entering and leaving a large Federal-style house on N Street, or so claimed a neighbor. He had been seen having coffee at a patisserie on Wisconsin Avenue, or so claimed the woman who had been seated at the next table. He had even been seen having dinner at the Four Seasons on M Street, as if the great Gabriel Allon, with his endless list of deadly enemies, would ever dream of eating in public. There was also a report that, like Paul Rousseau, he had been inside the National Counterterrorism Center at the time of the attack. The Israeli ambassador, who was almost never at a loss for words, failed to return phone calls and text messages, as did his spokeswoman. No one bothered to ask the NCTC for comment. Its press officer had died in the bombing, as had its director. For all intents and purposes, there was no NCTC anymore.

And there the matter might have faded into the void were it not for an enterprising reporter from the *Washington Post*. Many years earlier, not long after 9/11, she had revealed the existence of a chain of secret CIA detention centers—the so-called black sites—where al-Qaeda terrorists were subjected to harsh interrogations. Now she sought to answer the many unanswered questions surrounding the attack on Washington. Who was Dr. Leila Hadawi? Who had killed the four terrorists in Café Milano and the five terrorists at the cottage in Hume? And why had a dead man, a legend, been inside the NCTC when a thousand-pound truck bomb leveled it?

The reporter's story appeared one week to the day after the attack. It stated that the woman known as Dr. Leila Hadawi was in fact an agent of Israeli intelligence who had penetrated the network of a mysterious ISIS terror mastermind called Saladin. He had been in Washington at the time of the attack but had managed to escape. He was now assumed to be back in the caliphate, hiding from the American and coalition air bombardment. Gabriel Allon, she wrote, was in hiding, too—and very much alive. Israel's prime minister, when asked for a comment, managed only a crooked smile. Then, cryptically, he suggested he would have more to say about the matter soon. *Very* soon.

IN THE OLD CENTRAL JERUSALEM NEIGHBORHOOD OF NACH-laot, there had been doubts about the circumstances sur-rounding Allon's death for some time, especially on leafy Narkiss Street, where he was known to reside in a limestone apartment house with a drooping eucalyptus tree in the front garden. On the evening the story appeared on the *Post*'s Web site, he and his family were seen dining at Focaccia on Rabbi Akiva Street—or so claimed the couple who had been seated at the next table. Allon, they said, had ordered the chicken livers and mashed potatoes, while his wife, an Italian by birth, had opted for pasta. The children, a few weeks shy of their first birthday, had displayed exemplary behavior. Mother and father appeared relaxed and happy, though their bodyguards were clearly on edge. The entire city was. Earlier that after-noon, near Damascus Gate, three Jews had been stabbed to death. Their killer, a young Palestinian from East Jerusa-lem, had been shot several times by police. He had died in the trauma center at Hadassah Medical Center, despite heroic efforts to preserve his life.

The following afternoon Allon was seen lunching with an old friend, the noted biblical archaeologist Eli Lavon, in a café along the Mamilla Mall, and at four o'clock he was spotted on the tarmac at Ben Gurion Airport, where he met the daily Air France flight from Paris. Documents were signed, and a large wooden crate, flat and rectangular, was placed carefully in the back of his personal armored SUV. Inside the crate was pay-ment in full for an unfinished job: *Marguerite Gachet at Her Dressing Table*, oil on canvas, by Vincent van Gogh. One hour later, after a high-speed journey up the Bab al-Wad, the can-vas was propped upon an easel in the conservation lab of the

Israel Museum. Gabriel stood before it, one hand to his chin, his head tilted slightly to one side. Ephraim Cohen stood next to him. For a long time, neither spoke.

"You know," said Cohen at last, "it's not too late to change your mind."

"Why would I want to do something like that?"

"Because she wanted *you* to have it." After a pause, Cohen added, "And it's worth more than a hundred million dollars."

"Give me the papers, Ephraim."

They were contained in a formal leather folio case, embossed with the museum's logo. The agreement was brief and straightforward. Henceforth, Gabriel Allon renounced any and all claim to the van Gogh; it was now the property of the Israel Museum. There was, however, one inviolable proviso. The painting could never, under any circumstances, be sold or lent to another institution. As long as there was an Israel Museum—indeed, as long as there was an Israel—*Marguerite Gachet at Her Dressing Table* would hang there.

Gabriel signed the document with an indecipherable flourish and resumed his contemplation of the painting. At length, he reached out and trailed a forefinger lightly across the face of Marguerite. She required no additional restoration; she was ready for her coming-out party. He only wished he could say the same for Natalie. Natalie required a bit of retouching. Natalie was a work in progress.

76

NAHALAL, ISRAEL

THEY RETURNED HER TO THE place where it all began, to the farmhouse in the old moshav of Nahalal. Her room was as she had left it, save for the volume of Darwish poetry, which had vanished. So, too, had the outsize photographs of Palestinian suffering. The walls of the sitting room were now hung with paintings.

"Yours?" she asked on the evening of her arrival.

"Some," answered Gabriel.

"Which ones?"

"The ones with no signatures."

"And the others?"

"My mother."

Her eyes moved across the canvases. "She was obviously a great influence on you."

"Actually, we influenced each other."

"You were competitive?"

"Very."

She went to the French doors and gazed across the darkened valley, toward the lights of the Arab village atop the hillock.

"How long can I stay here?"

"As long as you like."

"And then?"

"That," said Gabriel, "is entirely up to you."

She was the farmhouse's only occupant, but she was never truly alone. A security detail monitored her every move, as did the cameras and the microphones, which recorded the awful sounds of her night terrors. Saladin appeared often in her dreams. Sometimes he was the wounded, helpless man whom she had encountered in the house near Mosul. And sometimes he was the strong, elegantly dressed figure who had so gleefully sentenced her to die in a cottage at the edge of the Shenandoah. Safia came to Natalie in her dreams, too. She never wore a hijab or abaya, only the gray five-button jacket she had worn the night of her death, and her hair was always blond. She was Safia as she might have been if radical Islam hadn't sunk its hooks into her. She was Safia the impressionable girl.

Natalie explained all this to the team of physicians and therapists who checked in on her every few days. They prescribed sleeping pills, which she refused to take, and anti-anxiety medication, which left her feeling dull and listless. To aid in her recovery, she led herself on punishing training runs on the farm roads of the valley. As before, she covered her arms and legs, not out of piety, but because it was late autumn and quite cold. The security guards kept watch over her always, as did the other residents of Nahalal. It was a tight-knit community, with many veterans of the IDF and the security services. They came to regard Natalie as their responsibility. They also came to believe she was the one they had read about in the newspapers. The one who had infiltrated the most vicious terrorist group the world had ever known. The one who had gone to the caliphate and lived to tell about it.

The doctors were not her only visitors. Her parents came often, sometimes spending the night, and early each afternoon she had a session with her old trainers. This time, their task was to undo what they had done before, to flush Natalie's system of Palestinian enmity and Islamic zeal, to turn her into an Israeli again. "But not *too* Israeli," Gabriel cautioned the trainers. He had invested a great deal of time and effort transforming Natalie into one of his enemies. He did not want to lose her because of a few terrifying minutes in a Virginia cottage.

She was visited, too, by Dina Sarid. During six interminable sessions, all recorded, she debriefed Natalie in far greater detail than before—her time in Raqqa and the camp at Palmyra, her initial interrogation at the hands of Abu Ahmed al-Tikriti, the many hours she had spent alone with the former Iraqi intelligence officer who called himself Saladin. All the material would eventually find its way into Dina's voluminous files, for she was already preparing for the next round. Saladin, she had warned the Office, was not finished. One day soon he would come for Jerusalem.

At the end of the last session, after Dina had switched off her computer and packed away her notes, the two women sat in silence for a long time as night fell heavily over the valley.

"I owe you an apology," said Dina at last.

"For what?"

"For talking you into it. I shouldn't have. I was wrong."

"If not me," said Natalie, "then who?"

"Someone else."

"Would you have done it?"

"No," answered Dina, to her everlasting credit. "I don't think I would have. In the end it wasn't worth it. He beat us."

"This time," said Natalie.

Yes, thought Dina. *This time . . .*

MIKHAIL WAITED NEARLY A WEEK BEFORE MAKING HIS FIRST appearance at the farm. The delay was not his idea; the doctors feared his presence might further complicate Natalie's already complicated recovery. His initial visit was brief, a little more than an hour, and entirely professional, save for an intimate exchange in the moonlit garden that escaped the sharp ears of the microphones.

The next night they watched a film—French, Hebrew subtitles—and the night after that, with the approval of Uzi Navot, they went for a pizza in Caesarea. Afterward, while walking in the Roman ruins, Mikhail told Natalie about the worst few minutes of his life. They had occurred, oddly enough, in his homeland, at a dacha many miles east of Moscow. A hostage rescue operation had gone awry, he and two other operatives were about to be killed. But another man had traded his life for theirs, and they all three had survived. One of the operatives had recently given birth to a set of twins. And the other, he said portentously, would soon be the chief of the Office.

"Gabriel?"

He nodded slowly.

"And the woman?"

"It was his wife."

"My God." They walked in silence for a moment. "So what is the moral of this awful story?"

"There is no moral," answered Mikhail. "It's just what we do. And then we try to forget."

"Have you managed to forget?"

"No."

"How often do you think about it?"

"Every night."

"I suppose you were right after all," said Natalie after a moment.

"About what?"

"I'm more like you than I realized."

"You are now."

She took his hand. "When?" she whispered into his ear.

"That," said Mikhail, smiling, "is entirely up to you."

THE FOLLOWING AFTERNOON, WHEN NATALIE RETURNED FROM her training run in the valley, she found Gabriel waiting in the sitting room of the farmhouse. He was dressed in a gray suit and a white open-neck dress shirt; he looked very professional. On the coffee table before him were three files. The first, he said, was the final report of Natalie's team of doctors.

"What does it say?"

"It says," answered Gabriel evenly, "that you are suffering from post-traumatic stress disorder, which, given what you went through in Syria and America, is entirely understandable."

"And my prognosis?"

"Quite good, actually. With proper medication and counseling, you will eventually make a full recovery. In fact," Gabriel added, "we are all of the opinion you can leave here whenever you like."

"And the other two files?"

"A choice," he answered obliquely.

"What kind of choice?"

"It concerns your future."

She pointed to one of the files. "What's in that one?"

"A termination agreement."

"And the other?"

"The exact opposite."

A silence fell between them. It was Gabriel who broke it.

"I assume you've heard the rumors about my pending promotion."

"I thought you were dead."

"It seems the reports of my demise were greatly exaggerated."

"Mine, too."

He smiled warmly. Then his expression turned serious. "Some chiefs are fortunate enough to serve during relatively quiet times. They serve their term, they collect their accolades, and then they go forth into the world to make money. I'm confident I won't be so lucky. The next few years promise to be tumultuous for the Middle East and for Israel. It will be up to the Office to help determine whether we survive in this land." He looked out at the valley, the valley of his youth. "It would be a dereliction of duty if I were to let someone of your obvious gifts slip through my fingers."

He said nothing more. Natalie made a show of thought.

"What is it?" he asked. "More money?"

"No," she answered, shaking her head. "I was wondering about the Office policy regarding relationships between coworkers."

"Officially, we discourage it."

"And unofficially?"

"We're Jewish, Natalie. We're natural matchmakers."

"How well do you know Mikhail?"

"I know him in ways only you could understand."

"He told me about Russia."

"Did he?" Gabriel frowned. "That was insecure on his part."

"It was in service of a good cause."

"And what cause was that?"

Natalie picked up the third file, the one with the employment contract.

"Did you bring a pen?" she asked.

77

PETAH TIKVA, ISRAEL

THE END WAS NEAR, IT was plain to see. On the Thursday, Uzi Navot was seen lugging several cardboard boxes from his office suite, including a lifetime supply of his beloved butter cookies, a parting gift from the Vienna station chief. The next morning, during the nine a.m. senior staff meeting, he acted as though a great weight had been lifted from his sturdy shoulders. And that afternoon, before departing for the weekend, he made a slow tour of King Saul Boulevard from the top floor to the underground recesses of Registry, shaking hands, patting shoulders, and kissing a few damp cheeks. Curiously, he avoided the dark, forbidding lair occupied by Personnel, the place where careers went to die.

Navot spent the Saturday behind the walls of his residence in the Tel Aviv suburb of Petah Tikva. Gabriel knew this because the movements of the *ramsad*, the official abbreviation for the head of the Office, were monitored constantly by the operations desk, as were his own. He decided it was better to show up unannounced, thus preserving the element of surprise. He slid from the back of his official SUV into a pouring rain and pressed the call button of the intercom at the front gate. Twenty long wet seconds elapsed before a voice answered. Unfortunately, it was Bella's.

"What do you want?"

"I need to have a word with Uzi."

"Haven't you done enough already?"

"Please, Bella. It's important."

"It always is."

Another prolonged delay ensued before the locks opened with an inhospitable snap. Gabriel opened the gate and hurried up the garden walk to the front entrance, where Bella awaited him. She wore an elaborate flowing pantsuit of embroidered crushed silk and gold sandals. Her hair was newly coiffed, her face was discreetly but thoroughly made up. She looked as though she were entertaining. She always did. Appearances had always mattered to Bella, which is why Gabriel had never understood her decision to marry a man like Uzi Navot. Perhaps, he thought, she had done it simply out of cruelty. Bella always struck Gabriel as the sort who enjoyed pulling the wings off flies.

Coldly, she shook Gabriel's hand. Her nails were blood red.

"You're looking well, Bella."

"You, too. But then I suppose that's to be expected."

She gestured toward the sitting room, where Navot was working his way through the latest edition of the *Economist*. The room was a showpiece of contemporary Asian design, with floor-to-ceiling windows overlooking the waterworks and manicured shrubbery in the garden. Navot looked like one of the workmen whom Bella had so terrorized during the long renovation. He wore wrinkled chinos and a stretched-out cotton pullover, and the gray stubble of his hair had encroached on his cheeks and chin. His disheveled appearance surprised Gabriel. Bella had never been one to permit weekend negligence when it came to grooming and dress.

"Can I get you something to drink?" she asked.

"Hemlock," answered Gabriel.

Frowning, Bella withdrew. Gabriel looked around the large room. It was three times the size of the sitting room of his little apartment in Narkiss Street. Perhaps, he thought, it was time for an upgrade. He sat down directly opposite Navot, who was now staring at a silent television. Earlier that day, the Americans had launched a drone strike on a house in western Iraq where Saladin was thought to be hiding. Twenty-two people had been killed, including several children.

"Think they got him?" asked Navot.

"No," answered Gabriel, watching as a limp body was pulled from the rubble. "I don't think they did."

"Neither do I." Navot switched off the television. "I hear you managed to convince Natalie to join the Office full-time."

"Actually, Mikhail did it for me."

"Think they're serious?"

Gabriel gave a noncommittal shrug. "Love is harder in the real world than in the secret world."

"Tell me about it," murmured Navot. He plucked a low-calorie rice treat from a bowl on the coffee table. "What's this I hear about Eli Lavon coming back?"

"It's true."

"As what?"

"Nominally, he'll oversee the watchers. In truth, I'll use him as I see fit."

"Who gets Special Ops?"

"Yaakov."

"Good call," said Navot, "but Mikhail will be disappointed."

"Mikhail isn't ready. Yaakov is."

"What about Yossi?"

"Head of Research. Dina will be his number two."

"And Rimona?"

"Deputy director for planning."

"A clean sweep. I suppose it's for the best." Navot stared blankly at the darkened television screen.

"I heard a rumor about you the other day when I was in the prime minister's office."

"Really?"

"They say you're moving to California to work for a defense contractor. They say you're going to make a million dollars a year, plus bonuses."

"When searching for the truth," said Navot philosophically, "the last place one should look is the prime minister's office."

"My source says Bella has already picked out the house."

Navot scooped a handful of the rice treats from the bowl. "And what if it's true? What difference does it make?"

"I need you, Uzi. I can't do this job without you."

"What would you call me? What would I actually *do*?"

"You'll run the place and see to the politics while I run the ops."

"A manager?"

"You're better with people than I am, Uzi."

"That," said Navot, "is the understatement of the year."

Gabriel gazed out the window. The rain was lashing Bella's garden.

"How can you go to California at a time like this? How can you leave Israel?"

"You're one to talk. You lived abroad for years, and you socked away plenty of money restoring all those paintings, too. It's my turn now. Besides," Navot added, "you don't really need me."

"I'm not making this offer out of the goodness of my heart. My motives are purely selfish." Gabriel lowered his voice and added, "You're the closest thing to a brother I have, Uzi. You and Eli Lavon. Things are going to get rough. I need you both at my side."

"Is there no depth to which you won't stoop?"

"I learned from the best, Uzi. So did you."

"Sorry, Gabriel, but it's too late. I've already accepted the job."

"Tell them you've had a change of heart. Tell them your country needs you."

Navot nibbled thoughtfully at the rice treats, one by one. It was, thought Gabriel, an encouraging sign.

"Has the prime minister approved it?"

"He didn't have much of a choice."

"Where will my office be?"

"Across the hall from mine."

"Secretary?"

"We'll share Orit."

"The minute you try to cut me out of something," warned Navot, "I walk. I get to talk to you whenever and wherever I please."

"You'll be sick of me in no time."

"That much I believe."

The rice treats were gone. Navot exhaled heavily.

"What's wrong, Uzi?"

"I'm just wondering how I'm going to tell Bella that I've turned down a million-dollar-a-year job in California to stay at the Office."

"I'm sure you'll think of something," said Gabriel. "You've always been good with people."

78

JERUSALEM

WHEN GABRIEL RETURNED TO Narkiss Street, he found Chiara dressed in a dark professional pantsuit and the children strapped into their carry seats. Together, they made the short drive across West Jerusalem to the Mount Herzl Psychiatric Hospital. In the old days, before his remarriage, before his unwanted celebrity, Gabriel had slipped in and out of the facility unnoticed, usually late at night. Now he arrived with all the subtlety of a visiting head of state, a circle of bodyguards protecting him, Raphael wriggling in his grasp. Chiara walked silently at his side, Irene in her arms, her heels clattering over the paving stones of the forecourt. He did not envy her this moment. He took her hand and squeezed it tightly while Raphael tugged at his earlobe.

In the lobby waited a rotund, rabbinical-looking doctor in his late fifties. He had approved of the visit—in fact, Gabriel reminded himself, it was the doctor who had suggested it in the first place. Now he didn't seem so certain it was a good idea.

"How much does she know?" asked Gabriel as his son reached for the doctor's spectacles.

"I told her that she's going to have visitors. Otherwise . . ." He shrugged his rounded shoulders. "I thought it would be best if you were the one who explained it to her."

Gabriel handed Raphael to Chiara and followed the doctor along a corridor of Jerusalem limestone, to the doorway of a common room. It was empty of patients except for one. She sat in her wheelchair with the stillness of a figure in a painting while behind her a television flickered silently. On the screen Gabriel briefly glimpsed his own face. It was a still photo, snapped a thousand years ago, after his return from Operation Wrath of God. He might have looked like a kid were it not for the gray hair at his temples. *The smudges of ash on the prince of fire* . . .

"Mazel tov," said the doctor.

"Condolences are more appropriate," answered Gabriel.

"These are challenging times, but I'm sure you can handle it. And remember, if you ever need someone to talk to"—he patted Gabriel's shoulder—"I'm always available."

Gabriel's face vanished from the screen. He looked at Leah. She had not moved or even blinked. *Woman in a Wheelchair*, oil on canvas, by Tariq al-Hourani.

"Do you have any advice for me?"

"Be honest with her. She doesn't like it when you try to mislead her."

"What if it's too painful?"

"It will be. But she won't remember it for long."

With a nudge, the doctor cast Gabriel adrift. Slowly, he crossed the common room and sat down in the chair that had been placed at Leah's side. Her hair, once long and wild like Chiara's, was now institutionally short. Her hands were twisted and white with scar tissue. They were like patches of bare canvas. Gabriel longed to repair them, but could not. Leah was beyond restoration. He kissed her cheek softly and waited for her to become aware of his presence.

"Look at the snow, Gabriel," she said at once. "Isn't it beautiful?"

Gabriel looked out the window, where a bright sun shone upon the stone pine of the hospital's garden.

"Yes, Leah," he said absently as his vision blurred with tears. "It's beautiful."

"The snow absolves Vienna of its sins. The snow falls on Vienna while the missiles rain down on Tel Aviv."

Gabriel squeezed Leah's hand. The words were among the last she had spoken the night of the bombing in Vienna. She suffered from a particularly acute combination of psychotic depression and post-traumatic stress disorder. At times, she experienced moments of lucidity, but for the most part she remained a prisoner of the past. Vienna played ceaselessly in her mind like a loop of videotape that she was unable to pause: the last meal they shared together, their last kiss, the fire that killed their only child and burned the flesh from Leah's body. Her life had shrunk to five minutes, and she had been reliving it, over and over again, for more than twenty years.

"I saw you on television," she said, suddenly lucid. "It seems you're not dead after all."

"No, Leah. It was just something we had to say."

"For your work?"

He nodded.

"And now they say you're going to become the chief."

"Soon."

"I thought Ari was the chief."

"Not for many years."

"How many?"

He didn't answer. It was too depressing to think about.

"He's well?" asked Leah.

"Ari?"

"Yes."

"He has good days and bad days."

"Like me," said Leah.

Her expression darkened. The memories were welling. Somehow, she fought them off.

"I can't quite believe you're actually going to be the *memuneh*."

It was an old word that meant "the one in charge." There hadn't been a true *memuneh* since Shamron.

"Neither can I," admitted Gabriel.

"Aren't you a little young to be the *memuneh*? After all, you're only—"

"I'm older now, Leah. We both are."

"You look exactly as I remember you."

"Look closely, Leah. You can see the lines and the gray hair."

"Thanks to Ari, you always had gray hair. Me, too." She gazed out the window. "It looks like winter."

"It is."

"What year is it?"

He told her.

"How old are your children?"

"Tomorrow is their first birthday."

"Will there be a party?"

"At the Shamrons' house in Tiberias. But they're here now, if you feel up to seeing them."

Her face brightened. "What are their names?"

He had told her several times. Now he told her again.

"But Irene is your mother's name," she protested.

"My mother died a long time ago."

"I'm sorry, Gabriel. Sometimes I—"

"It's not important."

"Bring them to me," she said, smiling. "I want to see them."

"You're sure?"

"Yes, of course."

Gabriel rose and went into the foyer.

"Well?" asked Chiara and the doctor simultaneously.

"She says she wants to see them."

"How should we do it?" asked Chiara.

"One at a time," suggested the doctor. "Otherwise, it might be overwhelming."

"I agree," said Gabriel.

He took Raphael from Chiara's grasp and returned to the common room. Leah was gazing sightlessly out the window again, lost in memory. Gently, Gabriel placed his son in her lap. Her eyes focused, her mind came briefly back to the present.

"Who is this?" she asked.

"It's him, Leah. It's my son."

She gazed at the child spellbound, clutching him tightly with her ruined hands.

"He looks exactly like—"

"Me," interjected Gabriel hastily. "Everyone says he looks like his father."

Leah trailed a twisted finger through the child's hair and placed her lips to his forehead.

"Look at the snow," she whispered. "Isn't it beautiful?"

A T TEN THE FOLLOWING MORNING, the Israel Museum announced it had acquired a previously unknown work by Vincent van Gogh—*Marguerite Gachet at Her Dressing Table*, oil on canvas, 104 by 60 centimeters—from the estate of Hannah Weinberg. Later, the museum would be forced to acknowledge that, in point of fact, it had received the painting from an anonymous donor, who in turn had inherited it from Mademoiselle Weinberg after her tragic murder in Paris. In time, the museum would face enormous pressure to reveal the donor's identity. It steadfastly refused, as did the government of France, which had permitted the transfer of the painting to Israel from French soil, much to the dismay of the editorialists and the cultural elite. It was, they said, yet another blow to French pride, this one entirely self-inflicted.

On that Sunday in December, however, the painting was soon an afterthought. For at the stroke of noon, the prime minister announced that Gabriel Allon was very much alive and would be the next chief of the Office. There was little surprise; the press had been buzzing with rumors and speculation for days. Still, it was a shock to the country to see the angel in the flesh, looking for all the world like a mere mortal. His clothing for the occasion had been carefully chosen—a white oxford cloth shirt, a black leather jacket, slim-fitting khaki trousers, a pair of suede brogues with rubber soles that made no sound when he walked. Pointedly, the prime minister referred to him not as the *ramsad* but the *memuneh*, the one in charge.

The flash of the cameras was like the glow of his halogen work lamps. He stood motionless, his hands clasped behind his back like a soldier at ease, while the prime minister delivered a highly sanitized version of his professional accomplishments. He then invited Gabriel to speak. His term, he promised, would be forward-looking but rooted in the great traditions of the past. The message was unmistakable. An assassin had been placed in charge of Israel's intelligence service. Those who tried to harm the country or its citizenry would face serious, perhaps lethal, consequences.

When the reporters attempted to question him, he smiled and then followed the prime minister into the Cabinet room, where he spoke at length of his plans and priorities and the many challenges, some immediate, some looming, confronting the Jewish state. ISIS, he said, was a threat that could no longer be ignored. He also made it clear that the previous *ramsad* would be remaining at the Office.

"In what capacity?" asked the foreign minister incredulously.

"In whatever capacity I see fit."

"It's unprecedented."

"Get used to it."

The chief of the Office does not swear an oath; he merely signs his contract. When the paperwork was complete, Gabriel traveled to King Saul Boulevard, where he addressed his troops and met briefly with the outgoing senior staff. Afterward, he and Navot rode in the same armored SUV to Shamron's villa in Tiberias. The steep drive was so jammed with cars they had to abandon the vehicle far from the entrance. When they stepped onto the terrace overlooking the lake, there arose a great cheer that might very well have carried across the Golan Heights into Syria. It seemed that everyone from Gabriel's tangled past had made the trip: Adrian Carter, Fareed Barakat, Paul Rousseau, even Graham Seymour, who had come from London. So, too, had Julian Isherwood, the art dealer who had provided Gabriel's cover as a restorer, and Samantha Cooke, the reporter from the *Telegraph* who had quite intentionally blown the story regarding his death.

"You owe me," she said, kissing his cheek.

"The check is in the mail."

"When should I expect it?"

"Soon."

There were many others, of course. Timothy Peel, the Cornish boy who had lived next door to Gabriel when he was hiding out on the Helford Passage, made the trip at Office expense. So did Sarah Bancroft, the American art historian and curator whom Gabriel had used to penetrate the courts of Zizi and Ivan. She shook Mikhail's hand coolly and glared at Natalie, but otherwise the evening proceeded without incident.

Maurice Durand, the world's most successful art thief, popped in from Paris and somehow managed to avoid bumping into Paul Rousseau, who surely would have remembered him from the brasserie on the rue de Miromesnil. Monsignor Luigi Donati, private secretary to His Holiness Pope Paul VII, was in attendance, as was Christoph Bittel, Gabriel's new ally inside the Swiss security service. Half the Knesset came, along with several senior IDF officers and the chiefs of all the other Israeli intelligence agencies. And watching over it all, smiling contentedly as though the entire production had been arranged for his private amusement, was Shamron. He was happier than Gabriel had ever seen him. His life's work was finally complete. Gabriel was remarried, a father, and the chief of the Office. The restorer was restored.

But the evening was more than a celebration of Gabriel's promotion, it was also the children's first birthday party. Chiara presided over the lighting of the candles while Gabriel, playing the role of proud father, recorded the event on his secure mobile phone. When the entire gathering erupted into a rousing version of "Happy Birthday," Irene wept hysterically. Then Shamron whispered a bit of Polish-accented nonsense into her ear, and she giggled with delight.

By ten o'clock the first cars were moving slowly down the drive, and by midnight the party was over. Afterward, Shamron and Gabriel sat in their usual spot at the edge of the terrace, a gas heater burning between them, while the caterers cleared away the debris of the celebration. Shamron refrained from smoking because Raphael was sleeping soundly in Gabriel's arms.

"You made quite an impression today at the announcement," Shamron said. "I liked your clothing. *And* your title."

"I wanted to send a signal."

"What signal is that?"

"That I intend to be an operational chief." Gabriel paused, then added, "That I can walk and chew gum at the same time."

With a glance toward the Golan Heights, Shamron said, "I'm not sure you have much of a choice."

The child stirred in Gabriel's arms and then settled into sleep once more. Shamron twirled his old Zippo lighter in his fingertips. *Two turns to the right, two turns to the left . . .*

"Is this how you expected it would end?" he asked after a moment.

"How what would end?"

"You and me." Shamron looked at Gabriel and added, "Us."

"What are you talking about, Ari?"

"I'm old, my son. I've been clinging to life for this night. Now that it's over, I can go." He smiled sadly. "It's late, Gabriel. I'm very tired."

"You're not going anywhere, Ari. I need you."

"No, you don't," replied Shamron. "You *are* me."

"Funny how it worked out that way."

"You seem to think it was serendipitous. But it wasn't. It was all part of a plan."

"Whose plan?"

"Maybe it was mine, maybe it was God's." Shamron shrugged. "What difference does it make? We are on the same side when it comes to you, God and me. We are accomplices."

"Who has the final say?"

"Who do you think?" Shamron laid his large hand across Raphael. "Do you remember the day I came for you in Cornwall?"

"Like it was yesterday."

"You drove like a madman through the hedgerows of the Lizard. We had omelets in that little café atop the cliffs. You treated me," Shamron added with a note of bitterness, "like a debt collector."

"I remember," said Gabriel distantly.

"How do you suppose your life would have turned out if I hadn't come that day?"

"Just fine."

"I doubt it. You'd still be restoring paintings for Julian and sailing that old ketch down the Helford to the sea. You would never have come back to Israel or met Chiara. And you wouldn't be holding that beautiful child in your arms right now."

Gabriel did not take issue with Shamron's characterization. He had been a lost soul that day, a broken and bitter man.

"It wasn't all bad, was it?" asked Shamron.

"I could have lived my entire life without seeing the inside of Lubyanka."

"What about that dog in the Swiss Alps that tried to tear your arm off?"

"I got him in the end."

"And that motorcycle you crashed in Rome? Or the antiquities gallery that blew up in your face in St. Moritz?"

"Good times," said Gabriel darkly. "But I lost a lot of friends along the way."

"Like Hannah Weinberg."

"Yes," said Gabriel. "Like Hannah."

"Perhaps a bit of old-fashioned vengeance is in order."

"The deal is done."

"Who's going to handle it?"

"I'd like to see to it personally, but it's probably not a wise move at the moment."

Shamron smiled. "You're going to be a great chief, my son."

BETHNAL GREEN, LONDON

IN EVERY OPERATION THERE ARE loose threads, small problems that for one reason or another slip through the cracks. Jalal Nasser, talent spotter, recruiter, long arm of Saladin, fell into that category. An arrest was out of the question; a trial would expose not only Gabriel's operation but the incompetence of the British and French security services as well. Nor was deportation an option. Were he to return to Jordan, he would have gone straight to the cellars of the Fingernail Factory—and then, in all likelihood, to an unmarked grave in a potter's field. Such an outcome might have been acceptable during the earliest days of the global war on terror, but now that cooler, more civilized heads had prevailed, it was unthinkable. There would be international outrage, perhaps a lawsuit or even criminal prosecution of the spymasters involved. "Collateral damage," intoned Fareed Barakat gravely. "And you know how His Majesty feels about collateral damage."

There was a simple solution, a Shamronian solution. All that was required was the connivance of the native service, which, for the above stated reasons, was not difficult to obtain.

In fact, the agreement was reached during a private interlude in Shamron's kitchen, on the night of the party. Much later, it would be regarded as Gabriel's first official decision as chief.

The other party to the agreement was Graham Seymour of MI6. The operation could not go forward, however, without the cooperation of Amanda Wallace, Seymour's counterpart at MI5. He secured it over martinis in Amanda's Thames House office. It wasn't a difficult sale; MI5's watchers had long ago grown weary of chasing Jalal through the streets of London. For Amanda, it was little more than a manpower decision. By moving Jalal off her plate, she would have additional resources to deploy against her primary target, the Russians.

"But no messes," she cautioned.

"No," agreed Seymour, shaking his gray head vigorously. "No messes, indeed."

Within forty-eight hours, Amanda terminated all surveillance of the subject in question, which later, during the inevitable inquiry, she would describe as mere coincidence. Graham Seymour then rang Gabriel at King Saul Boulevard and informed him that the field was his. Secretly, he wished it were so, but that wouldn't have been appropriate, not for a chief. That night he drove Mikhail to Ben Gurion Airport and placed him aboard a flight for London. Inside Mikhail's false Russian passport, Gabriel had concealed a note. It was three words in length, the three words of Shamron's eleventh commandment.

Don't get caught . . .

JALAL NASSER SPENT HIS FINAL DAY IN LONDON IN MUCH THE same way he had spent the previous hundred, seemingly unaware of the fact he was blown to kingdom come. He shopped in Oxford Street, he loitered in Leicester Square, he prayed in the East London Mosque. Afterward, he had tea with a promising recruit. Gabriel forwarded the recruit's name to Amanda Wallace. It was, he thought, the least he could do.

By then, Jalal's flat in Chilton Street had been emptied of its hidden cameras and microphones, leaving the team across the street with no option but to observe their quarry the old-fashioned way, with binoculars and a camera fitted with a telephoto lens. From afar, he seemed like a man without a care in the world. Perhaps it was a bit of performance art. But the more likely explanation was that Saladin had failed to inform his operative that the British, the Americans, the Israelis, and the Jordanians knew of his connection to the network and to the attacks in Paris, Amsterdam, and Washington. At King Saul Boulevard—and at Langley, Vauxhall Cross, and an elegant old building on the rue de Grenelle—this was seen as an encouraging sign. It meant that Jalal had no secrets to divulge, that the network, at least for the moment, was dormant. For Jalal, however, it meant that he was expendable, which is the worst thing a terrorist can be when his master is a man like Saladin.

At seven that evening the Jordanian spread a mat upon the floor of his tiny sitting room and prayed for the last time. Then, at seven twenty, he walked to the Noodle King on Bethnal Green Road, where, alone, he ate a final meal of fried rice and spicy chicken wings, watched over by Eli Lavon. Leaving the restaurant, he popped into the Saver Plus for a bottle of milk and then set off toward his flat, unaware that Mikhail was walking a few paces behind him.

Later, Scotland Yard would determine that Jalal arrived on his doorstep at twelve minutes past eight o'clock. It would also determine that, while fishing his keys from his coat pocket, he dropped them to the pavement. Stooping, he noticed Mikhail standing in the street. He left the keys where they lay and, slowly, stood upright. He was clutching the shopping bag defensively to his chest.

"Hello, Jalal," said Mikhail calmly. "So good to finally meet you."

"Who are you?" asked the Jordanian.

"I'm the last person you're ever going to see."

Swiftly, Mikhail drew a gun from the small of his back. It was a .22-caliber Beretta, with no suppressor. It was a naturally soft-spoken weapon.

"I'm here for Hannah Weinberg," he said quietly. "And for Rachel Lévy and Arthur Goldman and all the other people you killed in Paris. I'm here for the victims in Amsterdam and America. I speak for the dead."

"Please," whispered the Jordanian. "I can help you. I know things. I know the plans for the next attack."

"Do you?"

"Yes, I swear."

"Where will it be?"

"Here in London."

"What's the target?"

Before Jalal could answer, Mikhail fired his first shot. It shattered the bottle of milk and lodged in the Jordanian's heart. Slowly, Mikhail moved forward, firing nine more shots in rapid succession, until his target lay motionless in the entrance, in a pool of blood and milk. The gun was empty. Mikhail rammed a new magazine into the grip, placed the barrel to the dead man's head, and fired one last shot. The eleventh. Behind him, a motorcycle pulled to the curb. He climbed onto the back, and in a moment he was gone.

*T*HE BLACK WIDOW IS A work of entertainment and should be read as nothing more. The names, characters, places, and incidents portrayed in the story are the product of the author's imagination or have been used fictitiously. Any resemblance to actual persons, living or dead, businesses, companies, events, or locales is entirely coincidental.

Visitors to the rue des Rosiers in the Fourth Arrondissement of Paris will search in vain for the Isaac Weinberg Center for the Study of Anti-Semitism in France. Isaac's granddaughter, the fictitious Hannah Weinberg, created the center at the end of *The Messenger*, the first novel in which she appeared. Hannah's van Gogh painting, *Marguerite Gachet at Her Dressing Table*, is also fictitious, though its tragic provenance is quite obviously drawn from the terrible events of Jeudi Noir and the Paris Roundup in July 1942.

I wish I could say that the anti-Jewish attacks described in the first chapter of *The Black Widow* were cut from whole cloth. But sadly they, too, were inspired by truth. Anti-Semitism in France, much of it emanating from Muslim communities, has compelled thousands of French Jews to leave their homes and emigrate to Israel. Indeed, eight thousand departed in the twelve months following the brutal murder of four Jews at the Hypercacher kosher market in January 2015. Many French Jews pass their afternoons in Independence Square in Netanya, at Chez Claude or one of the other cafés that cater to a growing francophone clientele. I can think of no other religious minority or ethnic group that is fleeing a Western European country. What's more, the Jews of France are swimming against the tide, moving from the West to the most dangerous and volatile region on the planet. They are doing so for one reason only: they feel safer in Israel than they do in Paris, Toulouse, Marseilles, or Nice. Such is the condition of modern France.

Alpha Group, the secret counterterrorism unit of the DGSI portrayed in *The Black Widow*, does not exist, though I hope for all our sakes that something like it does. For the record, I am aware of the fact that the headquarters of Israel's secret intelligence service is no longer located on King Saul Boulevard in Tel Aviv. I have chosen to keep the headquarters of my fictitious service there in part because I like the name of the street much more than the current address, which I shall not mention in print. There is indeed a limestone apartment building at 16 Narkiss Street in Jerusalem, but Gabriel Allon and his new family do not live there. During a recent visit to Israel, I learned that the building is now a stop on at least one guided tour of the city. My deepest apologies to the residents and their neighbors.

There was once an Arab village in the Western Galilee called al-Sumayriyya, and its current condition is accurately rendered in the pages of *The Black Widow*. Longtime readers of the Gabriel Allon series know that it first appeared in *Prince of Fire* in 2005, as the family home of a female terrorist named Fellah al-Tamari. Deir Yassin was in fact the site of a notorious massacre that occurred during the darkest days of the sectarian conflict in 1948 that gave birth to both the modern State of Israel and the Palestinian refugee crisis. The old village is now the home of the Kfar Shaul Mental Health Center, a psychiatric hospital that utilizes some of the old buildings and homes vacated by Deir Yassin's original Arab residents. Kfar Shaul is affiliated with the Hadassah Medical Center and specializes in the treatment of Jerusalem syndrome, a disorder of religious obsession and delusion that begins with a visit to God's fractured city upon a hill. Leah Allon's condition is far more serious, as are her physical wounds. I have always been slightly vague about the exact address of the hospital where she is a permanent patient. Now we know its approximate location.

There is no Gallerie Mansour in downtown Beirut, but the Islamic State's links to the trade in looted antiquities have been well documented. I first explored the concept of terrorists raising money by selling stolen or illicitly excavated antiquities in *The Fallen Angel* in 2012. At that time there was no proof, at least not in the public realm, that terrorists were actually lining their pockets by selling treasures from the past; it was merely something that I suspected was occurring. I take no satisfaction in being proven correct, especially by the likes of ISIS.

But ISIS has not been content merely to sell antiquities; it destroys them, too, especially if they conflict with the group's interpretation of Islam. After sweeping into Palmyra in May 2015, ISIS holy warriors promptly destroyed many of the city's glorious Roman temples. Forces loyal to the Assad regime recaptured Palmyra as I was finishing the first draft of *The Black Widow*. Having sworn at the outset that I would not chase the shifting sands of the conflict, I chose to leave chapter 39 as originally written. Such are the hazards of attempting to catch history in the act. I regret to say I am confident the civil war in Syria will continue for years, if not decades, much like the war that almost destroyed its neighbor, Lebanon. Territory will be won and lost, captured and abandoned. Thousands more will become refugees. Many more will die.

I did my utmost to explain the roots and explosive growth of ISIS accurately and dispassionately, though I am confident that, given America's divided and increasingly dysfunctional politics, some will quibble with my portrayal. There is no doubt that the American invasion of Iraq in March 2003 created the seedbed from which ISIS sprang. And there is also no doubt that the failure to leave a residual American force in Iraq in 2011, combined with the outbreak of civil war in Syria, allowed the group to flourish and spread on two sides of an increasingly meaningless border. To dismiss the group as "un-Islamic" or "not a state" is wishful thinking and, ultimately, counterproductive and dangerous. As the journalist and scholar Graeme Wood pointed out in a groundbreaking study of ISIS published in the *Atlantic*: "The reality is that the Islamic State is Islamic. Very Islamic." And it is rapidly taking on many functions of a modern state, issuing its citizenry everything from driver's permits to fishing licenses.

At least four thousand Westerners have heeded the clarion call to come to the caliphate, including more than five hundred women. A database maintained by London's Institute for Strategic Dialogue finds that most of the women are teenagers or in their early twenties, and are likely to be widowed at a young age. Others face the very real prospect of losing their own lives in the violent world of the caliphate. In February 2015, three radicalized teenage girls from the Bethnal Green section of East London slipped out of the United Kingdom on an Istanbul-bound flight and made their way to the Syrian city of Raqqa, the caliphate's unofficial capital. In December 2015, as the city came under both Russian and

American air assault, all contact with the girls was lost. Their families now fear the three teenagers are dead.

Many Western ISIS recruits, men and women, have returned home. Some are disillusioned; others remain committed to the cause of the caliphate. And still others are prepared to carry out acts of mass murder and terror in the name of Islam. In the near term, Western Europe faces the greatest threat, in no small measure because of the large and restive Muslim populations living within its open borders. ISIS has no need to insert terrorists into Western Europe because the potential terrorists are already there. They reside in the banlieues of France and the Muslim quarters of Brussels, Amsterdam, Copenhagen, Malmo, East London, and Luton. At the time of this writing, ISIS had carried out devastating attacks in Paris and Brussels. The perpetrators, for the most part, were born in the West and carried European passports in their pockets. More attacks will surely follow, for the security services of Western Europe have proven themselves woefully unprepared—especially the Belgian Sûreté, which has countenanced the creation of a virtual ISIS safe haven in the heart of Brussels.

The American homeland, however, is ISIS's ultimate target. While researching this novel, I was struck by the number of times I heard someone say that an attack on a U.S. city is imminent, sooner rather than later. I was struck, too, by the number of times a high-level government official told me that this state of affairs is "the new normal"—that we must live with the fact that bombs will occasionally explode in our airports and subways, that we can no longer expect to be fully safe in a restaurant or a concert hall because of an ideology, and a faith, born of the Middle East. President Barack Obama seemed to express this point of view after the attack on the satirical magazine *Charlie Hebdo* and the siege at the Hypercacher market. Cautioning against overreaction, he dismissed the perpetrators as "a bunch of violent, vicious zealots who behead people or randomly shoot a bunch of folks in a deli in Paris." It was not a deli, of course; it was a kosher market. And the four victims were not "a bunch of folks." They were Jews. And for that reason alone they were targeted and mercilessly slaughtered.

But how did the West arrive at this place? In the afterword of *Portrait of a Spy*, I warned what would happen if America and its allies mishandled the so-called Arab Spring. "If the forces of moderation and modernity prevail," I wrote in April 2011, "it is possible the threat of terrorism will gradually recede. But if radical Muslim clerics and their adherents manage to seize power in countries such as Egypt, Jordan, and Syria, we might very well look back fondly on the turbulent early years of the twenty-first century as a golden age of relations between Islam and the West." Unfortunately, the promise of the Arab Spring has been broken, and the Arab world is in turmoil. With the age of oil in retreat, its future is bleak. If history is a guide, a leader of destiny might arise from the chaos. Perhaps he will hail from the biblical cradle of civilization, near the banks of one of the four rivers that flowed from the Garden of Eden. And perhaps, if he is so inclined, he might refer to himself as Saladin.

ACKNOWLEDGMENTS

I AM INDEBTED TO MY WIFE, Jamie Gangel, who listened patiently while I worked out the plot of *The Black Widow* and then skillfully edited the enormous pile of paper that spilled from my printer after seven months of intense writing. She has been at my side from the very beginning of the Gabriel Allon series, a warm sun-dappled morning in Georgetown when I first had the idea of turning an Israeli assassin into an art restorer. Now the morose, grieving man we first met in *The Kill Artist* is the chief of Israel's secret intelligence service. It is an outcome I never could have imagined, and I would not have arrived at it without Jamie's constant support. Nor would it have been possible without the love of my two children, Lily and Nicholas. Each day, in ways large and small, they remind me that there is more to life than words and paragraphs and clever plot twists.

To write sixteen books about a man from Israel has required me to spend a great deal of time there. I have traveled the country from end to end, and parts of it I know as well as my own. Along the way I have made many friends. Some are diplomats or academics, others are soldiers and spies. Without fail, they have treated my family with enormous kindness and generosity, a debt I have repaid by slipping bits and pieces of them into my plots and characters. I turned a friend's historic farm in the moshav of Nahalal into a safe house where I prepared a woman for a mission no one of sound mind would undertake. And when I think of Uzi Navot's beautiful home in the Tel Aviv suburb of Petah Tikva, I am actually seeing the home of a friend who lives a short distance away. I also think of my friend's brilliance, his pitch-perfect sense of humor, his humanity, and his amazing wife, who bears absolutely no resemblance to the domineering Bella.

I, too, have been summoned with scant notice to the old hotel in Ma'ale Hahamisha—not by Ari Shamron but by Meir Dagan, the tenth director general of the Mossad, who died as I was finishing this novel. Meir painted in his spare time and, like Ari, he loved the northern Galilee, where he lived in the historic town of Rosh Pinah. The Holocaust was never far from his thoughts. In his office at Mossad headquarters hung a haunting photograph of his grandfather taken in the seconds before he was shot to death by the SS officers. Mossad agents were made to look at it one last time before departing on missions abroad. On that afternoon in Ma'ale Hahamisha, Meir gave me a tour of the world I will never forget and gently chided me for some of the plot choices I had made. Every few minutes an Israeli in a swimsuit would pause at our table to shake Meir's hand. A spy by nature, he did not seem to relish the attention. His sense of humor was self-deprecating. "When they make the movie about Gabriel," he said with his inscrutable smile, "please ask them to make me taller."

General Doron Almog and his beautiful wife, Didi, always open their home to us when we come to Israel and, like Chiara and Gilah Shamron, they prepare far more food than we can possibly eat. I did not know Doron when I created Gabriel's physical appearance, but surely he was the mold upon which my character was based. One never quite knows who might show up at Doron's dinner table. Late one evening a very senior IDF general stopped by for a nightcap. Earlier that day, in a European port, a threat to Israel's security had been quietly and cleverly eliminated. When I asked the general whether he'd had anything to do with it, he smiled and said, "Shit happens."

The remarkable staff of Hadassah Medical Center allowed me to roam the hospital from its rooftop helipad to its new state-of-the-art operating suites far beneath ground. Dr. Andrew Pate, the eminent anesthesiologist, helped me save the life of a terrorist under less than ideal circumstances. Thanks to his expert instruction, I now feel that, in a pinch, I could treat pneumohemothorax.

I am forever indebted to David Bull, who, unlike the fictitious Gabriel, truly is one of the world's finest art restorers. A heartfelt thanks to my legal team, Michael Gendler and Linda Rappaport, for their support and wise counsel. Louis Toscano, my dear friend and longtime editor, made countless improvements to my manuscript, and my eagle-eyed personal copy editor, Kathy Crosby, made certain the text was free of typographical and grammatical errors.

We are blessed with many friends who fill our lives with love and laughter at critical junctures during the writing year, especially Betsy and Andrew Lack, Caryn and Jeff Zucker, Nancy Dubuc and Michael Kizilbash, Pete Williams and David Gardner, Elsa Walsh and Bob Woodward. Also, a special thanks to Deborah Tyman of the New York Yankees for taking a chance on an untested right-hander with a bad shoulder. For the record, I didn't bounce it.

I consulted hundreds of books, newspaper and magazine articles, and Web sites while preparing this manuscript, far too many to name here. I would be remiss, however, if I did not mention the extraordinary scholarship and reporting of Joby Warrick, Paul Cruickshank, Scott Shane, and Michael Weiss. I salute all the courageous reporters who have dared to enter Syria and tell the world of the horrors they have seen there. Journalism—*real* journalism—still matters.

It goes without saying that this book could not have been published without the support of my team at HarperCollins, but I shall say it anyway, for they are the best in the business. A special thanks to Jonathan Burnham, Brian Murray, Michael Morrison, Jennifer Barth, Josh Marwell, Tina Andreadis, Leslie Cohen, Leah Wasielewski, Robin Bilardello, Mark Ferguson, Kathy Schneider, Carolyn Bodkin, Doug Jones, Katie Ostrowka, Erin Wicks, Shawn Nicholls, Amy Baker, Mary Sasso, David Koral, and Leah Carlson-Stanisic.

Finally, a special thanks to the staff of Café Milano in Georgetown, who always take good care of our family and friends when we are fortunate enough to get a table. Please forgive the fictitious unpleasantness in the climax of *The Black Widow*. Let us hope a night such as that never comes to pass.

ABOUT THE AUTHOR

DANIEL SILVA IS THE AWARD-WINNING, #1 *New York Times* bestselling author of twenty novels, including *The Confessor*, *The Messenger*, *Moscow Rules*, *The Rembrandt Affair*, and *House of Spies*. His books are published in more than thirty countries and are bestsellers around the world. He lives in Florida with his wife, CNN Special Correspondent Jamie Gangel, and their two children, Lily and Nicholas.